Ta

Challedon Publishing
1294 Diamond Springs Road
Virginia Beach, VA 23455

tel·o·mere **– A compound structure at the end of a chromosome.**

tell-uh-meers or tee-low-meers

This book is a work of fiction. Names, characters, places, and incidents either our products of the author's imagination or are used fictitiously. Any resemblance to actual locales, events or persons living or dead is entirely coincidental.

Connect with author R.N. Shapiro at:
Website: www.RNShapiro.com
Twitter: @tamingtelomeres

V5117

Book Club Reader Praise

I am an avid reader of thrillers by Baldacci, Grisham, Connelly and others, and after finishing the manuscript, "Taming the Telomeres," I would tell any fiction enthusiast it is a "Must Read." The story line was refreshing, the characters believable, and the plot was not too simple with several unexpected twists. I would say this book is as good as any novel I have read on the best seller lists! I hope the author has a sequel. --Doug M.

I found the book intriguing from the very beginning. I loved the characters and Amanda was very believable because she never wavered from her strength, determination, and can-do type spirit. I also found myself clearly visualizing events, situations, character, reactions.....making me hopeful it is a huge success and becomes a movie. I would love to see it in that medium! It is action packed yet filled with such intrigue that you want to follow the details. The ending.....well, at first I kept trying to use my Kindle to find the next page, chapter, comments. Then I read the final few screens again and thought it felt incredibly open-ended and intriguing. --Diane F.

I thought it was quite the page turner. I could not put it down. From the medical breakthroughs to the legal twists and turns....as the reader you were always in suspense. The author's style is similar to a John Grisham novel; however, I would compare the suspense factor of the book to a Gillian Flynn novel. *--Diane G.*

"Taming the Telomeres" is a spellbinding page turner, with twists and turns that kept the reader guessing. I could not put it down--a tribute to fast paced, often-titled episodes. The author juxtaposed common reality with a tease of "sci fi" with references to NDE phenomenology and cutting edge medicine, legalities, and espionage. I kept thinking I had it figured out, only to be enthralled by a new plot. Good stuff. –Cathryn S.

Taming the Telomeres is an amazing story, only bettered by the intro in which the author claims it is based on a true story. This book reminds me of Robert Ludlum's *Jason Bourne* series with its major plot twists and the main characters not knowing the truth until the end. Like the *Bourne* series, I think this book would be a great movie. --Mary H.

Acknowledgements

For: Terri, Rachel & Dillon (ideas!).

The author thanks: "Peter Lucent," "Andy and Amanda Michaels," "Barbara and Steve Simon," Mary Hall, Manny, Sharon, Steve, Raven, Terry, Muse, Cathy, Bob, the NSA, CIA and FBI. Greg Johannesen for your inside illustrations. Erika Gizelle Santiago of Sugarskullcandy for the book cover designs.

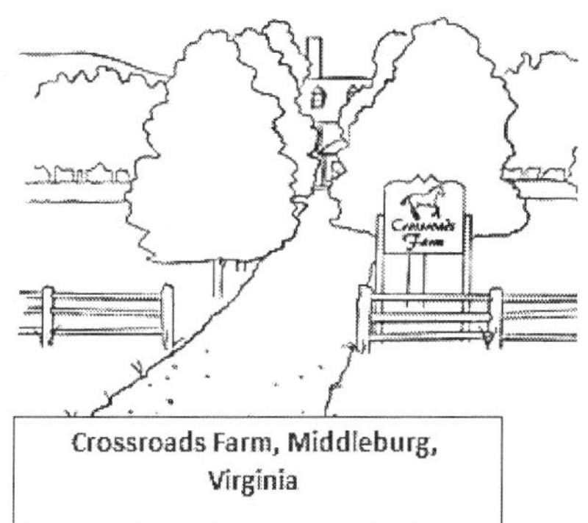

Crossroads Farm, Middleburg, Virginia

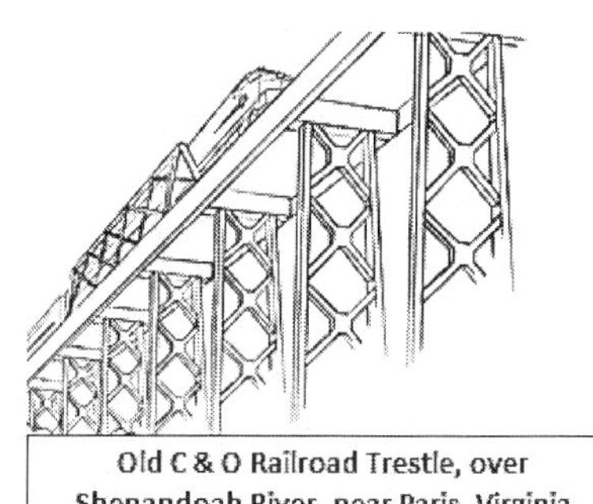

Old C & O Railroad Trestle, over Shenandoah River, near Paris, Virginia

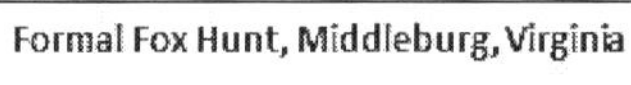

Formal Fox Hunt, Middleburg, Virginia

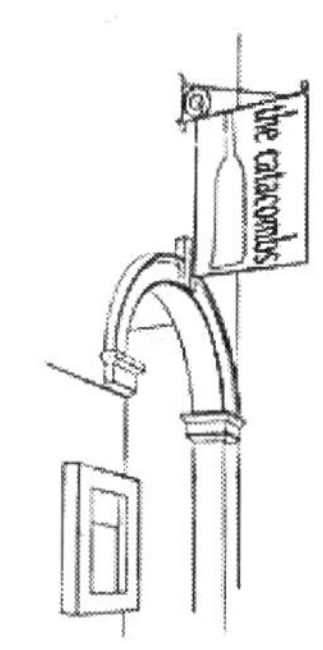

Catacombs Tavern, Georgetown area Washington, D.C.

Foreword

I am a lawyer, inventor, and now a writer; that much is 100% true. It's also 100% true that I have traveled a lot – in the United States, Europe and the Far East. When my son got older, he told me he thought I was a spy when he was younger because I was gone so much. I assured him he was mistaken, it was his youthful imagination, but the twinkle in my eye made him doubtful. In his mind, where I was all those times I was gone will be one of life's enigmas.

Another enigma is where this story began. Having completed a doctor's deposition at Georgetown University Medical Center in Washington D.C., I saw a flyer tacked on a crowded bulletin board in the hallway outside of a conference room. It read, "Unexplained Enigmas: The Near-Death Experiences of Children." It just so happened I had a few hours to kill and this symposium was scheduled to begin nearby in Regents Hall at 2:00 pm. I listened intently as Dr. Peter Lucent talked about his book, *The Inner Light*, covering the fascinating near-death experiences of children – from toddlers to teenagers – all whose souls literally "came back" from death.

After his lecture ended, I bought a signed copy of his book and voraciously read it in one day. One character in particular fascinated me. She survived a horrible catastrophe, and during her clinical experience she chronicled her amazing story of survival, heartbreak, depression, rebirth, and ultimate redemption. I contacted Dr. Lucent and asked if he might arrange for me to meet his former patient, whom I shall call "Amanda Michaels." He said I could if I agreed to never use her real name, or any friends or family members' names, and I readily consented. Over the weeks and months that followed I had unfettered access to "Amanda," her uncle "Andy," and most of her key acquaintances. About two years after the final interview, I completed this manuscript.

-- R. N. Shapiro

@Part I

The difference between a dream, a fantasy and reality is not always discernible.

--Amanda Michaels

Semi-conscious

Whoosh.

Heat like in hell, eyes sealed shut. Then cold – freezing, frostbitten, frozen.

Whoosh.

Four young Dorothys. Matching blue and white dresses, braided hair, four little Toto baskets.

Whoosh.

On a jet. People screaming in terror. The lady in the aisle seat beside me squeezes my hand, tight. She's talking to me calmly. Mom? What? Please, what—

Whoosh.

His small, cluttered home office. Little mosquitoes swarming around his table. A six-year-old asking him what he's doing.

Whoosh.

Holding a picture book reading to a baby boy on the bottom bunk. Justin and I laughing at the pictures. He's shaking my car keys in his tiny hands. Wait...?

Whoosh.

The little baby girl, pink dress, with tiny slip-on sneakers, wedged between two twin dads, one on each side of – me?

Whoosh.

Scenic overlook. Autumn-colored trees dotting the valley below. His leg barely touching mine creates static electricity.

Whoosh.

Bright light…blinding whitest light ever. Floating closer to the seductive white light. The other three Dorothys floating with me. Blissful. Then I suddenly pull away from them. Someone, something, tells me, "Go back."

Whoosh.

"Tracey, is all the hardware organized for the halo?"

"Ready, Dr. Wrightson."

"Drill please." The surgeon fires the drill bit into my skull. "Anterior skull screws," he says.

"Freaking amazing she survived," the nurse comments while handing over the screws. "Have they identified her?"

"Haven't heard yet. They took pictures of her just before surgery," Wrightson answers.

*Whirrrr….*Looking down at the doctors and nurses. Feeling the drill vibrate in my skull, shaking me. Smelling the drill's heat, the burning bone. Is this for *real*?

Andy

Reaching across her desk covered with small stacks of legal pleadings and letters, Angie Tipton reduces the volume of the music playing through her cell phone and presses the speaker button on her office phone.

"Myra, have you seen Andy?"

"Not yet."

"Okay, let me know when he shows. He'll stop here before his 11:00 o'clock hearing at D.C. Superior because I have the file he needs."

Angie checks the clock on her monitor, and then sips from her coffee cup. 10:15 a.m. Typical she thinks. I wonder if he forgot. He famously forgets stuff, even when I remind him the day before. Better text him, she concludes.

Where r u? Jones hearing at 11.

She turns the music back up and fingers her way through the Jones file, assuring everything is in place in each divided file, the way he likes it.

"He just walked in," Myra reports through the intercom.

"Good morning Angie, got the Jones file?" Andy asks a few seconds later, peering into her office.

"Here you go. Cutting it a little close aren't you? Uh, where are your socks?" She says, feeling motherly. But Angie is not a mother. Angie was a model in college during her college years at Georgetown. Never super model stuff, just magazine shoots, but only because of school. After graduating at the top of her class, she took a job on Capitol Hill as a congressional aide, but her Congressman lost his reelection bid. That's when she applied for the paralegal job and Andy hired her. Just months before 9/11, when terrorism changed the U.S. forever.

Andy hates dressing up and despises ties and suits. That's one of the things she likes about him. Monkey suits, he calls them.

"Don't need socks. I'll just throw on my back-up shirt, tie and blazer in my office."

Right, Angie thinks. He keeps the emergency gear in his small office closet – usually. Pressed shirt, a couple ties, and a stand-by blue blazer.

"You're not dressing like the Tort Prince, more like the court jester." Angie says as Andy heads toward his office.

At just 35, Andy was crowned the "Prince of Torts" by *Capitol Law* magazine for his masterful representation in the groundbreaking suit of the families of three Pentagon workers killed in the 9/11 jet crash. Having sued two airport security firms and Hemispheres Airways in D.C Superior Court, he and the families refused to settle, despite being given the option to tap into the victims' funding set up by Congress. Only crafty pleadings allowed the case to stay in D.C. Superior Court rather than being shifted to federal court like the others.

After five years the case went to trial. Andy tried the victims' case for a week – just long enough to expose the appalling lack of security by everyone involved – then the families agreed to settle. Getting their day in court is what the families had demanded from day one. Millions were eventually paid to each family, and millions were earned by Andy and his Georgetown personal injury law firm. It was the next to last of all the 9/11 victim cases to settle, according to the cover story in *Capitol Law*.

He became the youngest of three partners after the case settled. The framed magazine cover hangs over the brown leather couch in the small but cozy reception area of their law firm, Wilson, Hopper & Michaels. The headline reads: "Prince of Torts: How Andy Michaels Made Them Blink."

The reason he got the case in the first place was Angie. It just so happened that Angie was the cousin of one of the Pentagon victims. Angie told her cousin's wife, Georgia Jones, that Andy was perfect to handle the case: he worked on Capitol Hill as an aide for a couple years, graduated at the top of his Georgetown law school class, had been a law clerk for a D.C. Superior Judge, and was young and hungry. She pointed out that Wilson, the firm's managing partner, was a former U.S. prosecuting attorney who had handled many high profile cases, including major white-collar crimes and those involving Hollywood stars. Andy himself was a rising star. As his paralegal, Angie respected his ethics, ability and energy. Two other families signed with Andy after Georgia retained him and the stage was set.

Andy quickly surveys the paper stacks on his desk that only he could decipher, powers up his pc, and hits the voicemail button on his phone. He listens to two messages and forwards them to Myra with a brusque message about how to handle each. He grabs some other files on his desk and shoves them in his leather satchel as he walks quickly toward the door.

"Andy, Mrs. Erwin's on line two about her Medicare lien," Myra announces on the speakerphone.

"Not now, I'm walking out. See if Angie can help her."

Andy bolts out of his office, bounds down the stairway and out the door of the two-level row house, and hails a cab, mentally organizing the points he will cover at the hearing.

In the cab, his phone vibrates. He glances down and reads the text from Angie.

Just got tweet. Hemispheres commuter jet crashed in PA. DC-NY flight.

He ponders a moment. Hmm, maybe a new case?

Where in PA?

Dunno.

Will talk after court.

The cab stops in front of the sprawling courthouse.

"Keep the change," Andy says, slapping a ten in the cabbie's palm and sliding out of the cab. He dashes into the courthouse and up the escalator to the third floor.

Pulling his D.C. Bar Association card out of his wallet, he flashes it at the bailiff and bypasses the long line at the screening area. Moments like this make him happy to be a lawyer, but there are other moments he isn't so proud.

Andy had clerked in this courthouse for a year for Judge Hoffman, a great job. He had soaked up the lawyers' techniques in court and drafted Judge Hoffman's legal opinions. Hoffman now had senior status, sort of semi-retired. Andy learned a boatload from him – how to be prepared, never to dodge a judge's question even if the answer hurt, and answer honestly but in a way that helps your own case.

He stops reminiscing and pushes the heavy doors to the courtroom open, feeling a rush of air and having no clue that this motion hearing would be the least important part of his day.

Air Disaster

The loud beep on her desk phone startles her.

"Angie, there's someone with Hemispheres calling for Andy."

Angie wonders why Hemispheres airline would be calling *him*. Andy was presumably *persona non grata* to the airline.

"Put them through. I'll see what they want."

"This is Hemispheres Airline calling for Mr. Andy Michaels. Is he in?"

"This is Angie Tipton, his paralegal. Andy's in court. Can I help you?"

"No, I need to speak directly Mr. Michaels. Do you know how we can get in touch with him right away?"

Angie hears the serious tone in his voice. "I can try to reach him as soon as he's out of his hearing. Or, do you want to try his cell phone?"

"Yes please, what is his number?"

"Can you tell me what this is about?" Angie asks after giving the caller Andy's number.

"Unfortunately not, I have to speak with Mr. Michaels himself."

After hanging up, Angie has a sick feeling in the pit of her stomach.

After his hearing, Andy exits the courthouse through the heavy doors. His cell phone rings and he notices an odd area code. As is usual for a lawyer, he decides to take the call since it might be an expert or even a client.

“Hello, Andy Michaels here.”

"Sir, this is Hemispheres Airline calling. I would like to confirm that you are Andy Michaels, an emergency contact for Ron Michaels.”

"Yeah, that's me," Andy replies.

"Ron Michaels is listed as a passenger on Hemispheres Flight 310, which has just crashed in Quarryville, Pennsylvania. We're contacting every emergency contact listed for each passenger. Are you also related to Rochelle Michaels?"

"She's my sister-in-law, why?" Andy responds.

"And Amanda Michaels? What's her relationship with you?"

For some reason Andy suddenly feels dizzy and notices the wind blowing along the front of the building. The cabs on the street and the people are all moving in slow motion. He stops and leans against the side of the courthouse.

"Mr. Michaels, are you still there?"

Andy hangs up, then re-dials the same phone number.

"Hemispheres Emergency Response Center. Is this an emergency call?" Andy hangs up again.

Still leaning against the granite blocks of the courthouse, he stares trancelike at the street ahead. Memories of his brother Ron flash through his mind. Wearing the same clothes in elementary school. Playing in the park, on the playground. Playing soccer together. Ski trips, triathlons, celebrating every birthday together. He and his brother – under two years apart in age – were virtually inseparable.

Andy tries to decide whether to call Barbara, his older sister who lives nearby in Reston, Virginia. Instead, Andy waves down the first taxicab he can.

"31st and M Street," Andy barks at the cabbie as he gets in the back. He scrolls through the missed calls on his cell phone and sees that he's missed a call from his sister Barbara Simon and two calls from Angie.

"Hey, I seen you before! You're that lawyer that sued the airlines over the 9/11 crash. That's you right? I saw you on TV a bunch a times." The cabbie is staring at Andy in the rearview mirror, but Andy won't look up from his cell phone.

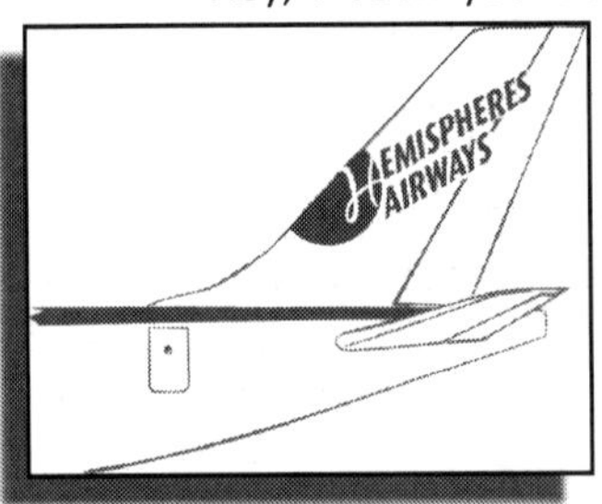

"Hey, you gonna be in business again. All they're talkin' 'bout is another plane crash on the radio. You goin' to go after them again?"

"That depends on if I get hired." Andy finally says.

"Ha! I knew it was you!" the cabbie says excitedly.

Andy's mind refuses to focus. After paying the cabbie he trots down the sidewalk and up the stairway to the second floor of his office building. Myra spots him.

"Angie's looking for you."

"I know." Before Andy can set his briefcase down beside his desk, Angie is there.

"You didn't return my calls. Have you talked to Hemispheres?"

"Yeah. They told me my brother, sister-in-law and niece were on the Hemispheres flight that just crashed. Have you heard anything about survivors?"

Angie ignores Andy's question. "Oh my God! All of them?" This doesn't happen to them. It happens to the unlucky strangers, the strangers that then somehow connect the degrees of separation and become their clients. Her eyes travel over to the framed pictures on Andy's credenza, the one of Andy and Ron at Andy's Georgetown law school graduation, one of Ron and his family. They aren't twins but Ron could easily be confused with Andy if you didn't know them both well. They both attended Georgetown, but Ron went the biology route rather than the law route.

"I didn't even know they were going anywhere. I talked to Ron a couple days ago and he didn't say anything about going to New York."

Andy stares out the window for a minute. "I'm going to make a couple quick calls. You see what's on CNT and let me know what they're saying."

Angie turns on the TV and watches footage from a chopper hovering over the rural accident scene.

"This is Natalee Spalding for CNT with breaking news. A Hemispheres commuter jet, Flight 310, departing Reagan National Airport outside Washington D.C., destined for New York City's Kennedy Airport, has crashed with 23 passengers the crew aboard. The crash occurred in Quarryville, Pennsylvania, which is southeast of Lancaster. We know it's an Embracer twin engine jet but have no information yet on the cause of this crash. We have helicopter video footage showing fire and rescue squads at the accident scene. As you can see, there is smoke and fire coming from certain parts of what is left of the jet fuselage and some pieces that broke away from the plane. We do not have any reports yet on survivors. We will keep you updated here on CNT."

Angie rushes back to Andy's office and finds him partly turned away from the door, looking at his credenza. He holds one of the pictures of Ron, Rochelle, and Amanda. Unlike his brother, Andy has no kids.

"Andy, they just showed footage of the scene and they aren't saying anything about survivors. Instead they're just showing the jet broken apart, some fires, the whole scene is---"

"Horrible," he interjects as he dials on his cell phone. "I'm calling my contact at NTSB. Maybe he'll know something."

After a brief conversation that provides no additional information, Andy ends the call. He is not relishing calling his sister, but he knows he has to do it. To say that she'll freak out is an understatement.

"Barbara, it's Andy. Hemispheres just called me about a plane crash. Have you heard about it?"

"No, I'm actually walking out of the grocery store right now. What about it?" Barbara responds.

"There's no easy way to do this, so here goes. One of their jets crashed in Pennsylvania and their records show that Ron, Rochelle and Amanda were all on it."

"No. Oh God. Oh God! Rochelle texted that she was taking Amanda to New York to shop and see a show for her 18th birthday. Are you sure they were on that flight?"

"The airline called me because I was the emergency contact on Ron's ticket, so I'm pretty sure. They mentioned Rochelle and Amanda too. No names have been released to the media yet, and there's no word on survivors either."

"Oh no. Oh no." Barbara stammers.

"I'll call you when I know more."

Middleburg Sadness

Angie and everybody else in the firm are glued to the conference room TV. Andy walks in.

"Are you sure you want to watch this?" Angie asks, noticing the gray color that has crept into his face.

"Yeah, I want to know."

CNT is reporting live from outside the perimeter of the plane crash site. Natalee Spalding is again reporting from their studio:

> "We still cannot get information from Hemispheres or rescue personnel on the number of crash survivors. However, Hemispheres has now contacted all the passengers' families and released a complete manifest. Among those listed as passengers are Roger Miller, the CEO of software company Omega Computers, and several employees. Also, Ron Michaels, a biologist from Reston, Virginia, his wife Rochelle Michaels, and Amanda Michaels, their daughter who attends Middleburg Academy in Northern Virginia. Greg and Arlene Roberts, and their three-year-old from Gainesville, Virginia..."

Andy loses focus as Spalding reels off more passenger names and details. He walks out of the conference room, back toward his office. He can feel the stares piercing his back like lasers.

The phone rings in the office of Middleburg Academy private school in Loudoun County, Virginia, 35 miles west of Washington, D.C. A reporter with CNT asks to speak with Headmaster Johnson about a senior named Amanda Michaels.

"Mr. Johnson, this is Natalee Spalding with CNT. I don't know if you have heard that a Hemispheres jet originating in DC and bound for New York City has crashed. The passenger manifest has just been released and it shows Ron, Rochelle, and Amanda Michaels as passengers. A quick search shows Amanda is a student at your school. I'm calling for some comments from you about Amanda Michaels."

"Wait one second now. That's a lot to digest. And how do I know it's true?" Johnson asks firmly but politely.

"Well, that's my job, sir. We have reporters at the Pennsylvania crash site and are covering it live if you want to turn on your TV. Will you allow me to record this conversation?"

"Well, you've caught me completely by surprise. I don't see any reason why I couldn't comment, but it'll have to be on things that are considered public information. Are you sure Amanda was on the flight?" He has watched news reports by Spalding for several years and knows she has a good reputation.

"The info is from the airline directly. She and her parents are on the passenger manifest. We don't have any further information except rescue personnel are on the scene."

Not being able to come up with any privacy issues, Johnson agrees to be recorded.

"I can tell you that Amanda Michaels is an honor student, a member of our soccer team and was, I mean is, one of the starting players on the team. As far as I know she's well-liked here at school. I better not make any further comment until we know more."

"I understand, and I may get back to you. Thanks for speaking with me," Spalding says and hangs up.

Within minutes, CNT includes clips of the phone conversation on the air, followed by video footage of the school and its grounds. Next there is footage of formally attired men on horseback, preparing for a Middleburg, Virginia fox hunt.

"Middleburg Academy is the oldest private school in America, located just outside the beltway of Washington, D.C. in Loudoun County, Virginia, the wealthiest county in the country. This is upscale horse country, where polo is played and fox hunts remain a storied tradition."

Headmaster Johnson watches the report and considers making a school-wide announcement, but he just doesn't know enough yet. He picks up the phone and pages Coach Ricci, who doubles as an upperclass English teacher.

"Coach Ricci, I just got horrible news from a reporter with CNT. Apparently Amanda Michaels and her parents were on the Hemispheres flight that just crashed. Have you heard anything?"

"What? Oh no! I knew Amanda was going to New York with her mom because she asked for the homework she was going to miss. Wait—did they survive?"

"They haven't said officially, but I just looked online and the rumors are there were no survivors."

"Are you going to make an announcement?" Ricci asks.

"I haven't decided. I'll let you know."

As Johnson turns to walk away from the administration office he is met by Iris Bailey, a senior on the girls' soccer team.

"Headmaster Johnson, I know I'm not supposed to be on my cell phone, but between classes I checked my phone and saw that a Hemispheres jet crashed. Amanda Michaels texted me earlier and said she and her mom were flying Hemispheres to New York. Now I'm totally freaking out because CNT named her as one of the passengers. She told me she was leaving on an earlier flight with her mom, but got delayed. Maybe there's a mistake and maybe she really wasn't on that one, because she texted me about the delay. Plus, her dad wasn't going with them either," she finally pauses, but nervously shakes her right foot side to side, awaiting his response.

"Iris, we've got to try to remain calm. You're right. I was contacted by a CNT reporter for a statement about Amanda. She said that the passenger list was released and the Michaels were on the flight. I'm going to make an announcement but I want to know more first."

"How are we supposed to do anything in our classes?" Iris has tears welling up in her eyes. Johnson knows and respects Iris, a top student and star athlete on their state champion soccer team.

Johnson pauses before speaking, and glances down the hall. He sees several other girls down the hall watching Iris' conversation with him as the bells sound for the next classes. Johnson knows the word has spread like wildfire.

"Your teachers will handle things appropriately."

"Alright." Iris dutifully turns and walks down the hall, but he hears her softly sobbing. That hits Johnson hard. Moments later, Johnson is back in his office. Surfing the internet on his tablet, he sees the headline: "No Survivors on Hemispheres Jet, Per Rescue Personnel."

He turns back to the TV for a live update:

> "This is Natalee Spalding with breaking news on the Hemispheres crash. According to rescue personnel at the Quarryville crash site, no survivors have been found. The jet went down with 27 people aboard, including crew. We do not have any information yet on the cause of this. Rescue personnel are sifting through the wreckage and are looking

> for the black boxes that will tell them more about what happened. NTSB officials will be analyzing the transcripts of the cockpit communications with air traffic control, and we are advised that Homeland Security is involved. No one is saying that this was a terrorist act. Again, if you have joined us in the last few minutes, rescue personnel at the scene have found no survivors from this crash."

Johnson briefly confers with some of the other staff in his office, then relays the sad news about the Michaels' family over the school intercom. He invites the entire school to the chapel and asks the teachers to handle their classes as they see fit until then.

Hand of Fate

A ribbon runs along the bottom of the TV stating: "Breaking News: Quarryville, PA Jet Crash."

> "Natalee Spalding reporting on the Hemispheres jet crash. One of our reporters in Quarryville, Pennsylvania, has an exclusive interview with a rescuer."

The frazzled looking rescue worker, wearing a hardhat and his yellow and gray firefighter uniform is on camera. The graphic below the image says, "Dale Peterson – Quarryville Fire-Rescue."

> Peterson: My team was checking for pulses on people near the center part of the plane but we weren't finding anything. And then we're placing a young female into a body bag and I noticed her arm was twitching. So I reached down and felt a very faint pulse on her and hollered over to some of the guys. We got an oxygen mask on her and the doc took over. I can only say that this female passenger was alive.
>
> Reporter: Was there any type of identification? Can you describe the female any further?
>
> Peterson: She was covered with soot and blood, laying kind of face down in the aisle under portions of luggage and debris and stray parts of – that uhh, I can't really talk about – it was just so bad. But I, I would say she was probably somewhere between 16 and maybe 25 years old, brown shoulder-length hair. We did find...she had a necklace on with a hand-like charm thing that...uhh...the doc has it now. I'm not sure what they're called, but it's got a hand-shaped thing on it.
>
> Reporter: Was she awake? Was she able to communicate with rescue personnel or the doctor?
>
> Peterson: No sir. She's being transported by rescue copter to a trauma center.

Reporter to camera: I can tell you that an air rescue helicopter was seen inside the perimeter, where we have not been given access. Reporting from Quarryville, this is Roger Summers for CNT.

Rules are meant to be broken, but violating the no-cell-phone policy in class at MA can mean suspension. Today that doesn't matter. Several of the students secretly check their cell phones for texts or tweets, including Iris Bailey. Right now she doesn't care. This is an emergency. Let them kick me out, she thinks, they will have to throw out half of the upper-class today.

She looks down at her phone and sees a news alert: *"Quarryville rescue personnel report female survivor."*

She continues to scroll on her phone and sees another report that says: *"Survivor-No ID, Wearing Hand Charm Necklace."*

Iris literally leaps up from her chair wildly waving her hand, like a third grader.

"Mr. James, Amanda might be alive and uh, please, uh, can I be excused? I would like to go tell Headmaster Johnson about what is going on."

Everyone in the class, as they see the updates on their own phones, joins in her request. "They found one female survivor." "I think it may be her." "Can I go down to the front office?"

"Class, please...please! Everyone be quiet. Iris, you, and you alone, can go."

Iris immediately hugs Charlyne Bennington, and then squeezes the hand of Amber Fields, both soccer teammates, and she races toward the headmaster's office. Bolting in, she blurts out, "CNT just reported that they found a female survivor. It's Amanda! She wears that necklace. I swear it's her!"

"Iris, slow down, slow down. Wears what?"

"CNT just said that a crash survivor has a necklace with a hand charm on it. It's Amanda, it has to be. She wears a hand necklace."

Headmaster Johnson asks, "What kind of hand?"

"You know, it's like a little hand on a necklace, it's a charm. Amanda was the only person I know who wore one. She's Jewish and she told me what it was. It's supposed to ward off the evil eye or something. Can you call the CNT reporter? Please?"

"I...I'll have to locate her phone number." Johnson says, while thinking what to do.

"I know," Iris says, "we should call Amanda's Aunt Barbara, or her dad's brother, Andy. I am sure they know she wears a hand necklace so they can confirm it's her."

"That's a good idea," Johnson agrees. He asks his office secretary to look up the next-of-kin contact information. "Iris, I need you to set a good example. Please go back to class. Trust me, I will make an announcement when I have all the information."

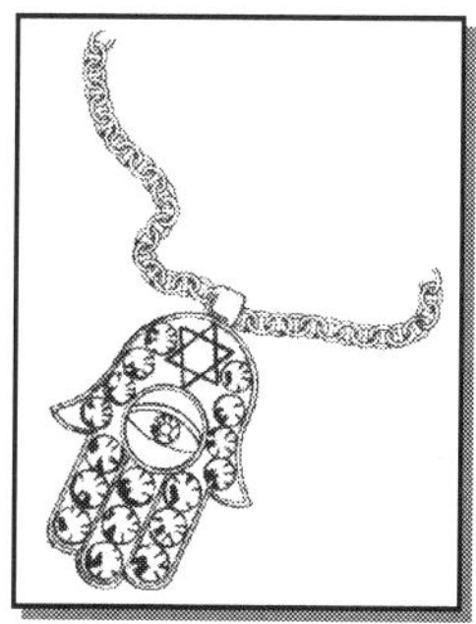

Swiveling his chair around, Andy stares at the pictures on the credenza. The D.C. triathlon. Himself, Ron, and Alex, one of their closest buddies. His cell phone rings, and he sees "Perry Carson" on the screen. Carson wrote a series of stories on Andy's handling of the 9/11 cases, which ultimately landed Andy on the front of *Capitol Law*. Can't burn a bridge, Andy grudgingly concludes.

"Andy Michaels here."

"Andy, this is Perry."

"I know Perry, what's up?"

"First, I want to express my deepest condolences about the news involving your brother and sister-in-law. But, did you see the news on CNT just now that there is one female survivor? There is speculation it's your niece."

Andy feels his heartbeat spike.

"No, I just stepped away from the TV a few minutes ago."

"They just interviewed a rescue worker. There is definitely a female survivor, but she isn't conscious. She's young and was wearing a necklace with a hand charm. Do you think that it could be her?"

Andy thinks for a moment. Yeah, a hamsa. "Where are they taking her?"

"All they said is that a rescue chopper was taking her to a trauma center."

"Amazing, thanks! Talk with you later." Andy replies.

"Wait Andy, I know now is not the time, but I hope you'll talk with me when the time is right. It's obvious you're going to be representing your family members in the cases."

Andy goes catatonic. Sure, he is eager to get the big injury cases---but he had never contemplated the thought of marching into court representing his own brother or any family member. He runs through the massive number of legal permutations.

"Are you still there?" Carson asks.

"Look, totally off the record, of course I will talk to you first. But there's a lot I need to do now. Thanks for the call."

"Great. I wish you the best with your family." Perry says. "Call me if you need anything."

"Andy, Alex Erickson is here to see you." Myra announces on his speakerphone.

"Send him back."

Alex Erickson is one of Andy's best friends, but was even tighter with Ron. Ron and Alex were tennis, skiing and triathlon mates, and Andy often joined them. For five consecutive years, Alex, Ron and Andy proudly finished the Ironman triathlon of Georgetown, running and biking through Rock Creek Park and swimming the Potomac. It had been grueling, but their sense of accomplishment was immense. They had survived a number of boys-only ski trips together. Once Alex and his wife had kids, Amanda had been Alex and Denise's favorite babysitter.

"I left work as soon as I heard," Alex says as he enters Andy's office. Andy begins to get up from his seat, awkwardly trying to decide whether to come around toward Alex.

"Don't get up. I'm so sorry Andy. Has there been any further news?"

"Yeah, actually we just heard some great news from CNT. There is one survivor and it may be Amanda."

"Fantastic, amazing! What's her condition?"

"No one knows, the rescue guy at the scene said the survivor wasn't conscious. But she was wearing a hand necklace, which fits Amanda's description."

"That's awesome. Are they sure there is only one survivor?"

"That's what they're saying."

Alex just shakes his head back and forth. "Can I do anything for you? Have you called Barbara or Becca?"

"Barb, yes. I haven't called Becca yet, and right now I'm hoping to find out where they are taking Amanda. I'm going to call Hemispheres back right now."

"Of course."

After Andy's call, the Hemispheres Emergency Response Center communicates with the chopper pilot. The patient will be carried to the major trauma center at Loudoun Memorial Hospital near Reston, Virginia. Hemispheres tells Andy to appear at the hospital to provide a possible ID. Possible, not positive. Alex tells Andy to text or call him if he needs him.

En route to the hospital, Andy fields a cell phone call on his Bluetooth from Angie.

"Sorry to call, but do you have Amanda's medical history with you? I have the file from your office in front of me."

"Good call. I forgot all about that. I'm driving and can't write, so can you text me the stuff?" Andy asks.

"Will do."

Andy speeds down the road toward the hospital, and possibly Amanda.

High-level Meeting

One of the three men gazes out the tinted windows, admiring the neatly manicured grounds surrounding the building. He had never really noticed how nicely the grounds were maintained before. This may be my last day, maybe my next to last day, he thinks. He decides he will miss the place. The other two men wear nondescript dark blue business suits. Sitting at the conference room table, they flip through the papers before them, not really reading because they have already read the material. Nervous tension fills the air. Since the most basic pleasantries were exchanged, nothing has been said. The loud second hand on a clock incessantly reminds them of each second and minute that passes.

The door opens. A fourth man enters the room. His hair is gray, close cropped to his head, and he is neatly dressed in a dark suit. The three men in the room promptly give him their full attention as he sits at the head of the table. They have come to respect him as a thoughtful, hard-working man.

He briefly flips through his copy of the report. He takes his glasses off and places them on the report while rubbing the bridge of his nose. Finally he speaks.

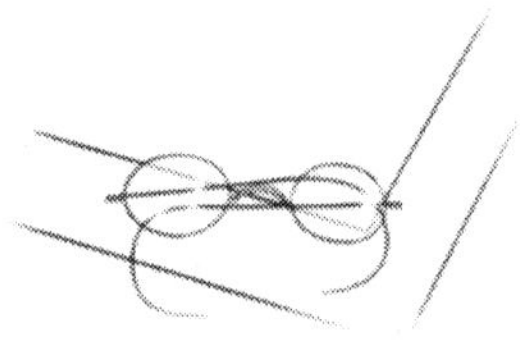

"No use in mincing words. We all know this was a colossal failure. Colossal! When we do our jobs properly, we cover *all* the details, none escape our attention." He then looks into the eyes of each of the three men.

The man who had been gazing out the window earlier speaks up.

"Here's my letter of resignation. I accept full responsibility as the team leader." He respectfully slides the typed letter toward the head of the table.

The senior man glances down at the letter disdainfully, but doesn't read it.

"Not now. However, I'll hold on to it pending what develops in the next several weeks. It is imperative that none of this leaks. Not one word. Do you realize what will occur if any part of this gets out? All the good we've done, all the good we're trying to do, won't matter. It will be irreparable. We will be blamed, bashed, bludgeoned. Won't matter that we aren't responsible. Heads will roll." The end of the last word echoes off the conference room walls.

One of the other men in the room asks the inevitable question.

"Sir, are we staying the course?"

"I've given that a great deal of thought." He pushes back from the table and stands up straight. He walks toward the window and stares out at nothing apparent except the slight movement of oak tree leaves.

"Yes, the goal remains the same," he says, turning back toward the conference room table. "This is important. We need answers. Not one more mistake. Not one. Understood?"

He looks now to his right at his general counsel, the only man yet to utter a word.

"Bob, have you calculated the potential cost of the crash, assuming we discreetly pay the lion's share?"

"Yes sir. I did significant cost analysis on the crash and on the Phoenix's technology. On the losses, I can safely say the gross valuation is between 160-200 million dollars. I recommend we cover three-fourths of that, which is still a huge number."

"Hell yes, that's a huge damn number! One we never anticipated. Let me ask you this: what's the value of the Phoenix technology?"

"It wouldn't be less than five billion dollars in the first five years, assuming we can replicate the Phoenix's initial research and results."

"So the Phoenix numbers mean this: yes, it's worth it. That's all, gentlemen," he abruptly says, sweeping up his papers and exiting the room.

Positive ID

"My name is Andy Michaels and I'm trying to find out if the survivor is my niece, Amanda Michaels. I saw the chopper outside. Is she already here?"

The meek receptionist looks up at him with sympathetic eyes.

"She's in triage right now. Please hold on a moment." She places a call, shields the handset partly with her hand and talks in a low whisper Andy can't quite hear. A supervisor walks through a set of swinging doors less than a minute later. The receptionist nods in his direction.

"Hello, my name is Barbara Smithson, and you are...?" Smithson extends her right hand.

"My name is Andy Michaels. The rescue worker's comments about the hand charm necklace make me think the survivor is Amanda Michaels, my niece. Can I identify her?"

"The young lady is in surgery now and I don't know exactly what her status is. However, the rescue personnel gave me the necklace to help with identification and we have photos of her. If you can describe your niece to me I will double check immediately."

"Brown hair to her shoulder, 5-foot 5-inches maybe. Petite. She wore a hamsa necklace her mother gave her for her bat-mitzvah. Do you have the necklace that you can show me?"

"Can I see your ID first, please?" After checking his license, Smithson has Andy follow her into a small conference room. She tells him she will be right back and soon returns with a baggie holding a necklace inside.

"Do you think this is your niece's?" she asks holding the baggie at eye level.

"Yes, this looks like what I remember. I just can't be 100 percent sure."

"The surgical team took a picture of her before the surgery started because we did not have identification." She flips open the folder and an 8-by-10 black-and-white photo shows a young girl laying on a hospital gurney surrounded by medical equipment with a swollen face, cuts, and bruises.

"Oh my God, that's her! What can you tell me?"

"I can tell you that she's in surgery," the nurse administrator says calmly. "She wasn't conscious when she was rolled in here but she is breathing with assistance. I don't know any more except that we've assembled a team of top trauma specialists and they're working on her right now," She presses her speakerphone button and calls for the triage nurse that assisted with transporting Amanda to surgery.

"Sir, do you have any medical history on your relative?"

"Yeah, it's on my phone," Andy says as he begins scrolling for the text from Angie. "She had a lower back spinal condition called a pars defect and, uh, she had something called vWD, a minor blood disorder."

"Oh, vWD could affect the outcome of her surgery, which is happening right now. What do you know about her case?" the triage nurse says, appearing concerned.

"I never heard her parents say it was a big deal, just that she had it." Andy says.

The triage nurse leaves to convey the information to the surgeons.

"Follow me back to my office and we'll fill out some paperwork."

Andy sees his sister as he follows the administrator back to her office. They rush together.

"Barb, it's Amanda! She's alive and they have her in surgery right now. They showed me a picture!" he says excitedly.

"Oh my God!" They engage in a long hug. Finally, Barbara asks, "Is she doing okay?"

"All I know is she's in surgery and I'm following this nice lady who works here."

"My name is Barbara, Barbara Smithson."

"That's easy, I'm Barbara Simon."

They fill out appropriate papers in Barbara's office, and she shows them to a family waiting area near the emergency room, where they can wait for news from the surgeons. They decide to review a list of family and friends to call. But first, Andy finds Iris outside the emergency room entrance and relays the news. They exchange a hug and he tells her he needs to get back inside to await news from the surgeons. She already has her phone out and is texting.

"What about her condition?" Iris shouts after Andy is almost out of earshot.

"Nothing besides the fact that she wasn't conscious before they wheeled her into surgery."

As Andy approaches the waiting room Barbara asks, "Andy, how are we going to get through this?"

"We don't have any choice. We'll get through it."

A nurse finally enters the family room. “Who is the next of kin of the crash survivor?”

Doctors Explain

Each of the doctors in the conference room wears a poker face.

"My name is Dr. Wrightson, I'm a neurosurgeon here at the hospital. This is my colleague Dr. Bill Burge, a general surgeon. This is Dr. Peter Lucent, a neurologist-psychiatrist, and we have been consulting with several other doctors. But first I wanted you to know that we've completed a six-hour surgery on Amanda who I understand is your niece, correct?"

"Yes that's, that's correct," Barb answers.

"We're all so sorry for your family's loss, but Amanda is quite an amazing patient. We did a lot of imaging when she first arrived here. Since she wasn't conscious when she entered, we did MRIs of her brain and CT and MRI scans of her spine. We have learned some troubling things.

"The MRIs showed that she has bleeding in the frontal area of her brain lobes. Then, in the series of CT scans and MRIs of her spine we found that there is a fracture of the vertebrae at C2, which is in her neck. We stabilized her and reduced the swelling in her brain."

Dr. Wrightson walks around the conference table and points to the scans that are clipped to a white board. Obviously, the doctors had been talking about these films before Barbara and Andy entered.

"With this type of fracture we have to be absolutely sure that there is no movement in her neck area. To do this we surgically attached what is called a halo. It encircles the skull and is attached with pins inserted into her head. Then we attach metal vertical rods to the halo and custom-fit a plastic jacket around her upper torso. Between the plastic jacket and the rods connected to the halo, any neck movement is prevented. We see a success rate of anywhere between 15 to 85 percent in halo patients. Success meaning that the cervical fracture heals itself and the bone fuses back together. I know I just covered a lot, do you have any questions?"

"Not yet..." Andy says.

"I had an infectious disease specialist at the surgery because Amanda had so many lacerations and contusions. We took some cultures and will follow up.

"Despite having multiple traumas, she had surprisingly little blood loss. I will need to reconfirm those figures. She did suffer a brain injury, which I'll have Dr. Lucent discuss."

"I'm Peter Lucent. We can tell you Amanda has suffered a mild to moderate brain injury, but not much else because she has not regained consciousness yet. The problem with Amanda's type of injury is that the front lobe of the brain controls many executive functions. It controls our impulses, and it plays a significant part in our general cognitive reasoning. Frankly, we will need to carefully reduce her medications and hope for the best. Although we are currently assisting her breathing and providing her nutrition, she'll hopefully be breathing on her own soon and will come out of the coma. But with the type of impact that she suffered it's just going to be a wait-and-see situation."

"When can we see her?" Andy asks.

"Once she's and we get her into a room, we will allow immediate family to see her. But she will be in intensive care for some time."

"Does this mean she's going to have permanent brain damage?" Barb bluntly asks.

"We can't tell at this point," says Dr. Lucent.

"With the halo, does she need a wheelchair? And how long does she need the halo?" Barb asks.

Dr. Lucent looks a bit uncertain and turns to Dr. Wrightson for an answer.

"She's definitely going to be in a wheelchair, at least—I'll just say for a while. Until she's up and responsive we won't know if she will have any paralysis. As for the halo, it could be 90 days or longer. We will conduct progress imaging to monitor the bone growth at the fracture site.

"The media is pressuring us for information on your niece, which is understandable given that she is the only known survivor of the crash. Do we have your permission to at least give general information about your positive identification, our surgery techniques, and her stable condition?"

Andy and Barb look at each other and ponder the question. Then, Andy answers.

"I see no problem with that."

"Do either of you want to attend the news briefing?"

"I don't think so," Barbara says, looking to Andy for his agreement. He nods affirmatively.

An administrative assistant, who had not spoken yet, produces a piece of paper with a short paragraph permitting the disclosure, which Andy signs. With that, the doctors rise from their chairs and one by one shake the hands of Andy and Barb before leaving.

"We want to thank you so much for everything you're doing for her." Andy says sincerely.

"Sure. Again, we are sorry for your loss," Dr. Wrightson offers.

Barb and Andy then walk back to the family room to pass the news along to those anxiously waiting for an update.

First View

"Mr. Michaels, the doctors say it's okay for the immediate family to come up to ICU now."

Andy and Barbara take the elevator up to the third floor and follow the nurse down the hall to a partially opened door. Amanda lays propped up slightly on the bed surrounded by medical equipment, and IV lines run everywhere. Her shoulder-length brown hair has been shaved away from her forehead in various places, and the metal halo has been affixed to her skull. Andy finally realizes that they actually screwed the thing into her skull to attach it. Yikes! Her face looks grotesquely bloated with random abrasions along her cheeks as well as along both of her arms. The blue hospital gown hangs loosely on her body, far too large for her petite frame. There's also a clear breathing mask over her nose and mouth. Her eyes are closed.

"The doctors have a breathing tube on her even though it's not clear she needs it. And she is being fed intravenously," the ICU nurse explains. Her eyes move back and forth from Amanda to the various monitors. One of them is beeping every several seconds so she reaches over and touches a button, observes another set of displayed figures, satisfies herself that they are okay and looks back at Andy and Barb. Her look is one of expectancy. As in what questions do you have?

Amanda's arms lie limply beside her motionless torso.

"Can I touch her?" Andy asks the nurse.

"Sure, just very gently."

Andy walks to Amanda's side and gently strokes her arm looking for a reaction. There is none. She remains motionless. Along the other side of the bed Barb also touches Amanda's arm.

"Can you hear me Amanda? It's your Aunt Barbara. Can you move or smile or do anything to let me know you hear me?" There's no movement from Amanda.

"We're going to have to sit and talk to her a lot and see what happens. I've heard amazing stories about relatives talking to someone in a coma and the person wakes up one day like nothing ever happened."

Andy forms an odd smile, one that indicates a mixed bag of emotions.

The nurse hovers impatiently in the corner of the room. She finally speaks up. "We're going to be monitoring her 24/7 and giving her the best possible care. You ought to try to go home and get some sleep, then come back in the morning."

Andy and Barbara walk out of the room and back toward the family room to explain the circumstances to everyone else.

It's a media circus on the first floor of the hospital and in the parking lot with all the press and TV reporters.

"I'm going to hire a security service to keep reporters out of Amanda's room. They'll be here first thing tomorrow," Andy says. Barb agrees, then insists that Andy be the one to go home first. She will sleep overnight in the waiting room on a chair or whatever she can find.

Andy Crashes

As he shuts and locks the door on his black Mini Cooper, Andy feels the exhaustion of the long day. Getting sleep is just about the only thing on Andy's mind, after the constant array of noises permeating the hospital waiting room, even though nobody else was there after midnight. Tossing his keys down on the kitchen counter he sees the blinking light on his answering machine and punches it to check messages. The first is from his father about traveling to the area to be with Amanda. Will dad behave himself, he wonders. It would be nice, for once. Then there is a message from Sarah, his ex-wife. He cringes but decides to listen.

"Andy, it's Sarah. I don't know what to say, this is such a horrible day for you. I'm so sorry about Ron and Rochelle. And then when I heard about Amanda I couldn't believe it. What a miracle! I don't know what else to say, but if there's anything I can do please let me know. I hope to hear from you."

Andy divorced Sarah in the middle of handling the 9/11 cases after five years of marriage. Sarah and Andy had met at Georgetown law school and he thought their marriage was meaningful until one day she announced that Andy wasn't paying enough attention to her and was too much in love with his job.

Sarah, being a lawyer herself, was the top Capitol Hill aide – commonly called an "AA" – to Republican Senator Mike Pierce of Indiana. She didn't want to have kids, not right away anyway; she said she felt it would interfere with her job, and she was probably right. It was only later, through happenstance that Andy learned that Sarah was having an affair with Sen. Pierce, a fact that still had never been made public. Although there is no such thing as a good divorce, the fact that they had no children made it a smidge easier. Psychologically it took a heavy toll on Andy, but he kept himself immersed in his cases.

Andy punches the button on the machine and listens to the next message. How ironic he thinks, when the next caller is Rebecca, the woman he's been dating for nearly two years. At least the messages are in chronological order with his life, he rationalizes.

"Andy, it's Rebecca again. I wanted to know if there's anything I can do to help. I'm definitely coming by the hospital tomorrow. When you get this message please get back to me. Love you."

Just hearing her voice brings a smile to his weary face. Rebecca and Andy have a good thing going. She owns and manages her chic clothing store, Becca's, right on Wisconsin. Amanda loves Becca's shop, and seems to love Becca too. Andy hovers in her store sometimes after work, waiting for her to close up. He tries to be invisible and patient, sitting in one of the comfortable customer chairs wedged between the clothing racks, near the full length mirrors in the rear of the store. He casually flips through fashion magazines she subscribes to that he would never really look at otherwise, but it's better than having nothing to read while he waits for her to free up.

After listening to his messages, Andy heads to his bedroom. He doesn't even remember his body hitting the bed.

The warm light streams through the hospital window between the slats of the vertical blinds, creating linear patterns on the hospital room wall. Barbara sits in one of the chairs reading the morning paper.

The security guard peeks in the room and tells her there are two men here to see her "from the government." Barb puts the newspaper down, and walks out the door to find two clean-cut official-looking guys in slacks and black shoes.

One of the men says, "Good morning, I understand you're the aunt of Ms. Michaels?" At the same time, he lifts a small billfold from the inside pocket of his jacket and flashes a badge. Barb notices the words "Federal Bureau of Investigation."

"I'm Charles Barnes, and this is Mr. Zelniak, from Homeland Security." Zelniak also slides a badge out of his inside pocket and holds it up for Barbara to inspect.

"Well, this is unexpected," Barbara says. "Are you here because...actually, why are you here?"

"This is really just routine due diligence. Because your niece is the only survivor of the jet crash, we're hoping to interview her, that is, if and when she's capable of talking with us."

Barbara scratches her nose a moment and looks past the both of them. "Are you suggesting that something like terrorism caused the crash?"

Zelniak speaks up. "Whenever there is any type of domestic crash and the cause is not yet identified, it's standard procedure to rule out any possibility of sabotage. Having said that, no ma'am, there is no evidence of any type of sabotage or terrorism here. Nonetheless, we would like to talk to your niece."

"We understand that she's in a coma now, but if she wakes up please give us a call. We'd like to ask her some routine questions so we can close this file." With that Barnes hands his card to Barb, and Zelniak follows suit.

Barb shuffles them in between her thumb and forefinger a moment.

"Right now the most important thing to us is that Amanda wakes up. But we'll definitely let you know if and when she can speak to you."

I wonder what that was really about, Barb thinks, as she watches them walk down the hall.

Awakened

Three full days have passed since Andy and Barb first saw Amanda in ICU. She is no longer in ICU because she is breathing on her own, but she's still on nutritional IVs and requires constant monitoring. Dr. Lucent and Dr. Wrightson have made their daily rounds. Lucent, the more upbeat of the two, has reinforced the idea that Amanda could regain consciousness at any time.

"Sure, go on in."

The security guard has gotten to know the young volunteer in the last few days and casually waves him into Amanda's small hospital room. He goes about his routine, changing the used towels and tidying the bathroom. Out of the corner of his eye he looks at the pitiful young girl in the blue hospital gown and metal halo. Hmm...kind of cute, he thinks to himself, admiring her hair with its uneven cuts around the halo and the fixation pins. He would have to be living under a rock to not realize how much the media has been covering her story in the last few days.

"Who are those guys on your shirt?"

Her eyes stare into his but she hasn't moved.

He can only stammer. "Uh...what? Uh...I need to go tell someone."

"Hey, wait!" she says as he darts out of the room, looking for the first family member or nurse he can find.

"Nurse, Nurse! The halo girl just opened her eyes and talked! Where's the doctor?"

The nurse dashes down toward the nurses' station with the volunteer trotting behind her. She quickly scans the nurse's notes relating to the patient and pages the neurosurgeon and Dr. Lucent. After they have a brief discussion, the nurse dashes down the hall to convey the news to Barbara Simon.

"Dr. Lucent asks that you please not enter her room until he and the other doctors evaluate her. You can go in as soon as they're done."

Barb hurriedly texts Andy: *"Amanda out of coma! Get here ASAP!"*

Andy responds seconds later that he's on his way.

Within minutes the doctors and nurses have assembled in Amanda's room. Dr. Lucent, the neurologist, is the first to speak as Amanda looks around the room in silence.

"Ms. Michaels, my name is Dr. Lucent. I'm one of the doctors treating you. I'd like to ask you a few questions in order to evaluate you."

"I want to know what I'm doing here and why my head is locked in place," Amanda says in an aggravated tone. "What's the thing on my head for? Can someone get me a mirror please?"

Lucent decides to ignore the mirror request. "You are a patient in Loudoun Memorial Hospital, and you were in an accident. Do you remember anything about that?"

"What are you talking about?"

"Please wrap your hand around my index finger. I want to check your strength." Amanda complies.

Next Dr. Lucent asks her to follow his pen as he moves it left and right, checking her vision. He completes several other quick bedside tests.

"I need to ask you a couple of questions. Do you know what kind of accident you were in?"

"I already told you no. I don't know what you're talking about."

"Tell me your name."

"Uh ...I'm not sure. What's my name?"

"It's Amanda Michaels. Do you know where you go to school?"

"No...tell me where."

"According to our notes it's called Middleburg Academy. Can you tell me what grade you're in?"

"No, I really can't."

"Amanda, do you know your parents' names and whether you have any brothers or sisters?"

"Umm...do I have any brothers or sisters? Do I?" Something shoots through her synapses. "Yes, I have a little brother named Justin. I can't recall my parents' names."

"Do you know who the president of the United States is?"

"No."

"Can you tell me how many states there are in the United States?"

"Fifty, and that's a really ugly jacket you have on. Same for the other guys hovering around behind you. Why are all these people here?" Amanda asks.

Dr. Lucent motions with his finger to the other doctors and nurses and they huddle at the corner of the room, whispering.

"I don't like when people tell secrets, stop it!" Amanda says.

Dr. Lucent walks back over to her bedside and places both hands on top of the white linens.

"Do you play any sports in school?" he asks, trying to trigger her memory.

"I like swimming. I like riding bikes."

"Do you know your address?"

"Nope. Where is the guy with the T-shirt I was talking to?"

The doctor holds up his pen. "What is this?"

"It's a pen, duh. Where's that kid that I was talking to?" Amanda again asks.

"I'm not sure who you're talking about," Dr. Lucent says, turning to the nurses with a quizzical look.

One of the nurses pipes up. "I think she's referring to Kent Perless, one of our hospital volunteers."

"Oh," Dr. Lucent says. "I can send him back in here later. Do you know him from before your stay here with us?"

"I just like his T-shirt," Amanda replies, not really answering the question. "And my little brother Justin — why isn't he here? How long have I been here, anyway?"

"It was great talking with you, and we'll talk again real soon," Lucent says, eyeing the door.

"How soon? I'm hungry."

"I'll get you some food right away, and I'll be back in just a few minutes." Lucent tells one of the nurses to give Amanda some soft foods as everyone files out of the room.

In the hall, Andy rushes at them from the other direction.

"Hey you guys, what's the deal? Is she talking? When can we see her?"

"We are just figuring that out now, your timing is great."

Once Andy and Barb are seated inside the conference room with the doctors, Dr. Wrightson takes the lead.

"It is fantastic news that she has come out of the coma. Her first words were to a hospital volunteer who was tidying up the room and Dr. Lucent just conducted an initial neurological evaluation. She exhibited very promising cognitive signs, but I will turn this over to Dr. Lucent to explain her condition."

Dr. Lucent takes over. "As is typical with a brain injury, Amanda has amnesia, which currently is very significant. She is oriented to understanding basic things around her and can handle present cognitive functions, but she has no memory of the jet crash, who her parents are, where she lives. Except she did ask to see Justin."

Lucent notices that Andy has a quizzical look on his face, but he forges on.

"This could be temporary and her memory could start coming back slowly day by day, or it could be more long term. We just don't know. We will have to work with her to see if we can coax these memories back. I want to do a thorough neuro-evaluation, but I can do that after you are introduced to her. And yes, I mean introduced because she probably won't know who either of you are."

"Is there anything we should be doing as her family to help her? I mean, especially about her amnesia?" Barb asks.

"Oh certainly. Empirical data shows that talking with her and sharing pictures of family members and past events can help bring memories back to the conscious state. However, I can tell you, based on my experience, patients vary. Memories could come back within days, weeks, months or never, unfortunately. I am far past predicting these things, as the brain still holds a lot of mystery. I have a special interest in near-death experiences or NDEs."

Dr. Wrightson shoots a disapproving look at Dr. Lucent.

"Peter, can you give them further guidance about memory loss?" Dr. Wrightson directs the discussion away from NDEs. Unbeknownst to Andy and Barb, Wrightson and many of the other doctors at Loudoun Memorial aren't happy with Lucent's personal obsession with near-death experiences.

Barbara looks curiously at the faces of each doctor and then asks: "Will seeing her close family and friends and talking with them help jog her memory?"

"Certainly won't hurt, and hopefully will help." Lucent responds. He then explains that family members should be escorted into Amanda's room by one of the nurses to observe her reactions.

"I will evaluate her further tomorrow morning. Let's withhold any information about the jet crash, her parents and their deaths. She is too fragile for that." Lucent says. "Actually, I'll go back to the room with you."

One of the nurses leads the three of them into Amanda's room and Andy and Barb both stand bedside while Amanda stares at them. Dr. Lucent stays near the entry door with the nurse.

"Where's the kid with the four guys on his T-shirt?" Amanda asks all of them.

"Amanda, I am your Aunt Barb. Do you remember me?"

"No."

"I'm your dad's sister."

"Hi Amanda, I'm your Uncle Andy. Do you recognize me?"

"No. And I really don't want to talk to either one of you right now. Where's that guy? You, the doctor near the door, where is he?"

The doctor leans in and whispers to Barbara. "With someone who has a brain injury it's best not to push. Also remember that they will say strange things. Impulsive stuff, so don't be surprised."

"I don't like people telling secrets. What are you hiding from me?"

"Nothing," Lucent says.

Barb turns to make eye contact with the doctor and then follows him out into the hall.

"Where should we start?" Barb asks.

"Bring lots of pictures of her family. I may refer to some of them in our sessions too, if you leave them here."

"Sure, I'll go by their house and collect some stuff," Barb says.

"How can we start showing her pictures but still keep from her that her parents were killed in the crash?" Andy chimes in.

"She doesn't have these events in sequence like you think she does. Her brain has been scrambled. It's okay to show her pictures, just don't talk about what has happened to her parents yet. I'll deal with that in her therapy. I will break the news to her very soon, but in a way that works. Possibly later today, or tomorrow morning." Lucent says.

"Oh, okay," Andy says, secretly glad he doesn't have to do that tightrope walk.

First Session

"Do you remember anything about your accident?" Dr. Lucent asks.

"I remember being dead, but nothing about any accident. Like, stuff flashed through my mind and I knew I was dying. But I don't remember how I almost died. I know something really bad happened by the way everyone's acting, so... are you going to tell me now, or just keep asking mysterious questions? Did I drive my car off the road or smash into somebody?"

"Do you remember what kind of car you drive?"

"No. Why won't you guys let me see Justin? I want to see my brother. What about my parents? No one is saying anything about them. Are you going to tell me where they are or when they're coming to see me? Oh, something just popped in my brain. Four Dorothys. There are Four Dorothys and they all are dressed the same. I was with them and that's one of the last things that happened I think."

"Last things?" Lucent prompts her.

"Yeah, before they were drilling into my skull."

"What do you remember about that?"

"I just remember feeling it. Watching them from up above. Oh, I guess that doesn't make any sense. But, you asked me. And that's when I saw the four Dorothys."

"Do you know who the Dorothys are? Are you referring to the *Wizard of Oz* movie?"

"Blue and white dresses." Amanda's eyes begin to dart around the room. Lucent is staring at her. She appears deep in thought. "I don't know if I knew the others, but we all look the same in blue and white dresses. We had baskets for the little dog."

"You mean for Toto?"

"Yeah! We all had baskets for Toto. I was one of the Dorothys, we were all floating, or flying I guess."

"Amanda, what you are describing is a near-death experience, or NDE for short. They can be real things that happened to you, or fantasies that incorporate portions of your life into the recollection."

Lucent has been warned by Andy and Barbara about Justin. It is important that he prod Amanda's memory rather than confront her about him. He decides to dig deeper.

"Tell me about Justin. Why do you want to see him so badly?"

"I make him laugh. I like playing with him. I'm much older so, you know, there's no competition. I just like to do stuff with him."

"What kind of stuff do you like to do with him?"

Amanda thinks a second or two. "I know I read picture books to him. I guess it's not really reading since the pictures are the main deal. I can't remember much of anything else right now."

"Do you remember why your parents decided to have another baby?" he asks.

There is no response, just a glazed-over look in Amanda's eyes. Lucent refuses to talk, wanting to find out as much as he can and as early as he can.

"No." Amanda finally says.

"Would you be surprised if I told you that you don't have a brother named Justin?"

"Now you're the one who sounds crazy. Just ask anyone in my family."

Dr. Lucent has been trained never to confront a patient with deep-seated delusions like Amanda's. He wants to be gentle.

"I've spoken to your Uncle Andy and Aunt Barbara, and I've asked them to verify some of the records as well. There's no evidence that your parents had any children besides you. Is this possibly just a dream you've been having?"

"No, it's not a dream, he's my baby brother. I know it. I used to do lots of things with him. Read picture books, play with his toys with him."

Lucent pretends to help her recollect what he already knows is fantasy. "Can you recall Justin's room in your house?"

"No, just the one time I was reading to him when he was really little. It hurts when I try to remember."

"We'll work through this. You had an amazingly significant impact to your skull and to tell you the truth, it's a miracle you survived. Every day you'll get better."

"Are my parents dead? That's why my aunt and uncle are here but not them, right? And don't lie to me."

Lucent has noticed that Amanda lacks typical emotion and manifests an effect of detachment that can occur with her type of injury, so he knows her reaction will not be normal.

"You were all on a commuter jet that crashed traveling from Washington to New York. Of everyone on the plane, you are the only survivor. It's terribly tragic. We are so sorry for you and your family."

Amanda says nothing for a few seconds. "How come I survived?"

Lucent does not know whether this is survivor guilt or just a simple question from a girl suffering from amnesia.

"We honestly don't know. You were unconscious, but had a pulse. You were airlifted from the crash area. There are all kinds of reporters here who want to talk with you or just get pictures of you. Stories about the crash and your survival have been all over the internet and in the newspapers."

"That's why I have this halo on my head."

"That's right. You fractured your neck, and you are fortunate you have full use of your arms and legs. Anyhow, we covered a lot. I want you to rest tonight and I'll come back tomorrow. You have nice family members who have been here around the clock, watching out for your best interests. I'm astounded with how well you are progressing. I will see you tomorrow morning."

Preservation Motion

It's Angie who reminds him that but for the fact that his family was involved in this jet crash, he would have been down at the courthouse within 24 hours after being retained by a client, seeking to preserve every bit of evidence from this crash.

What is torturing Andy is that this would likely take place even before his brother and sister-in-law's funerals. Finally, he concludes that if he would do it for a third-party client, how the hell could he justify not doing just as much for his own family. As he is preparing to file a motion to preserve, his senior partner calls him.

"Andy, don't just file the motion, file a complaint for your niece's injuries. You would just be creating more work for yourself not to file the injury complaint along with the motion to preserve now."

"But we don't have any hard evidence from the NTSB or the FAA." Andy responds.

"Jets don't crash without a mechanical failure, Andy. You know it, I know it and the judge will know it. The law doesn't require us to have all of the proof in advance." That seals it for Andy, and they rush the injury complaint and the motion to court.

At the courthouse, Andy vaguely recognizes a couple faces, and then sees Perry Carson. Carson catches his eye and walks toward him.

"Andy, just for background, not for quotation: What do you think is going to happen today?" he asks.

"Well, my motion to preserve evidence is on the docket. The defense agreed to the hearing on far less than normal notice so I'm not sure what Franklin may have in mind."

"Franklin told me he's not agreeing to anything. What about that?"

"Really? Anything to obstruct. You know what their game is all about. And that is not for attribution."

Andy makes his way to the front of the courtroom and spreads the papers out in front of him on one of the attorney tables.

Paul Franklin, already seated at the nearby counsel table, steals a glance over at Michaels.

Franklin has a history with Andy, having defended the 9/11 crash case for almost four years. They are like generals who have met on a battlefield before, acrimonious prior skirmishes between worthy opponents.

The bailiff loudly announces, "Oyez, oyez. Please rise, the Honorable Judge Rhonda Easton is now presiding. All those having pleas to prosecute shall now be heard."

A tall, thin African-American woman in a black robe enters the courtroom from behind the bench.

"You may be seated. Is everyone here? Please introduce yourselves and your clients for the record," the judge states.

"Andy Michaels, for the estate of Rochelle and Ron Michaels and on behalf of Amanda Michaels."

"Paul Franklin of Leftwish and Franklin, counsel for Hemispheres."

"Counsel, are we ready to proceed?" The attorneys both nod in agreement.

"All right Mr. Michaels I'll hear from you on your motion to preserve."

Andy stands again and begins. "Judge Easton, may it please the court. My firm has been retained to represent the interests of Ron and Rochelle Michaels, who died in the Hemispheres crash. We filed this motion to ensure that Hemispheres preserves evidence in the crash, and that the victims' families will have access to important materials including the event recorders, personal possessions, and any other items that Hemispheres currently controls. We also want to be sure that there is no testing, no alteration of any of the evidence, and so forth.

"Mr. Franklin informally agreed to some of these items but we'd like a court order entered immediately so there are no questions down the road. At the appropriate time we hope to have an aviation expert analysis done as part of our investigation." With that Andy sits, knowing judges appreciate brevity.

"Thank you Mr. Michaels. Mr. Franklin?"

"Judge we don't have a problem with most of Mr. Michaels' motion to preserve. But we think it's burdensome and will keep us from doing some expert testing. Also, he wants us to have the evidence available in some kind of warehouse, but we want all testing done where the items are located now. We also object to producing the event recorder printouts within seven days, which does not give us enough time to have the results analyzed by our experts first. Lastly, he lists items that may not even exist, as the physical evidence is still being catalogued and Homeland Security agents are still exercising jurisdiction over everything. So we ask that you deny everything except what both sides already agreed on, which is outlined in our response." Franklin ceremoniously drops his papers on the table and sits down.

The judge fiddles with her reading glasses and sets them down. "Mr. Michaels, any brief rebuttal?"

"Your Honor, there's no real defense to our motion to preserve, we would ask that you enter the order we submitted and overrule any delay that Mr. Franklin seeks to impose on us and anyone else who decides to file a claim. There is no reason why he can't have the event recorder printouts to us within seven days, and then I can work with him on our experts getting access to the physical evidence."

"On the motion to preserve I am going to grant most of Mr. Michaels' requests. A few of them go too far, but the physical evidence from the crash needs to be maintained for expert inspections. I'll mark up this order and then you can have it entered at the clerk's office. Thank you, gentlemen."

Some judges ask the attorneys if there is anything else. Not Judge Easton. After handing the file over to the courtroom deputy clerk, she disappears through the door behind the judge's bench.

As they pass each other at the swinging double doors in the back of the courtroom Franklin turns to Andy. "My condolences to you and your family, and I mean that."

Andy shoots a cold stare back at Franklin. Is that professional courtesy? Can I really take him seriously? Cold-hearted, defense prostitute of a lawyer. Franklin uses every legal trick in the book. Never actually broke a promise to me, Andy admits, but he almost never makes any either. Andy knows why companies like Hemispheres use Franklin. He looks good in front of juries, doesn't take outrageous positions like some insurance lawyers. He is masterful at making cases about anything but human loss and suffering. Make it about legal defenses, stumbling blocks, maneuvers that assure no jury will ever pass on the human toll. And, unfortunately he's good-looking too, kind of Brad Pitt mixed with a little Clint Eastwood poured into a 50-year-old barrister.

"Thanks. It isn't going to change how hard I'm going to go after your client."

"I would never assume any less of you." Franklin says as they separate in the hall.

Undercover

Easy money, the former SEAL thinks to himself. It's like hiring a plumber. You're paying for their experience, even if they really don't spend a lot of time solving the problem. But you can't do it yourself, so it's worth the money. That's why Franklin hired him.

Pitch dark. There's barely any light in the alley behind the Georgetown law firm. He sits in his SUV with the lights out and scans the narrow alley ahead. It's 3 a.m. and he knows there should be nobody on the street, but some of the row houses facing the alley on the opposite side have a few lights still on. For $350 an hour this is pretty low-risk work, especially compared to what he used to do on the SEAL team for a fraction of that per hour.

He taps the accelerator enough to crawl up directly beside four large trash cans conveniently marked with the street number for the law firm. He lifts the hatch of the SUV and takes out eight large trash bags full of shredded paper. He lifts the lid of the municipal trash cans, pulls out several trash bags from each and places them into the back of his SUV. Then he places the bags he brought into each of the receptacles. It's just a backup measure. Somebody from the firm will throw some other bags in there tomorrow, he figures.

Trash isn't private. It's sitting on the curb and heading for a refuse dump. Ryan prides himself on clean private investigations. He knows where the legal line in the sand runs and will step right up to it. Should be interesting to see what turns up in all this crumpled up discarded trash.

The next day he sits at the head of a long rectangular table in his basement home office. Crumpled up piece of paper by crumpled up piece of paper, he pours through each and every item. Dunkin' Donuts discarded breakfast. Coffee remnants. Bills and invoices. And many marked up legal drafts. Part investigator, part archaeologist on a dig.

Eventually, he locates Andy Michaels' trashcan, which isn't hard since the discards clearly show who the mail has been sent to or from.

Telephone surveillance is a bit trickier. Sitting in the SUV for hours on end is incredibly boring. There are so many calls from the law firm that can be picked up in the alley. Getting what his principal is looking for on Michaels or his paralegal is like finding a needle in a haystack. Hours on end can be spent for nothing. But eventually, he always comes up with something.

He wonders to himself what it is that Franklin will learn from this surveillance. Sure, it's a high-profile aircraft crash case with millions at stake. But it is ironic that Franklin, a supposedly ethical well-respected lawyer, would hire a private investigator to snoop his opponent as opposed to some supposedly greedy victim. Snooping on personal injury victims in a big case to confirm the seriousness of their injuries is understandable. He's uncovered some real gems. But this is a first for him, attorney vs. attorney. Whatever, the money is good and easy.

Recording phone calls is probably illegal in the District of Columbia without a court order or a subpoena. Ryan doesn't really intend to use the recorded phone conversations, he just wants information. He never needs to let anyone know how he got it, and he'll delete the digital recordings once he figures out what is juicy. What Franklin doesn't know shouldn't hurt him.

He agrees to meet Franklin at Dumbarton Oaks Café on Wisconsin Avenue just north of Georgetown's epicenter. It's a busy place and often requires a wait. After they get to the table Franklin starts the conversation.

"Anything interesting to report?"

"Yeah, looks like they retained their expert, heard Michaels talking to..."

Franklin quickly cuts him off. "Just give me the key information and never tell me anything about how you got it, roger me?"

Ryan glares back at Franklin. What a condescending ass. He's hired me to do surveillance, but he doesn't want to know the details? What bull crap. Only from a lawyer.

"Are you kidding me?" Ryan says.

"No, I'm not. They've got these rules that prohibit lawyers from doing indirectly what they can't do directly. I know because I am on one of the ethics committees for the Bar. Even if what you do isn't illegal like you say, I've got a bunch of ethical standards to worry about that don't apply to the general public. So, yeah, I'm dead serious." Franklin looks to his right and his left as if someone at the adjacent tables may be listening.

"Whatever. Okay, the facts. Michaels has been talking to an aviation guy and he plans to give him the black box data. They've been talking about that and what might have happened."

"They don't have any theories yet do they? The NTSB hasn't said a word yet."

"Nothing solid yet, but they discussed electronics."

"Okay, great. Probably the same guy he used during the 9/11 cases. A known entity."

"The guy told Michaels he thinks it was an electrical defect but he'd need to inspect various parts of the plane. Michaels told him it would take forever to get permission."

"Yep, we fight them tooth and nail when they want an inspection. Okay, what else?"

"You told me to look for stuff involving his paralegal. I found all kinds of stuff. They've got several different families that may hire them and she's requesting info from them."

"I figured as much. The press has been covering Michaels and his firm every day. Anything more interesting?"

Ryan drinks some coffee before answering. "She issued a Freedom of Information Act request to Dulles International Airport. It's for all the surveillance videos at the gate before and after the departure."

"Hmmm...We don't get a copy of that because it's not issued in the lawsuit. That's good intel. I will be sure to ask for it during discovery. I wonder why they want it?"

"How do you want your bill written up? I mean, the company name will be Litigation Support Associates, but..."

"Yeah, let's discuss that. It can't have any details. Just put something vague, like 'document review,' the total hours spent and amount owed. We have all kinds of outside litigation vendors and you need to be just another. And don't give me anything else in writing."

"Roger."

"Let's meet again in a couple weeks, I'll call you."

"I'm sure I'll have something even better for you by then."

Bond Formed

Amnesia has wiped out everything from before the crash, but nothing since.

"Hey, I remember you!" Amanda says.

"Yeah, I hear you're doing well." Kent replies.

"You had that T-shirt on with four guys walking."

"Those four guys were famous. They were in a band. You really don't know who they are?" Kent says.

"Nope, I can't even remember who my family members are. I just liked the picture."

"You really don't know who the Beatles are?"

"No. Do they play around here?"

"Wow. I don't know where to start. They were, like, the most popular band in the 60s. I cover a few of their songs. My dad has this coffee shop with a music store in the back that you may have been to. You know Café Loco in Middleburg? Anyhow, he has the same poster of the Beatles crossing the street. The road was called Abbey Road and they named one of their albums after it. 'She came in through the bathroom window, protected by her silver spoon...'"

"I don't know Café Loco, and I don't know the Beatles. What about the bathroom window, is that a song?"

"Can you listen to music?"

"No one has said I can't, and my aunt, the one who's always here, she would've told me. She's always telling me what I can't do."

"When I'm volunteering here I can't listen to music. They want me to give all of my attention to my work, which I guess makes sense.

"Here I'll put my ear buds in your ears so you can hear 'Strawberry Fields Forever.'"

Kent delicately places the small buds inside Amanda's ears and she listens to Ben Harper's version of the song.

"How cool would it be to walk around in strawberry fields?" Amanda asks Kent loudly because the music is filling her ears.

"Very cool. They wrote the song about a specific place in England, but we could probably find some strawberry fields somewhere around here and walk through them. Not while you have that halo on your head, but maybe one day. In the meantime, I'll put together some music for you."

"What instrument do you play?"

"I play guitar. Acoustic, electric, and I have a 12-string guitar, which is like playing two guitars that are an octave apart. Sometimes I play at my dad's café or his music store, Ramblin Kyle's. If you ever get out of here you can come hear me. I play with a couple friends in a band."

"I wonder if I've been to the café before."

"Hard to say. A lot of kids from the local high schools come in, so it's possible, but I don't remember seeing you there."

Amanda notices that Kent, who is sitting in the chair beside her bed, is wearing one of the most wrinkled pairs of khakis she's ever seen. His light blue polo shirt says 'Loudoun' and is less wrinkled." He has short chestnut brown hair and she decides he's cute.

"You're cute, do you have a girlfriend?" Amanda asks, her filter removed by her amnesia.

"Wow, you're pretty direct. I go out, but I don't have a girlfriend really."

"Do we go to the same high school?"

"No. I finished high school. I'm 20. I went to JMU for a year, but withdrew and came back here. You go to Middleburg Academy, right? That's a snooty private school. I don't mean you're snooty, but a lot of the kids there are. Did you know you were a star soccer player?"

"Really? That's weird. How do you know that?"

"It's been all over the news. I also talked to your aunt. Anyway, I need to go visit some more rooms."

"When will you come talk to me again?" Amanda asks urgently.

"I volunteer twice a week so it'll be a couple days. I also work at a stable with horses."

"Really? I think I love horses. Please come see me soon."

"Sure. I have to turn you on to some music. I will ask your aunt if you own a phone or something," he says while starting to leave.

"Remember me," Amanda says.

"Halo girl, how could I forget you?"

@Part II
Second Session

Dr. Lucent enters Amanda's room, and Barbara Simon picks up the *Washington Post* and her magazines and walks out.

"Good morning Amanda. Are you ready for another session with me?"

"I'm ready for you to tell me when I can get this halo thing off."

"That's Dr. Wrightson's jurisdiction. Have you asked him?"

"No I haven't, since I don't know which one he is. As for your first question, I'm babbling all kinds of madness and can't remember squat. Is that enough for today's session?" She asks sarcastically.

"You're not in a great mood this morning."

"You wouldn't be either if you were trapped in this hospital bed with metal all over your head and could barely move. Not to mention everybody but me died on that plane and I can't remember my own parents. But everything's great doctor, thanks for asking!"

"Unfortunately, I can't change what happened. I can try to help you work through where you are now. Help you make sense of things."

"Yeah, sure."

"Look, my interest is not just in helping restore your memory, but also making some sense of your NDEs. While I would have been treating you for your brain injury regardless, I've treated a number of young kids and documented their NDEs, and I'd like to do the same for you."

"What do you mean?"

"One 10-year-old patient got her hair caught in a powerful pool drain and drowned. She was given CPR for 45 minutes and, miraculously, her pulse came back. She told me she floated right out of her body and traveled up through a narrow, brightly lit tunnel. When she got to what she called heaven, a nice man asked her if she wanted to stay."

"I know, she didn't stay, duh..." Amanda interjects, sipping on the straw in her cup then placing it back on the tray.

"Right, she told him she wanted to be with her family, and then came back. Then I had Adam. He was 15 or 16 and had a rare heart condition that had never been diagnosed. He coded in the hospital waiting room. In the intensive care unit, doctors employed chest compression and injected epinephrine and got his heart working again.

"A couple days later he told me he had an out-of-body experience. He also described moving fast through a tunnel, and at a certain point a tall white-haired man offered him two large buttons. At first, he wasn't sure which one to press because he didn't know whether he wanted to go forward or return, or even which button would do what. He ultimately decided he wanted to see his family and friends again. Somehow he knew at that moment which button to choose and he came back when his pulse returned."

"I remember a bright white light, but not any choice about which way to go. Like, whether to come back or not, or whether I did it for my family or what."

"What is the bright light? What does it represent? No one knows." Lucent then reduces the volume of his voice to little more than a whisper. "Unfortunately, the hospital is not supportive of my research."

"Why don't they want you to study it?"

"A few years ago I published a short book discussing kids' NDEs. The title was *The Inner Light*. There is no real-world explanation for many aspects of NDEs. I've been exploring whether there is an unexplained phenomenon of the human soul. Any time you challenge medical science you're treated like an outsider because people are uncomfortable with things they don't understand.

"Do you remember the children's book called *A Fish Out of Water*? Oh, I guess you wouldn't," he says, catching himself before Amanda can answer. "I still remember when I was little, my mom would read me that book and I loved it. There's the famous scene in the book where this man who runs a pet store, Mr. Carp, jumps into the pool with a giant goldfish named Otto that had grown huge after a little boy fed it too much. Otto filled up the whole pool, but Mr. Carp jumped in with his snorkel gear and the next thing you knew he made Otto small enough to fit in his original goldfish bowl again. I loved that book mainly because I never understood how Mr. Carp did it. Unlike kids, I think my grown-up colleagues don't like me writing about NDEs because they are confused and the mere concept threatens their tidy view of reality.

"This is especially true when it comes to the concept of a person's soul. It's something that has not been peer-reviewed or proven in an operating room. So, the entire thing is dismissed. I got off on a tangent, sorry. Let's get back to you. You told me about the Dorothys, you told me about Justin. Have you remembered anything else new?"

"Just last night I either dreamed or remembered something. I was on a plane —before it crashed I guess — and I'm looking next to me and see a pretty lady. She has a peaceful look on her face, and she's holding my hand."

"Your mom?"

"I guess so."

"Did you see a man, perhaps your dad, on the plane too?"

"No." Amanda stares at the wall.

"That's a significant dream," Lucent hands her a tablet. "Take this note pad and keep notes of any dreams you have, or if you recall any NDEs, and we can discuss them later."

"I don't know about a soul, Dr. Lucent, I need to think about that. I mean everyone talks about a soul, but I never heard anyone say that it might slip out of your body. I don't understand why I survived either. Hey, can I read your book?"

"Sure, I'll bring it by tomorrow. It'll be interesting to see what you have dreamed or remembered by our next session."

Speed Bump

It was never made clear to her just why she was selected for this role by the Chief Justice of the U.S. Supreme Court. It remains challenging, though whistleblower Edward Snowden single-handedly made her "top-secret" Intelligence Court job far less secret. She stares again at the affidavit on the screen of the government-supplied laptop sitting on her desk on the third floor of the Alexandria Federal Courthouse.

TOP SECRET
UNITED STATES
FOREIGN INTELLIGENCE SURVEILLANCE COURT
In Re Application of the Federal Bureau of Investigation for a Special Order
AFFIDAVIT 2165

She flips to the second page and re-reads the outline. Then she scrolls a few more pages and looks over the order requested. Unbeknownst to the public, Judge Lisa Bondakopf serves as one of only a dozen secret United States Foreign Intelligence Surveillance Act judges who review Patriot Act and intelligence surveillance requests. This is the only speed bump all CIA, NSA, and FBI requests hit in their pursuit of the covert dirt. The FISA and Patriot Act provisions allow them to bypass unwieldy grand juries, pesky probable-cause mandates and all search and seizure protections afforded Americans by the Fourth Amendment of the U.S. Constitution. In other words, Bondakopf and her eleven colleagues serve as the only internal control over the government's often warrantless requests under the acts.

"We need to be at the judge's chambers at 2:00 p.m. today for Affidavit 2165," Department of Justice Intelligence Counsel Braningham reiterates to FBI Special Agent Solarez.

"She's never asked to talk to us before. Do you know how many FISA affidavit requests and orders she has reviewed and signed?" Solarez protests.

"Of course I do. I talked to her. But she said she's not signing anything until she gets a satisfactory explanation."

"I can't remember one single time when an FISA judge has requested details of our ongoing operations."

"That may be true, but a number of the judges have modified and narrowed our requests. Usually they work with us, but this time she said she won't. So the deal is, if you want the order, we have to be there at 2:00 p.m."

"Why don't we just submit it to one of the other..."

"I'm going to pretend you didn't ask me that. Do you know how quickly she would find out if I tried an end-run around her with another judge?"

Braningham and Solarez are ushered into the judge's chambers. Judge Bondakopf is waiting. She shakes their hands and offers them seats in large tufted leather chairs in front of her desk. There is no need for the courtroom today since there is no opposing party or court reporter.

"I realize this is unusual. However, this is not a usual affidavit. I've reviewed it carefully and I'm not going to sign it."

"Never going to sign it, Your Honor? Why would you call us here then?" Braningham asks.

"I didn't say never. I just said I'm not signing it based on what's currently in it."

"Judge, I'm a bit baffled. Just a few weeks ago you signed Affidavit 2163, covering telephone metadata of millions of cell phone subscribers for three months. This is only three people."

"Counsel, this is a completely different animal. This covers three select individuals, one of whom is an attorney here in Washington. Essentially you're seeking to wiretap all electronic communications of Michaels, his niece, and this other individual, Kent Perless. Don't you see the contrast?

"And, I'm sure you remember the Maypole case on the West Coast, when you hit, let's say, a few snags with an attorney designated as a terrorist? My FISA colleague on the West Coast granted the secondary order because you supposedly had a fingerprint hit. Only it wasn't really Maypole's print. Your colleagues were positive he was the terrorist mastermind behind the Spain subway attacks because he had converted to Islam. Let's not forget how much money the U.S. paid him for that mistake. Do we understand each other?"

Braningham looks sheepishly at his notes. "That was a very rare, unfortunate mistake. And frankly, Your Honor, I still contend that this affidavit falls under the clear provisions of the Act, just like all the others you have reviewed and signed."

"Look, everyone not living in a cave knows that Andy Michaels lost his brother and sister-in-law in the Hemispheres crash. You're asking me, with no factual basis that one might dare to call probable cause, to give you permission for an open-ended search of him, his niece, and this other person, who I have no idea what role he plays. I'm not signing this secondary order without further evidence." The judge drops the affidavit on her desk for dramatic effect.

"Why don't you guys go to the conference room and make some calls. Someone is going to tell me exactly what provision of the Patriot Act or FISA this request falls under, and more importantly, how, before I sign this order. The Fourth Amendment still means something to some of us. This boilerplate, formulaic affidavit is not enough for me, and Counsel, I'm sure I don't have to remind you that all of the FISA judges engage in a secure conference call every other week."

Braningham and Solarez leave her chambers, have an animated conversation in the hallway, and then disappear into the conference room. Fifteen minutes later the buzzer goes off and a U.S. Marshal in the outer reception area lets the two of them back into her chambers.

"Now that you have had time to confer, which provisions of which act authorize me to sign this order?"

Braningham looks down at his notes and over at Solarez. "Judge, the anti-terrorism provisions and –"

"Are you suggesting to me that Andy Michaels is involved in terrorism? I hope you are prepared to explain."

"Judge, I don't contend that. However –"

"Are you suggesting that a terrorist act was involved in the Hemispheres crash? There has not been a word about it from either the FBI or the NTSB. Is there credible evidence?"

"We don't know yet is the best answer we can give you."

"Well then, if you're not suggesting Andy Michaels or his niece are involved in any type of terrorism, how does this fit under any Patriot or FISA provision?" she asks.

"Your Honor, we're not of the belief that they were actively involved, but you didn't let me finish. We do believe that the basis of this request fits better under the clandestine intelligence operation provision."

"Wait a second. Isn't it either one or the other? We either have terrorism or we have a covert intelligence operation," she says, holding her left and right hands palms up in front of her as a visual aid.

"Not necessarily, Your Honor. We suspect there is active surveillance already, so we need to determine who may be monitoring their electronic communications. I don't really want to divulge any national security information unless you require us to do so."

"I'm still not going to sign. If you want to disclose more, perhaps I'll change my mind."

Braningham leans over and whispers to Solarez. "Agent Solarez will address your concerns."

"Judge, I understand why you may be skeptical. Let me tell you where this whole thing starts. Andy Michaels' brother, Ron Michaels, was a biologist with Biological Blood Services, a research group just outside Washington. Michaels has developed some very significant breakthroughs having to do with telomeres, one of the basic structures in the human cell chromosome. We were running a counter-intelligence operation involving Ron Michaels before plane went down. We believe that some of the highly classified research he developed was somehow pilfered by at least one foreign nation, and we need to know how. The purpose of this affidavit is to continue an ongoing operation involving counter-intelligence and clandestine activities. That is why we need to monitor all of the individuals outlined in this affidavit."

The judge stands up and walks several steps over to the single window of tinted bullet-proof glass overlooking Courthouse Square. She ponders for what seems like an eternity, then turns back to them.

"So, the category is biological. And the authority would be 'clandestine intelligence operations.' Are you suggesting the Michaels brothers may have been involved in assisting a foreign nation?"

"There are many unanswered questions, but the Michaels brothers are not our targets, Your Honor," Solarez says.

“As to Andy Michaels and his niece, you are monitoring them to prevent a future terrorist act and for counter-intelligence?”

“Yes, Your Honor.”

"And you're convinced, Agent Solarez, that this roving electronic surveillance is going to lead you to information regarding a foreign country trying to steal biological secrets?"

"Precisely."

"This third person, Kent Perless, what is his involvement?"

"At this time, he is only a person of interest. We're unsure how he fits in, but he's an acquaintance of Amanda Michaels we're watching."

"I'm still not going to authorize these open-ended sneak-and-peek warrants and electronic communication surveillances with no notification to the persons being searched, especially without a sunset provision. I'll give you three months to get what you need, but then you're going to have to notify them."

"Judge, you know that an ongoing intelligence operation can be compromised as soon as we have to notify..." Braningham whines.

"Like I said, I'll modify the proposed order and give you 90 days before you have to notify the three individuals. By that time you'd better have everything you need and solid evidence of the benefit of this fiasco or you're going to have hell to pay. And that's just to me, not the subjects of these warrantless searches. This better not be another Maypole fiasco."

Infectious Process

Dr. Wrightson flips through the clipboard with the pathology results and blood tests. He briefly talks to Amanda, mentions she will be starting an antibiotic, and within a couple of minutes, leaves the room. Unfortunately, the blood test results indicate MRSA, a particularly dangerous flesh-eating infection. Only a few antibiotics have been proven effective against MRSA. Two medical residents stand beside Dr. Wrightson, and he assigns one to monitor the blood over the next 48 hours.

"As long as this is being treated, put the usual infection warnings on her door, discuss it with all the nurses, and be sure everyone thoroughly sanitizes their hands before they come into the room and after they leave. This kind of infection must be treated very seriously," he explains to them. "We're going to administer vancomycin, one of the best antibiotics for fighting this infection. Let's have blood draws twice a day for the next 7 to 14 days. She had multiple open wounds with numerous stitches and, unfortunately, MRSA is insidious in a hospital setting."

The next morning, the resident monitoring Amanda's blood has startling news.

"Dr. Wrightson, the blood test done this morning on the Michaels patient shows no counts for the MRSA infection. I couldn't believe it so I ran it again. What am I missing?"

"It's a mistake. You must have the wrong chart. Or you could be looking at an earlier test before she developed the infection."

"I checked everything twice — date, time, and patient. I also searched through all the blood records. Did you know that she had no blood administered between the crash site and the hospital?"

"That's probably a paperwork mistake. You know rescue squads are notorious for poor notes because of what they do and the conditions they work under. You'll have to talk to them."

"But remember, she was the only patient airlifted out of that crash site, it's not like they were triaging a bunch of people."

"MRSA doesn't just disappear. In fact, part of the reason it's so dangerous is because it multiplies. Double-check everything again and let me know what you find."

Team Scrapbook

Barbara and her husband spent several hours poring through family pictures collected from Ron and Rochelle's home and organized them into several scrapbooks for Amanda. They also found a few CDs with family videos. Barbara purchased a new cell phone for Amanda and found her laptop at the house, full of Amanda's own pictures, email and schoolwork. Both Barbara and Andy have since gone through the scrapbooks with Amanda several times, but have made no progress in restoring her memory of anything before the crash.

A daily stream of well-wishers continues to visit Amanda. Alex Erickson brings his wife Denise and their three kids to see their favorite babysitter, but the kids are upset and confused—despite having been warned of Amanda's amnesia. Becca brings Amanda two blouses from her shop, which fully button to get around the halo. But Amanda shows zero interest in them. Barbara, always the optimist, remains excited about Amanda's soccer teammates coming by as a group with a new scrapbook.

"We brought something very special with us," Iris Bailey says, waving a thick scrapbook in front of Amanda. Iris is followed by several other players from the MA soccer team, all of whom have played with Amanda and had classes with her. David Owlsley, arguably the smartest student at MA, and John Parkinson, who dated Amanda before the crash, are also there.

Iris sits on the hospital bed on one side of Amanda, and Charlyne and Amber sit by the other side of the bed, sharing a chair.

One of the few players on the team who has played club soccer with Amanda since they were 12, Amber has helped put the memory book together, including captions of places and names shown in the photos. Amber and Amanda are both Type A personalities and are like oil and water. "Look at this group picture here. We were what, 12? This was where I met you, Amanda. Do you remember Coach Bobby?" Amber asks, pointing to a picture of young girls in a team picture. "This is you right here, and I'm right next to you. We all had the same color ribbons in our hair."

Amanda stares at the picture, trying to smile. She recognizes no one and can't remember anything.

Iris knows that the moment is uncomfortable. She flips the page to the next picture. "This was when we played for the Loudoun Strikers team. Do you remember this Memorial Day tournament? It was raining ridiculously. One time you took a shot and completely wiped out and landed on your butt in a mud puddle. But the shot still rolled in past the goalie." Iris excitedly says. "Or how about this group picture of the whole MA team and Coach Ricci?"

"Coach Ricci?" Amanda asks.

Iris steals a glance over at Amber and Charlyne.

"Coach Ricci is one of your favorite teachers. He teaches English. We're hoping to win the State Championship this year. You are one of the starting forwards, along with Amber. We hope to have you back with us," Charlyne says, knowing it may never happen.

"School's not the same without you," John says after the soccer players exhaust their efforts to jog Amanda's memory. "We all miss your sense of humor. The teachers keep asking how you're doing, especially Coach Ricci."

Amanda looks at John and decides he's is a really good-looking guy. He's tall, has dirty blonde hair, and is wearing a faded T-shirt and pair of jeans. "What do you do for fun at school?" she asks him.

John looks at her and David with a perplexed smile. "Uh, I play baseball, and hang out." He thinks it's too bizarre that she asked that question when they were virtually inseparable before the crash.

"How long did I go out with you?" Amanda asks John, as serious as can be.

"Well, we started dating the spring of ninth grade and have been together pretty much since then."

"I don't know what we would have in common." The comment is biting and sarcastic, and it hits John like a ton of bricks.

John is ready to defend their relationship, but David puts up his hand like a crossing guard, motioning John to keep quiet. He flips down the screen of his laptop on his lap, saying, "Amanda, maybe it will start coming back to you. You don't remember now, and your emotions are out of whack too. Let's just move on to something else."

"Actually, I'm pretty tired. I should probably get some rest."

Just then, Barbara comes into the room and the teens say their goodbyes and head for the hallway.

"This scrapbook is great. We really appreciate you doing this. And it's so nice that you want to have a party. We'll talk to Amanda and let you know."

As the group walks down the long hall toward the hospital exit, Charlyne mumbles to the others. “I’m so bummed. I can’t believe she doesn’t remember us.”

“Tell me about it,” John says. “She treats me like I’m nobody.”

Charlyne says, “Oh, I left my phone in the room. I drove myself so you don’t have to wait for me.”

The rest of the group departs, and Charlyne walks back inside. Actually, she has her phone in her pocket. She just wants to spend some more time with Amanda, alone. A few minutes later she is talking with her again.

“I really wasn’t that tired, I was just bored and bothered with the whole trying to remember stuff,” Amanda tells Charlyne, simply because she’s there.

“Can I ask you a weird question? What was I like? I mean was I your best friend? Was I nice, or a bitch, or what?” Amanda asks.

“Uh, well, we weren’t really BFFs.” Charlyne says.

“What’s a BFF?”

“‘Best friends forever.’ You were always with John. So yeah, we’ve always been good friends, but you were with him the most.”

“Like all the time?”

“Yeah.”

“John, the guy that was just here?”

“Yeah.” Charlyne opens the scrapbook and points out numerous pictures of Amanda and John.

“Do you know if I, uh, did it with John? He looked at me a certain way, and I was freaking out thinking what if I did? So, did I?”

“I don’t know. It’s not like you walked up to me and said, ‘Hey, John and I did it.’ That’s not the kind of thing you would’ve told me.

I know you were intimate with him…” Charlyne thinks it’s time to get off this tangent, and fast. “Do you know you’re the only vegan on the soccer team? You turned a lot of girls onto vegan stuff.”

“Are you kidding? I didn’t eat anything but vegetables? What about cheeseburgers?”

“No. You were obsessive. Frankly it was a royal pain in the ass.” Charlyne says.

“But I love cheeseburgers and eggs and stuff like that. I can’t see eating just plants and green stuff.”

“Crazy. Now we can finally eat somewhere together, no special orders necessary.” Charlyne laughs.

Barbara slips back in and agrees: "It's true. You've been a vegan since you were 16, or should I say you used to be."

After discussing many other pictures, Charlyne leaves. Sadness envelopes her as she walks alone to her car, depressed at the loss of camaraderie. She resolves to do what she can to restore Amanda any way possible.

Who Listens?

After the depressing hospital visit with Amanda, David decides to hang out with John and do some gaming at his house. They run through a virtual burned-out warehouse in a snowy war zone.

"Watch out David, there's a sniper entering behind us."

David's online persona, a military warrior, whirls around and guns down the invading sniper with a machine gun.

After lobbing C4 and grenades into different rooms and terminating the virtual lives of innumerable opponents, they finish that particular mission. John scrolls through the onscreen menu looking for another war zone to conquer.

"John, I want to show you something in my car." They put down the controllers and walk outside.

Before they get to the car, David says, "I really don't have anything to show you in the car, I just didn't want to talk inside."

"Why?" John asks.

"You know I'm a computer nerd, right?"

"I wouldn't call you a nerd, at least not to your face, but I'll take your perfect 800 in math, reading and writing on the SAT any time. And your dad works for that computer snoop and spy company, right?"

"Yeah, my dad always has computer gear around, and it's been pretty useful. Look, there's a lot of stuff about me and computers that I don't tell anybody about. Can I trust you?" David stares at John with a very serious look on his face.

"Sure, you can trust me. Why?"

"Well, sometimes I'm just paranoid, but I have reason to be now. Can you think of any reason why there would be a bug hidden in Amanda's room?"

"What are you talking about? Like a thing to spy on her with? How do you know?"

"Every time I've gone to see her I've brought my laptop, and I have detection equipment installed on it, along with a small USB device that works as a receptor. I did some analysis and there's more going on than just Wi-Fi. I'm as sure as I can be. Any ideas on who'd bug her or why?"

"Who would bug Amanda's room?" John repeats, thinking. "Well, the press has wanted to talk to her. They're so desperate for interviews, they even tried me. So maybe the *National Enquirer* or something?"

"I don't know," David says. "But somebody wants to know everything that's going on in her room."

John looks back at the house from where they are standing beside David's car. Could someone actually bug his room? Is David being paranoid? No, David is nobody's fool.

"Have you told anyone else about this besides me?" he asks David.

"Not a soul."

Funeral News

Angie has her TV tuned into CNT as she gets ready for work. The news correspondents are discussing the crash and the video images behind them are helicopter footage of the wreckage.

> "This is Natalee Spalding, reporting on the Hemispheres crash aftermath. There have been a number of funerals held around the Washington, D.C. metropolitan area and in New York by families mourning the loss of those who died in the crash. We are specifically covering the funeral for the parents of the sole survivor, Amanda Michaels. A joint funeral is being held today in Loudoun County, Virginia.
>
> "I want to turn to our legal correspondent, Jeff Rossman, for an update on identification of the passengers who died in the Hemispheres crash. Jeff, what can you tell us about identification issues?"
>
> "Forensic investigators had the difficult task of finding remains of the victims and comparing them with existing records, such as dental records. After a lot of painstaking work, all passengers and crew members have been identified."
>
> "Thank you, Jeff, I may come back to you in a few minutes. We have not been told whether or not Amanda Michaels will attend her parents' funeral. Up to this point, the lone survivor has not made a public appearance."

Angie grabs the remote and turns off the television. After zipping up her black skirt, she reaches for her phone and texts Myra: *"Just saw news story on the Michaels funeral. Meet at corner of Wisconsin & Oak at 10 a.m.? Will be tough day."*

Angie finishes getting ready, pausing to read Myra's response:

Agreed. What R U wearing?

Black skirt, white blouse, black jacket, black shoes.

K

Joint Service

Angie accelerates onto the ramp entering Interstate 66 West.

"You don't have to haul ass, we have plenty of time."

"I'm not speeding, I just have a fast car."

"Where is the service being held?"

"Temple Beth El, on the edge of Reston. I don't know about you, but this is going to be one of the worst days of my life." Angie adds, just thinking about Andy's eulogy.

"I stuffed half a box of tissues in my purse. I've never been to a Jewish funeral. Have you?"

"Never. But I called a friend of mine who's Jewish and asked what to expect. She couldn't think of anything that would be that different. I asked her about the service inside the temple and she said there usually isn't one."

"Amanda's going to be there, right?"

"Andy said she would be. He asked if she wanted to speak and she said 'no way.'"

They slowly pull into a large parking lot, guided by men in black suits. "Oh my God, I've never seen so many people," Myra says.

"What'd you expect? It's all over the news."

They find a seat about a third of the way back on the left side. Angie recognizes several D.C. lawyers as she scans the sanctuary.

Angie flips open the funeral pamphlet and scans through the names of those delivering eulogies. An organ begins playing at a barely audible level. Myra can't see where it's hidden. The rabbi, in a long traditional robe not unlike a judge's, speaks:

"We come here today with heavy hearts and in sadness with regard to the passing of Ron Michaels and his wife and soul mate, Rochelle Michaels."

Angie tries to let her mind wander to avoid breaking into tears. She knows that once there is a crack in the dam, it will turn into a flood. She tilts her head to the left and sees Andy's head and Amanda's halo from the rear.

Andy walks up to the lectern. "We try to make sense of this tragedy, but it's impossible. How could people so good, that we respect and love so much, be taken from us this way? Ron was a wonderful brother. We were born only a year-and-a-half apart, as many of you know, and we were the ultimate competitors. We competed in skiing, triathlons, squash and tennis. He found Rochelle during college, and I remember the first day I met her I had a feeling she was the one. We've made so many wonderful memories..."

Tears are rolling down Angie's face behind her dark sunglasses.

"Here, more tissues." Myra whispers.

"Amanda, you're a survivor," Andy continues, "and you're my inspiration. Even though you have suffered terrible injuries, we know that you will make a great recovery."

Andy leaves the podium, and the congregation watches him return to the front row with his family members. The pamphlet indicates Andy was to deliver the last eulogy. Then, there is a rustling from the front of the temple. Myra and Angie crane their necks. They see Andy slowly walking Amanda up to the podium. The rabbi steps up to the other side, assures that Amanda is okay, and adjusts the thin gooseneck microphone down to her height. Once she is steady, Andy backs away a couple steps.

"Hi. My name is Amanda Michaels. I wasn't going to speak, but something changed my mind. First, I want to say my aunt and uncle have been great, really great. They have given me scrapbooks and mementos and even videos of my parents. And I am sorry, really sorry if I have seen you and didn't remember you or things we did. I can't do anything about it but wish I could. Anyhow, I read over everything about my family and I found one birthday card my mom gave me. It says on the cover, '13th Birthday.'" Amanda holds the card up for a moment. "And I know this was before I had my bat mitzvah, because of what she wrote: 'Amanda, I have never seen someone more dedicated and focused than you. I have listened to you singing the prayers over and over outside your bedroom. You are going to succeed not just at your bat mitzvah but in everything you put your mind to in life. You inspire me every day. Love, Mom.'

"This is what my mom did to inspire me. My dad probably didn't write gushy things like this, but I can tell he was happy in all the pictures and videos we have.

"So, on behalf of my family, my aunt and uncle, and on behalf of Justin, thanks for being here."

Andy walks back over to the podium but Amanda waves her hand, indicating she wants no help. She walks down the five carpeted steps from the podium, turns, and pauses to run her hands over each of the two closed caskets. She then takes her seat with Andy on one side of her and Barb on the other.

Myra notices the rabbi is again speaking.

"The Michaels family invites all of you to their home at 121 Rock Place, Reston, Virginia, after 4:00 p.m. where the family will sit Shiva today, tomorrow, and the following day. The address is printed on the back of your pamphlet. The graveside service is for immediate family only."

The funeral home representative softly shuts the door of the limousine after Andy. They have really done a nice job, he realizes. There was nothing about this whole thing that had not been painful for Andy, but meeting with the funeral home director was high on the agony list. Ron and Rochelle had never bought cemetery plots, and working out the language on the tombstones with Barbara was surreal. Barbara and her husband Steve were also selfless, handling most of the arrangements since he was fairly overwhelmed with the legal details of the lawsuits.

The rabbi delivers very brief remarks at the grave. As soon as he finishes, the funeral home representatives slowly turn some sort of pulley that lowers each casket in cadence. Andy can hear sobbing but looks straight ahead, hiding behind his dark sunglasses. He looks over his right shoulder and sees Amanda, with the ubiquitous halo, still standing beside the black limousine about 25 yards away. She had refused to walk with him over to the grave insisting on staying away, over beside the limo. The rabbi then explains the symbolic custom of taking a scoop of dirt and dropping it into the freshly dug holes.

Andy counts the times that he has had to do this in his life: his mother, granddad, and one uncle. He takes the first scoop of dirt and pours it gingerly right beside the casket of his brother. And he takes a few steps over and does the same into the open hole beside Rochelle's casket. Struggling to compose himself, he then stabs the shovel back into the mound of dirt where the rabbi has gestured. One by one, other family members do the same, including Rochelle's parents and Andy's father.

After softly plunging the shovel back into the dirt mound his father walks over and touches Andy's shoulder.

"That was a beautiful eulogy," his dad says in a whisper.

"Thanks Dad." Andy can't think of anything else to say without breaking down, so he decides not to try. Since his mom's death years ago, his dad had been on kind of a wild streak, acting more like a bachelor than a widower. Barbara and Andy are glad that he came up from Naples, Florida, and that he came alone.

As soon as he is back beside the limousine, Andy talks to Amanda, while Becca stands a respectful distance away.

"Are you okay?" he asks.

"Yeah, that's the problem."

"What do you mean?"

"Don't worry about it. I don't know really..."

"But I do worry about it, we are all worried about you."

She has something folded up in her right hand that she is nervously tapping along her right thigh. He looks down and notices the cover of the birthday card. At that moment he understands exactly what Amanda is saying.

Shiv-er

“How many blocks away are we? There’s already cars parked on both sides,” Angie says as they inch through the residential neighborhood to get to Barb’s house.

“Just find a parking space, we’re not far,” Myra responds. “Hey, who is this Justin that Amanda mentioned?”

“I have no idea,” Angie says.

Andy and Barbara each face the full range of emotions greeting family and friends near the front door.

As soon as Alex walks through the door and faces Andy, their eyes lock. He embraces Andy while his wife hovers a few feet away.

"We’re so sorry. I don't know what else we can say."

"There really isn't anything...," Andy whispers.

Then Alex’s wife, Denise, hugs Andy in silence. Andy breaks the embrace, asking “How are your kids?”

"We didn't bring them. We decided that they were too young. They had enough trouble seeing Amanda in the hospital with that halo, especially since she didn’t remember them.”

“I agree.” Andy nods. “Why subject them to this.”

"How are you holding up?" Alex asks.

"As good as can be expected."

Alex leans into Andy and touches his upper arm. "Andy, if there is anything we can do for you, for Amanda...”

"Thanks guys, I appreciate it." Several other couples are hovering nearby to pay their respects.

Alex leans closer to Andy. "I checked with the human resources manager at work. She can call you and go over Ron's insurance benefits."

Alex was not only one of Ron's longtime friends, they also worked together at Biological Blood Services, or BBS for short. The CEO, Michael Jacoby, attended the funeral.

"I also talked to folks at the office about getting Ron's things, and I can help get them to you whenever you want," Alex offers. “We’d been training together for the next Ironman event..." he says, his eyes welling up with tears.

Andy notices the sudden surge of emotion and consciously turns the subject to happier memories. "I have the picture behind my desk of all three of us in our first triathlon together. Ron was so proud of doing the Ironman and he trained so hard, particularly for the swim under Memorial Bridge. He bested both of us every time, remember?"

"Of course I do, although I hate to admit it."

They are standing at the rear of the room near the open doorway and their attention moves to the large TV playing a slide show of Rochelle and Ron. At least 20 other people occupy the room, nibbling on food and watching the photos.

"Do you remember that it took them, what, a year and a half of in vitro for Rochelle to finally get pregnant?" Alex asks Andy.

"Yeah, it seems like ancient history now."

A slide showing Ron and Rochelle standing side by side on a strange-looking rocky coastline appears.

"I love that picture," Andy says.

"Yeah, that was when they visited the Galapagos Islands. Rochelle loved nature and exotic plants and animals. She was fascinated with the Blue-Footed Booby. I think it's only found there. I'm sure you need to talk to some other folks. If you need anything, don't hesitate to call me."

Sarah, his ex-wife, has been in the house talking with a number of Andy and Barb's relatives and finally works her way over to Andy. Becca has been watching her every move, though unobtrusively, from the kitchen area. Sarah reaches out to give him a heartfelt hug, which she holds a couple extra seconds.

"I'm so sorry, Andy." She whispers in his ear. "I'd really like to see you again soon. I'll call you."

Without waiting for an answer, she then respectfully moves away to allow someone else to greet him.

"My condolences to you," Angie says when she finally gets her face time with Andy.

"Andy, so sorry for your loss." Myra says.

"Thanks both of you. And thanks for coming today. We have all kinds of food, so help yourself."

"We've had three different families call who want to meet with you. I set up appointments for the day after tomorrow. Is that okay?" Angie asks.

"I guess so. Sitting here every day would probably be worse."

Angie and Myra say their goodbyes, leaving Andy to accept more condolences, and help themselves to a fruit tray in a different room.

Myra asks Angie, "Is Amanda going to live here?"

"It's the obvious choice. They're a lot closer to Middleburg Academy than Andy's place in Georgetown."

Andy looks for Becca, and as she walks past him toward the kitchen she whispers, "Did you really need to be that friendly to her?"

Andy wheels around and follows her into the kitchen, where they are momentarily alone.

"Look," he whispers back while she puts some dishes in the dishwasher, "it's not like she wasn't part of my life before. I wasn't going to be nasty to her for coming here. But please, Becca. That was then. Now, it's you and me that matter, not her. And I mean that."

As Andy says this to Becca, he can only hope that Sarah knows this too.

Viral Video

Just about all of the soccer players are surrounding Amanda's wheelchair. David Owlsley is also hovering, along with John Parkinson.

Kent Perless enters the den and slowly walks over. David notices that he has a suit on with a light blue shirt, but unlike the rest of them he is not wearing a tie.

"Amanda, I wanted to come by tell you how sorry I am."

"Thanks. These are friends from school. I've been meeting them all over again. Everyone, this is Kent from the hospital."

"I'm Amber Fields. I'm one of the forwards on the soccer team." She shakes Kent's hand.

The remaining girls each introduce themselves.

"Didn't you go to MA a few years ago?" Amber asks.

"Just for part of a year. Things didn't work out, so I transferred to Loudoun High, where I graduated."

David pulls Jonathan over to a quiet corner of the room.

"That's the guy that did the viral fox hunt video! It's hilarious!"

David opens YouTube on his phone. He types in "red fox hunt spoof." Moments later a video comes up with 1,000,600 views, and he holds the phone so John can see. Riders wearing traditional fox hunt attire galloping on horses across a large, open pasture fill the screen. The camera view moves in front of the galloping horses. Running for its life is a tiny hamster, furiously scampering away from the horses. Crafty video editing shows a close-up of the desperate hamster as it runs around trees and even leaps over a brick half-wall. The riders appear baffled in their attempts to capture the small critter.

Several comments accompany the video. One is by Kent, the lead horseman, who exhorts his posse in a faux British accent: "He's turned, we must re-double our efforts!"

"This is crazy!" John says. "How did he come up with this?"

"I don't know, but look, it's gotten over a million views. A complete spoof on the traditions of Middleburg, and it went viral. He won't win any popularity contests in Middleburg with this. Hey, let's ask him about it."

They find Kent over at the dessert tray eyeing the Napoleons and brownies.

"Hey, I was just talking to David here. We just realized that you were the fox hunt spoof guy."

"I figured someone would bring that up."

"It's hilarious! Where did you come up with the idea?" John asks.

"I don't know. I guess you could say I like to swim upstream."

"It's so funny when all of a sudden you realize these serious riders are chasing a gerbil," David says.

"It was a hamster actually, but no hamsters were harmed in the making of the film," Kent jokes.

"Well, it's pretty twisted. I heard you were the first one to actually talk to Amanda," David says.

"Yeah, I was just changing some bedding during my rounds when she woke up and asked me a question. Actually, it completely freaked me out, but I'm looking forward to getting to know her better," Kent says, glancing over at John.

NTSB

Several hours before the official NTSB announcement, Andy's source leaks the information to him. So Andy had told Angie to expect a news release from the NTSB giving its official preliminary findings relating to the crash. Angie surfs to the NTSB website.

> **NTSB News Release:**
> **Hemispheres Flight 310 Crash, Quarryville, PA**
> Washington, D.C. — The NTSB, based on its preliminary findings relating to the circumstances of the Hemispheres Flight 310 crash, has found no evidence of sabotage or a terrorist act. NTSB investigators continue to work to find the cause and are analyzing the black box data, the voice recordings, and all forensic evidence recovered from the crash site. At this time the NTSB is ruling out any type of bomb or explosion as a cause of the crash. However, NTSB investigators caution the media and the public that no official conclusions have yet been reached on the precise cause of the crash.

Angie downloads the message and buzzes Andy on her speakerphone. "I just printed it off. Full steam ahead, right?"

"Yep. Obviously sabotage would've made our jobs 10 times harder," Andy notes.

"So are you calling Bob Garrison, or should I?" Angie asks.

"I'm on it," Andy says, his mind churning with all the different things that he wants to push forward on as far as legal strategies. Calling his aviation expert, Bob Garrison, is just one of a dozen other items in his brain's rolodex under "plane crashes."

Foreign Made

Inside a secure room in the Embassy off Massachusetts Avenue, the three men each listen to the taped conversation on small headphones.

Wait a second. Isn't it one or the other? We either have terrorism or we have a covert intelligence operation.

Not necessarily, Your Honor. We suspect there is active surveillance already, so we need to determine who may be monitoring their electronic communications. I don't really want to divulge any national security information unless you require us to do so.

Mr. Braningham, I'm still not going to sign. If you want to disclose more, perhaps I'll change my mind.

Judge Bondakopf, Agent Solarez will address your concerns.

The man in the center listens for another couple of minutes and jots notes on the pad in front of him. He then takes the headset off and drops it on the table.

"Jiang, you have done incredible work. The FISA Court is a totally secure courtroom, and I am sure FBI agents sweep that room before every hearing. Since the Snowden leaks, we have been unable to successfully hack the federal computers to obtain the FISA applications and orders. How did your team get this intelligence?" Mr. Chun, the supervisor, waits for Jiang's response.

"Sir, first, our team placed no listening devices inside the courthouse. Does that make it even harder for you to imagine how we did it?" Jiang says.

"You had no listening device inside? How can that be? This was recorded in chambers. Please explain."

"I said my team placed no listening devices inside the courtroom or judge's chambers. We conducted surveillance on this judge and two male judges because we knew they were the three FISA judges in the D.C. area. What better way to get critical information on the counter-intelligence efforts of the NSA and CIA than from their own top-secret hearings?

"We studied the shoes that the male judges wore each day until we could predict which pairs would most likely be worn. My team embedded a very tiny, non-detectable listening device into the soles of at least five pairs of shoes for each of the male judges. This was more effective than bugging their cell phones because we weren't sure they'd carry a phone into the hearings. We also mounted a tiny wireless relay device outside the window to increase our listening abilities."

"How did you get that device mounted?" Chun asks.

"Quite simple, actually. An agent posed as a window washer. The plan for the female judge was even better. After extensive surveillance at her regular courtroom, we determined that she keeps her cell phone with her at all times in her purse. Given the phone is manufactured in our country, we've had access to every component in the phone. We easily obtained her cell phone number, and when she appeared at FISA court we remotely activated the recording device built into her cell phone. When the hearing was over we turned the recording function off, waited a bit, then hacked into the phone again and commanded it to wirelessly transmit the entire recording to our listening station."

"Amazing, Jiang, particularly the part about using our mobile phone technology against the Americans. Chun says with a smile. "In light of this new intelligence information, will we be modifying our surveillance of these subjects?"

"Since the judge signed this order, we have already altered our operations, and I'm implementing several new plans to ensure that any electronic surveillance is undetectable," Jiang replies.

"This information is highly valuable to our ongoing operation. I will report this to the director. Excellent work," Chun says. "Continue to provide me weekly updates."

"Yes sir, with pleasure."

Jailbreak

"She'll have the cell phone you gave her, right?" Andy asks Barb. She is in the hallway, out of earshot of Amanda, and Andy is at his office.

"Yes, and he has a cell phone too. But it'll be the first time she's been out of this hospital on her own, and I just worry...after what's happened..." Barbara mindlessly paces.

"At some point we've gotta let go, at least a little bit. She's recovering great, and he's going to use a hospital-supplied van and wheelchair." Andy says.

A security guard still sits at Amanda's hospital room door because of the fairly constant pressure from the press for interviews and pictures. Amanda's celebrity status has been the talk of not only the talk shows and news networks, but *People* and *Us* magazines.

Barb moves the phone away from her mouth. "All right guys, it's okay so long as both of you have your cell phones and Amanda is back here by dark."

As part of the deal with Barb and Andy, Amanda is to remain in the wheelchair the entire time they are gone even though she is perfectly capable of walking. They move down the hall with Kent pushing the wheelchair to the elevator. Fortunately, the hospital has a basement level they can access by the service elevator, avoiding the press. Minutes later, Kent is driving out of the garage with his special cargo.

"How long will it take to get there?" Amanda asks.

"About 20 minutes."

At the entrance to the farm there is a white split-rail fence on both sides of the gravel entryway and fronting the farm. A small sign says "Crossroads Farm" and has a horse silhouette above the name. Kent drives the van slowly down the long drive past a horse stable. They pass a small old house, then a farmhouse with a New England style covered front porch.

"Who lives here?" Amanda asks. She notices the long open porch with a hammock and a few rocking chairs.

"I do. Manuel lives in the other house beside the stable, which he maintains, and my buddy Zander also helps part-time. My dad pays Manuel, and we board some other families' horses with ours."

They continue on down the lane to another stable. Kent parks the van, opens the side door, and turns on the pneumatic lift that holds Amanda's wheelchair. He lowers the wheelchair to the ground beside the van, pushes Amanda a few feet away from the van, and closes it back up.

"Let me introduce you to a couple of the horses."

He pushes the wheelchair into the middle of the stable where horses begin nickering, having recognized Kent's presence. Kent enters one of the stalls and walks out with a horse toward Amanda.

Amanda stands up from the wheelchair.

"I told your aunt that I'd keep you in the wheelchair, so please sit back down."

"There's nothing wrong with my legs. I'm going to pet this beautiful horse."

Amanda runs the back of her right hand along the jaw line of the horse and then along her neck, admiring her beautiful brown-and-white coat.

"Do you know anything about horses?" Kent asks.

"Not that I remember. I probably did a pony ride at some birthday party but I don't know if I've ever ridden a horse before."

"This is Roxy. She was my mother's horse."

"She's beautiful," Amanda says, still stroking her neck.

"Let me show you my horse," Kent says, walking Roxy back into her stall, releasing the lead from the halter, and closing the stall door. He walks across the aisle to the opposite stall. Moments later he produces a gelding with a white blaze between his eyes and nostrils. The only other white on him is the four white socks above his hooves; the rest of him is nearly black. "This is Voodoo. My mom got him for me when I was 14."

"Why'd you name him Voodoo?"

"I was learning to play 'Voodoo Child' by Jimi Hendrix on guitar, so I thought it was a cool name."

"I really want to ride Voodoo."

"Amanda, there's a snowball's chance in hell you're riding this horse tonight. You must have lost your mind. Well, I guess you did lose your mind, sort of, but riding is out of the question," Kent says, a bit agitated.

"You ride him then," Amanda virtually orders.

"Well, I don't know. I came here to introduce you to the farm and show you the horses." Kent mildly protests while stroking Voodoo's neck.

Amanda watches with intense interest as Kent walks Voodoo over to the area where the saddles are stored.

After saddling Voodoo, Kent slips off halter and replaces it with a bridle. He finally walks out of the stable leading Voodoo loosely by his reins, and a few steps away from the stable he swings up into the saddle. "I'll just ride in a loop."

Kent trots off about 50 yards into the open grassy field. He begins a loop counterclockwise to warm up Voodoo, and then breaks into a gallop, gradually increasing speed. Watching Kent and his horse, Amanda feels privileged. She realizes again that she's the only survivor of the plane crash and knows that some karma was behind it.

"He's a great horse, isn't he?" Kent says, slightly out of breath from the brisk ride around the pasture.

"I enjoyed watching you ride," Amanda says, really meaning it.

Kent dismounts Voodoo and walks him back toward the stable. Amanda wishes she didn't have the halo on her head because she feels like getting closer to Kent. But it would be pointless with the halo. As they enter the stable, Amanda notices that another man has walked through the opposite side.

"Hey there, Manuel. How are you?" Kent says.

"Didn't know you were coming out here today," Manuel says. Amanda can tell English is not his first language.

"This is my friend Amanda. She got sprung from Loudoun Memorial to see the horses." Kent says, as he untacks Voodoo and returns him to his stall.

"Yes. I've heard about you, Amanda. You are all over the news."

"You have beautiful horses here."

"Yes, we love this stable and the farm. Hopefully we can stay here, but I really don't know what will happen." Manuel says.

"What did he mean by that?" Amanda asks as Manuel walks into one of the stalls, and she and Kent walk out the other side of the stable.

"The farm has been for sale for months. My dad doesn't really want to sell, but he says he needs to. Between this and the café, the expenses are adding up. Can I show you around the main house?"

"Sure."

"Then get back in the wheelchair, halo girl, I can't leave it here." He pushes her the short distance along the gravel drive toward the main house.

When they near the porch Amanda says, "I'm getting out here. I'll be fine."

The exterior of the house is hardy cedar plank with wooden entry stairs that creak slightly as they both walk up the porch steps. They go in through the front door.

"This is the great room," he waves his hand toward the room. "Nice fireplace, isn't it?"

"Does your dad live here?"

"No, he has an apartment in town, near the café, a block or so behind the Red Fox Inn."

Kent walks down the hall, pushes open his door and walks into his room. Amanda follows a few steps behind. Once inside she notices a very cool wooden guitar rack holding a line of six instruments.

"What's that instrument with the metal on the front?"

"That's a dobro, it's like a guitar but has a little country rock sound to it," Kent explains. He picks it up and strums it a few times to demonstrate. It rings with a twang. The bright silver metal along the guitar face gleams.

"Cool. Hey, you've got one of those old fashioned players, too. What's it called again?"

"A record player, or turntable. Yeah, I collect some old rock. I have like 50 vinyl records. Hendrix, Led Zep, Stones, Mott the Hoople. Bowie, Van Morrison."

"Can you play something on it?"

Kent grabs a Led Zeppelin album, places it on the turntable and presses the play button. The music begins playing at a moderate volume. Amanda, still standing in the middle of the room, scans the place. Stacks of books scattered along a three-shelf bookcase, a few posters. Not too sloppy, not too neat either. Numerous incense sticks stand upright in a small glass container on the night stand. On the wall, Amanda notices small index cards taped to the wall. She steps a little closer and reads the handwritten words:

Nothing's beautiful from every point of view. - Horace

Money often costs too much. - Ralph Waldo Emerson

"Are these just reminders or your favorites?"

"Both I guess. When I read something or hear something I like, I write it down. Some are on the wall, and some I put in my journal."

Kent never takes a seat, appearing slightly uncomfortable, and Amanda is uneasy herself. The song has not even ended when he tells Amanda he has another place he wants to take her, and within a couple minutes, they're out the door, back in the van and heading down Route 50.

"We're heading to Red Rocks State Park, about 10 miles away." Kent says.

"Yeah, what's special about it?" Amanda says.

"You'll just have to see for yourself," Kent says.

Kent fiddles with his phone and a playlist of tunes begins.

"This song sounds almost like orchestra music," Amanda says.

"It's called 'Oh Yeah' and was written by a British guitarist, Peter Bluemon. The guy started Fleeting Woodwinds. My dad wrote some music for that band and some others. In England, they were as big as the Beatles and Stones in 1969. Peter was amazing on guitar. But at the band's peak around 1970, he just left to live in Germany on a hippie commune. My dad was one of his best friends in London, so he went with him. They both lived at this commune for a couple years. I've read a lot about how Peter Bluemon freaked on too much acid when he was there, but my dad never talks about it."

They both listen to the chorus:

But don't ask me what I'm gonna do,
you won't like the answers I am giving you...
Oh Yeah.

"Acid? What do you mean acid? Why would someone want acid?"

"I don't mean spill acid. I mean LSD, it's a drug. It was called acid in the 60s. Lots of people, including musicians, took it. Peter never rejoined the Fleeting Woodwinds, and my dad never wrote any more songs after they went to Germany either."

"Do you think it made their music better? You know, the acid?" Amanda asks.

"Good question. I've never taken it, so I can't say."

Finally they pull into a very small parking area in Red Rocks State Park.

"I'm not using the wheelchair if we're not going far."

"No hiking. There is a scenic overlook just a couple hundred yards away. You'll probably be okay without the wheelchair if we take it slow."

"So what are we overlooking?"

"You'll see."

Overlook

Kent and Amanda walk down a pathway toward the overlook. Leaves of every color form a slightly padded walkway under the tree canopy. Kent has his phone in his hand.

"I brought my ear buds so we can listen to my favorite playlist when we get there."

"Cool. This is beautiful out here."

They walk a few more steps and Amanda impulsively taps Kent on the shoulder. Kent turns, and as soon as he is facing her, Amanda leans forward, halo and all, and presses her lips against his. Kent seems taken aback. Because of the halo, he moves his hands to half hold her around the shoulders. She pulls a few inches away from him, staring into his eyes.

"Surprised you, didn't I?"

"Pleasantly."

She leans forward again and softly brushes Kent's lips, and he kisses her back, his tongue darting inside her mouth. She responds, and their tongues caress.

No words are exchanged as they continue walking down the path toward the overlook, hands clasped. The only sounds are the crinkling leaves underfoot and an occasional whistle of the breeze through the tree branches.

They clear the canopy and Amanda looks at the breathtaking view before them.

"Wow! It seems like you can see for miles. How far can you actually see?"

"Not sure. But on a clear day you can see some tall buildings in D.C.," Kent says, pointing with his right hand.

The small town of Middleburg lies in the foreground. They are sitting on a well-worn bench that was once a tree trunk, mounted just a few feet from the edge.

"It's pretty windy right here," Amanda says.

"Yeah, I guess that's typical when you have wind blowing across an open area like this. I come up here every once in a while and put on my headphones and just think."

"I know a little about your dad, but what about your mom? You really haven't talked about her," Amanda says.

"Well, she was one of my heroes. I guess you know she was a doctor at the hospital." Kent says.

"Yeah, my aunt told me she was an emergency room doctor at the hospital and she died of cancer. What happened?"

Kent lifts the single ear bud out of his ear and holds it in his hand.

"I'll never forget the day she and my dad came into my room after school. She told me she had breast cancer and that she was going to have chemotherapy and radiation. I remember the look on her and my dad's face like it just happened. They were brave about it. I'd never once thought about cancer before. So I go on the internet, searching everything I can find. What the treatment is, what the survival rate is." Kent chokes up and Amanda decides not to ask any more questions. They both look out over the valley for a while.

"Have you ever sat in a chemo room?" Kent asks.

"No. Never. What's that like?"

"Well, I can't think of what would be worse. Uh, torture? You won't forget it once you visit one. Hers was in the building right beside the hospital. My dad didn't want me to go but I told him I wanted to see it. I just wanted to be with my mom. All these people in the room are poisoning themselves, on purpose, with these drugs that drip from bags hanging on IV poles. But they were all really nice to me. It made me think a lot."

"Think about what?" Amanda asks.

"About how unfair life is. My mom didn't deserve it. We thought at one point she was cured, but she got it again, and that time it spread. It hung over our heads like a cement cloud. Every day in school I would think about it, even though I tried not to. It was a really good day when I forgot about it even for a few hours. But when I got home it was always there."

"With my mom and dad," Amanda says, "I don't feel anything. It's weird, I can't remember them, even after staring at their pictures. I know their faces now, but all the memories were stolen right out of my head. I don't have that sense of loss like you. Wow, I swear I just remembered being right here before. I mean, I think I had a dream or NDE about us being here. That sounds dumb but..."

"Not dumb. This is special being here with you." Amanda moves slightly closer to Kent so their bodies are touching.

"Volunteering at the hospital since my mom died is the first thing I've done that wasn't motivated by me selfishly trying to get myself somewhere."

"If you weren't a volunteer, we would never have met! Maybe that was karmic." Amanda says, smiling at Kent. She runs her hand lightly through his hair a moment, then adds: "My friend David from school says you went to MA for a year and that you either got kicked out or quit or something. Was that when your mother was doing chemo?"

"Yeah. My dad and mom enrolled me there the year before my mom was diagnosed. I wanted to get kicked out. There were so many snobs, and I couldn't focus on anything. But, yeah, the reason that I quit was because my grades were terrible. I was flunking two of the classes, but I couldn't have cared less, I was numb. They let me finish the semester but weren't going to let me come back, and I was pretty happy because I didn't want to," Kent says, letting a few seconds pass. "Some people think I do crazy stuff, but to me it's not crazy. I'm just not going to waste my life sitting around doing nothing."

Whippers-in

"David also showed me your video. That's the most I've laughed since I woke up from the crash. What made you do that?" Amanda asks.

"I wanted to throw mud on all of the highbrow people in Middleburg and Upperville. You know, the whole thing with fox hunts and their snobby traditions. I had no idea it would go viral, I just sent it to a couple friends." Kent says.

Amanda chuckles. "That's pretty twisted Kent."

"Well that's just my mojo." Kent says. "There were a lot of pissed off people in Middleburg. I actually participated in a bunch of real fox hunts, even the exclusive Orange County hunt."

"When you were a teenager?"

"Yeah, I went when I was 13 years old with my uncle on my mom's side. It's like a rite of passage here."

"Did you have to wear, like, special horse riding clothes?"

"Oh yeah. You have no idea how formal this stuff is. Do you know what the MFH is? Or what a whipper-in does?" he asks.

"No idea. Tell me."

"Well the MFH is the master of foxhounds, the leader of the hunt. He's in charge of the entire thing. But the huntsman has a horn and actually directs the foxhounds and the whippers-in," Kent says.

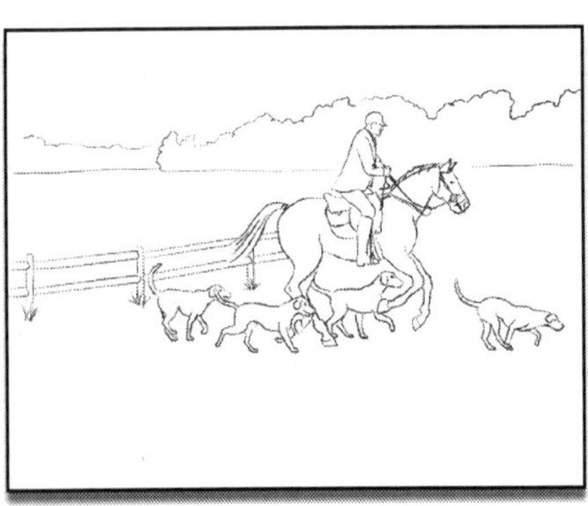

"Whippers what?"

"The whippers-in are the horseback riders who kind of keep the hounds together and keep everything going with the flow. They release a red fox, which gets a little head start, then everybody takes off."

"Do you carry rifles to shoot the fox?"

"No, no one shoots at the fox. Sometimes, though, the foxhounds will just tear the fox apart. That even has a name. I left a lot of stuff out, but what happens is the foxhounds track the scent of the fox, and the riders follow the dogs. If they get to the covert — it's pronounced 'cover,' but has a 't' on the end — that's when the huntsman makes the key decisions.

"None of the riders can get ahead of the draw. When the foxhounds actually find the fox, everyone is supposed to be silent because the foxhounds make a distinctive sound, or 'speak,' so everyone knows that the fox is in the covert. If the huntsman decides to cheer the hounds all together, he makes a series of short blasts, called 'doubling the horn,' that calls the hounds all together. At that point the fox is jumping around in the covert, pretty much surrounded and sometimes the foxhounds just tear into the fox. They also used to do something called blooding."

Amanda is almost afraid to ask. "Good God, what is that?"

"I'll never forget when they actually did it to me. Blooding is when the hounds have all torn the fox to pieces, and the lead huntsman takes some of the blood from the fox and symbolically rubs a little bit of it onto the youngest riders' foreheads. Also, they will cut off the fox's tail, paws, and head, as trophies. Then they throw the remaining carcass to the dogs."

"I think I'm going to puke. That seems horrid. Why did you let them do it?"

"I didn't know any better. I was 13. My uncle was into all this stuff. It was what Middleburg was all about."

"When they do those hunts now, do they still do that?" Amanda curiously asks.

"No, they don't do the blooding ritual anymore. And sometimes they don't even kill the fox at the end. Foxes are smart, some of them know that they should run along a stream, or run along the top of fences. That throws off the hounds, and they can get away. Really, the only fun thing about it was galloping along trying to find the fox and leaping over low fences."

"So, that's why you did your video. You were making fun of them because of all that."

After making their way back to the parking lot from the overlook, they go through the ritual of getting Amanda into the van. Kent starts driving down the road as the sun is setting in the western sky. Bands of sunlight stream through the tall trees, creating a strobe effect inside the van.

"I have one more place I want to stop, and I can still get you back in time." Kent says.

He pulls the van up to a little country roadside café, and asks Amanda what she would like.

"Just get two of whatever you're getting and I'll try it."

Amanda surveys the area and sees some picnic tables in front of the café. Kent returns a few minutes later and helps her out of the van. There's a family with a little boy who looks to be about three years old at one picnic table and another young couple at another. Amanda suddenly feels self-conscious about the metal halo around her head and notices a few furtive glances in her direction.

"I got you green tea with some brown sugar, is that okay?"

"Guess I'll find out."

They situate themselves at one of the picnic tables with a large umbrella over it. Shortly after they start sipping their drinks, Kent asks a question he has obviously been thinking about a while.

"You really can't remember anything about your parents? Nothing about your dad's job, your mom's job?"

"Nothing. I keep flipping through the scrapbooks hoping I'll remember something."

"Do you feel sad about that?"

"I mean, some of my family members tell me things that make me smile or make me sad when I hear them, but it's not because I'm remembering anything."

"Can you remember anything about the plane crash, like getting on the plane, where you were going, being at the airport?"

"Not really. They tell me it was my birthday present, we were going to shop in New York. But I will tell you something that I haven't told anyone else but Dr. Lucent. I've been having these dreams, or maybe they're really near death experiences, I don't know. Lucent said he thinks they're NDEs."

"That's pretty spooky," Kent says, twirling the circular cardboard protector on his cup.

"A couple of my flashbacks, are really weird. I remember something from the *Wizard of Oz* movie, but I can't even remember my parents or the crash."

"How can you remember the *Wizard of Oz*?"

"No clue. Why can I remember the color of the dress Dorothy was wearing and that her dog's name is Toto? Brain damage is what Dr. Lucent says."

Kent begins to wolf down a white chocolate brownie. Suddenly, they both notice the lady standing beside the picnic table.

"I'm sorry to interrupt, but are you Amanda Michaels?" she asks. Kent realizes that the metal halo surrounding her head is a fairly big giveaway.

"How did you know that?" Amanda asks.

"We've seen you all over the news. I just wanted to tell you that my husband and I are amazed at how strong you are and we just want to wish you a speedy recovery. We know that you have been through so much."

"Thanks, you are very kind," Amanda responds. The lady walks back to her picnic table where her husband waves to Amanda and Kent.

"You're a celebrity now," Kent says.

"I really just want to be invisible. I didn't ask for this. And I really want to get this halo off my head and get back to whatever I was doing before."

"I hope you guys had fun. And Kent, I want to thank you for taking Amanda," Barb says.

"I had a great time," Amanda says, "and I got to meet Roxy and Voodoo and see the farm."

"I heard that your family's farm is up for sale," Barb says to Kent.

"Yeah, it's been listed for a while now but there haven't been any offers."

"That beautiful farm, you should never let him sell it," Amanda says.

"Well, I definitely agree but it's my dad's business and his finances that are involved, not mine."

"Are you volunteering tomorrow?"

"Day after tomorrow," Kent responds.

"See ya then," Amanda says.

Amanda watches him walk down the hall, wondering what he could possibly see in her.

Surveillance

"I've reviewed all the surveillance tape. When would you like to talk about it?" Angie asks Andy through speakerphone.

"Do I need to look at it with you?" Andy asks back.

"Like I told you, there isn't much of anything there." They already know that the plane crashed, and watching video of the people in the waiting area at the gate probably is not going to shed any light on why.

"I still want to look at it. Let's go in the conference room and view some of the footage and you can tell me what your preliminary thoughts are."

Andy enters the conference room, and Angie is already there with the remote in her hand.

"I used the family pictures and tried to locate each of our clients in the gate area. One surveillance camera shows everyone leaving the gate, going down an escalator, and gathering on a lower level. The second cam shows the representative that checks the tickets, and then they all get on a shuttle bus that takes them out to the jet on the tarmac."

Angie points the remote at the flat screen on the wall and they both look at some footage.

"So in this first section here you see Rochelle and Amanda in line to go down the escalator. Notice that Rochelle is on her cell phone. What's interesting is that we've got the cell phone records so we know the last call she made was to your brother. Ron is nowhere to be found. He must have been running late. Let me fast forward here and I'll show you where he comes in."

Angie fast forwards the video to the time she has in her notes as correlating to Ron's arrival. "Here is the footage where Ron gets to the gate and hurries down the escalator. He was one of the last passengers. The second cam shows him presenting his ticket and heading out to the shuttle bus. They sent the last shuttle bus with Ron and the last couple passengers, none of whom are our clients."

Angie hits the pause button on the remote control.

"Why weren't they together?" Andy asks.

"Yeah, that's kind of weird. Rochelle and Amanda were moved to that flight because their earlier flight was canceled. As best as I can tell, your brother was scheduled on this flight. It's odd they weren't booked on the same flight in the first place."

“Yeah, that is strange,” Andy agrees.

Black Box

"Andy, we received a stack of documents and cds on the Hemispheres black box data. I know you want to look at it right away."

"I don't need the cds right now, but I want to see the transcripts," Andy responds.

Moments later Angie drops them on the corner of Andy's desk.

"Here you go. Are you calling Garrison to tell them they're here?"

"Yeah, and I may ask you to take the stuff to him. He lives in Arlington somewhere, I think." Andy locates the transcript from the pilots. He flips through a few pages and quickly finds the first relevant communication before the crash:

> *Pilot: Mayday mayday!*
> *ATC: Hemispheres 310, state your position and souls on board.*
> *Pilot: Near Lancaster. 27 souls on board.*
> *There is a four-second pause followed by the following:*
> *Pilot: Declaring an emergency, want to land immediately. Control problems.*
> *ATC: I see you. Recommend Lancaster.*
> *[Second Voice – likely co-pilot] Smell electrical smoke and controls acting weird, not responsive.*

He reads a little further:

> *Pilot: Smoke getting thicker, loss of control, losing altitude and control of jet.*
> *Pilot: Nothing's responding. Can you get any control over there?*
> *Co-pilot: No response here either.*

Five seconds later per the timestamp on the transcript:

> *Pilot: Okay, I've got the airplane.*

Three seconds later:

Co-pilot: Smoke's getting thicker, we're going down.

Another timestamp indicates the time of the crash as seven seconds later when there is no velocity reading whatsoever.

Andy paws through several transcript pages from the other event recorder, which records air speed, altitude, power settings and other parameters he doesn't understand. He scrolls through his address book on his phone for Robert Garrison.

"Robert, Andy here. We have the Hemispheres event recorder printout on the Flight 310 crash. We also have the logs of all cell phone calls made by the passengers for a period of time before the crash. I didn't even know they did all of that, but in any case, it's a ton of stuff. I'm going to have Angie bring it all to you in Arlington. Is that okay?"

"That will be fine," Robert responds. "If you get them to me today I should be able to give you some preliminary thoughts tomorrow."

"The press has been doing a lot of theorizing about an electrical cause, but once you look through this we'll obviously have a better idea."

"Exactly, I will talk to you tomorrow." Garrison says.

Next, Andy presses the speakerphone button on his phone for Angie. "I just spoke with Garrison and I need you to take everything to him."

The next day, Garrison calls Andy with a preliminary report. "Andy I've studied all this material. To me, it clearly was an electrical issue. For the pilot and co-pilot to lose all of their controls on this type of Embracer aircraft, there's no question that a wiring bundle completely failed. A complete failure like this is extremely rare because of the secondary engineering put in place specifically to avoid this type of disaster. Hard to say what caused it, especially since there's no evidence of a bomb or sudden explosion. That makes it harder to figure out.

"Without a forensic analysis of all kinds of parts from the aircraft it's hard to determine anything else. Is there any chance you could get me in to do an inspection of the aircraft parts being held by Hemispheres?" Garrison asks.

"Fat chance, you know that."

"Well, we can definitely make some assumptions based on what we currently have, but I sure would like to look at some of the actual electrical system if you can get me access to it."

"Let me see what I can do in the coming days or weeks. Thanks a lot for your help so far." Andy ends the call.

He buzzes Angie to give her the update and to see if she has any interesting information about the cell phone log.

"I just got off the phone with Garrison. He says it was definitely an electrical failure, but he can't say much more than that without examining the parts that were collected after the crash."

"I can't imagine how many motions and hearings that would require," Angie says, rolling her eyes at the thought of it.

"I'll probably file a new motion for a detailed expert inspection just to see where it goes. Are there any interesting calls on the cell phone logs?"

Café Loco

Iris had promised Amanda to take her by Café Loco on one of their strolls. Dr. Wrightson had given Amanda permission to walk a few days ago, and Amanda delighted in any opportunity to get out of the hospital.

"You remember the Red Fox Inn, don't you?" Iris asks as they walk down the sidewalk in the center of Middleburg.

Amanda looks at the small metal icon on top of the post in front of the inn. It's a man holding a lantern.

"Pretty cool design, but I don't remember it."

"It's one of the oldest landmarks here in Middleburg. It's been here since the 1700s or something. It's a pretty ritzy joint."

They continue walking until they find the slightly recessed entrance to Café Loco just off Jefferson Street. Amanda notices the small sign above the doorway that looks worn and battered. In the entryway, posters about past and future shows adorn the walls. As they open the second swinging door, the smell of coffee reaches Amanda's nose. To the right she notices a large open area with small tables. Straight ahead is a typical coffee house staging area, to the left she sees another group of tables near a window. On the window ledge, numerous newspapers and random magazines are stacked up for the patrons' enjoyment. As they walk in, Iris points to a small stage on the right.

"That's where the bands play when they have music in here. And Ramblin' Kyle's is down that hallway there. We've been here a bunch of times. Anything coming back to you?"

"No. But I like the atmosphere in this place. Hey, there's Kent." They get in line behind a young woman who is just finishing her order. As she moves to the side Kent says, "Hey you guys. Thanks for coming. Can I get you anything?"

Iris orders both of them a skinny vanilla latte. "You'll like this."

"I'll get a break in a minute or two and come talk." Kent says.

"Okay, great," Iris says.

He confers with a pretty young barista, and within a few minutes all three of them are sitting at one of the tables near a window. Iris looks at some of the magazines on the window ledge and says, "Hey, Amanda, you're on the cover of *People* magazine! You're like a rock star."

"I don't feel like one."

Amanda gets up from the table and gestures for Kent to follow her. She looks up at the framed pictures hanging on the wall. “Who are the guys in the concert hall?”

"That guy is my dad, back in the early 70s. This is at Royal Albert Hall, when David Bowie played with Mott the Hoople."

"Did your dad play in a famous rock band?" asks Iris, who has now come over to hear the commentary on some of the pictures of Kyle Perless, Kent's dad.

"No, but he wrote a lot of tunes for these guys and hung out with a lot of them.”

"Is your dad here?" Amanda asks.

"Yeah, I think he's back in the little office behind the kitchen." A few minutes later, a man walks out from the kitchen and Amanda surmises that it must be Kent's dad. She figures he must be in his late 50s. He's wearing a pair of faded jeans and a well-worn T-shirt that has a picture of a surfing scene and says “Endless Summer.” He has a chiseled face with appears to be a day of stubble. Definitely handsome, Amanda concludes. And Kent does show some resemblance. She also notices the gold stud earring in his left ear and very short ponytail.

"I know who you are. Your costume is a dead giveaway," Kyle says, reaching his hand out to shake Amanda's.

"I can't imagine what you mean," Amanda says playfully. "Kent was just telling us how you knew all these famous guys, and that you teach guitar here."

"Oh yeah, I was Mr. Shooting Star back in the day, but that was long ago. I'm just a washed up rocker running a café now.”

"Are those your guitars?" Iris asks, pointing to five instruments hanging on the wall.

"Some of those are mine, and a couple I saved from way back when. Ian Hunter gave me that old mandolin. Supposedly one of the guys in Mott the Hoople played it on ‘I Wish I Was Your Mother.’ The great sound at the beginning and end of Rod Stewart's ‘Maggie May’ is done on mandolin.”

"Will you play it for us?" Amanda meekly asks.

"Sure." Kyle walks over and unlocks the rack, freeing the mandolin. He rolls right into the repetitive mandolin lick at the end of “Maggie May,” singing as he plays.

"Maggie, I wished I'd never seen your face..."

"Oh, that song. I didn't know the name of it, but now that you're playing it I know I've heard it on the radio," Iris says.

Kent chimes in, "My group mixes in some classic rock with John Mayer, Coldplay, Mumford & Sons and anything else we happen to like. But none of the new stuff is as adventurous as the stuff from the early 70s."

"Ditto that," Kyle says as he walks back over to the wall and carefully places the mandolin back on the rack and snaps the lock in place. "Good to meet you," he says, and walks back toward the kitchen.

"Who's the pretty girl behind the counter?" Amanda asks.

"That's Sienna. She's been with us a few weeks."

"I noticed she has a slight accent."

"Yeah, she's originally from France but went to college here. Seems nice."

Amanda checks her out and wonders if Kent is interested in her.

"When can I hear your band?"

"We play here once a week. We're mediocre at best, but it's a blast. I'm sure you'll get to see us soon."

"They're actually really good Amanda, he's just being modest." Iris says, pushing her hand against Kent's shoulder.

"We suck, she's just being nice." Kent laughs and playfully shoves her back. "I've given Amanda most of the songs we play, she probably just doesn't remember their names," he teases.

"Not true, I've learned a couple!" Amanda says, getting up to go to the restroom.

Have you talked to your dad about the party we want to have here for Amanda's 18th birthday?" Iris asks Kent.

"Oh yeah, my dad said that's absolutely cool. Two Saturdays from now is best. My band will play and we'll have a DJ. It should be very cool."

"I heard your dad has set up the entire café before with strobe lights and black lights and made it a big 1960s psychedelic room."

"Yeah, that was a couple years ago. We can do it again. "

"Why don't we make up some posters calling it 'The Psychedelic Rave for Amanda's Halo Charity' and ask people to give donations? Then we can donate the money to a charity like 'Healing Heroes' or wherever Amanda thinks would be good," Iris says.

"That’s a great idea," Kent agrees.

“She's already told us not to do anything big, but we're ignoring her. You only escape death and turn 18 once, right?"

Healing

Dr. Wrightson leans back in his leather swivel chair and stares again at two large monitors. On one screen are the full-size CT scans and thumbnails of various other test panels. An MRI image occupies the other large monitor. With his mouse he scrolls around the 3-D images looking at both axial and sagittal views of the cervical fracture sight. Hmm, there's no question that there's good – no, great – bone growth. He continues to review the images for a few more minutes, and then pushes the speaker button on his phone.

"Bobby, are you in there?"

"Yeah, why?"

"Do you have a second to take a look at some scans of one of my patients?"

"Sure, be right there."

A minute later the other neurosurgeon is standing by Wrightson's desk.

Wrightson points at his monitor. "Look at how solid that bone has fused at the cervical site."

"Yeah, what about it?"

"This is not after months of healing, this is after two weeks. It's Amanda Michaels."

"Two weeks? I'd categorize that as remarkable. Is that what you're asking me?"

"Yep."

"Amazing. She is young though. She's what, 18?"

"Yeah, but you should've seen it the night of the surgery."

"Everyone is different," Dr. Canton responds, already backing a few steps out of the office. "Anything else?"

"I've got to decide if this changes my timetable for removing her halo."

"Can't answer that one for you," Canton replies.

"Did I tell you that we thought she contracted MRSA?"

"No, what about it?"

"Did you ever have a patient develop MRSA and then it just disappeared, literally the moment you started antibiotics?"

"MRSA doesn't disappear, everyone knows that. It takes days, even weeks for the vancomycin to have any effect on the blood counts. Did you talk to an ID doc about it?"

Wrightson closes his eyes and leans back again in his swivel chair. "Yes I talked to an infectious disease doc. He told me exactly what you told me. But I went back and looked at the blood counts and tests myself."

"And?"

"I don't know. There had to be a false positive or something. The tests were positive for MRSA, but a day later it was gone."

"Sounds like a *CSI* episode. Maybe someone secretly switched the blood tests." Canton laughs.

"Something else, kind of off topic," Wrightson continues. "Have you heard about Lucent meeting with Amanda Michaels, even for unscheduled visits, about NDEs?"

"He's like a witch doctor," Canton agrees.

"Have you ever talked to him about it? He was talking to me one day about how he actually thinks the soul may temporarily depart the body during an NDE. Then apparently the soul just sneaks back into your body. The whole thing is way outside of the scope of what he ought to be doing with his patients, especially when they're our patients too. And on a high-profile case like this it's even worse. This smears all of us, don't you think?" Wrightson questions.

"Maybe you should confidentially discuss it with administration."

"Hmm...maybe so."

New Clients

"Andy, the Richmans are here," Myra announces through the speakerphone.

"I'll be there in a minute. Please tell Angie too." Andy scans back over the yellow pad at the bullet-point reminders of what he wants to cover in each meeting: liability/fault, damages, choice of state laws, cause of crash, recording a statement, legal documents to sign.

As they discussed at lunch, he and Angie have prepared a PowerPoint presentation with embedded video clips from some of the previous settlement conferences and mediations the firm has conducted in some of its more high-profile cases. Heading down the hall, he peeks into Angie's office and asks, "Ready to go?"

"Yep." She follows Andy down the hall to the reception area where he greets the couple on the reception couch.

"Good morning Mr. and Mrs. Richman. I'm Andy Michaels and this is Angie Tipton, my paralegal." Andy and Angie each exchange handshakes with the Richmans. "As we head back to the conference room, I want to express our heart-felt condolences to you for your loss."

"Thanks," Mr. Richman begins slowly. "Lauren had just graduated from UVA in Charlottesville. She was working for the Department of Justice in Washington, and had been accepted to both Harvard and Yale Law Schools. She was on her way to visit one of her friends from UVA in Manhattan."

Mrs. Richman is refusing to look at Andy, staring down at the conference room table instead. Andy decides to stick to the formalities and stay away from family details for now.

"I'd like to tell you a bit about our firm and how we handle a wrongful death case..."

"Mr. Michaels, we already know who you are and what you've done." Mr. Richman interrupts. "We know you are the only lawyer who took a 9/11 case involving the Pentagon crash to trial. And we also know about your brother, sister-in-law, and niece. You don't have to convince us that you're going to tear into this airline."

Andy's emotions start to get the best of him as his mind wanders, not toward the Richmans' daughter, but his brother Ron.

"When we handle wrongful death cases we normally charge a one-third contingent fee. The contingency part is that we only get paid if we recover for your family. Do you have any questions about the economic part of our representation?"

"No," Mr. Richman answers.

"Lauren was our pride." Mrs. Richman breaks her silence. "This airline has stolen away the daughter that we loved. Do you have any idea what that means?" Her voice trembles with emotion.

Mr. Richman reaches to his left and places his hand over his wife's clenched fists on the tabletop.

"I want you to know, Mrs. Richman, that we are going to do everything possible to obtain justice for you and your family," Angie says. A little bold, Andy thinks, but it's actually reassuring to the Richmans.

"Here's the bad part," Andy says. "This airline will drag things out, and they will fight us on every effort we make to determine what caused the crash. In a wrongful death case we must prove some negligence of the airline or some defect or faulty part on the jet itself. The airline will most likely try to point to sabotage or equipment failure, basically anything that would deflect the blame away from them."

"You mean to tell me that the airline isn't going to have to pay if we can't show precisely what caused the plane to crash? The jet broke up into thousands of pieces," Mr. Richman says incredulously.

"Not quite. We don't necessarily have to show an exact cause, but we do need to develop a good, plausible theory backed by corroborative evidence. I've already contacted a forensic aviation expert. We also spend an incredible amount of time marshaling the evidence and figuring out how to present it in a way that conveys our clients' enormous loss and ultimately serves as a catalyst to get a big case settled," Andy explains. "I can show you examples of previous presentations we have created."

"Will you be willing to go to trial and prove the neglect of the airline if necessary?" Mr. Richman pointedly asks.

"Absolutely. I'm not afraid to try cases, but events will dictate whether we need to take this all the way. If you retain me, we will promptly file the lawsuit, but if we develop good evidence, many times the companies or insurers want to settle before trial. They may offer substantial compensation to your family. Based on my experience with this airline, I don't foresee that happening, but it could."

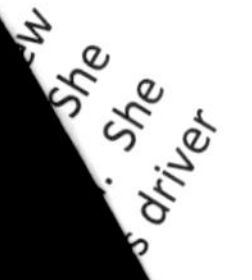

[illegible]ill do," Andy says, wondering how Amanda will react when [illegible] Bobby Vail's request.

"We want you to get to the bottom of it. Neither of us is scared to testify," Mrs. Richman says, with as much bravery as she can muster.

"Angie is going to review the necessary paperwork with you and record your statements relevant to the case. Thank you so much for allowing us to represent you, and remember that there will not be any settlement negotiations or any action on any offer from the airline without your permission." Andy shakes both of their hands and exits the room.

Next is Mr. and Mrs. King, who have lost their 28-year-old son Sam, an information technology supervisor working for a D.C. bank with numerous branches. His fiancée asked him to join her at a friend's wedding in New York City. Even though this is the type of client Andy would crawl across hot coals to represent, he just can't summon up his usual exuberance.

The last meeting of the day is with Mr. and Mrs. Perkins from Chevy Chase, Maryland, who lost their son, Charles, a regional manager for the Porsche dealership in Bethesda, Maryland.

While Angie goes to bring Mr. and Mrs. Perkins back to the conference room, Andy's sorrow over the loss of his own brother and sister-in-law gets the best of him. He runs out of the conference room and bounds down the stairs.

The Park

Andy finds himself at Dumbarton Park, the one hidden from the busy streets. The circular slide, the monkey bars, and the jungle gym are all still there. It has even been spruced up a bit with a few nice touches, like wood chips covering the area, some new paint on the bench where he decides to sit.

Tears wet his cheeks, but he remains silent. Just what he wants, he thinks, the Dumbarton park bench. Alone.

"Hey mister, why are you sad?"

The small voice startles Andy. He quickly wipes the tears off both his cheeks. "Oh, nothing. Nothing really."

"You must be crying for something," the little girl says, jumping up and plopping herself down on the park bench a few inches away from Andy. She is deep inside his personal space, having crossed a line that most adults respect but many kids are oblivious to. Her little 8-year-old feet dangle back and forth, not reaching the ground.

"Something bad happened, tell me what. I cry sometimes too."

Andy looks out and notices a couple of other kids, eight, maybe ten years old. One chases the other up one side of the jungle gym, down the other. On the opposite park bench across the playground sit a couple of adults, and in the middle of the park stands an older grandparent-looking lady peering in his direction.

"Well, are you going to tell me?" the little girl asks again, her swinging legs shaking the park bench.

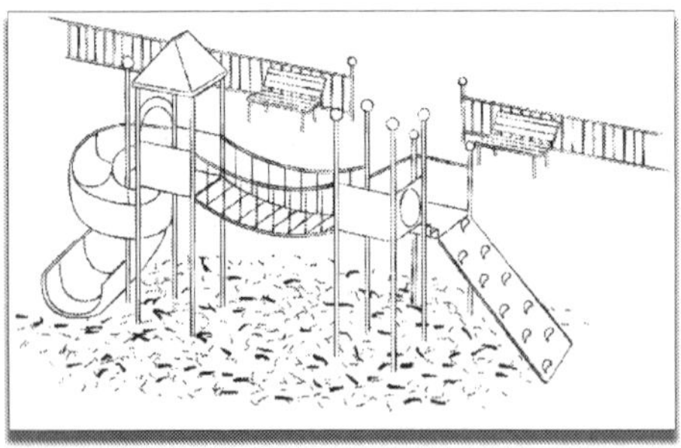

"Some people lost their daughter, and I lost my brother." Andy says, just staring out at the playground.

"We can find them. I find stuff that I thought was lost too. I lost a Barbie doll. My mom found it behind the toy box. I thought I'd never see it again."

Andy feels the slightest ripple of a grin. Such awesome innocence.

"Did they just get lost? Was it around here near the playground? Grammy and I can help you find them. She's right over there." The little girl waves her right hand toward the elderly lady in the middle of the playground.

"My brother and I played on that snake slide. Do you like the snake slide?"

"I love it. Will you go on it with me now? I got Grammy to go on it with me one time, but she won't do it anymore. C'mon, please?"

"It was a long time ago when my brother and I used to slide down."

"He didn't just get lost today? I thought that's why you were crying."

Andy decides against some deep discussion about life and death, opts instead to just be grateful her innocent mind has lifted him up in some strange way.

"Mister, are they really lost or are you crying about something different?"

"You ever played the game 'Troll' on the jungle gym before?" he asks her.

"No, let's do it. How do you play?" she asks.

"Well, you have to have a ball. It can be small or big."

"We have a ball!" She jumps off the park bench, runs across the wood chips, sending errant chips flying, past Grammy to the other side of the playground where she grabs a little bouncy ball. After running all the way back, she proudly holds it up in front of Andy.

"Here it is, let's play!"

Andy hadn't thought this through. Oh, God. Memories with Ron come flooding back.

She then tosses the ball right at his chest, and he grabs it at the last second.

"Okay, if your Grammy will let you, I'll teach you how."

The little girl turns and sprints to the jungle gym, where she climbs to the top and waits for Andy.

"Come on, Mister."

Andy sheepishly carries the ball toward the lady she calls Grammy.

"Hi. Your granddaughter wants to play a game with me. Will it be all right?"

"Sure, she was horning in on some of the other kids before and could use a distraction."

The other kids still tirelessly run around other parts of the playground. Low humidity, sunshine, and limitless energy, the perfect playground combination.

The little girl has her hands raised over the jungle gym rails, leaning her head against the vertical bars that support them.

"How do you play?" she asks through the bars.

"Here's the deal. I'm the troll. The object is for me to throw the ball and make it land on the floor where you are on the bridge, but it has to land between this side here," Andy points to a crack along one side, "and here," he says, walking a few steps and then pointing to the crack at the other end of the bridge. "I get one point every time I throw the ball and it lands up there on the bridge."

"How do I get points?" the little girl asks excitedly.

"Simple. You bat the ball away and stop it from landing on the bridge. You get two points if you catch it or bat it away, and I get one point if I land it. We play until one of us has 12 points."

"What's a troll?"

"Uh, old time stories talk about them. A troll is a strange type of person that hides under a bridge and messes with the travelers that cross it. The troll tries to rule the bridge by asking riddles or demanding money before someone can cross."

Andy's sadness temporarily lifts. He knows he can duck under the elevated walkway and run around the other side and try to surprise her, just like he used to do with Ron. He runs under the elevated landing, and before the little girl can get to the edge, he lobs the ball just inside the bridge zone, scoring his first point.

"Ha, I got a point."

The little girl picks up the ball with a crooked grimace on her face and tosses it down onto the wood chips. "I wasn't ready. Not fair!"

Andy grabs the ball and starts looking off in one direction, then the other, trying to fake her out. "Are you ready this time?"

"Ready."

Andy moves his arm quickly and fakes the ball toward the right and then tosses it to the far left, but the girl quickly bats the ball away from the scoring zone.

"Ha ha! Gotcha that time. Two to one. I'm winning!"

And so Andy and the little girl play the game of Troll, while Grammy sits on the park bench, happy to have a rest. When the score is 11 to 10 in Andy's favor, he lets off a little bit, knowing that he has to let the little girl win. And she does, 12-11. She is happier than if a rainbow of candy had appeared in her bedroom. She demands that they play again, but Andy needs to leave. Grammy's and the girl's smile make Andy happy too.

"Next game is yours, Grammy," Andy says with a big smile as he walks away.

"Hey Mister, where are you going? Let's play Troll again." She balances the bouncy ball atop the bridge rails.

"I gotta go now," Andy says, spinning around and beginning to walk off the playground. When he looks back, the little girl is still standing on top of the jungle gym, and she raises her arm in a big wave. He waves back before turning again. Grammy can take over now since she watched the entire game.

Andy walks through the opening in the park's metal fence, crosses the sidewalk and street, and then turns down the block to his house. As he approaches his house he sees Angie standing on the sidewalk beside her car, facing him.

"I've been looking everywhere for you. You didn't answer your phone, and the Perkins were sitting at the office waiting for you. What gives?"

"I left it on my desk. All my stuff is there. I don't even have the keys to my house, come to think of it."

"I told them we would have to reschedule, that you had a sudden emergency. Totally embarrassing. Were you in the park?"

"Sorry. I just couldn't shut it out anymore."

Angie has a fairly confused look on her face. Then it dawns on her.

"Andy Michaels, you mean...?"

"Yeah."

"Is that why you were in the park?"

"Used to come here with my brother."

Angie sees that Andy's eyes are red. She feels really bad for accusing him of walking out on the Perkins family. Instead of walking toward his house Andy leans against her car, head down toward the strip of grass adjacent the street, and starts sobbing. Angie takes a few steps and places the fingers of her right hand on his shoulder. She doesn't say anything because nothing appropriate comes to mind. She takes her hand from his shoulder, quickly walks over to the car's driver side, grabs some tissues and comes back.

"Here, some tissues."

He takes them from her, barely looking up, and dabs his eyes. A long minute passes.

"I'll take care of rescheduling. Do you want me to tell them to come back tomorrow?"

"Yeah, whatever."

They hear a ruckus across the street. Andy looks up and the little girl is running in his direction.

"Hey, Mister!"

Grammy is trying to keep up with her.

"Look both ways before you cross!" Grammy shouts.

The little girl quickly looks both ways, then bolts across the street toward Angie's car.

"Mister, I wanted to give you this. It's a sparkly rock I found at the park. Look at all the colors it makes when you move it around." She demonstrates how the light makes the rock appear shiny and iridescent.

"I hope the sparkles make you happy. You know, I saw the Lion King movie, when Simba was really sad, that part. His dad got runned over by the herd. He heard his dad's voice say that it was part of the circle of life. Simba knew he would see his dad again. And that's what made Simba feel better. Mister, keep that sparkly rock, and when it shines, maybe you won't be sad about your brother anymore."

By now Grammy stands behind her holding the playground ball under one arm. She reaches out for the little girl's hand.

"We've got to go Gracie. Let's leave the nice man alone now."

"Mister, thanks for teaching me Troll. We should play again. See you at the park."

The two of them are halfway down the block the next time Andy looks up. Andy glances back down at the little rock in his palm then drops it into his pants pocket.

"What a precious little thing. Do you know her?" Angie asks.

He never answers that question, but thinks somewhere, sometime, he must have met her or someone like her. Then Angie asks a new question.

"So you played in that park as a kid?" The wind blows a few wisps of her hair across her face and she moves them away from her nose and mouth.

They are both leaning against the passenger side of her car, facing the sidewalk.

“We lived a couple blocks from here, and there was a cut-through between two houses, so we used to ride our bikes to the park.”

“Is that why you live here now?”

“I don’t know, maybe it was subconscious. Maybe the wind just blew me in this direction.”

"How are you going to get into your house?"

"I have a hidden key. I'm fine. I'll see you tomorrow morning at the office. Just reset the Perkins appointment for 10 a.m. or whenever they can come back, will you?"

Andy walks away from her, rubbing his fingers over the rock in his pocket.

@Part III
Amanda's Halo

Although it was Iris' idea initially, "Amanda's Halo," the Facebook page chronicling Amanda's survival of the plane crash and the charity set up in her honor, was created by both Iris and Charlyne. They uploaded all kinds of pictures of Amanda at soccer games and parties, hanging out at school, you name it. Once launched, it took on a life of its own as other seniors started adding photographs and comments.

The online charity enjoyed similar success. Once the media jumped on the bandwagon, $10,000.00 in donations for Amanda flooded in within 24 hours. Andy was quickly appointed to handle the charitable contributions and a trust was created. When he announced that Amanda was going to donate the money to charity, Healing Heroes asked him to consider their charity for the funds. This fund had been started in the aftermath of 9/11 and was devoted to helping those who survived some kind of disaster. The honorary chair of Healing Heroes, Bobby Vail, called Andy himself.

"Andy, this is Bobby Vail. I don't know if you've heard of me, but I'm the chair of the Healing Heroes group. How are you today?"

"I'm fine, and I'm honored you called me," Andy replies.

"I don't know if you've seen our program before, but we've started an annual show at the Kennedy Center that honors survivors of unfortunate circumstances who have made a difference. We'd like to have Amanda appear on this year's show."

"Well, it would certainly be an honor, but I need to run it by Amanda. Her condition is still a little uncertain. I think she'd be thrilled to do it, but I'll have to get back to you."

"Great, let me know what she says. And please keep us in mind as a possible beneficiary of Amanda's Halo."

"Will do," Andy says, wondering how Amanda will react when he tells her about Bobby Vail's request.

Snatched

Becca watches the "Real Housewives" of somewhere on Bravo in the great room, sipping her decaf green tea, and Andy sits at his desk in the spare room, trying to focus. How does Becca watch those fake housewives with their fake controversies? He would rather watch rust form on metal. Andy's desk affords him a view out the window, and from a certain angle he can see part of Dumbarton Park. He has been reading the latest 30-page brief to be rolled out by the Franklin deforestation paper mill, arguing why no family member, attorney or their experts should get to inspect any part of the wreckage until the NTSB has issued a final report on the crash.

During one of his many gazes out the window, he sees the little girl he befriended walking down the sidewalk toward the park with Grammy.

"I am going over to the park for a few minutes, Becca."

"What? Why?" she asks, not taking her eyes off the screen.

As he walks through the opening in the metal fence surrounding the park the little girl sees him. She begins running toward him and yells, "Hi there, mister. Let's play Troll!"

"I didn't bring a ball," Andy says.

"I'm sure we can find one somewhere." Her eyes dart around the park. Andy also looks, but there are no balls around.

"I actually came to give you something. Here you go." He hands her the little white plastic bag.

"What is it, what is it?" She opens the plastic bag containing a pink, green, and red Power Ranger. "Oh, cool! I love Power Rangers. We have all the episodes on DVD at home."

The girl beams from ear to ear. "That's real nice, mister." She walks up to him and hugs his legs with one arm. "Will you be here tomorrow? I try to come after church on Sundays."

"I'm not sure," Andy says, feeling great satisfaction in making her happy. She runs over toward Grammy and proudly holds the bag open to show her the gift. She leaves the bag there and runs back over toward Andy.

"Do you know my name?"

"Yes, it's Gracie, right?"

"How'd you know?"

"Your Grammy said it that first day I met you. I have your shiny stone on my desk at my office."

"I was wondering, what's your name?" she asks.

"Andy. Andy Michaels."

"My Grammy says you are famous or something 'cause you're a lawyer for people who got killed in a plane crash. What's a lawyer do anyway?"

Andy thinks about how to simplify things so his little friend will understand. "If someone runs over a person in the street with their car, and the driver who did it doesn't want to pay, we try to make them pay the person who got hurt," he finally explains, thinking about Gracie crossing the street herself.

"Well, if they hurt my Grammy when she was crossing the street, they know they need to apologize and pay for what they did wrong, don't they? We learned that in Sunday School."

A little girl on the jungle gym yells at Gracie, "Are you playin' or not?"

She looks at Andy, fidgeting.

"Are you comin' to play chase with us or not?"

Andy helps her out. "I've got to get going, go ahead and play, Gracie."

"Coming! Mister, thanks a lot for the Power Rangers," she shouts, running off to the jungle gym. Andy gives a wave to Grammy, seated on the bench on the other side of the park, and walks back home.

The little girl and Grammy never see it coming. As they walk along the sidewalk heading home from the park, a man jogging toward them swerves, rips the white bag right out of Gracie's little hand, and momentarily slows his pace.

"Hey! Gimme back my bag!"

Grammy immediately yells "Hey!" and instinctively wraps her arms around his left arm in an amazingly powerful grip, hard enough that the jogger can't shake her loose at first.

Then with martial arts precision the thief frees his left arm and cracks back viciously against Grammy's face. Her body goes limp, and her head, followed by her body, crashes down on the sidewalk.

Gracie sees Grammy's head strike the sidewalk, bounce up once, then land again on the sidewalk. A noticeable amount of blood leaks from Grammy's ear.

Gracie stoops down over her. “Grammy? Grammy? Are you okay?”

Her eyes are wide open but no words come out to reassure her granddaughter.

A lady who witnesses the mugging jams on her brakes in the middle of the street. She runs over to the sidewalk.

“What happened, what happened to her?”

"A man just stole my bag of toys, then he smacked Grammy. Grammy won’t answer me now. Grammy, can you hear me?”

“Huh...huh...ahhh...” Grammy tries to communicate but can’t.

"I’m calling 911,” the lady tells Gracie. “They can help your grandmother.”

"It's right around here. He lives somewhere on that side of this street. I remember. Let's go find him."

“Find who?” the lady asks. “The bad guy ran off. Do you mean he lives near here?”

“No, my friend Andy Michaels. He lives somewhere near here. He will help us find the thief.”

“We need to get your Grammy help first.”

Tears soak Gracie’s face.

"I didn't even get time to play with them. Why would that man do that?"

"Nothing is safe anymore," the lady tells Gracie. "Bad guys will steal anything from anyone, even from little kids.”

The man literally throws the pieces of the Power Ranger figures across the room, right at the man in the jogging suit. The jogger ducks and holds both his hands out instinctively as the various pieces hit him, the wall and the shelf behind him.

"There's no chip, no embedded information, no anything. You stole toys from a little kid walking down the street for nothing. Worst of all, what if she tells Michaels, and this tips him off to our surveillance?”

The agent tries to defend himself. “We've had 24-hour surveillance on him. I'm telling you he is using that park as a drop. There’s no other reason he would have gone there. How can we be sure there is nothing embedded or hidden anywhere in those toys?"

"We have broken every piece down. We've done cross-sections, axial sections, metallurgy, chemical composition. There's nothing there," Chun says.

"Then he must have dropped something somewhere and this was a ruse or a decoy."

Chun begins to pace around the small room. "You haven't turned up one clue, one item for us to go on. He must know something about what his brother was doing. They did everything together. We have to find something. Our key contact clearly doesn't have all the details to reproduce the results."

The jogger dares to suggest, "It's possible he doesn't know anything."

Chun immediately disagrees. "I don't believe that for a second. We need to pursue Michaels in addition to our mole. No telling who or what will lead us in the right direction."

The Rave

The traffic is gridlocked for a few blocks on all sides of Café Loco. The limousine carrying Amanda and her entourage is stopped by a local cop. The limo driver rolls the window down.

"Can we get through here, Officer?"

"Yeah, I'm going to wave you through. Give me a few seconds to clear up a lane for you."

Massive numbers of high school kids – together with many parents – have come to the charity event, excited that it has garnered national news coverage. CNT has discussed it in several broadcasts over the last two days. A line snakes out the entrance of Café Loco and down the street.

The limo containing Amanda, Iris, Charlyne, David, and John crawls down the last block-and-a-half and parks in front, and the entourage – in their psychedelic garb – get out. They push through the heavy drapery toward the dance room, which is by no means large. The entire room is dark, lit only with black lights. The noise from the PA system is loud and pulsating, and everything appears to be in motion because of the disco ball mounted to the ceiling. A number of fluorescent hippie-like 1960s posters line the walls. There are already people standing in all corners of the large room and around several tables at the far side. Charlyne and Iris quickly guide Amanda over to the table reserved for them. It has a place card on a metal stand marked "VIP." They see Andy, his girlfriend Becca, and Barbara and Steve Simon, along with some of their friends, and introductions are exchanged.

"Hi Amanda, do you remember me? My name's Angie Tipton. I'm Andy's paralegal. This is Myra, one of the firm assistants."

"Okay, yeah." Amanda says. The next step Amanda takes finds her face to face with Perry Carson, the reporter with *Capitol Law* magazine.

"Amanda, great to see you. I still want that interview. Will you give me your first interview?"

Before Amanda can answer, Andy steps in between them.

"Perry, we'll get you that interview, but not now."

The DJ is playing "I've Got a Feeling" by the Black Eyed Peas. The dance floor is already so packed with bodies that any errant movement causes unintended contact. There are several news crews shining lights on the dancers. Over by the door, Kent is standing beside

Sienna, who is collecting donations from those without advance tickets. All of the café employees are wearing matching tie-dyed T-shirts. Kent wears a vest with black and purple paisley over his, and his faded jeans are virtually sparkling under the black lights. He stealthily makes his way over to Amanda, who is talking to someone else, and taps her on the shoulder. Amanda wheels around.

"Kent, you look really, uh ... sparkly."

"You look smashing. What color is your dress?"

"Canary yellow, but you can’t tell in here. You guys did an amazing job with this place. I don't think I've ever been in a psychedelic room before."

"Wait until you see the dancers up on the pedestals."

As they make their way toward the dance floor, they notice the high Lucite. Four similarly dressed leggy women in mini dresses with sequined fringe dance on each pedestal.

Kent leads Amanda onto the dance floor and dances as near to her as he can given her halo. In the middle of gyrating on the dance floor, Amanda suddenly freezes.

Kent leans toward her and shouts, "What's the matter?"

After a few seconds Amanda snaps out of it and walks off the dance floor followed by Kent.

"Something about the black lights...I just remembered something."

"What was it?" Kent asked.

"It must be my dad. I’m a little girl and he's got black lights on in this little lab, like in a house or something."

"What's it mean?"

"I don’t know," Amanda says. “There were bugs flying around inside a netted area or cage-like thing.”

“How do you know it’s at home?”

“Because it wasn’t at a laboratory, it was like a room in a house.”

“Your house?”

“How would I know? I guess so.”

Kent begins to pull her back to the dance floor.

"Wait,” she leans toward his ear. “We are in a little office. And he's sitting at his desk."

"Did he have a lab at home?"

"I don't know. I guess I can find out later." Amanda leads Kent back into the sea of flesh.

Moments later David Owlsley approaches them.

Revelation

"I need to ask you something pretty weird," David yells toward Kent's ear. "Do you have some kind of bug or camera hidden in Amanda's hospital room?"

"What? What the hell are you talking about?"

David studies Kent's reaction but can't quite read him. He knows Kent was able to mastermind his viral video, and he befriended Amanda at the hospital. A lot of coincidences, perhaps too many.

"All I can tell you is that someone bugged Amanda's room, and they might even have video of her, although I'm not positive about that part."

"How do you know that? And why would you accuse me?"

"I can't tell you how I found out."

"Well it wasn't me." Kent says as he quickly turns and pushes through the crowd. He is fuming about the accusation but decides not to start an argument at the party.

The DJ is mixing in old 60s and 70s psychedelic era music, and "Purple Haze" by Jimi Hendrix blasts through the sound system. Kent then hears the opening part of "Iris" by the Goo Goo Dolls. He walks straight to Amanda and leads her toward the dance floor. When he pulls her toward him she feels the electricity of his body just barely touching hers. Soon, the song breaks into the up-tempo chorus.

When everything's meant to be broken, I just want you to know who I am.

As the song ends Kent whispers in her ear, "I really enjoyed that. I hope you did too."

"Of course I did. Are you going to play with your band later?"

"Oh yeah. We're going to play a couple tunes, and we even have a surprise or two in your honor."

"I don't know if I like surprises!"

As they get back to the VIP table, Sienna is standing near the table, tidying up. She is wearing a tight black mini skirt and a small black satin vest with her requisite tie-dyed shirt. Amanda's jealousy antennae go up, because she has seen Kent talking to her several times.

"Can I get anyone anything? We have little chocolate chip cupcakes and brownies here. They are excellent."

Several of the people at the table have already partaken, as evidenced by the empty spaces on the platter.

No one knows who notices it first. Iris and Charlyne are laughing and giggling. And they can't stop.

"Have you noticed that we're laughing at everything?" Iris says.

"Yeah, I don't know why, but my cheeks hurt from laughing," Charlyne responds.

Around this time David pushes through some other revelers over to the giggly girls.

"I'm not totally sure, but I think somebody spiked something. Either our drinks or something we ate." David says with an ear-to-ear grin.

"Oh my God. I was kind of thinking the same thing," Iris says.

David reviews the evening's events in his mind that is already addled by pulsating strobe lights and pounding music. They hadn't all had dinner together before they arrived, so that left something they drank or ate at the party. John walks in front of David.

"Do you feel high on something?" David asks John.

John stares at the flashing lights, contemplating David's question. "That's a good question. Since I don't do drugs, I don't know how it feels to be high, but I've been dancing like a fool and the room is making me dizzy."

"Aren't you that reporter with *Capital Law* magazine?" Kent asks Perry Carson, who is hanging with a group of parents.

"Yeah, I think I met you at the Simons after the funeral," Carson says, practically yelling over the pulsing music.

"Hey, I want to talk to you about some stuff pertaining to the Hemispheres crash."

"I'm all ears," Carson says, sensing something really good.

"Not now, not tonight. I've got to check on a couple other things. Do you have a card or something?"

"Sure do," Carson says, and fishes one out of his wallet and hands it to Kent.

"I'll call you soon," Kent says, sliding it into his pants pocket and quickly moving back into the crowd of people.

Even though Amanda has no recollection of her long relationship with John Parkinson, she finds herself on the dance floor with John for a number of the songs.

Kent takes the stage, and his band launches into their first song, covering Coldplay:

Look at the stars,
Look how they shine for you,
And everything you do,
Yeah, they were all yellow.

Looking down from the elevated stage Kent sees John dancing with Amanda. This is exactly what he had hoped would not occur. The real insult for him is that he is playing a song that makes him think of Amanda, and she is dancing with her former boyfriend.

"At this time, we would like to introduce a special guest, Mr. Kyle Perless, and his friend, Nils Lundgren. Both are here as part of the fundraising event in support of Healing Heroes and Amanda Michaels."

Kent's band, Paris VA, launches into a David Bowie classic, "Ziggy Stardust," with Kyle playing lead guitar and Nils on vocals:

"Ziggy played guitar,
Jamming good with weird and Gilly..."

After "Ziggy Stardust," the band immediately segues into "Heroes" as the dance floor packs out.

"I'm pleased to be here in support of the Healing Heroes," says Nils, who is wearing a sequined sport coat. "We'd like to do this special song for Amanda."

I, I will be king
And you, you will be queen
Though nothing will drive them away
We can be heroes just for one day
We can be us just for one day.
We can be heroes ...

They repeat the chorus from "Heroes" and Kent joins in on his mike. Amanda is sandwiched between Iris, Charlyne, David, John and other MA seniors amidst a sea of people. Toward the end of the song,

Nils lifts a saxophone and adds a few short riffs. Soon after, Kyle, Nils and Kent's band leave the stage for a break. The DJ cranks up a current dance song and the dance floor remains packed for another 45 minutes. Amanda looks for Kent and finds him clear across the dance floor, dancing with Sienna, who apparently is no longer serving.

Soon David tells Amanda the limo is ready to depart. Amanda finds Kent.

"I have to go. The limo is leaving."

"Why don't you just stay and I will give you a ride home later?"

"I really can't. I, I need to stay with the group. I have felt really weird all night. I think someone spiked something because all of us feel high."

"Medicinal marijuana," Kent says.

"What?" Amanda yells.

"I have it on good information that the cupcakes and brownies were spiked." He leans forward and gives her a quick kiss on the lips, a mischievous smile, and then turns to walk through the mass of bodies on the dance floor.

Protection

Sometime later, Sienna, Kent, and several other staff are cleaning up the carnage from the party. Kyle is hovering around, pitching in. Once matters are mostly under control, Sienna prepares to leave.

"Kent, can you walk me to my car please? It's late." True, she never works this late, he thinks. Then she runs her hand along his forearm to emphasize the personal request. Kent can smell her perfume.

"Sure, where are you parked?"

"I'm on Main Street down past the Red Fox Inn."

Kent says goodbye to his dad and the others and follows Sienna outside. The street is now deserted.

As they walk down the street toward Main, Sienna purposely walks right against Kent, occasionally touching him and playfully caressing her fingers along his back several times.

"You and the band sounded really good tonight. Having Kyle and Nils play at the café was amazing too."

Kent's fairly high on the cupcakes, and he can smell alcohol on Sienna's breath. She must have been tapping some booze hidden away from the high schoolers.

Once they arrive at her Jeep, she says "Get in, I'll take you to your car. Where'd you park?"

Kent climbs in the passenger seat.

"Everybody had a great time, at least it seemed that way." Sienna says.

"Yeah, for sure. It will be hard to top."

"So, you've been seeing Amanda some? Are you guys, like, going out or what?"

"We just hang out."

"Does she remember anything from, like, before the crash? Like her friends, stuff like that?"

"No, she doesn't recall anything, not people. Not music. Not her friends from school. Nothing." Kent pauses, and then continues on a slightly different tangent. "I'm looking into the jet crash and what may have caused it."

"What are you talking about?"

"Um...can't really say. I'm just looking into some things and I'm meeting with a reporter soon. He was there tonight, did you meet Perry Carson?"

"No. Where's your car? "Sienna asks resting both hands on the steering wheel. "And what about the crash could be that interesting to you that hasn't been all over the news?"

Kent directs her the couple blocks. "I'm not really sure yet. It might end up being nothing."

Before Kent gets out, Sienna grasps his left arm, causing him to turn toward her.

"Thanks for walking me." She leans toward him quickly and gives him a quick peck on his left cheek. He freezes a moment. Then, he turns toward her and they exchange an awkward look that occurs when two members of the opposite sex aren't quite sure what just happened. Kent exits the Jeep and waves to her as he turns on the Alfa's headlights and watches her pull away.

Surprise Visitor

"Well, hello stranger!" Myra says, quickly admiring the visitor's stylish black trench coat.

"Hi Myra, can you tell Andy I'm here?"

"Sure thing." Myra presses a button and then speaks softly into her headset. "Andy, Sarah is here." There is a brief pause. "Okay." She looks back at Sarah. "He said come on back."

Myra waits until Sarah is out of sight before she rockets out of her chair to find Angie.

"What's going on? Sarah just went into Andy's office. Did you know she was coming?"

"No."

"She was dolled up like she was attending a formal. Black trench coat, matching pumps, stockings with seams running down the back. She's on her way to Andy's office."

"Knowing her, she wants something. We'll find out."

Sarah finds Andy's office door and stands on the threshold for a moment.

"Can I come in?" She asks rhetorically. She knows his office well from before their split. She suggestively removes her coat and closes the door, knowing that the hook is on the back of it, and that Andy will get a good look at her seamed stockings and the rear view of her tight black pencil skirt. A loose-fitting gold chain belt divides the skirt and her long-sleeved sheer black top, unbuttoned to generously reveal her cleavage. She turns and walks over to one of the client chairs.

"You look really great," Andy says as she sits in the chair and crosses her legs. He figures Sarah knows she looks good, but gratuitously reinforces it.

"Thanks."

Sarah keeps herself in amazing condition and is always mindful of her God-given assets, especially amongst the sex-starved congressmen and lobbyists on Capitol Hill.

"What's going on?" Andy asks, and he means it because he has no idea why she is here.

"It's been on my mind ever since I saw you at Barbara's after the funeral. I keep thinking about it Andy, and I just wanted to tell you

I'm so sorry. I mean I'm so sorry about your brother and Rochelle, but I'm also so sorry about what happened between us. It really hit me hard when I was at Barbara's house and I saw all your family and everybody. It made me realize how much I miss you."

Sarah stops for a moment trying to decide what to say next. "I never told you I'm sorry. I also never told you it was my fault, so I'm doing it now."

She looks straight at Andy, wanting him to say something, but he doesn't. His anger is so vast; he knows if he even starts to explain his pain, it will result in a nasty tirade that he will never be able to take back.

Sarah then gets up from the client chair, and walks around his desk towards him.

"Sarah, don't."

She ignores his weak protest and sits on his desk blotter, facing him, her legs dangling, uncrossed. She runs her hand briefly through his hair, gently touching his ear and neck for a moment before pulling it away and grasping his hand. She holds it between both of hers, resting it right at the bottom edge of her black skirt between her thighs.

"I need to tell you something," she says in a mere whisper. "Whenever I'm alone, I don't fantasize about anyone else. It's always you and me. That's the truth, and I know you must still think about me too."

Sarah releases his hand. She begins unbuttoning her blouse, staring into Andy's eyes, but not finding the look she longs for.

Andy suddenly pushes his chair back toward the credenza, standing and turning toward her.

"I can't do this, Sarah. I can't just turn it on like this – like you can. You don't have any idea how you wrecked me. I can't just forgive you and make everything vanish from my brain. Sure, I think about you. But I just can't. Things are good with Becca."

Sarah slides down off the desk, and then slides right into Andy's own chair, as she re-buttons her blouse.

"Andy, I know one of the things that got between us was starting a family. That's not a problem anymore. I know that's important to you and I'm ready."

Andy has plopped down in one of the client chairs. He briefly ponders the juxtaposition. She's now in the attorney's seat, but he's not sure he wants to be counseled.

"Here's all I ask. Let's just have dinner, see if we can start over."

He stares at her, but doesn't commit.

"Just tell me you'll think about it please?"

"Okay. I will."

Less than 30 seconds after Sarah has exited the reception area, Angie's in his office. "Well, what was that all about?"

"Nothing. She just wanted to talk to me about something confidential."

"Andy, do you think I'm an idiot? She was dressed like she was going to Ladies Night at an exclusive club. She must've put the major blast on you. You gotta tell me."

"Well, assume she did 'blast' me, what do you think I should do?"

"I'm not inside your relationship with Becca, and was never inside your relationship with Sarah either. So I don't know. Are you going to start seeing her again?"

"I don't know, I didn't commit to anything."

"She really puts some kind of spell on you doesn't she?"

"No," he says, but even he is unconvinced.

Coincidences

Kent notices that Sienna has a routine. It's not exactly extraordinary, just a little weird. During her ten-minute breaks, she gets her laptop out of her backpack, powers it up, and does some browsing. That's not a lot of time to catch up, he thinks. She also sits right by the window every time.

Today, while contemplating Sienna's choice of location, Kent notices a black SUV with dark tinted windows pulling into the space right in front of Café Loco. He thinks a black SUV was parked in the same spot yesterday. But Kent isn't sure when exactly he saw it, and who knows, maybe the owner just needed to stop in a shop or office nearby two days in a row.

Then he sees Sienna pull a thin card out of her backpack. She plugs it into a USB port in the laptop. Kent finishes ringing up his customer and walks from behind the counter toward Sienna because his curiosity is piqued. As he approaches Sienna, her back is to him and she is facing the window.

"You know we have free Wi-Fi…" he says.

Sienna actually jumps in her seat. She quickly closes the screen of the laptop, too quickly, in fact. She slides the card out of the USB port and puts it back into her backpack.

"Oh, uh, the password didn't work for me the last time I tried it," she says.

Kent notices that the black SUV is pulling out of the parking space. It was only there a minute or two and no one got out.

"Did you know the person in that black SUV?"

"What are you talking about?"

"I thought I saw that same SUV right there yesterday."

Sienna has already zipped up the laptop in her backpack, and is headed toward the counter. Kent stares out at the now empty parking space, wondering if he is just paranoid.

Released

The process of removing the halo and the shoulder harness was simpler than Amanda or her family members imagined. It was done in the outpatient surgical center at Loudoun Hospital. The only tricky part was removing the screws penetrating her skull. But Wrightson had no trouble, and in about 30 minutes the halo and harness were gone. Amanda's biggest concern then was the holes left from the screws. She demanded a brush to try to cover them up but some of the areas simply didn't have enough hair.

About a half hour after Amanda was moved to recovery, Wrightson spoke to Amanda, Andy and Barb. "Everything looks excellent as far as bone growth and stability. We took some images in the operating room once we removed the halo. All is good. So here are the main restrictions. Absolutely no driving for 30 days. No athletics, no exercise whatsoever, except for walking, which is encouraged. After 30 days I want to see you at my clinic to determine if I can lift any of the restrictions."

"Why can't I drive? How's that different than being in a car with someone else driving?" Amanda asks.

"We want no sudden head-turning."

The staff had already informed the family that Amanda would be free to leave after 2:00 p.m., once the doctors went over her instructions. The press conference would begin at 2:30 p.m. Andy had discussed this earlier with Amanda, and they decided not to participate. Rather, they would use that time to escape so Amanda wouldn't be mobbed by reporters.

Iris, Charlyne, Kent, John and David all stand in the hall outside Amanda's room waiting to walk out with her. The doctors walk into the news conference, where at least 12 video cameras, dozens of microphones, and more than 30 reporters patiently wait. The hospital staff never disclosed that Amanda isn't coming, so the reporters are eagerly awaiting her appearance.

"Dr. Wrightson, is it unusual for a patient with a neck fracture to be released so soon? What are the medical risks?" These are the first questions posed to the five doctors seated behind the table on a small stage.

At the same time, Amanda and her entourage walk through the hall, in an almost parade-like atmosphere. Amanda pauses many times to receive hugs from the staff. As they hit the doors at the service exit of the hospital, Natalee Spalding, her cameraman, and one young cub reporter are there, having been tipped off to Amanda's departure.

"Amanda, how do you feel about finally being released?" Spalding asks, pressing a large microphone in her face.

"A lot better than I did at the beginning!" Amanda says sarcastically. "I'm really excited to finally have the halo off my head."

"How about your memory, Amanda? What do you remember from before the crash?"

"Unfortunately, still very little. But I have a bunch of great friends and family and I'm just moving on."

"When will you be returning to high school?" Spalding asks.

"Right away I think."

Barbara and Andy both put an arm on Amanda's shoulder and indicate that they would like to move her toward the car. Her Uncle Steve has pulled Barb's car right up into the circle and Amanda prepares to climb into the backseat. She turns, looking for Kent.

"Kent, are you going to come over?"

"No, I think your family wants to be with you alone. Text me and we'll make some plans."

Just then several of the TV reporters come sprinting down the hospital sidewalk in their direction, realizing that the guest of honor just sneaked out through the service exit.

Within 15 minutes, the exclusive interview and video footage from the hospital news conference appear on CNT's continuous news coverage.

> "Today, Amanda Michaels had her cervical halo removed and was released from Loudoun Memorial Hospital, just about a month after the Hemispheres crash in Pennsylvania. At a news conference today, her doctors called it nothing less than a miracle. One of the most significant lingering problems is her amnesia, according to her doctors. As for the cases filed against Hemispheres, possible electrical issues continue to be where the accident investigation is focused. The NTSB has offered nothing on the cause since its preliminary news release. Most of the family lawsuits are

pending in D.C., although a few cases have been filed in other jurisdictions. This is Natalee Spalding, reporting for CNT from Loudoun County, Virginia."

Steve Simon has opened the front door to their home, and Barbara and Andy stand beside him in the foyer with Amanda. Steve holds the small rolling bag from the rehab hospital, but everything else has already been placed into the room upstairs that they have set up for her. The awkward scene plays out almost like foster parents bringing home a foster child.

"Your room is at the top of the stairs to the left. We hope you like it. We brought a lot of your things from your room in your own house," Barb says, leading the way.

Amanda silently follows Barbara, and Steve and Andy bring up the rear. Once they enter the room she sees a number of posters on the wall. There is one of a female soccer player kicking a ball near a goalie, a picture of a female musician with flowing red hair, and there are a couple of mirrors with metal star shapes around them. Amanda stares around the room.

"Does it bring back any memories?" Steve asks her.

"Who is that soccer player?"

"Mia Hamm, a famous American soccer player."

"How 'bout her?" she asks, pointing to a red-haired musician.

"She's Florence, from Florence and the Machine, a rock band you like," Barb answers.

Everything is set up the same way it was in her old room, but Amanda doesn't remember any of it.

"Why don't you settle in and we'll eat together later." Barb says, backing out of the room with Steve and Andy.

Amanda lays down on the bed and looks around the room, at the posters and the books. She wonders about her own taste. She resolves to get some Florence and the Machine music on her phone and laptop.

Paris

Kent had been promising for some time that he would take her to Skyline Parkway to show her places he had described in their conversations. One of them was the old B&O Railroad bridge trestle over the Shenandoah River. Kent arrives at Barb's place. The sky is a deep blue with a couple wispy clouds and the temperature is pleasant. Amanda is standing in the front foyer, ready to leave. She has already said goodbye to Barbara, who was baking in the kitchen.

"I am taking you to Paris," Kent says.

"The doctors will never let me go," she replies longingly.

"Not France. Paris, Virginia, just west of Upperville. That's how we got the name of our band."

Huh. I thought you just made it up."

"Nope, it's real." He closes the front door after her.

As they walk out to the street, Amanda eyes the little red two-seater convertible Kent has brought. "What kinda car is this?"

"Alfa-Romeo, don't see 'em around much anymore. Great car, even though it's stick and not totally reliable anymore." Kent walks around and gently closes her passenger door.

"We'll head out 50 West. Ever been to Paris?"

"Kent!"

"Sorry, that was pretty brainless. It's a farm town. We'll stop there then head west. I want to take you to this overlook near the old B&O Railroad bridge."

"Why an old bridge?"

"The view's amazing. It's really high, like a couple hundred feet above the Shenandoah River. Someone told me it's been there since before the Civil War. The train comes all the way down from Harper's Ferry, which is actually in West Virginia. It's got a little walkway down one side. We lived a mile or two away until I was in seventh grade, and I used to play by the river under the trestle."

There's a song on Kent's phone playing through the car's speakers.

Hey where did we go,
Days when the rains came
Down in the hollow,
Playin' a new game.
Laughin' and a runnin' hey, skipping and a jumping ...

"If you're walking on the bridge, which is like half a mile long over the river, and you hear a train whistle, you've gotta take off running as fast as you can for the other side. Or else jump in the river, and it's a long way down. Scary but kinda cool. Like Huck Finn or something."

"Almost getting hit by a train is cool to you?" Amanda asks, looking at Kent as he stares intently ahead.

"If you never take risks, life's boring. I told you I've got a twisted view of the world. Probably because of what happened to my mom." They both look ahead at the farms and cornfields dotting Route 50 on each side while listening to the close of "Brown-Eyed Girl."

"Not to freak you out or anything, but when I was in middle school a girl and a guy got killed on the trestle. They lived in my neighborhood. The guy got hit, and I think the girl actually jumped, but she drowned because she wasn't a good swimmer. Or maybe the impact of the water knocked her out. It was all over the newspapers here. First friends of mine that died."

"Were you with 'em?"

"No, we'd moved six months before, but I'd been there with 'em. We used to ride our bikes and then climb up there."

"Were they trying to outrun the train?"

"No one ever figured out what happened."

A few minutes pass and Kent downshifts the Alfa, hits his blinker and navigates a right turn just past a sign reading "Paris, Virginia - Population 51."

"Wait, there're only 51 people in Paris?"

"Yep. There's a street fair today."

Once they park they make their way onto the busy single block of town. They hear music from a fiddle, bass and drum. A couple guys walk toward them and Amanda notices their cowboy boots and jeans. Another couple and their toddler are walking down the center of the road.

Street vendors line both sides of the road selling funnel cakes, barbeque, and snow cones. One vendor is selling all kinds of jewelry on a cloth-covered table.

Amanda stops and admires the bracelets, many of which have small colorful stones and charms.

"All handmade," the thirty-something lady seated in the folding chair says.

"Pick one. I'm buying," Kent says.

Amanda holds one up to her wrist. It has three peace-sign charms and small colorful stones

"How about this one?"

"Yeah, it's totally you. How much?" he asks the lady.

"$25.00."

Kent hands her $40.00 and she makes change.

"Wanna bag Honey, or are you gonna wear it?"

"I'll wear it," Amanda responds, and Kent helps her hook it around her wrist. They walk down a short distance to a street vendor selling chocolate and candy-coated apples, some with rainbow sprinkles.

Kent stops and points. "Split a candy apple with me?"

"Sure."

Moments later, Kent pushes the candy apple toward her face.

"Go for it, it's awesome." They stop walking and she takes a bite. Little pieces of sprinkles and red candy stick to her lips on one side.

"Let me help you with that," Kent says. Instead of using his fingers he pulls her close, kisses her momentarily, then pulls away slightly and nibbles the small candy pieces off her mouth.

"Hold it to your mouth, I'll get a picture." He quickly snaps it with his phone. Then she gets one of him doing a goofy bite.

They finish strolling along the short block that comprises the Paris street fair, and are back in the Alfa within 20 minutes.

"That was a pleasant little surprise," Amanda says once they are leaving town.

Kent follows several back roads and they end up in Delaplane, the tiny town where the overlook is located.

"Let's get walk up. I want you to see the view back to Paris," Kent says.

"I've never been to Paris, France. I wonder if this is as good," Amanda muses.

"It ain't the promenade on the Eiffel Tower, but it's one helluva view." Kent walks past a small number of gravel parking spots and along a narrow trail. Amanda follows close behind until they reach a clearing no more than 50 yards away from where they parked Kent's car.

"Look straight ahead and you'll see the red roof of a really old church. That's the old Methodist church, been there since the Civil War."

Amanda looks into the distance and notices the bright red roof and the colors of the trees dotting the valley. The sun is setting and the view is breathtaking.

"Well?" Kent reaches for her hand and wraps his fingers through hers. Amanda feels electricity from his touch.

"This is really nice. Kent, what do you see in me?"

"Don't ask me questions like that. Why do women ask guys questions like that?" He stares toward the red-roofed church.

"Okay, whatever."

Before they leave the overlook Kent walks over to a waist-high tree stump and places his phone there with the photo timer set. He tells her he wants one picture and runs over to her right before it flashes. Kent checks the photo and then reaches over and shows her.

"Let's go. You haven't seen the bridge." Kent says, pulling her toward the car.

Once they're belted in, Kent peels out in reverse, shooting gravel in several directions, then quickly shifts back into first gear and squeals back onto the roadway.

The stereo is cranking out tunes and the wind is gusting. Over the din Kent finally says, "I'm infatuated with the fact that you're the only survivor. Is that weird? I keep thinking maybe a little bit of your magic fairy dust'll land on me. And you're hot." Kent laughs.

A warm smile comes to Amanda's face.

"What're you gonna do with the rest of your charmed life anyway?"

Amanda's first impulse is to say spend it with you, but she doesn't. She is proud that she is able to keep the thought from leaving her lips. "Dunno. Maybe charity stuff. I'm way behind in my classes, so I may never graduate."

"You'll graduate. And go big, whatever you do. But be sure to use the fairy dust a little at a time so it lasts."

"Ha ha... funny."

Trestle

Kent parks along the shoulder of the road. After opening the passenger door for her, he grabs her hand and says, "We gotta get moving. The sun's going down soon and you have to see it in good light."

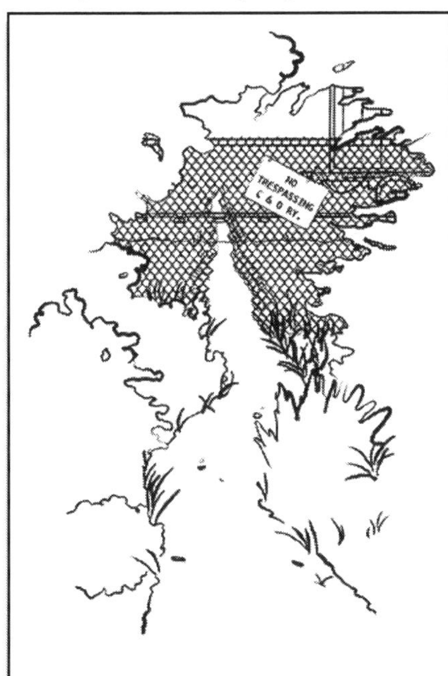

They walk near each other along a thin but well-worn dirt path. Maybe 100 yards down the trail, they come to a sign partially covered by brush. Kent stops and points.

"Can you read that?"

"Yeah, 'No Trespassing.'"

"The other part says 'Walking on bridge strictly prohibited. C&O RR.' C&O Railroad hasn't existed for decades."

"I'm not so sure we should..." Amanda says, but Kent persists.

"Come on, I'm just going to show you the scenery, not sit in the middle of the trestle."

Kent pushes back part of the old fence. "Go."

Amanda partly ducks through the narrow space and Kent follows. Then he lets the rusty fence spring back. Up ahead she can see a clearing in the distance.

"Look," Kent says.

She and Kent stand right beside the gravel ballast rocks lining a single railroad track, and she looks down the track and sees rusty metal supports in a reverse U-shape over the track.

"The right side is the walking side."

"There's no way you can walk on that if a train's coming. I'm not sure even a cat could."

"The railroad built it so there's gotta be enough space for someone to walk. Besides, they have to blow their whistle well before they hit the bridge. If you hear the whistle, you should have plenty of time to run to the opposite side."

Amanda inches forward a few steps to look down the trestle and she sees the greenish-brown water of the Shenandoah River.

"Does anyone ever do anything in the water? Like, I don't see any boats."

“Small fishing boats or canoes. It's sundown so they're not around right now.”

“You guys knew better than to ever go out on that bridge when you were kids. So why’d you do it?”

“Why do kids do anything? We used to paint turtles too, caught ‘em in a creek that ran near our neighborhood.”

"It’s really pretty up here," Amanda admits, gazing out at the river. The water is so calm the reflection of the entire tree line on the opposite side of the river is reverse-imaged on it.

Suddenly Kent begins to walk out along the pedestrian path of the bridge. He walks about 20 feet away and then turns back toward her and waves with his arm, indicating she should come along.

"No way. Come back here!"

"C’mon, you chicken, just a little ways. If we hear a whistle we’ll run back.”

"The bridge curves. I can't even see the other side." Amanda edges out barely onto the pedestrian side of the trestle, not even past the edge of the elevated embankment.

"Oh my God. There's no handrail or anything."

"No, but if you lost your balance you could just hold onto one of the metal supports. Can you swim?"

“I guess so. As you can imagine, I haven’t tried lately. You don’t forget how if your brain gets scrambled, do you? Like riding a bike?”

"Don’t know. I don’t want you to find out. It’s a long way down.”

After following Kent no more than 10 yards, Amanda chickens out. She turns around and starts slowly walking back.

“Did I just hear a whistle?” Kent says.

What a smart ass, she thinks. Never one that was comfortable with heights, Amanda quickly returns to the embankment. She turns and notices that Kent is still walking in the opposite direction on the pedestrian side of the track.

"Kent, get off of the bridge. Now!"

Kent stops and turns, wearing a funny smile on his face. He holds both arms outstretched, moving them up and down playfully in an airplane motion, like a soccer player who scores a goal.

"You're a killjoy" Kent begins to walk toward her.

"You're a lunatic."

"Actually, it's probably not any riskier than being on a busy highway. And this is way more fun."

Amanda impulsively puts her arms around Kent and stares into his eyes. He looks back at her and they hold each other's gaze for a moment. She initiates the forward motion and barely touches his lips with hers. Then she moves away and stares back into his eyes. He then pushes forward, his lips against hers in a passionate kiss. He runs his hands under her hair and softly touches her ears and the nape of her neck. He presses his body against hers. It is dusk, the sun no longer visible on the horizon. After a few minutes he grabs her hand and they start walking back to the car. He helps her in and closes the door. He comes around to his side, cranks up the car and pushes the accelerator directly to the floor. He looks over at her with a worried look.

"Um, it didn't do anything."

"Are you kidding? Try again."

The same thing happens.

"That's the problem with these old sports cars. No reliability."

"Now what? Do you have any tools?"

"Hang on." Moments later Kent has popped the hood and is looking around. In the dusk he can see a little but could really use a flashlight. A few minutes later, he gives up on the engine. Amanda watches him as he walks and stares at the gravel beside the road.

"What're you doing?" Amanda shouts.

There's no answer, even though Kent obviously hears her. He continues looking carefully at the ground. Finally, he reaches down and picks something up. He waves in the air what appears to be a long discarded shoelace.

"I don't believe it. We're so lucky!" Kent excitedly exclaims.

"How are we lucky, stranded in the middle of nowhere?"

"Just wait." Kent peers under the hood. After a few minutes his hand appears and Amanda sees part of the long shoelace that he has fished from under the left side of the hood through to the driver's side of the car. He lowers the hood back down but leaves it slightly open.

Kent returns to the driver's side, picks up the dangling shoelace, and pushes it through his open window. As he opens the driver's door he holds the shoelace and then closes the door again.

"If this works this is going to be our accelerator cable."

Kent turns the ignition, pulls the shoelace slightly and they both hear the engine start.

"This is our ticket home tonight," Kent says gleefully.

"You mean the shoelace is going to make the car go?"

"Yep. I'm gonna have to juggle between shifting gears and using the shoelace as the accelerator," he says as the car edges out onto the road. "You ever drive a stick-shift before?"

"Once again, I don't know. Just tell me what to do."

"Okay, just move the gear shift down or up when I say so."

"Right."

"Pull down," Kent says and Amanda dutifully shoves the gear shift. "Excellent, now up and to the right."

Once the car is in top gear, Kent simply holds the shoelace near the left side of the steering wheel. After traveling along the rural road at 55 miles an hour for a bit, their unusual shifting procedure doesn't seem unusual at all.

"Seven Devils" by Florence and the Machine wind-tunnels through the air:

Seven devils all around you, seven devils in your house
See I was dead when I woke up this morning,
And I'll be dead before the day is done
Before the day is done.

"I've never heard of painting turtles."

"No? There were plenty of yellow-bellied sliders in the creek. We'd tie some fishing line and a hook to a branch and try to catch 'em. Sometimes we'd rest the stick in a tree while we were playing, and if you hooked one, your pole would pull right out. We'd run and try to grab the pole before it fell in the creek. Sliders aren't fast, so most of the time you could grab it before the turtle swam away with the pole."

"How'd you paint 'em?"

"We'd put 'em in a bucket and hang it from our handlebars on the ride home. Katie'd get some white fingernail polish, and when their shells were dry we'd paint our initials on them."

“Did you keep them as pets?”

“No, none of our parents would let us, but we’d feed them and take them back to the creek and let them go. We painted them so we’d know if we ever caught them again. Let’s stop by the farm for a few minutes."

"Cool, I'd like to see the horses again.”

"I’ll borrow a car so I won't have to use the shoestring method to get you home," Kent adds with a grin.

Kennedy Center

Bobby Vail and his brother had both played for the Boston Celtics, but his brother perished in the 9/11 collapse of the Twin Towers. That motivated him to get involved with those making a difference in others' lives. Bobby and his associates took care of all the details relating to Amanda's appearance for the annual "Healing Heroes" TV special sponsored by CNT. He had personally talked to Andy, and then Amanda, about her appearance. He explained that they would have a collage relating to the Hemispheres crash and her survival, and then a presenter would introduce her and present her with a Healing Heroes award. He also promised limousine service to and from the event and backstage VIP passes for Amanda and her family.

Everyone meets at Andy's place, including Kent, whom Amanda invited as her guest. Once they get to the venue there is a large room backstage for all of the featured persons and their families and friends. There is even a roving videographer doing a back story and interviewing people as well. The event is being aired live and will be shown a couple of other times by CNT.

Finally, one of the production assistants with an earpiece tells Amanda it's time to move to the ready room just off the stage. Everyone wishes Amanda the best of luck, and she follows the assistant. Inside the quiet room is a large screen showing the ongoing presentations on the stage.

Vail begins to introduce Amanda Michaels' piece by first stating, "The next story of survival needs little introduction. We are all familiar with the lone survivor of the Hemispheres Airlines plane crash earlier this year. Before we bring out our next guest, please watch this short video clip."

Helicopter footage shows the Hemispheres crash, the smoke and fire and parts of the aircraft strewn through the wooded area. The video montage then cobbles together the interview of the rescue worker, helicopter footage showing the Nightingale chopper landing at the hospital, and video of the gurney with Amanda being rushed into the hospital. Her first interview is shown when she has the halo, and then an interview is shown with Natalee Spalding when she was released from the hospital. When the video is complete, the large Kennedy Center audience claps enthusiastically. Bobby Vail then says "I'd like to introduce to you the survivor, Amanda Michaels."

The production assistant indicates its Amanda's moment to walk onto the stage. Once she is at the podium beside Bobby Vail, her first words are, "Thank you, thanks so much." Before she can say anything else, Bobby Vail leans into the microphone.

"Amanda, we have arranged a little surprise for you."

At that moment a man, perhaps in his 40s, comes walking from the other side of the stage toward them.

Vail leans back toward the microphone and says "Ladies and gentlemen, this is Dale Peterson, the fire and rescue worker who rescued Amanda Michaels at the crash site. Let's give him a hand."

Amanda is shocked. She has never actually "seen" Peterson, except for watching the news footage of him. Looking completely surprised, she immediately embraces Peterson, and he hugs her back for what seems like several minutes.

Peterson breaks the embrace and looks into her face.

"I guess you don't remember me?" he asks into the live mike.

"I've seen the video, so I know you're the one," Amanda says.

Bobby Vail leans toward the mike. "Anything you would like to say to Dale?" he asks.

"Thank you so much for everything. I don't know what else I can say — you saved my life, I know it."

"Can you tell us what you are doing with your own charity, the Amanda's Halo Charity?" he asks.

Amanda says, "We hope to help people who need rehabilitation, particularly those with brain injuries."

"Let's give a round of applause for Dale Peterson and Amanda Michaels, a true survivor's story," Vail says.

The crowd at the Kennedy Center loudly claps and gives a standing ovation to both of them. A few moments later they both walk off the stage together to the ready room and then into the back room where all of the other VIPs are waiting. Within seconds the backstage videographer is interviewing Amanda and Peterson. Later, there is an after party sponsored by CNT at the Kennedy Center Ballroom. The entire event is a blur for Amanda as every other worthy survivor or admirable person involved in charitable work jockeys to speak with her during the reception.

It is early Sunday morning when the limousine drops their entourage back at Andy's house. The Simons say their farewells immediately and depart. Andy and Becca have set up the guest room to have Amanda stay over. Andy offers to let Kent sleep downstairs on the couch, but Kent declines, explaining that he's working the morning shift at Café Loco.

Amanda walks outside with Kent before he drives from D.C. to Middleburg. Once the door closes they stand on the porch, press in to each other, and passionately kiss.

"I like running my hands through your hair," he says pulling away from their embrace, and continuing to run his fingers down the back of her head and shoulders, making her tingle with excitement.

"It feels really good," she says, then presses her lips to his, inserting her tongue inside his mouth. She runs her hand along his chest and then she lets it slide down his back past his belt line to the left side of his butt, just grazing it but not grabbing it. Kent lightly caresses her earlobe and her neck as they continue kissing.

"I guess I need to hit the road, probably going to take 45 minutes."

"I wish we could stay together tonight," she whispers.

"Your uncle is protecting you, and I can appreciate that. We'll get together soon. Good luck at school Monday."

"Call me or text me." She gives him a short goodbye kiss and steps back.

Before even turning off Andy's street, Kent remembers he put Perry Carson's card in the unused ashtray of the Alfa, and he fishes it out and places it just in front of the gear shift where he'll remember it. The time is right to call Perry and arrange a meeting, he decides.

Hard Rain

As Sunday evening turns to night, rain falls in heavy sheets. Blackness covers the open pasture of the farm. Walking away from the sports car and the lifeless body in the driver's seat, he looks vigilantly ahead and hears only the squishing sound of his plastic booties each time they meet the thick, soggy grass in the pasture. Because of the rural location and the new moon, there is no artificial or natural light. The outline of the sports car is barely visible, he thinks, as pelting rain buffets his tight-fitting black hoodie and forms long streaks running down his cheeks.

Once partly back in the driver's seat of his black BMW, he slowly and deliberately lifts his feet up off the roadway. He slides the booties off his shoes and stuffs them into one pouch of his small black backpack. He then removes his rubber gloves, stuffs them inside another pouch, and puts on a new set of gloves before touching any part of the vehicle's interior. He taps in a confirmation message on his wireless device and places it back into the backpack on the front passenger seat.

Less than 100 yards behind the black BMW is a black SUV, well hidden by the sheets of rain. The two men in the front seat have been watching the man walking toward the BMW through their night-vision goggles and have their self-contained breathing apparatus at the ready. The man in the SUV's passenger seat stares down at his wireless device. The device silently lights and the word "proceed" appears.

They observe that the BMW has started to move very slowly, evidenced only by a very brief flicker of the brake lights. A few seconds pass. The driver of the SUV then commands his colleague: "Initiate the dose!"

The man reaches for a wireless phone doubling as a remote control. Once activated, the device takes over certain electronic components of the BMW, preventing operation of the electronic windows, locking the doors, and reducing the car's speed down to a crawl before it loses all power. An odorless gas begins to permeate the car's interior. Seconds later, the BMW veers toward the right shoulder and rolls down into a small, water-logged drainage ditch.

The SUV pulls up behind the BMW. Both men exit the SUV and approach the BMW, which has its right front end tilted down into the grassy ditch. The SUV driver, wearing his night-vision goggles and breathing apparatus, trains his Glock pistol ahead of him and slowly approaches the driver's door. He holsters it only after confirming there is no movement from the driver, whose head is slumped forward. He nods to the other man, who unlocks the doors with the remote. He also crouches down and locates a tiny device magnetically attached to the undercarriage and places it in his small backpack. Carefully opening the passenger door, he surveys the front seat area for any loose or collectible items and grabs the man's backpack. He pops open the glove compartment, but finds nothing except a registration, which he immediately puts in his backpack. He scours the floor, the back seat and the center console, taking several random objects and placing them in the confiscated backpack. The men exchange several words before laying a poncho-like covering over the body and carrying it back to the rear hatch of their SUV. They carefully lay the body onto a tarp in the back and fold up the tarp. With the driving rain and tinted rear window, there's little risk of it being seen. He softly closes the rear hatch. At the same time his partner walks back to the BMW and completely circles around the car before entering the driver's seat again. After cracking each of the front windows slightly, he turns the bi-level air controls to max. Reaching under the dashboard, he removes the remote delivery system and jamming device and places it in a thick resealable plastic bag before stashing it inside his backpack. He starts the car, maneuvers it slowly back onto the road, and the two men caravan to their assigned destination.

@Part IV

Pasture Spider

The orange ball of the sun just shows itself over the tree line on the east end of the pasture. Loudoun County Detective Holmes feels the moist air against his face as he captures a 360-degree view around the pasture, from the farmhouse to the tree line to the roadway entering the farm, and back to the small red sports car beside him. His homicide detective partner, Rogers, stands on the driver's side of the small sports car. Homicides are common in nearby D.C., but they are very infrequent in Loudoun County, and this one is definitely not routine, Holmes quickly decides.

"Are you going to call the medical examiner before we do anything?" Rogers asks Holmes.

"Yeah, right now, actually. But I want to explain the situation accurately so I'm thinking it through."

"We don't got all day. You've got the number, right?"

"Yeah, it's in my phone." Holmes and Rogers are not a homicide "team," because there aren't enough murders in Loudoun County to justify one. They are two detectives who work together on various cases when the police chief tells them to.

Holmes reaches into his pocket, scrolls through his numbers and finds the Manassas office of the Virginia medical examiner. Figuring that the office is not open yet he calls the emergency number. The operator patches it through to the assistant medical examiner working that office who is probably still at home.

"This is Dr. Greenman, can I help you?"

"Hey, Paul. This is Detective Holmes, we need some advice."

Greenman and Holmes have worked together before. There aren't too many suspicious deaths in Loudoun County, but when you work in homicide investigations for a decade you get to know most of the players.

"We're standing in a pasture at a horse farm outside Middleburg. We've got a dead victim inside an Alfa Romeo, early 20s. Could be an accidental OD, or maybe a homicide."

"What makes you think you've got a drug overdose Rob?"

"He's slumped over in the driver seat in the middle of a pasture. Rogers found a small baggie with several patches in his pocket. We think they're Fentanyl patches. We've had them turn up in several drug cases and there's been at least one other OD with Fentanyl fairly recently. It's one of the new drugs of the year."

Holmes moves his head left and then right, while peering into the driver's side area, still holding the phone to his ear. "I wanted to call you before we did anything else, like move the body, especially if you wanted to come to the scene."

"Just take as many pictures as possible before you move the body. And have forensics sweep the car for every type of fiber or anything else in case it isn't..."

Holmes interrupts. "But here's the thing. Why would he drive to the middle of the pasture? Why not just have your high with your buddies in the house?"

"Yeah, that's strange. What about the farmhouse? Did he live there?"

"Yep, but his father lives in town. When the 911 call came in, the father was notified, and now he's here looking for answers. We're gonna interview anyone that lives or works here." Holmes says.

"I'm not going to come out. I'll get everything during my autopsy. Sounds like an overdose. Get the background on the kid from his dad and any other witnesses, and I may make some calls to his doctors to see if he had any history of drug abuse."

"Gotcha Doc. We'll be in touch later."

"He's not coming," Holmes tells Rogers. "Just wants us to do our thing. Get forensics out here and I'll go interview the people at the farmhouse."

As Holmes starts to walk away to confirm the terrible news with the kid's father, he stops and turns back to Rogers. "Do you think it's a coincidence that it was raining really hard when this kid OD'd last night?"

"I dunno, why?" Rogers asks.

"Well, any experienced killer knows that a hard rain is perfect for washing away the evidence."

"What the hell're you saying Holmes? That somebody staged this?" Rogers asks sarcastically.

"Just sayin' that it was raining hard as hell last night. It's a little weird that he'd do Fentanyl in his car moments after leaving his house and end up in the middle of a horse pasture. We need to see who he was with last night. If he'd been going to see his honey, for example, then I might..." Holmes trails off.

Rogers looks up from his notebook. The car door is propped open and the kid's lifeless body is still slumped where it was found. "We've got no evidence of anything except Fentanyl patches. We've got no footprints, no evidence of another car in or out of here. Don't ya think we need a sliver of something to suggest foul play?"

"Just wanted to float it out there."

Holmes looks over toward the farmhouse. This is one of the worst things about this job, he decides. People die. Parents need to be told. Holmes begins his long slog over to the farmhouse and sees a couple of forensic technicians walking across the pasture toward the sports car. Recognizing both, he waves. He replays the short sequence of events in his mind.

A 911 call came into dispatch from the farm. The caller identified himself as "Zander, a good friend of Kent Perless." He said that when he went out to feed the horses at the crack of dawn like he always does he saw Kent's car in the middle of the pasture. He had no idea why it was there. After trudging through the field, he was shocked to see Kent slumped over in the driver's seat. He claims he reached over instinctively and touched his neck and felt nothing, so he ran back to find his cell phone and called 911. After that, he called his friend's dad, Kyle Perless, who is now sitting with a younger kid and another man on the set of five steps leading up to the porch.

A female deputy from the Loudoun County Sheriff's office walks toward him as he approaches the house.

"The guy over there with the short ponytail says he's the father. His name's Kyle Perless. The young man beside him called 911, Zander Hickson. Says he works here part-time, and the other man works here in the stable. Manuel something, can't recall his last name."

"Thanks, let's see what else I can find out." Holmes says in a whisper.

The older gentleman stands up and begins to take a few steps down off the porch. Holmes looks him in the eye and waits until they are a conversational distance from each other.

"Sir, my name is Detective Holmes. They tell me you may be the father of the young man in the Alfa Romeo?"

"Zander says it's Kent. Can I see him?" Kyle Perless asks.

"Mr. Perless, I'm not sure that's a good idea right now. Maybe you would like to sit down inside first because the news is not good."

The reality of the situation suddenly overwhelms Kyle Perless. He plops himself back down on the steps and places both hands over his eyes and forehead. The sound of a grown man sobbing is something Detective Holmes hates to hear. But his job has taught him to hide his own emotions and maintain a professional demeanor around grieving family members.

"Would you like to go sit down inside so I can ask you some questions?"

"I have questions for you. My only son is gone. Are you going to find out who did it?" Kyle's voice is quivering. He is valiantly trying to hang on, but big tears wet his cheeks.

"Let's go inside. I think it will be better."

Perless slowly stands up, turns around and leads the detective inside to the kitchen table.

"Mr. Perless, we always consider homicide in a suspicious death like this, and we're going to look at it from all angles. However, there's no obvious sign of foul play, and we found some evidence that suggests he may have taken some drugs. Did your son have a prescription for any pain medications?"

"That's insane! My son did not abuse prescription drugs. I worked with him regularly at the café, and there was no sign of a drug problem."

"Most parents don't think their son or daughter could possibly be abusing drugs. It's a very difficult thing to imagine..."

"My son may not have been an angel. He may have smoked pot. But that's it. No way was he doing harder stuff. What do you think he was taking?"

Holmes decides he's not going to disclose the specific type of drug found with the victim. That is a particular card that needs to be held back. There are many advantages to not immediately disclosing key details of an accidental death or homicide.

"The only thing I can tell you right now is that we found some signs of drug use."

"You're really not going to tell me what drug you're claiming he OD'd on? Don't I have the right to know? My kid's dead out there! Someone is responsible."

"We've talked to the medical examiner and he's going to do an autopsy. Then we'll transfer the body to the funeral home of your choice. We'll do everything with the utmost dignity and respect for your son. Now I'd like to ask you a few questions that might help us. Is that okay with you?"

"Yes, of course."

"Good. First of all, this fellow Zander. Is he a good friend of your son's?"

Holmes

"Did you know of any money issues between Zander and your son?"

"Huh-uh. We provided Zander a place to stay in exchange for helping out with the horses. They were best friends, surely he's not involved in this. I do have the farm up for sale but I don't think that means anything."

"Any other person been here in the last 24 hours, or anyone else that you think I need to know about?" Holmes asked.

"None that I can think of. My son worked regularly at the Café Loco that I own. You could talk to some of the people there. Oh, he did befriend Amanda Michaels, the Hemispheres survivor."

"How did he meet her?" Holmes asks, trying to process that strange fact.

"He started volunteering at the hospital before she was a patient. My wife used to be a doctor there, so we have deep ties there."

Holmes listens carefully to what people say because you never know what might roll your way. The thing about his wife captures his interest. He continues to jot a few notes down on the notepad.

"What happened to your wife?"

"She passed away from breast cancer a number of years ago."

"Terribly sorry about that. Just horrible in light of the situation."

After asking permission, Holmes examines all the entry doors to the house, finding no sign of forced entry. Then he circles the entire exterior perimeter of the house, and meets Kyle again on the front porch.

"Who'd know about your son's whereabouts for the last 24 hours?"

"He was with Amanda and her family at the Kennedy Center Saturday night, he worked at my café during the day yesterday, and as far as I know he was here at the farm last night. His friend Zander may know more."

"I'd like to take a look at your son's room, do you mind?"

"No problem." Kyle gets up from the kitchen table and starts leading Holmes toward Kent's room. The detective asks him to wait a moment as he walks back out on the porch and asks a forensic tech to join them.

The bedroom door is open and Kyle steps inside, followed by Holmes and the female forensic tech carrying a plastic box in her rubber gloved hands.

Holmes notices rock-and-roll posters on the wall, a bookcase with all kinds of books, more books scattered near the nightstand, a number of guitars and musical instruments on a rack, and an old-style turntable. The bed is partially made. He spies a laptop with its lid closed, still plugged in. The door leading to the adjacent bathroom is open a crack, so he lightly taps the door open and takes a look. Certainly not well-cleaned, but not unusual for a kid in his 20s without a maid or parental cleaning service. Holmes walks back out of the bathroom, carefully surveying everything.

"Your son was, uh, into music?"

"Oh yeah, he's quite the guitarist and songwriter."

Holmes notices the present tense of his language. That's something that a lot of family members do when absorbing a sudden and untimely death.

"Learned from you?" Holmes asks.

"I was a songwriter and I play a lot of instruments. I helped him learn guitar, although he really didn't want my input once he got to be a teenager. More recently we'd played together a little, mainly at my café. He had his own band, Paris VA, with Zander and another kid."

"Kathy and her team'll get formal pictures and search for fibers and fingerprints. I'd like your permission to retain his laptop so we can analyze the data on it. We'd also like to analyze the cell phone found on the front seat of his car. That okay with you?"

"Sure. Please let me know what you find, okay?"

"We will."

Holmes notices one of the two windows in the room is cracked open a couple inches. "Do you know if that window was open all night or if someone just opened it this morning?"

"No idea."

"Would it be unusual for your son to leave a window open?" While asking, Holmes carefully checks out the window sill, careful not to touch anything. He also looks at the floor for marks or scuffs, but doesn't see any. However, he notices that both of the floor vents to the HVAC system are closed.

"Probably not unusual, since we don't have any safety issues out here," Kyle responds.

"Do you have central air here?"

"Yeah."

Holmes entertains the thought that the victim's death may not have occurred inside the car, but his partner's skepticism of any foul play quickly leads him away from that notion. He looks at the wall and sees some handwritten index cards with pithy notes and quotations. He scans some of the books stacked on the bookcase. Freud, Shakespeare, *Fahrenheit 451*, *Fear and Loathing in Las Vegas*, *The Kool-Aid Acid Test*, *Life of Pi*, *The Catcher in the Rye*.

Holmes decides to have a look at *The Catcher in the Rye*, and flips through some of the pages randomly. He notices careful underlining in two different colors.

"Are these your son's books? Did he read all these?" he asks.

"Oh yeah, he's a very inquisitive kid."

The detective picks up *Fear and Loathing in Las Vegas* because he's familiar with Hunter S. Thompson and knows that he glorified drug use. Again, certain portions have yellow highlighting. Holmes randomly focuses in on one page. Thompson is talking about ether and various drugs as he and the attorney are speeding down the highway.

"How long did your son have the Alfa?"

"About three years. He loved that car."

"I'm sorry to have to ask this, but where were you last night and this morning before you got the call about your son?"

"At the café until closing time, then home. I watched some television, slept. I was getting ready for work when they called."

"Kathy, put some tape on this door and do your thing. Take some of the books with highlighting and any diaries or journals you find. We'll return them later, Mr. Perless, along with the laptop." Holmes heads out of the bedroom followed by Kyle.

"Here's my card. I'm sure I'll want to talk to you further, and if you think of anything, please give me a call. Do you have a ride, and can someone be with you today?"

"I'm okay, but thanks."

Holmes puts his card in Perless' hand, nods slightly and walks down the front porch stairs out toward the investigators still with the Spider in the pasture.

"Did you look at his phone yet?" Holmes asks Rogers when he gets back to the car.

"Yeah. There's nothing on it since a day ago, which is a little weird isn't it?"

"Is the rest of the data still on it?"

"I haven't had time to do a detailed analysis. I did look through his pictures, and there are some of Amanda Michaels and the Kennedy Center, probably at that Healing Heroes thing. What's he doing with her?"

"According to the dad, they were seeing each other. We've got company," Holmes says, spotting a news truck with its satellite high above it on the two-lane road.

"What's our story?" Rogers asks.

"Not a word about the Fentanyl patches. Just that it's a suspicious death and we're looking at all angles. Until we hear from the M.E. we can't mention overdose."

"Gotcha."

"His dad doesn't believe his kid abused drugs. But we've heard that one before, haven't we? I'm going to talk to the friend who called 911." Holmes then walks back toward the farmhouse and sits on the porch on a long outdoor sofa. He begins talking to Zander Hickson who has made no effort to leave the porch.

"I'm really sorry about your friend. I feel terrible for you and for his dad."

Hickson stares straight ahead.

"I know this is hard for you, but can you tell me how you realized something was wrong this morning?"

Zander proceeds to explain how he was heading to the stables and saw the Spider totally out of place in the middle of the pasture. He describes the horror of going over to the car and finding his friend with his head bent forward in the front seat of the car with no pulse.

"Any reason you can think of that Kent would get in his car in a driving rainstorm and drive it into the grass?"

"No idea," Zander says.

After thoroughly covering things, Holmes closes out the interview and hands Zander his card.

"Call me anytime with questions or information."

Holmes walks back toward his colleagues still working on the car. He stops 20 yards away and again thinks about the situation. Zander doesn't give off any vibes that make him suspect. Sure, it's totally conceivable the kid overdosed. But to think this kid could be wasted and drive across the pasture and moments later just collapse on his steering wheel? Strange, really strange.

Rogers stands beside the car observing one of the forensic techs methodically collecting various fiber samples in small bags, writing details with a permanent marker on the exteriors of the bags.

"Should we impound it?" Holmes asks.

"Why? Everything points to an overdose, so why bother?"

"I guess you're right."

HQ Summons

Franklin had worked closely with the CFO of Hemispheres defending the company during the 9/11 case. Nonetheless, he had only been to corporate headquarters for two meetings. This time he was personally summoned to discuss the numerous cases arising out of the Quarryville crash.

Franklin's legal team had worked up a long, detailed evaluation of the company's liability defenses based on the preliminary information relating to the cause. Part of the evaluation also included what the government was doing and what its preliminary findings were. Based on this data, Franklin contended that the cases were highly defensible, and he further outlined that the passengers' families would have great difficulty proving the precise mechanical cause of the crash. Finally, he noted the company could argue the possibility of sabotage.

Exiting the elevator on the 31st floor, Franklin introduces himself at the reception area. After flipping through some magazines and the *Wall Street Journal* for a couple of minutes, the receptionist tells him that his meeting will be convening in the main conference room one flight up. He takes a circular staircase up to a massive conference room. Upon entering the room, he exchanges pleasantries with CFO Andrews and is surprised to see the airline's CEO, David Merland, as well as a couple of executives that he is not familiar with. Darn, he should have studied the officers' pictures before he came. They all shake hands, and he sits at one side of the immense table and immediately removes several files from his briefcase.

"Mr. Franklin, thanks so much for coming today," CEO Merland says.

Sensing that he should immediately outline some points of the formal evaluation he already provided, Franklin jumps in as soon as the CEO stops speaking. "Great to see all of you. I think the headline of this meeting is that these cases are highly defensible and we look forward to..."

Franklin has not even finished the first sentence of his well-rehearsed presentation when CEO Merland cuts him off mid-sentence.

"Actually the main purpose of this meeting might surprise you. We've reviewed the data and decided we are setting up a fund to compensate all of the crash victims' families. We want you to settle every case as quickly as possible. Optimally within 30 days."

Franklin looks past Merland over to the CFO in shock. How could the company misinterpret his bullish evaluation given the huge stakes with all of the death cases?

"This is the road we want to pursue on this one," Andrews agrees.

"We haven't even gotten one discovery-related answer in any case yet. We have highly defensible cases..." Franklin starts again, and for the second time is cut off by the CEO.

"The decision's been made, Paul. We brought you here today just to go over how to best achieve the most reasonable and rapid settlements." For a split second Franklin imagines a dark open field, a huge bonfire using massive bales of $100 bills for kindling, representing his legal fees going up in smoke.

"Our insurer is paying a total contribution of $50 million. We are contributing another $110 million, gathered from some of the potentially responsible parties, creating a $160 million settlement fund. Your job is to settle every claim as far inside that as possible."

"But we've only just answered the first few suits. We don't even have any settlement demand packages, no information on the extent of each family's losses, nothing." Franklin almost whines. "And the insurer, why would they..."

"Yes, it's unusual, but we met with the vice president last week, and they simply decided that their coverage would be wiped out, given the number of claims and the early evidence pointing to an electrical cause. This way they'll save tremendous attorney fees. Paul, we read your reports, but what we want you to do is go to each claimant's attorney and tell them that we want to entertain an early possible settlement. Tell them to submit a comprehensive demand package within seven days. Then set up a settlement conference with an agreed-upon mediator and every lawyer representing the families of the passengers, pilots and crew," Merland says.

"But that's completely contradictory to the usual strategy. We wear each claimant down, create doubt and fear about their case and its value, and only then can we get the best deal. If we do it your way, we won't get anything close to the best numbers on these cases."

"There's no other way to do this, you'll just have to expedite everything the best way possible. You do have the know-how, don't you?" Merland pointedly asks.

"Yes. We're definitely capable of getting these cases resolved quickly," Franklin responds. He can't stop thinking about his fees going straight down the rat hole, because fast settlements simply mean less hours.

The CEO looks around the room and back at Franklin. "Here's the bottom line. We don't want to give any discovery information under oath about the cause of the crash. Just object and delay on all that material and pursue settlement as quickly as possible. No depositions either."

"Right. They've got nothing right now that hurts us. As a matter of fact, my sources report no evidence yet of any electrical or mechanical issue that would have caused the crash." Thinking as he talks, Franklin adds, "I will be asked which suppliers are contributing to the settlement funding, and whether their attorneys will attend any settlement or mediation conferences. What can you tell me about that?"

The CFO looks over at the CEO, who answers carefully.

"Look, I don't want to tell you anything that's going to require you to disclose something confidential. We're not at liberty to disclose that due to a confidentiality agreement. And no, there will be no other supplier or parts manufacturer party or their attorneys at any settlement conference. So, do your best to get every case settled within the next 30 days. End of story. If you run into problems, feel free to talk to Andrews here for authority, but I don't foresee you having any difficulty."

CEO Merland rises from his chair and shakes Franklin's hand. Franklin understands the meeting is over and he shakes hands all around, quickly slides his unused folders back into his briefcase, and heads for the spiral stairs completely baffled.

He is astounded that the insurance company is contributing only $50 million. In prior cases he's dealt with, the company always maximizes the insurance payment and minimizes any self-retained portion of settlement funding. It just makes the most sense. No company wants to pay money out of its own operating accounts that it is insured for - especially not Hemispheres based on the 9/11 cases he handled. Not only is Hemispheres paying $110 million of the $160 million fund out of its own operating accounts, he knows from his prior experience that Hemispheres is self-insured for the first $10 million of any air disaster, and then the insurance kicks in 100 percent over the first $10 million. The settlement pot is completely backwards.

As Franklin waves down a taxi, all of these equations flash through his head. The only way the scenario makes sense is if Hemispheres is, what? It dawns on him. Only if Hemispheres is paying no more than the self-insured $10 million. And if the insurance company is only paying $50 million, that means that another party, perhaps a major parts supplier or the aircraft manufacturer, is paying $100 million! Merland made it clear that Hemispheres already has the commitment to the $160 million fund, and that the company saves money if he brings in the total claims for less than that.

Franklin imagines contacting all of the victims' attorneys and feels nauseous. He hates feeling weak or powerless. Their jaws are going to hit the floor when they hear he wants a settlement demand before even receiving their initial information disclosures on the case. The red flags will be waving big time.

The Return

Ever-efficient Barbara calls Headmaster Johnson the Friday before Amanda's return, reviewing her medical restrictions and how she will make up the missed schoolwork. Johnson suggests tutoring to help her, and Barbara resolves to work on that also. Their home is further away from Middleburg Academy than the Michaels' home, but Amanda's friends have promised they will help with her transportation until she can drive.

For the big first day, Charlyne appears at the Simon home to give Amanda a ride. As they make their way toward school, Charlyne glances over at Amanda and says: "Aren't you excited about coming back? Everybody's excited about seeing you!"

"I'm actually pretty scared. I don't even know when to just smile or give a big hug to someone."

As the two of them walk across the road in front of the school Amanda can see the large "Welcome Back Amanda!" banner above the main entrance.

"I can't believe they did that," Amanda says meekly to Charlyne.

"We're so proud to have you back," Charlyne says, putting her arm around Amanda. Charlyne pulls one of the doors open and there is a huge roar from inside.

"Welcome back Amanda! Welcome back Amanda!"

"Amanda, I am Headmaster Johnson, in case you don't recall. We are so pleased to have you back at school."

"Thank you. I really didn't want this, but thanks."

At least 50 members of the senior class are organized on both sides of the hall, leaving a tiny walkway in the center. John, her former flame, stands next to David and both greet her loudly, and everyone claps her through the narrow walkway. Clapping an honoree on the way to, or from, a stage, is a time-honored M.A. tradition.

A number of the kids and teachers crowd around Amanda, wishing her well and telling her how glad they are to see her back. Charlyne and Iris escort Amanda to her chemistry class. Next, using a cheat sheet Charlyne made, Amanda finds her way to history, and then to study hall, where she rejoins Charlyne.

After the next bell rings, Charlyne guides Amanda left, then right, then left again to English Literature with Mr. Ricci. After the class ends, he calls Amanda to the front of the classroom as the other students file out.

"Here are a number of sheets that I'd like you to start looking through from the time you've missed."

"Okay," Amanda says despondently.

"How are you feeling?" Ricci asks.

"Okay I guess."

"I understand the doctor said that you can't drive for at least 30 days. What did they say about physical activities and playing sports again?"

"Well, I just got the halo off. I doubt I'll be able to play soccer again."

"How'd you feel about just coming to some of the practices or games? I could keep you on the roster. Might help to be around your teammates."

"I really don't know." Amanda says honestly.

"Well, it's something I think you should consider. I'd love to have you still be part of the team."

Once Amanda arrives in the hall, she has no idea where to go. As she unfolds the cheat sheet Iris see her and offers to help.

"C'mon, it's lunchtime."

Iris takes her over to Charlyne, Amber, and a couple other soccer players. They all stand in line, get their food, and head to a table.

As they all start eating, Amber starts laughing.

"What's so funny?" Amanda asks, not remembering Amber's name.

"What you're eating."

"Why's it funny?"

"You've got a cheeseburger and fries, which proves you don't remember anything from before."

Amanda takes a bite out of the cheeseburger, still not absorbing the comment, just realizing she is really hungry. She puts the burger down on her plate.

"I don't mean to be nasty, but what's your name again?"

"Mia," Amber says sarcastically, referring to the famous soccer player. All of the girls start laughing, but Iris stops herself.

"Girls, we need to be nice." Iris says.

“Do you know what it feels like?” Amanda bolts away from the table and rushes out of the cafeteria into the hall. Iris runs up behind her.

“Amanda! Wait! They’re just trying to come to grips with things. You don’t remember their names, and you were a hard-core vegan before. It’s nothing like you’re going through, but it’s different for us too.”

“They’re supposed to be my friends? They sure don’t act like it.”

"Come back and finish lunch with us. Please."

Amanda rummages through her small purse, locates the cheat sheet again, and studies the notes.

“No thanks. I’m going to read some, and I’ll find my next class myself.”

Broken

Amanda places her books from Algebra II into her locker and grabs the ones for her government class. A couple steps away, Charlyne also places and retrieves some books.

Amanda sneaks a peek at her cell phone. She was reminded of the no phone policy by Charlyne. She notices a text from her Uncle Andy.

Call me ASAP about the news.

What news? Amanda pulls up the local news and sees the headline:

"Middleburg Man Found Dead." She reads the first line, "Kent Perless, a Middleburg resident, was found dead..."

She stares at the screen in disbelief. The books drop from her hands, the cell phone clatters to the floor, and her body immediately follows.

"Somebody get help! Amanda fainted!" Charlyne screams at several of the students standing at their lockers nearby. She stoops and tries to talk to Amanda but she is unconscious.

"Call 9-1-1! Get a teacher over here!"

A teacher, Mrs. Robinette, rushes over and feels for her pulse, listens for respiration. "She's breathing."

Many of the seniors crowd around Amanda and the teacher. Within several minutes the rescue squad arrives with a gurney and the EMTs take over. They slide Amanda onto a flat brace board, lift it onto the gurney, and wheel her out. A bunch of the students as well as Headmaster Johnson have collected near the main doors where the ambulance is parked. Charlyne already has Amanda's Aunt Barbara on her phone.

Charlyne asks the headmaster if she can take a car to the hospital because she agreed earlier to be Amanda's ride. Minutes later, Headmaster Johnson makes an announcement over the loudspeaker explaining why the rescue squad came, and he promises to keep them posted on Amanda's condition.

Andy rushes to the hospital. After reading the news about Kent's death, he had managed to track down one of the detectives working the case. It was Detective Holmes. Holmes explained to Andy that he could only release limited information because the investigation was active. The detective revealed that there were no suspects yet, and that the evidence of foul play was thin. Holmes did inquire about the relationship between Amanda and Perless. Andy told him what he knew. Finally, Andy arrives and finds his way to where Barbara is, and the ER doctor finds them moments later.

"She's stable. We believe she simply fainted from shock, so we put her on appropriate medications. We didn't want to take any chances, so we have her restrained and a nurse is observing her. She won't answer me even though it looks like she can hear and understand everything."

"So, it's okay if we talk to her and make sure she's okay?" Barbara asks.

"Sure – that's fine. As a matter of fact, once I'm convinced that she's stable and the various testing comes back, we should be able to release her."

The doctor walks away and Charlyne hovers with David, who somehow got excused from class also.

Barbara and Andy talk with the teens, asking if they've heard anything about Kent's death or the circumstances surrounding it.

"I heard some people saying it was a drug overdose," David says, "but that's just some people talking and I don't really know what to make of it."

"I haven't heard that," Charlyne says. "And I'd have trouble believing it. Amanda and Kent were getting along great. There's just no reason he'd OD."

Andy soaks this in without voicing his opinion. Nor does he mention he spoke to Holmes since he really didn't divulge anything anyway. They all walk into Amanda's room.

Andy tries first, "Amanda, can you hear me?"

She is looking right at him, but says nothing.

"Is there anything we can do for you?"

Suddenly Amanda yells, "Why? Why would he ever do that? He wouldn't. Why...why? I don't understand. I can't understand!" Then she whispers, "Uncle Andy, get me out of here. Tell them to take the restraints off."

"I'll see what I can do." Andy walks toward the door. Barbara, Charlyne, and David follow him out into the hall.

An hour later the doctor releases her. He reviews basic instructions with Andy and Barbara, and a nurse goes over some drug interaction instructions with Amanda. Andy helps Amanda, who is somewhat wobbly on her feet from the meds, into the backseat of Barbara's car. Charlyne and David travel in Charlyne's car back to Barbara's house and Andy heads for his place in Georgetown.

Once they arrive back at Barbara's place, the three teens file into Amanda's room. Barbara asks Amanda if she can do anything for her. Amanda declines.

Once the door closes, Amanda walks right over to the closet where her clothes are, grabs an overnight bag and starts tossing clothing into it.

"Why are you packing?" Charlyne asks.

"Not staying here."

David gives a curious look over at Charlyne without saying anything.

"What's that supposed to mean?" David says.

"Just what I said. We're getting out of here. I'm not staying here anymore."

"What're you talking about?"

She finishes packing the bag, zips it up, and says, "Let's go."

"I'd like to know where you think you're going." Charlyne says. "You've just been released and you're on medication."

"I'll tell you when we're in the car," Amanda says and walks out the bedroom door and down the stairs. David and Charlyne shrug and start following her. Moments later Amanda has walked out of the house and down the driveway toward Charlyne's car. Barbara sees Amanda walk by and asks Charlyne and David, "What's going on? Where is she going?"

"She said she wants to leave. We're just following her," Charlyne says.

Barbara immediately trots out the front door and across the yard. When she gets near Amanda, she is still standing beside Charlyne's car.

"Amanda, what are you doing? We need to monitor you. You're still on medication and obviously have had a horrible, stressful day. We understand you're upset."

"I can't stay here. I'm ju-, I'm sorry, Aunt Barbara I can't do this anymore."

"Do what? Where are you going?"

"I'm going by the farm and I'm going to talk to Kent's dad. After that I don't know."

"Amanda, we're your family and we're here to take care of you. You can't just leave."

"Says who? I'm 18. I can make decisions like this myself. Charlyne, can we go?"

With keys in hand, Charlyne is standing by the hood of the car listening to the discussion; actually it's more of an argument. She stands motionless with a confused look on her face. Should she refuse to take Amanda?

"Charlyne, please get in the car!" Amanda shouts.

David hovers nearby because Charlyne has given him a ride. Charlyne finally starts moving toward the driver's side door and unlocks the car. Barbara says nothing, standing along the edge of driveway. She's fuming inside.

"I'm sorry, Mrs. Simon. We'll bring her back or let you know where we are."

The three of them get in the car. Barbara watches the car drive away and calls to report the events to Andy.

"Take me to Kent's farm."

From the backseat, David says, "What're you gonna do there?"

"I dunno," Amanda says, "But I'm not going back to my aunt's house."

After a ten-minute drive, mostly in silence, the three arrive at Crossroads Farm. As soon as the car stops, Amanda opens the door, grabs her bag and heads in the front door. There's no sign of anyone around. Charlyne and David follow Amanda, who is making a beeline for a bedroom. Yellow crime scene tape is stretched across the entry door. She pulls one side down, and once inside, she throws her bag down and sprawls on the bed. Some moments later, Charlyne and David enter the room.

"What now?" Charlyne asks.

Amanda never even looks up from her prone position on the bed.

"You leave, that's what,"

"Wait. Are you kidding?" David says.

"Dead serious. Leave. Goodbye."

David and Charlyne both look around the room and realize it's Kent's room. Neither has ever been there. They see the guitars, random books all over the bookcase, recording equipment. They both look at each other, not knowing what to do. David motions toward the door and they head out to the great room.

"What're we gonna do? We need to tell somebody," Charlyne says.

"Yeah, call her aunt."

Charlyne calls Barbara as they walk out on the front porch. "We don't really want to leave her alone, but she wants us gone, so we don't know what to do." Charlyne explains.

It's agreed that Barbara will drive over to the farm and talk to Andy. Charlyne and David sit on the front porch biding their time.

"I do have trouble believing he'd commit suicide," David says. "He was a little out there, yeah, but not like that."

"Me either. I mean, I can't believe what Amanda's already gone through, and now this."

Barbara pulls into the gravel driveway, and just a couple minutes later Andy pulls in also. They gather on the porch and exchange information with Charlyne and David. Andy explains that he tried to reach Kent's father, but was unsuccessful. While they're standing there, a man walks over toward the porch. It's Manuel.

"Hi, I'm Andy Michaels. My niece Amanda was friends with Kent."

"Oh, uh...I suppose you've heard the terrible news?" Manuel asks.

"Yeah, and now my niece is in Kent's room and refuses to leave."

"Why is she in there?"

"We're not exactly sure, she just demanded to come here. We're going to talk to her. She's depressed and not being very rational."

Everyone walks inside, and Charlyne points out the room. They see Amanda still lying on the bed.

"Amanda, we're trying to understand why you're here," Andy starts.

"Get out! I don't want you here. I don't want you asking questions. I'm okay, but I'll be better if you all get out...now!"

Andy and the rest of them retreat to the front porch.

"We can't leave her here. She could be suicidal." Barbara says.

"I agree; we can't leave her. One of us has to stay."

They walk over toward Manuel.

"She's insisting on staying in Kent's room. Can you call Mr. Perless and see if it's okay for her to stay here 'til tomorrow?"

Manuel nods. "I think it'll be fine."

A plan is cobbled together in which Andy is going to stay the night. Barbara will return later with some of his clothes, and come back in the morning to relieve him. Barbara resolves to take a few days leave from work to sort out Amanda's situation.

Why & How?

"Two questions. Why'd they kill him, and how? The director is going to be all over my butt!" Solarez says to his trusted field agent.

"We had ears on him, but not eyes," the agent responds, referring to listening devices versus visual surveillance.

"Where were our people?"

"Two agents were posted there. We're still not sure how their agent got inside, but they used gas. As soon as our guys figured out what was going on, they called in and followed instructions."

"And that's when they neutralized their own agent?" Solarez asks.

"Correct. They took the kid much more seriously than we thought, serious enough to kill him. We've listened to all of the kid's audio, checked his cell phone records and internet activity."

"No one was reviewing what the kid was doing in real-time?" Solarez asks.

"No, we didn't think he was a significant target. We assumed he simply stumbled into his friendship with Amanda Michaels."

"Who says he wasn't their asset?" Solarez demands.

"It's unlikely, but not impossible. His online searches show he'd bungled his way on to BBS and the fact that Ron Michaels worked there. Whether he really had connected the dots I can't say, but they decided he was too close when he set up a meeting with a reporter."

"Who?"

"Perry Carson, with *Capitol Law* magazine. Perless was to meet with him the next day. The local detectives know that, but they're convinced it was a suicide or accidental overdose. We had an agent copy the entire laptop and phone before the local cops got there."

"Did they wipe the laptop and phone clean?"

"No, they must've figured it would look too suspicious, so they hid the search history but left the hard drive."

Solarez gets up from his desk and paces a few steps, pondering. "Unfortunately, we're no closer to figuring out who their mole is."

"Nope. But, if we tighten the noose, something's bound to give."

"When and how we do that is the trick," Solarez says.

Winds Change

Andy checks his voicemail. The fourth message is from Paul Franklin.

"Andy, it's Paul Franklin. Please give me a call as soon as possible about the Hemispheres crash cases."

Andy calls Franklin back and is put on hold by his receptionist. A few seconds later he hears Franklin's voice.

"Andy, I'd like you to send me a settlement demand on all of your cases by the end of the week."

"Franklin, don't mess with me. I don't have any tolerance for this right now."

"Michaels, I'm not kidding. I seriously want a settlement demand for each of your clients."

"We haven't even finished discovery yet. This is completely...well, just not normal," Andy says, trying to pry something out of Franklin.

"Listen, I had a long talk with the airline. They want me to work toward settling all the cases. This isn't an indication of any problem with our defense. We're just going to give settling a try. These are my marching orders from Hemispheres. Hopefully we'll settle some of them and mediate the rest. I want as much information on each decedent as possible, their ages, earnings, families, everything you've got."

"Don't know if we can get them all done within four days, but we'll get started," Andy says, ending the call in disbelief. He buzzes Angie.

"Hey, that was Franklin. Would you believe that he wants a settlement demand on every one of our cases? Mix that in your drink."

"Holy crap! You know what that means, don't you?"

"Yep, they know something we don't."

Rock Creek

"Perry Carson on line two," Myra says.

"Okay, I'll take it." Andy answers.

"Hello, Michaels here."

"Andy, it's Perry Carson. I'm wondering if now's a good time to finally talk. A lot's gone down."

Andy ponders a moment. "I run most mornings in Rock Creek Park. You still run, don't you?"

"Yeah, couple times a week on Rock Creek Trail."

"How about tomorrow morning at seven? I usually drop in at Dumbarton near 27th. You know, where Dumbarton ends right there at Rock Creek Trail?"

"Yeah, I know that spot. 7:00 a.m., I'll be there."

The sun's barely up. Andy waits at the end of Dumbarton where the tree line starts to drop into Rock Creek Trail. He sees Perry running down the trail, and they join up and jog south. Neither says much at first, as joggers run past. After they run under the Georgetown overpasses and approach the Potomac, Perry finally breaks the silence.

"I heard Hemispheres wants settlement demands from everybody," Carson says.

"That's a fact. What about it?"

"Look, I've covered the legal scene long enough to know that's highly unusual. None of the lawyers have even answered the written discovery in the case. Obviously they know something bad or they would never do this. Do you know what it is?"

"Not yet, but I'm not standing still on it. My expert thinks it was electrical," Andy says, as men crew long narrow boats along the Potomac.

"Hey, you know that kid who was friends with your niece? The detectives officially said it was an accidental overdose. Did you hear that?"

Andy takes a quick look over at Perry.

"I'd heard that it was likely an overdose. Any details?"

"Fentanyl toxicity overdose."

"Bizarre. My niece is having a tough time with it. She had developed a relationship with him."

Through a pant, Carson says, "I don't think you knew this, but when I saw him at that party he said he wanted to talk to me about the crash. I never heard from him again. Now he's dead. I called the detective in Loudoun County and told him. But once they got the tox report, I guess it didn't matter."

They're looping around the Lincoln Memorial halfway through their run, and many runners are out. Andy stops when they near the lower end of Georgetown at the Potomac.

Still huffing, Andy says, "So that detective didn't think Kent's wanting to talk to you was connected?"

"Said it was interesting but that all he had to go on was a fentanyl patch he found on the body. He asked me if I knew what Kent wanted to tell me. Maybe he was just a publicity hound."

"Do you have any leads connecting him to the crash?"

"Nope. But, after Kent approached me I pitched a story to my editor about Kent, Amanda, and the crash, and he gave me the green light. I thought the story was even more justified after he died, but my editor killed the story entirely."

"Does that happen a lot?"

"Next to never."

"Did you ask him why?"

"Said it was too speculative since no one knows why the plane crashed."

"Let's keep digging, and sharing info."

Andy gets up from the bench and takes off. When they reach Dumbarton Oaks, Andy breaks off at 27th Street, and Perry waves and keeps running north up the trail.

Bumblebee

"We've got a big problem," the field agent tells Solarez, plopping down in a chair in his office.

"Great. What do you mean 'a big problem'?" Solarez says with a grimace.

"Our mole attended a meeting and someone referenced the wiretaps approved by Bondakopf. We've got a security breach. Could be an informant or a bug."

"You're kidding. We sweep the courtrooms every morning and again before each hearing. How could they be compromised? It's gotta be a leak."

The agent disagrees. "Actually, we're pretty sure it's a bug stuck outside the courtroom somewhere. It's possible it's inside, but we have no idea how or where it would be."

"If this is true, our asses are grass." Solarez says, thinking about his offered resignation that the director still holds. "Actually, we won't say anything 'til we know for sure. Do a sweep right away, inside and out. Use anyone you need to draw up a plan for a complete sweep, inside and out. This goes well beyond the Phoenix operation. Hell, this affects every hearing, every national security operation in the FISA courts."

"It's gotta be discreet so they don't know we're onto them," the field agent says.

"Right. Wait, I wonder if the bumblebee is online yet. See if it is and if we can use it."

Manned by experienced pilots working for the CIA, the borrowed news chopper hovers unobtrusively just above the federal courthouse near dusk. Several covert agents walk down the sidewalk near the courthouse. The small side door of the chopper opens, and the man in the front seat next to the pilot opens a small box. Operating a large laptop, another "pilot" in the backseat prepares for takeoff.

The drone, barely larger than an actual bumblebee, slowly but steadily rises out of the box and begins flying downward under the command of its pilot. The bumblebee's high resolution video camera hones in on the various cracks and crevices near the windows of the building, sending video back over a secure wireless frequency to the chopper laptop. Near one window of the main FISA courtroom, the drone pilot moves the bumblebee in closer with his joystick. He sees a tiny protrusion in a crevice next to the window. He zooms in for a better view. After no more than 180 seconds, the tiny device is directed downwards where it softly hovers at shoulder level near one of the agents walking on the sidewalk. He quickly reaches up and grasps it with a special webbed glove and places it into his jacket pocket, all without missing a step.

"I have the insect," he advises the team.

Within hours, all of the footage has been pored over by the field agent and his team. He places the key results on Solarez' desk.

"Got it," the field agent says. "Look in this picture. See that little wire in the mortar crack? That's a bug, just millimeters away from the window. They're probably camped out in the building here." He points to pictures of the building across the street. "We're going to check all the rentals from the third floor to the top."

"Not yet. We have some interesting options. I'll put together some suggestions for the director." Solarez studies a few of the pictures on his desk and formulates his next move.

Despondency

Andy ends the cell phone call with one of the Hemispheres crash widows about settling and his mind turns to Crossroads Farm. It's day three of Amanda's occupation of Kent's bedroom. She's been totally despondent and inconsolable, refusing to eat anything except the tiniest scraps of food and occasionally drinking a bit of bottled water. She stays inside the bedroom, and only grudgingly talks to anyone.

According to Barb, Amanda plays nonstop music and hasn't changed clothes since arriving. She's wearing one of Kent's T-shirts and a pair of his pajama pants.

In the midst of this personal crisis, Andy and his staff have been working 12-hour days to put together demand packages for all of the Hemispheres cases.

Andy parks his Mini Cooper along the drive in front of the farmhouse. Barbara's already on the porch. She starts talking before he reaches her.

"Andy, we don't have any choice. You have to sign the papers."

"This is a serious step. Committing her involuntarily, even for a few days, is going to be bad, bad, bad."

"She's not eating, she won't communicate. She needs counseling. We're the only family she's got left and we need to help her."

"Let me go talk to her."

As they near the bedroom, Andy hears loud music. He turns to look at Barbara before he opens the door.

"Alright, I'll be out in the great room."

Andy knocks but there's no response. He cracks the door open. Amanda is lying in bed, her head on the pillow, staring up at the ceiling.

"Amanda, we need to talk!" Andy says loudly above the music.

Amanda says nothing, so Andy walks to the side of the bed. Her pajama bottoms look wrinkled and he recognizes the Beatles' Abbey Road shirt she's wearing.

"We're really worried about you. You're not eating, not talking, not going to school. Something's got to give."

Amanda still stares at the ceiling.

"Have you ever listened to this song? Really listened?"

Andy recognizes "She Said, She Said" by the Beatles.

"She says 'I know what it's like to be dead.' Then he says she's wrong. When he was a boy everything was right. That's what I feel like. Everything was right before the plane crashed. Now everything is wrong and I know what it's like to be dead. I died. And I still remember some of the things I saw when I was dead. I'm not scared of it, it was really peaceful. Peter Fonda was tripping on LSD and he told Lennon he knew what it was like to die because he accidentally shot himself in the chest when he was young and nearly died. He freaked Lennon out. Fonda knew what I'm talking about..."

Andy has never heard this kind of crazy talk from Amanda before. He's no shrink, but maybe Barb is right.

"I know that you weren't breathing and all that, but I don't think you were dead."

"I was as dead as dead gets. You don't know, you have no freaking idea. I know. I'll never, ever forget what it was like, I remember everything. Justin, the four Dorothys, and my dad working in his office lab."

"Four Dorothys?"

"Yeah, I was one of them. We were floating up and up. I am still trying to figure that out. Hey, did my dad have a home office with a lab in it?"

"Uhh, he had a small office he used for doing biological stuff. Look, I understand you're devastated about Kent, but we're worried. If you won't go back to school and insist on staying in this room day in and day out, we'll have to get you some help."

"I don't need help. Haven't you ever wished you could get back to some time, some place, where everything was alright? That's what I'm telling you. Can you understand that?"

Andy shakes his head. He's got to break the news to her about the settlement discussions.

"Amanda, I know it's the furthest thing from your mind, but I need to talk to you about your case." No reply. "The Hemispheres lawyer called me and he wants a settlement demand number on your case and lots of information. Angie and Aunt Barbara have collected family pictures, information about you playing soccer, your school grades, medical records, everything we need for your case. Do you want to help put it together?"

Amanda sings along with the closing chorus to the song. "And you're making me feel like I've never been born..." She has the vinyl album cover in her hand and is studying the reverse side, ignoring him.

"I'm going to demand more on your case than any of the others. I know that sounds weird since you're still alive, but you may have permanent issues and a lifetime of medical expenses. What do you think?"

Still no answer.

Andy plows on, thinking he at least has to run the options by her. "It's a little early, but we need to think about how we'll safeguard any money you receive. I really want to put most of it into a structured settlement annuity because then the money grows tax-free. We'd keep enough in a bank account for college expenses too. We're assuming you'll eventually want to go..."

"Blah blah blah. I don't understand any of that. I trust you, just please stop." Then, she asks, "Are you going to the funeral?"

"I hadn't made up my mind. Why?"

"There's no way I can do it. I was hoping you'd go and tell me about it."

"We went through some mail from your parent's house," Andy says, changing the subject. "You did really well on your SATs. You've got a lot of options, maybe UVA?"

"Wow, I took the SAT? Nice..."

This is not the comment of someone who's mentally deranged, Andy decides. More like someone with amnesia who isn't listening. She's just focused on things that are important in her world.

"I'm gonna ask for $12 million in your case, but I can settle your case, or your parents' cases, without your approval."

Amanda has another old record cover in her hand and she's reading parts of the back.

"I don't know what we're going to do..." Andy says, starting to walk away from the bed. Then, he turns back around.

"Are you going to go to school tomorrow?"

"No."

Andy says goodbye and softly closes the bedroom door, then walks down the hall and motions to Barbara to head out to the porch.

"She's completely delusional. I mean, she hears me, she's listening. But she's acting bizarre." Andy says.

"You've got to sign the papers. She'll only be there for a few days, until she stabilizes."

"Barb, it's a lot more complicated than that. Stuff like this can really create long-term bitterness. Imagine being committed and having to be in a mental ward for even a few days. And it's complicated with what's going on in court. If she gets committed, that means she's incompetent, and I can't even settle her personal injury case without having a legal guardian appointed and possibly outside psychiatric evaluations."

"We have to be concerned about her health, not just about the settlements. How do you know she's not suicidal?"

Andy thinks for moment. "Okay, as long as she gets out within a few days...I guess she'd still be considered competent. Then she can approve whatever she wants."

"Then sign the papers," Barbara says. She opens the folder as they sit side by side on the porch swing.

Andy reads through the papers from the Loudoun County Courthouse.

"I can't do it." He lays the pen down on top of the folder in his lap.

"Well if you won't, I will. Because I know it's best for her." Barbara retrieves the pen and folder back from him with a cross look and signs the page requesting the involuntary commitment.

"You know this requires you to go down to the courthouse and actually appear before a magistrate," Andy mentions.

"Yeah, and I want you to come with me."

"It's not an adversarial deal. Just take the papers to the clerk. They'll get a magistrate to hear you and it's virtually done. I'm involved in too many legal battles and I'm not going be the one to commit her."

"You want me to be the bad guy. I can't believe you," Barbara says, standing up and walking a few steps from the porch swing.

"I'm not making you the bad cop. I've just been through too many wars. And this is a war I'm not sure we want to start. After all, you want her to come back and live in your house. What if she takes it out on you? I don't want her taking it out on me." Andy says. He gets up off the swing and walks a few steps down the porch.

"I'm not saying you're wrong."

Barbara leans forward on the wooden railing facing Andy. "What happened to the fierce litigator? You're making me do this alone? Thanks a lot."

"I've said my piece. Just do whatever you think is best for her."

Psych Ward

The anti-anxiety meds have Amanda's brain all fuzzy. Her eyes won't focus on the pages of intake questions the nurse patiently waits for her to complete. *Do you know why you're here? Do you have any thoughts of suicide? What are the most optimistic things on your mind?* What a bunch of rubbish, she thinks to herself. Do they really think they get honest answers?

"Ms. Michaels, you've got to fill out this questionnaire so the doctor can evaluate you."

"I just want to get out of here," Amanda says dropping the clipboard holding the questionnaire with a loud clatter on the side table.

"If that's true, you'll fill it out," the nurse says with a less than happy look. Amanda grudgingly picks up the clipboard and starts writing. When she finishes, the nurse looks through the answers. Although some are missing, she realizes it's probably acceptable for the psychiatrist.

"Look, I want to talk to my aunt or uncle. Are either of them here?"

"I'm not sure if any of them are here right now."

"How do I find out who put me in here?" Amanda asks.

"You can talk to one of the doctors about that. Do you want me to contact Ms. Simon?"

"I just want you to tell her that I want to see Dr. Lucent. He's the doctor who treated me after the plane crash."

"I'll try to get the message to her."

Amanda assumes that the nurse thinks she's crazy like the rest of them.

"I'm going to take you back to your room."

The nurse escorts her down a hallway. Amanda looks around, doesn't see any bars on the doors or anything, and half considers making a run for it. But she figures there must be outer doors that are locked, and if she does try it, they might make her stay even longer.

Amanda notices the room has another bed and a drape that can be pulled between the two beds like a partition. It's not even a private room, she thinks to herself. Great.

The nurse checks her area and says, "The doctor'll be in to see you during morning rounds. You must stay in your room until he does his initial evaluation. Here are the policies to follow while you're here." She lays a paper down on the bedside table.

"Well, I guess I have lots to look forward to," Amanda says sarcastically as she sits on a chair beside the bed.

She notices her overnight bag that she had brought to Kent's bedroom. As the nurse walks out Amanda unzips the bag and surveys the contents. Then she hears something from the other side of the room.

"Are you over there? I said, are you over there?"

Amanda has no intention of answering. A frail, ashen-looking woman with brown, shoulder-length hair pulls back the curtain between the two beds and scowls at Amanda.

"When I was 12 my mom told me I was smarter than Einstein," she says.

Amanda looks up. She has no idea how to respond.

"She took me to a place and they did an IQ test and she told me afterward that they said my score was higher than Einstein's. Like, I didn't know who he even was, but I found out he was a genius."

Who is this bottom dweller? Why is she babbling? She's probably on Paxil, Valium and who knows what else, Amanda thinks to herself. Just leave me alone...

"But I get him now. When Einstein said, 'how can you stretch time?' I know how. It's gravity and speed, like with trains and stars. It's relativity, and...it's physics. I get it. It's really simple actually. If you're traveling through space and you don't have a reference point, how do you know if something is moving toward you or you are moving toward it? Can you answer that?"

A few seconds of silence pass.

Finally, this freakazoid has stopped, Amanda thinks hopefully. Please go back to your space. She considers reporting to the nurse that her roommate is making her even crazier.

"Can you answer it or not?"

"Uh, answer what?" Amanda finally answers.

"How do you know if something is moving toward you or you're moving toward it? You know, relativity," she repeats.

"I'm not really following what you're saying."

"Cause you can't is the simple answer, but if I take a couple steps in your direction you can tell, you know why?"

"Are you, like, teaching me?" Amanda asks. "I'm not your student."

"I'm a tutor. But...whatever."

Oh no, she is shuffling further into my space, Amanda thinks anxiously.

Walking toward Amanda's bed, the woman plunks down papers full of numbers, equations and arrows.

"I just need some quiet time so I can work out all the details and then I can tell the world some of my theories."

"How long have you been here?" Amanda asks.

"About a week. It's my addiction. I stayed up for five straight days without sleeping. Have you ever stayed up five days with no sleep? Well, okay, I think I got 15 minutes here and there, but never slept at night."

"Can't say that I have ever, uh, been that deprived. What would make you stay up that long?"

"I cooked meth, well, my boyfriend did really. Once you start, it takes over your brain. You don't need sleep or food, just more meth. You're wired 24/7, like you're driving down a road and the trees are whizzing by you. Wait... are you whizzing by the trees, or are the trees whizzing by you? That's what the theory of relativity is about and really the trees could be whizzing by you, do you get that? It's really like, wham, when you do get that, it just hits you in the head like you ran into a pole or something." She smacks her right hand against her head for greater effect.

Amanda looks away from all the scribbled numbers on the papers. She wonders how this girl spiraled so far down. How old is she? She looks terrible, but not beyond repair. No makeup, her teeth have a gray tint. But Amanda can tell that she was pretty once, when she took care of herself. She looks a tad over 100 pounds, maybe 110 though she must be 5'6" or 5'8" tall.

"How old are you?"

"32, but meth makes you look older. It wrecked my marriage, and my ex has my 7-year-old."

"How'd you ever start doing meth?" Amanda asks.

"When I was going through my divorce, I met this guy at a bar in D.C. He was a musician, but he lost his gig from being a meth head. I didn't know he was an addict when I met him, and I made the mistake of trying it. I never finished my Ph.D. at George Washington, stopped showing up for my tutoring gigs. Once meth gets in your brain, it just needs more. I'm kinda glad they forced me in here cuz they know what drugs to give me."

"What's your name?"

"Brittney, Brittney Hayes. From Foggy Bottom, you know where that is right? It's not really foggy, not any more than anywhere else in D.C."

"Yeah. I'm Amanda."

"Why are you here?"

"I think my family got me committed. My boyfriend died a couple days ago. I stopped eating, stopped going to school, and I was crashing at his farmhouse in Middleburg. I was fantasizing about being with him, wasn't sure I wanted to live anymore."

"Sorry to hear that. What'd he die from?"

"The cops say he OD'd on Fentanyl, either by accident or he was trying to kill himself. I know that's a lie."

"Wow. I'm so sorry. Suicide stuff will get you put in here really quick too." Brittney says, sounding as if she's experienced on these issues. "I'm getting outta here any day. I know I can stay clean."

A noise, and the door opens. The nurse from before motions to Amanda.

"I need to take you for your evaluation." Amanda gets up to follow her.

"I'll teach you some more about Einstein when you get back," Brittney says.

The nurse leads Amanda to a small conference room and she bumbles her way through the evaluation with the doctor. She starts thinking about Andy's visit to the farm and the millions of dollars he's trying to recover in her case. A plan begins to formulate in her head and it starts to motivate her. A few minutes later the doctor finishes the evaluation and thanks her. She tells him she wants to see Dr. Lucent. He promises to notify the doctor, and also tells her he knows who she is, he watched the "Healing Heroes" special. His platitudes don't phase her. Only one thing is on her mind: get the hell out.

Amanda asks if she can make a phone call to Aunt Barbara. The doctor says that will be fine. Moments later she has her Aunt Barbara on the line. Amanda thinks about saying something about her aunt forcing her into this hospital, but she purposely decides not to bring it up knowing that it could blow the whole deal. Hey, rational choices, she just made one. That means she should get out, right?

Barbara assures her that Dr. Lucent is going to try to stop by before the end of the day.

"Aunt Barb, if he thinks I'm okay, will I get out of here?"

"That's a question I can't answer. The professionals will decide. We'd like to get you back home as soon as we can and get you back in school."

Amanda thinks to herself, over my dead body. "Can I ask you a question? Are you the one that got me put in here?"

"Amanda, you needed help and I had to do what is best for you. I hope you can forgive me for that."

Hell no, Amanda thinks to herself. Oh yeah, keep it inside. Right now she just wants to get out of this hellhole.

"Yeah, I guess I understand," she lies.

There's no escaping the incessant chatter from Brittney. Maybe she is smart, Amanda concludes, but jeez, she never shuts up. Wait, music. Amanda digs in the bag and finds her phone and ear buds and starts to put them in.

Brittney whispers from the divider curtain. "You've got to be careful what you say because they listen to everything."

Amanda is sure that Brittney has no idea she is the plane crash survivor, and has no intention of telling her that. Talking begets more talking. Brittney sees her fiddling with the ear buds.

"I know I talk too much. It's the drugs. They make you just want to pour everything out. Hey, have you ever read Nietzsche, and his Übermensch concepts?"

The door opens and the same nurse is there again.

"Ms. Michaels, there's a doctor here to see you in the conference room. Follow me." Amanda is sure it's Dr. Lucent, and feels rescued.

"Here's my address and number so we can stay in touch," Brittney says as Amanda leaves the room. "Remember, I can tutor."

Amanda virtually runs the last few steps to Dr. Lucent and gives him a big hug.

"God, I'm so happy to see you. I've been through hell. Can you puh-leeze get me out of here?"

"Whoa ... slow down. Let's go over some things."

Lucent has been fully briefed by Barbara and Andy on Amanda's depression. He knows about her inability to eat, her despondency, and her obsession with everything relating to Kent, including her ritual of sitting in the passenger seat of his car. Lucent follows the normal psychiatric evaluation protocol, covering suicidal idealities and every other facet of psychiatric disorder indicators that Amanda manifested over the prior week.

"What motivates me now is how I can make a difference someday," Amanda says.

"What do you mean by that?" Lucent asks, recognizing that this is not a suicidal person's psyche.

"My uncle told me the airline wants to settle and I started thinking about what I could do with the money."

Amanda is sketchy on the details of her future goodwill work. And that's okay with Lucent because his main goal is to assure himself that the patient is on the mend and that there is no suicidal tendency.

"Are you eating?" Lucent asks.

"Yep. I'm better...really better. That doesn't mean I don't want to stay at the farm for a few more days though."

"Have you had any more memories, dreams, or flashbacks?"

"Definitely not any memory recall. I've had some dreams with little snippets of things that might have been real but nothing I can really put my finger on."

“What about getting in Kent’s car and sitting in the front passenger seat?”

“What about it? I can’t drive a stick, or any car at all yet.”

“It’s not normal, you sitting in Kent’s car. Do you understand that?”

“I like sitting there. So what?”

"Okay, different subject. Your aunt and uncle want you to move back to your aunt’s house. To me, that seems to be the logical choice for the rest of your senior year at Middleburg Academy. Are you going to do that?"

"I don't want to commit to that, Dr. Lucent. I don't see how that has anything to do with whether I'm doing better or not. If I can get a ride to school from the farm, and if Kent's dad will let me stay there, why can't I? I'm 18, so legally I'm an adult now. Don't I have the right to live at the farm if I want to and Kent’s dad says it’s okay?"

"Well, it's complicated. I really don't want that to get in the way of you being declared competent and released from here. It's more of a family issue."

"Dr. Lucent, if you sign the papers to get me outta here, the first thing I'll do is talk to my uncle."

Lucent looks down at his paperwork and writes a few notes. He calls for the nurse to send Amanda back to her room.

"You are going to help me, aren't you?"

"Everything will be fine Amanda."

After she leaves he pulls out his cell phone and calls Andy.

"Andy, it's Dr. Lucent. Just finished my evaluation of Amanda. She's doing much better. I really don't think she's a suicide risk. I wasn't around to see how bad she was at the farm, but she seems competent now. She exhibited every indicator that she understands why she was involuntarily committed. She even admitted to me that she was deeply depressed. And one of the things motivating her is the possibility of you settling the lawsuits. She said she wants to talk to you about that. I'm ready to sign the release papers if you're in agreement."

"I don't want her in there any longer than necessary. Did you two discuss her moving back in with Barbara?"

"Yeah, you might have a problem there. She wants to go back to the farm, but I don't think that's reason enough to keep her here. I'm going to sign the release papers. Who'll be coming to pick her up?"

Andy looks at his watch – 3:30 p.m. He figures it'll take him an hour to get there with traffic.

"I will. How long until she is released?"

"I'll tell the staff you'll be here at 4:30."

"Okay, great. Thanks for getting there on such short notice. I'll relay the message to Barbara."

Drop for Drop

Detective Holmes reads over the autopsy and toxicology reports. No suspicious marks on the body like bruising, cuts, or abrasions. The medical examiner concluded that the cause of death was "Fentanyl toxicity." Holmes flips to the tox report. He scans over the various drugs and chemicals and blood levels. Positive THC, meaning some marijuana use. No surprise there. Nothing of note except 30 mcg of Fentanyl – over three times the potentially fatal dose. Holmes shakes his head. Another Fentanyl overdose death.

Holmes buzzes Rogers on his phone. "Have you read the Perless autopsy report?"

"No, what's it say?"

"You were right, it's Fentanyl toxicity death. Three times the fatal dose actually. I was still thinking there might've been some other angle here but I don't see it now. No bruising or exterior marking on the body to indicate any other type of injury. Nothing at all from the fiber analysis, and no fingerprints besides his own. I haven't heard anything about the laptop analysis, but we turned up nothing on his cell phone."

"I told you it's an overdose. No mysteries here. Users have no idea Fentanyl can kill them just as quickly as it gets them high."

Holmes thinks a moment and then says "I'm going to call Mr. Perless and set a time to give him the bad news in person."

Holmes reaches Kyle Perless at Café Loco and arranges to meet him there at 3:30 p.m., a slow time at the café so they can talk. It's a few blocks from the police station and Holmes wants the exercise, so he walks over. They sit at a small round table near the window.

"Can I get you some coffee or anything?" Kyle asks, trying to be a good host while inwardly hoping for news that will put the speculation about Kent overdosing to rest.

"No thanks, I'm good. Mr. Perless, the reason I've come is that we just got the autopsy and toxicology report. The medical examiner studied your son's body and found no bruising or signs of a struggle or anything consistent with foul play. Also, you may recall that we did find a small baggie with patches in his pocket that have since been tested and confirmed as Fentanyl pain patches. The toxicology screening showed that there was 30 mcg of Fentanyl in the blood drawn from your son. That's over three times what's considered a fatal dosage. The medical examiner concluded the cause of death was Fentanyl toxicity. Your son's death will be listed as an accidental overdose, and we're going to close the case. "

"I'll never believe that bull, Detective. What else have you done besides decide this was an accidental overdose? Did you look for suspects, someone who might want to kill my son? What if someone killed him?"

"What do you mean 'killed him'?"

"Like, gave him a toxic dose or forced it on him?"

"There isn't any evidence of that. There are no motives, no enemies...I'm very sorry..."

"What did you do to look for someone who could have..." Holmes cuts Kyle off mid-sentence.

"Well, we've done a lot besides get these reports. We interviewed the entire staff at your café."

"Yeah, but you never told me what you found."

"Well we found that there was nobody that knew anything. We found no motive for any of your staff to want him dead. Even so, we still checked alibis on everyone. We even tracked a few of the staff on surveillance cams. We found nothing."

"Well, Sienna quit a couple days after he died with no notice. What about her?"

"I'm glad you asked. We checked surveillance cams at her apartment and found nothing. She was home that night and came straight here the next day. Everything checked out."

"Well if someone was selling him illegal Fentanyl patches, did you try to find who sold him the stuff?"

"Drug dealers don't generally come out of the woodwork when something like this happens. Everybody clams up. Because the patches are legally prescribed it's difficult to trace them. We know what brand they are, but every pharmacy in this area can fill that type of script, and none of them had any thefts either."

Kyle looks down at the copy of the autopsy and tox report and flips through it without really reading it since it would be meaningless to him.

"I still don't believe any of this. It makes no sense."

"Well some things are self-evident. It's pretty evident that he got the Fentanyl illegally and died of an overdose. I've got nothing to support a homicide here, including no motive. I'm so sorry for your loss, and I wish I had better news."

Kyle stares out the window to the street, holding his jaw slightly upwards, wanting to cuss, to shout.

"You have no idea what it feels like, none." He pushes the chair back and walks across the café, through the swinging door, back to the music store for his next lesson.

Joker

7:30 a.m. on a school day is a frantic time in the Owlsley house. David pours cereal and milk in a bowl. Usually his dad joins him, but this morning he stands a few steps behind his seat, listening to his cell phone with a serious look on his face.

David is on his third spoonful of cereal when his mother whispers to him, "The cops just told Dad that someone broke into the office last night. He's on the phone with Ed right now."

David finally manages to swallow the spoonful in his mouth and robotically takes another bite.

"What about all of the diagnostic equipment, computers, everything on the desktops?" his dad asks Ed. "Do any of the network files appear corrupted or missing?"

He waits for a response. "Excellent, excellent. What about the locked evidence room?"

Another few seconds go by. "Amazing, no forced entry or missing evidence in there?"

Soon after, his dad ends the call.

"The cops talked to Ed. They couldn't find any evidence of forced entry, just one unlocked ground level window. Somehow the intruder downed the alarm system from outside without using our code. Ed fast-forwarded through all the surveillance camera footage, and there's a couple seconds where we can see the intruder wearing a mask and hoodie before he covered the camera," his dad says.

David's mom asks, "What kind of mask?"

"A Joker mask. The cops say there are thousands of them."

"That's good they didn't steal or trash anything. What do you think they would've broken in for?" David asks.

"Hard to say. It may take days or weeks to figure out. They swept the doors and other areas for fingerprints and couldn't find any."

David rinses his bowl in the sink and puts his backpack over his shoulder as he walks toward the door.

"See you guys for dinner," David says.

"Have a good day David, love you," his mom says.

"Love you David," his dad adds.

David takes the long way to Middleburg Academy and locates a dumpster behind a grocery store. While still inside the car, he pulls a Joker mask, rubber gloves and gray hoodie from a small plastic bag. He looks at the gray hoodie without any identifying logo or labels and decides to keep it. Then he cuts the Joker mask into tiny pieces and puts them back in the bag. After confirming no one is around and that there is no surveillance camera, he throws the bag and the rubber gloves into the middle of the half-full dumpster.

He cycles back through the events of the night before when he broke into his dad's office and located Kent Perless' laptop. He then downloaded all of the data from the hard drive. He stored it on a zip drive, then backtracked with another program to remove his digital fingerprints.

He figured the one person he would share his findings with would be Amanda, but definitely not yet, given her current frame of mind.

B&O Magnet

In "her room" at Aunt Barbara's, Amanda finds a small notepad and handwrites a note. She folds the note and puts it inside a small envelope. Then she texts Charlyne.

U R one of my BFFs, right?

Yep. U home?

Yeah. Got sprung tonight. Pick me up tomorrow after school? Want to visit B&O bridge overlook. Can U?

Sure. Be there at 3:30, K?

Text when U R a couple blocks away, I'm sneaking out. Kinda in lockdown.

The next morning Amanda texted David who was assigned to take her back to school. She said she was sick and wouldn't be going. When David never came by Aunt Barbara discussed it with Amanda, who said she just didn't feel up to going to school.

When she gets Charlyne's text, Amanda grabs her cell phone, puts a couple items in a small knapsack, and cuts through the back yard to find her.

"Thanks a lot for picking me up, and I know it was weird asking you not to come to the house."

"I know everything is weird for you. Everyone at school is saying you got forced into a psychiatric hospital. Did you?"

Charlyne puts the car in drive and starts pulling away.

"Yeah, for no reason really. My aunt did it. I just don't want to go to school, at least not yet."

"I get it. You've been through hell. I went to Kent's funeral with Iris and David. It was terrible."

Amanda puts her hand up. "No details please. I wanted to go but I just couldn't."

"So where exactly are we going now?" Charlyne asks.

"It's a beautiful park that overlooks the B&O railroad trestle on the Shenandoah River. Kent took me there. Have you ever been?"

"No, but I kinda know where it is. Just point out some turns at the end, okay? Are you getting any tutoring since you're ditching school?"

"I really haven't done anything since Kent died. I've just been trying to figure out things."

"Yeah, right. Why does something like that happen to a guy like Kent? I have trouble believing he OD'd."

"We didn't have any secrets. He would've told me if he was doing drugs like that."

"Some of the seniors think he wanted to commit suicide because of what happened to his mom."

"That's crap. He never talked about suicide or anything like that. Besides, I think he really liked me, so why...Up here at this next intersection is where you turn."

A few minutes later Amanda guides Charlyne into the area where she and Kent had pulled off. As they close the car doors, Amanda tosses her cell phone onto the front passenger seat. Charlyne notices.

"You're not bringing that?"

"No. I don't want to lose it out there."

However, Charlyne notices Amanda has a small knapsack slung over her shoulder. Charlyne pauses a moment, then decides to bring her cell phone. Amanda guides them along a path, the same one she walked with Kent.

"Been here a lot?" Charlyne asks.

"Just once."

As they walk along the path Charlyne looks back toward the road.

When they arrive at the top of the path near the edge of the embankment leading out to the railroad trestle, they stop and look out on the Shenandoah River. The water is shimmering because of the sun, which is fairly low in the western sky by this time.

"See that walkway along the trestle?" Amanda asks pointing.

"Yeah, what about it?"

"I'm thinking about walking along it. Wanna come with me?"

"Are you kidding?" Charlyne says, never being much of a daredevil herself.

"No I'm not. It's one of the things I did with Kent. Actually he walked along it but I was too chicken."

Amanda steps through the broken fence and starts toward the tracks. Charlyne still hovers on the opposite side of the fence.

"Hey, it says 'no trespassing.' You can't go in there," Charlyne partly screams.

Amanda moves onto the narrow walkway beside the track, which has no handrail whatsoever. She still has the small knapsack slung over her right shoulder. Could it be even three feet wide? She's got her back to Charlyne, who she knew wouldn't come with her.

"I'm just going partway, you sure you don't wanna come?"

"Don't Amanda! If this is why you wanted to come here, it's a really bad idea. Come back, please! You're starting to scare me."

Amanda ignores her pleas and starts walking along the trestle. Charlyne watches, knowing there is nothing she can do except go out there and force her to come back or wait for her to return.

"Amanda! Stop it! Come back!" After she walks another 50 yards at least, Charlyne cannot believe what Amanda does next. She sits down with her two legs draped over the edge looking out at the water. Charlyne has her cell phone in her back pocket. Who should I call? She is scrolling on her phone for Amanda's aunt or uncle when she hears a sound.

HONNN N-N-N-K-K-K! HONNN N-N-N-K-K-K!

At first she doesn't recognize the distant sound. But then she hears another horn blast, far louder. Terrified, she leans forward into the broken fence.

"Amanda! A train is coming! Come back now!"

She sees Amanda turn and look in her direction but she's unsure whether she hears her.

Then Charlyne feels the vibration, starting in her feet and working its way up through her body. Seconds later she looks to her right and sees the large blue and yellow locomotive heading toward the bridge trestle and Amanda. The train must be going 40, 50, maybe even 60 miles an hour. Charlyne grabs for her cell phone and waves wildly to whoever is in the huge engine, hopelessly trying to gain anyone's attention as the train barrels onto the trestle.

Inside the lead locomotive the CXT engineer and the conductor notice the person waving just as they approach the trestle. They again blast their horn, and suddenly the conductor sees something near the middle of the trestle.

"That's a person! Throw it into emergency!" The conductor yells. The 50-ton train is loaded with coal and trails for about a quarter mile behind three engines. The engineer applies air brakes to all of the train cars and the engines. A train with this tonnage will take at least a quarter to a half mile to come to a stop. Both of them watch as the human figure gets closer and closer.

The person now stands on the narrow walkway, not moving, not running, nothing.

Surely the person must hear them. The conductor and engineer catch one more glimpse just before the locomotive blasts past. The conductor nervously clutches his portable radio receiver and frantically calls the train dispatcher.

"Dispatch, this is CXT Train 1310, we may have just struck someone on the B&O trestle, in block, uh, 154, over the Shenandoah. The person was just standing in the middle of the trestle, never moved despite repeated horn blasts. Over."

"Train 1310, pull clear of the trestle. Examine front plow of the engine and determine what happened. We will await your reply to take action. Over."

"Dispatch, confirm you put a stop order on traffic on the block with the B&O trestle. Over."

"Train 1310, we have put a stop order on the track, giving you protection. Over."

"Dispatch, Thanks. Over."

Within a minute, the CXT conductor examines the plow on the side facing the walkway. There is a small but noticeable shear scrape no more than four inches long about four to five feet up on the plow.

He reaches for his radio and advises his engineer he is proceeding to the trestle.

Charlyne's hands shake so badly she can hardly dial the numbers for Amanda's uncle. Finally, his phone is ringing.

"Andy Michaels here."

"Mr. Michaels, this is Charlyne Bennington. Uh, I'm not far from Sky Meadows Park and I'm with Amanda, and she walked out on the railroad trestle and the train just went by, and I, I don't know if she's okay or not."

"What?! She's where and what happened?"

"I tried to stop her, I yelled, but she wouldn't stop or come back and she went onto the railroad bridge. It's the B&O bridge over the Shenandoah. I can't see her on the bridge. I don't see her in the water. I don't know what happened... God... I don't know what to say. Can you get here quickly?"

"The B&O railroad bridge over the river?"

"Yeah, that's it. "

"Charlyne, just stay put. Let me make some calls and I'll get back to you. Just stay there. Did you drive?"

"Yeah, I drove. You'll see my car, and I'm up a little path. I'm going to stay up here where I can see the bridge."

As he makes this walk the conductor believes that whoever was standing on the railroad trestle was there for a reason. Another despondent soul using a train as their means to an end. He sees a lump on the tracks as he nears the place where the person was standing. He carefully kneels down and grasps a girl's small backpack. It's the kind that you just cinch at the top, so he pries it apart with his fingers. He peers inside the bag and finds an envelope. He pulls it out, and then notices a small gold necklace inside as well.

Miller quickly concludes it's a suicide note. He stuffs the letter back inside the knapsack. He looks down at the water below, wondering how someone could survive the long fall, especially if they hit her. He gets on his portable radio.

"Dispatcher, Miller here. I'm at the middle of the trestle. There is no sign of the person, but I found a small backpack and what looks like a suicide note inside. There's also a little necklace. No identification, but it was probably a girl. I'm guessing we clipped her and she fell into the water, so we need a water rescue crew. Over."

Free Fall

The fisherman in the small boat hears the train rumbling across the trestle. Moments later the loud splash not more than 20 yards ahead startles him. He presses the electronic start on the small 10-horsepower outboard engine and puts it into forward gear. Approaching the splash area he sees her lifeless body face down in the water. He slows to a crawl, and once near the body he kills the engine.

Wrapping one arm around her upper torso and the other around her waist, he pulls her face-down into the boat. Quickly turning her over, he searches for her pulse, but doesn't feel it. He listens close to her nose and mouth for any air movement. None. He begins vigorous chest compressions.

Whoosh.

White light. Brighter and brighter. Then I see him. He touches my hand. I stare into his eyes - they look so happy. Then his hand lets go, he shakes his head no, and floats up and away from me.

Whoosh.

Whoosh.

A small burst of water suddenly erupts out of the girl's mouth and onto her neck and bloody arm. Seconds later, the fisherman talks to someone on his cell phone.

"Yeah. Get rescue personnel to the dock on the west side near the trestle. I pulled her from the water and she's been resuscitated."

"I just saw him. He touched my hand."

"Who are you talking about?"

"Kent. My boyfriend. He...he was just there. I just saw him."

"I'm not sure who he is or what you think you saw, but I just revived you. You're one lucky girl."

"You don't understand."

Amanda stretches out on the aluminum floor of the boat with her head against the hard wooden seat.

"I'm going to get you checked by the rescue squad," he says, directing the small boat toward the dock.

Rescued

While en route, Andy receives a cell phone call from Loudoun County Emergency Rescue Services. The dispatcher relays the news that Amanda was rescued by a fisherman and is stable. He quickly calls Charlyne and gives her the great news, but explains he doesn't know her exact condition.

He follows a narrow two-lane road to the river level and sees the medical rescue van. The rear doors are open and two rescue personnel are standing near a gurney tending to a girl with her back to him. As he trots toward her, the EMTs back off a few feet. The older of the two speaks first.

"She's going to be okay."

Andy wants to give her a huge bear hug, but he stops himself because he's unsure of her injuries. He delicately places his hands on her shoulders.

"Are you okay?"

Short, intermittent sobs come out of her mouth.

"What happened? What were you doing on the bridge?" he asks.

"I don't know," she says.

"Are you hurt?"

"Not really, just my right arm. It's fine, I'm fine. I'm really fine."

"What were you doing up there? Were you trying to die?"

"No. I didn't want to die...just almost die."

"Huh? What's that mean?"

"I wanted to know what it would feel like 'cause I don't remember before the crash, but I do remember some of the stuff when I was dead and then when I came back. Does that make any sense to you?"

"Not really, actually not at all. You dodged a train. Why would you do that?"

"I wanted to see Kent again."

"So you were trying to kill yourself."

"To tell you the truth, something told me I wouldn't die. I think I jumped but I don't know. I really don't remember. The point is I remember what happened after, when I almost died. I saw Kent again and now it's alright, Uncle Andy. I think I'm good now. Really, I mean it."

Andy turns from her and walks over to the nearest rescue squad worker.

"Should I take her to the hospital?"

"Frankly, the only problem we found was superficial wounds along her arm, and the bleeding was minor. We ran all of her vitals and conducted all our normal testing, so it's your call."

Andy walks back over to Amanda and touches her shoulder. "We should take you to the hospital."

"I don't want to. Can you take me to the cemetery where Kent's buried? He's at Springbranch Church, off of Route 7. Do you know where that is?"

Home Visit

Andy finds Peter Lucent's phone number on his cell phone.

"Dr. Lucent, sorry to bother you, but Amanda has been in an accident and I'm hoping you might be able to see her."

"Why don't you just take her to the ER?"

"Under the circumstances, I really don't want a record of the situation."

"Why?"

"She just fell off a railroad bridge. There's a lot more to it, but I'd rather tell you in person."

"Fell off a bridge?"

"She doesn't appear to be injured, but I want to be sure. Could you please see her at your home?"

"As long as you understand I'm not an ER doctor. I live at 101 Fox Lair Court in Reston. How long do you think it will take for you to get here?"

Andy considers his location for a moment. "Maybe 20 minutes."

Andy walks over to Amanda.

"Let's get out of here. I'm going to have Dr. Lucent examine you, then I will take you by Springbranch. I promise." He helps her over to his car. As she gets in she's already asking questions.

"Dr. Lucent? Why did you call him?"

"We don't want a medical record of this because it would raise questions about your competency. Got it?"

"Okay, whatever."

Peter Lucent opens the front door and ushers Andy and Amanda inside.

"Young lady, I understand you've had a bit of an accident. Let's go talk privately."

Lucent leads Amanda into his home office. He is carrying what looks to be a first aid kit.

"What happened?"

He has taken several of the items from the first aid kit and placed them on the table. He examines her arm, looking at the various cuts and bruises.

"I dunno. I went back to this railroad bridge I visited with Kent. And I walked out on it and..."

Lucent interrupts, "Why would you walk out on a railroad bridge?"

"I dunno. I just wanted to experience what I had with him. I can't give you a better explanation than that. I know it's stupid, but I don't care."

"And what happened after that?"

"A train came. I don't remember much after that. Some fisherman fished me out of the water. The rescue squad came to the boat ramp and treated me there. Come to think of it, I never got to thank that fisherman, I wonder if I'll ever find him again."

"Amanda, were you trying to get hit?" he asks sincerely in a low whisper.

"I really don't know. Kent told me about two friends of his who got killed out on that trestle. It was a girl and a boy from the neighborhood where he grew up."

"What about that? Why do you mention it?"

"It was just something I had been thinking about."

Amanda looks down at the first aid kit materials on the table and sees sharp scissors.

"Doctor Lucent, I don't bleed like I should."

"You don't bleed like you should? I'm not sure I..."

Before he can do anything she picks up the scissors, flips them open and slashes one of the razor-sharp edges against her wrist until blood starts spurting out all over her arm, the table, and the floor. She drops the now bloody scissors onto the desk.

"Amanda! What are you doing?" Lucent shouts, searching his first aid kit for gauze, a bandage, anything to stop the blood.

Andy hears the commotion from the adjacent room and runs in to find blood everywhere.

"What happened? What happened? My God!"

Dr. Lucent finally locates a bandage and tape. He rips open the bandage, but as he starts to press it to Amanda's wrist, she pulls it away and refuses to let him cover the wound. She holds her hand palm up in front of them both.

"Look. This is what I mean."

The blood has already coagulated and sealed the wound shut. Lucent is speechless. Andy doesn't know what happened but he stares at the wound too.

"What happened?" Andy asks.

"Your niece just slashed her own wrist. She's claiming that for some reason her wounds heal much faster than normal. So she was making a point."

"I knew it for sure when the rescue squad was treating me today, but I also kinda knew before that."

Andy looks at Lucent. "Is there any medical condition that she could have developed that would do that after a serious accident?"

"Nothing that comes to mind. What's even more amazing, her medical history shows she was previously diagnosed with Von Willebrand Disease, or vWD, which is marked by excessive bleeding. She has signs of the complete opposite now."

Lucent covers the wound with the bandage and secures it with tape.

"Well Andy, I think your niece is fine as long as she doesn't slash herself again anytime soon," Lucent says, eyeing Amanda.

Springbranch

The church, built more than 100 years ago, has a red brick exterior, oversized front doors and a high steeple. The cemetery sprawls over a hillock immediately adjacent to it. Amanda makes it clear that she does not want Andy to come with her, and he figures he'll just let this play out.

Amanda enters through one of the front doors of the church, and Andy texts Barb and Charlyne, assuring them that Amanda is safe and sound. A few minutes later a priest walks down the steps with Amanda and ushers her around the side of the building. His outstretched arm points to a certain area where there are lines of headstones. Amanda begins walking in that direction.

Andy decides to follow Amanda at a distance, just to keep an eye on her. As she walks through a series of gravesites, he walks just close enough so that he can still see her. He sees her looking around on the gravel roadway and picking up several stones.

Placing small stones on a headstone is a Jewish tradition. One explanation for placing the stones is to ensure that souls remain where they belong. Keep the soul down, don't allow it to wander back into the land of the living. But this is a Christian cemetery, Andy thinks to himself. I guess the deceased really don't mind what religion you are, and they certainly can't complain.

Finally, Amanda stands before a headstone and places two, maybe three, small stones on top of the polished headstone.

They're back on Route 7 driving toward Barbara's house.

"I want you to take me to Crossroads."

"Amanda, you can't keep going there. You've got to stay with your Aunt Barbara, and you've got to go back to school."

"I know you may hate me for it, but I just don't know if I can do it. I'm not sure I can walk back into M.A. again," Amanda says, looking right at him.

"What is it? I know terrible things have happened. But have you lost the drive to enjoy life? You're only 18, Amanda! I'm not telling you how to feel, but..."

"I'm moving on. I feel better now. And I have a plan. It's a plan that I really just figured out."

"What kind of plan?"

The white picket fences of the horse farms pass on both sides of the road. Amanda stares up at the huge trees, watching their branches move in the wind. She outlines her new plan as Andy listens incredulously.

"I'll have to talk about it with your Aunt Barbara. Then I'll look into a few things and we'll talk about it again," Andy responds.

"You guys can talk, but it won't change my mind. Are you taking me to the farm now?"

Andy thinks about his options. He knows that Amanda, at least before everything happened with the crash, had a good head on her shoulders. And he desperately wants to believe she has bottomed out.

"Yeah, I'll take you there. But I want to talk to Kyle Perless again. We need to make sure it's okay."

"He'll let me stay there as long as I want and you know it."

The Catacombs

Andy has trouble focusing on the long list of emails on his screen. His mind keeps mulling over the circumstances outlined by Perry Carson, a couple conversations he had with Amanda about Kent, and the newest revelation from David that Amanda's hospital room had been professionally bugged.

Andy decides there is one person who may be able to offer more insight. He texts, *Hi, Alex. Any chance you could meet me for a drink after work today? Thx, Andy.*

A few minutes later, Alex confirms, and they set a time and place.

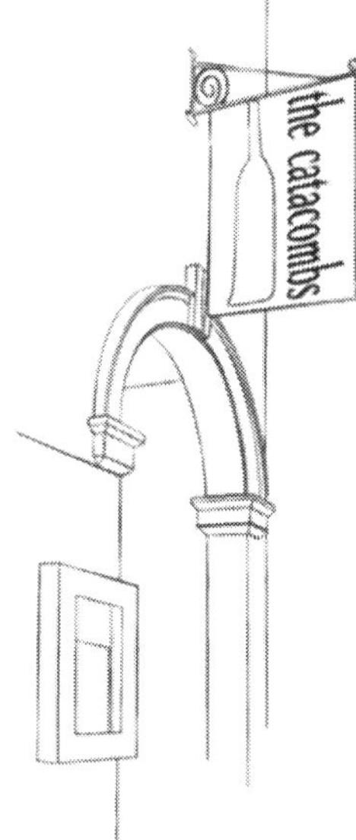

Andy enters the Catacombs a few minutes early and takes the staircase down to the dark, basement-level bar, a place he partied in many times during college. It is an institution for Hoya students and Georgetown alumni, well-hidden a few blocks off Wisconsin Avenue. He notices the musty beer smell as he scans the bar. Satisfying himself that Alex has not arrived, Andy slides onto a hardwood bench in one of the booths. "Yellow" by Coldplay is pumping through the speakers. Within a couple minutes he sees Alex walking down the steps. Andy holds his hand up to get his attention and Alex strolls over.

They exchange a quick hug before sliding into the booth opposite each other.

"Thanks for meeting me with such short notice. I know it was a hassle to come back into the city at rush hour." Andy says.

"No problem. I wanted to talk to you too." Alex responds.

"Oh yeah? About what?"

Before he can respond a young waitress, probably a GU student, asks for their drink order. Andy orders a Sam Adams, and Alex requests the same.

Once she leaves, Alex re-starts.

"It's finally kind of sunk in that your brother is no longer here and I'm having trouble dealing with that. I'm so sorry for you and the family."

"I just keep marching forward one step at a time myself. Because I'm representing so many of the other families, I can't let myself get down."

The waitress drops off the beers. "Having dinner, guys?" she asks, but they both decline.

"Okay," Andy starts, "I've got some really disturbing stuff that I need to ask you about. Someone bugged Amanda's hospital room. At first I thought it was the press, but now I think that theory was misdirected."

"That seems preposterous."

"Didn't you and Ron have a security clearance at your job?"

"Yeah, I still have one. Why?"

"I'm just wondering if there could be any connection between Ron's death and his research. Did you guys work together?"

"We didn't really work together, but he worked on blood biology research like I do, in micro-fluidics."

"Micro-fluidics? Never heard of it. What did he actually do?"

"Remember, BBS is a big company and I didn't work in his unit. Also, some of the classified stuff I can't talk about. Micro-fluidics is a big new area. It's taking a tiny tube, or a channel, and using technology to separate the blood components. It can also be used to monitor for bad stuff in the blood. Instead of needing big machines, a tiny channel and some high-tech engineering can do major diagnostics on blood."

"I know he patented one blood screening process before he even started at BBS. What about that research?"

"What about it? He assigned his first patent rights to BBS and I know they paid him for that. Everything developed at work is considered company intellectual property. So if you work on anything that's even partly related to the research at the lab the company's lawyers see to it that the new process or invention is patented through the company. You are listed as an inventor, sure, but the company owns and controls any patents and resulting income. That's pretty typical..."

Andy interrupts him. "How about the research he did at home for years? He mentioned it in passing, but he never told me what he was doing. Do you know?"

"Whatever he did at home, I'm not surprised he kept it to himself. If it had anything to do with work, he knew it would be assigned to the company and he would get little credit for it. The company could claim the basis of the idea came from work, even if he'd come up with something at home."

"Are you avoiding my questions?"

"I told you we didn't work closely together."

"You're holding back on me, Bro. I know you too well. And this is my brother, dammit!" Andy pounds the near-empty mug on the tabletop.

"Alex, a few years ago he went all the way down to Easter Island for two weeks and he told me it was a company business trip. Did you go down there also?"

"Yeah. We had a whole bunch of scientists on that trip. It was very cool."

"Why did your company send a bunch of biologists to Easter Island?"

"Easter Island is rich with biodiversity and all kinds of strange species. We were looking at biology relating to unique species located there. I really can't say anything more. If I disclosed things that were classified, I could get in some serious trouble. I know you understand."

"So the company sends a bunch of the biologists all the way out into the South Pacific Ocean, but you can't tell me why?"

"The company's always investigating new techniques, that's all I can say."

Andy stares into Alex's eyes and then back down at his own beer mug, deep in thought.

"Let me throw something else at you. Amanda befriended a young kid who was volunteering at the hospital. He was in his early 20s, and they became fast friends. This kid, her new friend, was found dead in his car a few days ago. There were drugs in his pocket, prescription Fentanyl patches, but he had no script for any of it. No suicide note. Cops think it was an accidental overdose, not foul play.

"So here's what we've got overlaid on that. My brother, my sister-in-law and my niece are in this crash. My niece survives, my brother and sister-in-law die. The kid that befriended my niece turns up dead weeks later, under very suspicious circumstances. So again, here is my question for you. Do you think someone could want to kill Ron because of his work?"

"You expect me to have an answer?"

"Yeah. What's the answer?"

"First, I have no idea if a lot of what you just said is true—I mean besides what we definitely know. I didn't know anything about this kid's death—Amanda's friend. But I don't think this stuff has anything to do with Ron's work." Alex says.

"I am not asking you to be sure. But is there a reason to wonder? You wouldn't be violating any security clearance to tell me that much...."

"Let me just speak in hypothetical terms. Biological breakthroughs are important to the U.S. economy. We don't want our competitors to own bio-genetic technology that we could have developed because we want the income. Did you know that if the U.S. government funds part of the research it earns some of the patent licensing fees?"

"No, I never knew that." Andy says. "Are you saying the U.S. sponsors your company's research?"

"No, but the U.S. puts up grant money for various projects, which is the same thing. You know I'd tell you if I knew something that would help."

Actually, Andy isn't sure about that at all, after attending a couple legal seminars discussing the micro-expressions of testifying witnesses. Micro-expressions can be telltale signs of lying or deception, and some of Alex's expressions belie his words.

"Alex, tell me the truth about your trip to Easter Island."

"This conversation is heading down trouble lane. I told you I can't breach security or I'll be toast." Alex pulls out a twenty-dollar bill and slaps it down on the table.

"I have to go. You're not listening. It's bad enough trying to deal with your brother's death. It's worse having you try to pry information out of me that I legally can't disclose. I think you are trying to connect dots that simply don't connect."

Alex gets up from the table and starts walking out of the bar. Andy gets up and follows him. Neither of them pays any attention to the young couple in the booth beside them who have been keenly interested in their conversation.

"Wait. One more question. Do you think the government or someone else could kill someone over what my brother was working on?"

They're both standing at the foot of the stairway heading up from the lower level bar to the ground level. Alex turns and looks at Andy.

"Andy, I've told you everything I can. Do you understand how much corporate espionage there is over medical and biological technology? Better ways to ensure that the blood donated is safe for operational use and transfusions. Better ways to analyze or screen transplant tissue. This stuff is big business. Do you have any idea how much money companies make on patented medical technology? Millions, maybe billions. So are the stakes big? Yes."

"So is that an answer or a background statement?"

"I don't know. Whatever you think it is."

"Do you think someone could get killed over Ron's research?" Andy asks one last time.

Alex starts walking up the steps. Andy tags along behind him and pokes him at the top of his shoulder blade. Alex turns around, completely pissed off.

"Leave it alone," his friend barks.

Alex wheels back around and continues up the steps. Andy stares up from the bottom of the stairwell for several seconds before walking back to the booth. He slumps back into the seat to nurse the few remaining sips from his beer mug.

Andy returns from a quick lunch the following day, still obsessing over everything he and Alex discussed. Sitting down at his desk he scans through his emails of the last hour or so. He sees an odd one with a return address that he doesn't recognize and a subject that says "Read this now." Andy immediately figures it's spam, but something keeps him from deleting it. He decides to click into the email. There is no greeting.

They know we met. Can't meet anymore.

Andy looks, but there's no name on the email. The only person who could possibly be the sender is Alex Erickson.

"Andy, it's Mrs. Allsop calling about the status of her case, can you talk to her?" Angie asks over the speakerphone. Andy knows he should take the call. But he wants to look a few things up on the Internet.

"Please cover for me and send me an e-mail with the details. I'm in the middle of some serious research."

Andy walks to the kitchen to make a cup of green tea while mentally outlining a quick research plan. Surfing on the Georgetown website he finds the Department of Biochemistry and Molecular and Cellular Biology. The webpage trumpets collaborative studies between the National Institutes of Health, the U.S. Department of Defense and other government research institutions. Hmmm.

Then Andy punches in the name of the company Ron worked for, "Biological Blood Services," and finds their website. It's fairly limited, but mentions that the company collaborates with major private companies and U.S. government institutions on biological research, biochemistry and cellular biology. The website indicates the company is a leader in the screening of blood, micro-fluidics, and the handling of human tissue. It's weird. In all the time Ron worked at this company, Andy realizes he never really had any idea what the hell he did there. And not once did Andy ever visit him at work.

Last, he considers Easter Island, a place he knows nothing about. Wasn't that where they tested some nuclear bombs underwater and the mushroom cloud could be seen hundreds of miles away in the 1950s? He types "Easter Island" in the browser and learns it is a Polynesian island in the middle of the southeastern Pacific Ocean. It's 2400 miles west of Chile, is only 69 square miles, and has only 2500 permanent residents who are considered the most remote population on the planet. The first recorded European contact with the island was in 1722 when a Dutch navigator visited for a week.

What would blood biologists be looking for there? There is discussion of the Polynesian rat, which apparently played an important role in the disappearance of the indigenous Rapanui palm tree. A number of other trees have also become extinct. A massive seabird population, perhaps the world's richest. Amazing petroglyphs, caves, unique stone platforms.

Then, eureka. Andy finds it:

> "The immunosuppressant drug sirolimus was first discovered in the bacterium Streptomyces hygroscopicus in a soil sample from Easter Island. The drug derived from this bacterium is also known as rapamycin, named after Rapa Nui, the native name of the island."

As Andy follows the footnote for more information, he notices goose bumps on his neck.

> "A peptide that was first isolated in 1975 from the bacteria strain Streptomyces hygroscopicus was found on Easter Island. Rapamycin has been found to have a number of

interesting properties, including a novel mechanism of immunosuppression. May help prevent rejection of organ transplants, may be effective in the treatment of cancer...."

Andy continues to follow footnotes and finds a number of journal articles, all reporting within the last several years on studies of the properties of rapamycin. He quickly copies and pastes abstract summaries and citations to the journal articles into an e-mail he sends to Angie.

He presses his speakerphone button. "Are you there?"

"Yeah, where else would I be?" Angie replies sarcastically.

"I just sent you a bunch of cites for medical journal articles. Can you go down to the Georgetown medical school library and get the complete articles copied for me please?"

"When do you need them, and what case am I billing it to?"

"This afternoon or tomorrow morning at the latest. As for the case, uh, no case yet, just general legal research."

Andy contemplates driving over to Alex and Natalie's house that evening, then decides it would be a bad move. He contemplates just what the right move may be.

Demi-vierge

It's the third time David has banged on the door at the farmhouse. He hears music from inside. He finally cracks open the unlocked door.

"Hello? Amanda! Amanda!"

He realizes the music is coming from the bedroom so he raps on the bedroom door. Still no answer. He goes in and the pungent smell of incense invades his nose. A couple of candles are burning and barely any natural light filters in. He can see Amanda is focused on the record player and still hasn't turned around to acknowledge him. Her overly long guy's button-down shirt doubles as pajamas. He walks close to her and she flinches a moment, somewhat startled.

"Hey, what're you doing here?"

"Actually I wanna talk to you about some stuff..."

"I'm really getting into these vinyl albums that Kent collected. Some of them have some really wild notes inside. Now it's just a tiny CD case that you can hardly fit any words inside. Did you know that these old turntables will auto-replay one side of a vinyl record too?"

Amanda flops down on the bed and turns back over the book she was reading. David leans across from the other side of the unkempt bed and looks at the book's spine: *Fear and Loathing in Las Vegas*.

"What's the book about?"

"It's about this crazy journalist who goes on this gonzo vacation with another guy to Las Vegas. Hunter S. Thompson wrote it. Ever heard of him?"

"No."

"He was crazy. Big on drugs. Ended up living in Aspen, Colorado. Eventually committed suicide. I think he was scared of getting old..."

"Amanda, can I change the subject a second? I don't think Kent committed suicide."

Amanda starts laughing. David is confused.

"What's so funny?"

"This part in the book. It's just insane."

"I just told you that I don't think Kent killed himself."

"Well, duh... thank you Captain Obvious."

Amanda never takes her head out of the book. Led Zeppelin is blaring. David likes the music blaring. Anyone listening won't hear his conversation. He lays down on the bed, angular to her, but their heads aren't far apart.

"Now, I was thinking also about how you're the only survivor of the plane crash..."

Amanda never looks up. David's head rests on top of his closed hands under his chin.

"What if the reason you survived that plane crash wasn't just good luck? Do you remember when you had that problem with your back when you were about 12 years old?"

"You know I can't remember. What problem?"

"You had to stop playing soccer because you had incredible back pain. Your parents sent you to an orthopedic doctor who said you wouldn't play soccer for at least a year."

The music continues to vibrate the room.

"But you were playing again in three months. What if there was a reason that you recovered so fast?"

Amanda never responds.

David touches her shoulder.

"What?" she says.

"I just asked you something."

"What...what did you ask?"

"Don't you see? I'm wondering if there's a reason you got better so fast."

"And I'm the one who supposedly has brain damage. What are you talking about?"

"About your dad. What if...like...what did he do where he worked?"

"I don't know. He was a biologist, you know that. They analyzed blood, did what biologists do..."

"What if his work had something to do with why you survived?"

"You've lost your mind." Amanda dog-ears a page of the book and closes it up. The record has stopped playing on the turntable. She walks over to it and lifts the record off of the turntable and places it back in its protective sleeve. She puts on another album.

"Do you know 'Wild Horses'? The original Rolling Stones version?"

"Yeah, I've heard it."

Amanda begins to sing along, "I saw her today at the reception...Glass of wine in her hand..."

"I wanna find out what your dad did in biology. Will you help me?"

Amanda again doesn't reply and seems content back inside the *Fear and Loathing* book.

"Hey, are you listening?"

She gets up and changes the record back to the Led Zeppelin album. The up-tempo song "Black Dog" pulsates through the room and David's body.

David again gets near her ear.

"Someone had Kent killed. I've done some homework. I also think this house is bugged, so I'm glad the music is blasting."

Amanda looks over at David, confused. "That's outrageous. Kent didn't kill himself, for sure. But for you to be right, there has to be bad guys. Really serious bad guys."

"If you saw something like this on TV, you would be saying, whoa, those things can't all be an accident, there's some connection. It's all too coincidental."

"I'm not sure..."

"Prove me wrong. Get your doctor's records. You're 18, so you can."

The song "Stairway to Heaven" has begun playing. Amanda climbs up off the bed and begins slowly dancing to the song with one arm stretched toward the ceiling and her other arm out in front of her. She begins turning slowly, swaying her hips. While her trancelike dance continues, she sings along, "And she's buying the stairway...to heaven."

"David come dance with me," she demands.

David has come to expect this kind of erratic behavior from her, and he gets off the bed and stands a few feet in front of her. She reaches her right hand out and takes his and they begin dancing together. She leads, he follows.

"Have you done it yet?" she suddenly asks him.

"What kind of question is that?" he says, amazed that she could move from the stuff he just told her to this.

"Do you know if I've done it? You're good friends with Jonathan, did he tell you? Come on, 'fess up." Amanda prods, maintaining her rhythm and moving closer. Her breasts just graze David, and he tries to get the hang of dancing with her in this odd setting. He feels relieved he didn't have to tell her he's never gotten laid, although he has gotten to third base with a couple girls.

"He never told me. I swear."

"You were always around us; do you think we did it?"

"I can say *something* happened. I just don't know exactly what. Why do you want to know?"

"Charlyne told me Amber has been making moves on him."

"I know she's been after him, that's old news. Jonathan misses you. He's told me so. Why won't you see him?"

"I don't mean to be nasty, but it's not going to happen. Break the news to him however you want," Amanda says without hesitation.

"I'm not going to tell him anything." David says.

"Alright. Doesn't matter. The funny thing is I don't really care about Amber and Jonathan because I don't remember feeling anything for him. It's weird, there can't be envy without recall. Maybe that's the first good thing to come from losing my memory."

Their dance continues.

"I think I'm technically a virgin anyway," she practically shouts over the music that has grown louder.

"Technically?"

"Being a virgin means doing it your first time. I can't remember whether I did it before or not so, yeah, I say I'm technically a virgin. I'm like a demi-vierge. Like halfway a virgin."

"Huh?"

"I looked up stuff on virginity online and learned that a demi-vierge is sexually promiscuous, she does everything except..."

"She won't go all the way?"

Suddenly, Amanda lifts her blouse up and over her head and tosses it on the bed, leaving just a sheer bra on.

"David, undo my bra please," she shouts over her shoulder, backing up toward him, still swaying to the music.

David is stunned and not sure what to do.

"What?" he manages to say. He has always worshipped Amanda, but something like this just can't be happening.

"Do it, David. Undo it."

So he does, and then Amanda shakes the bra forward and tosses it with one hand onto the bed.

"Do you think I'm attractive?" She asks, dancing toward him with both hands up until she is close enough to graze him with her nipples, which are erect. David's eyes fix on them as they sway along with her body.

"Well?" she demands.

"Hell yeah, of course."

Amanda wraps her arms around David and presses her naked breasts against him. She moves her body languidly left and right, accentuating the contact, in a sensual slow dance. She feels he is excited also. Sliding her left thigh between his legs, she feels him against her down there. Emboldened, she rakes her right hand down his chest and then plunges it past his navel and inside the front of his loose jeans. She finds his manhood.

"What?" He asks after the rapid-fire maneuver.

"I want to please you," she whispers just by his ear.

David's heart is beating like a drum. He enjoys her caressing and fights to maintain his composure.

The long Led Zeppelin song finally ends. She removes her hand from his jeans and gives him a big hug, awkwardly holding it a couple seconds longer than natural. David enjoys her closeness and her feminine scent, but before he can even decide how to react, Amanda has flopped back down on the bed with the Hunter S. Thompson book, still topless.

His arousal fades away as he considers her virtually nonexistent reaction to his big disclosure to her. Didn't he just spill to her his thesis of Kent being killed, and the whole deal about her dad's work and her survival? Did she hear any of that?

"Do you remember the stuff I told you?" he asks, not wanting to make mention of specifics since the music is not playing.

"Yeah. Let's talk soon," she answers.

"When?" he asks a bit impatiently, having made the not-insignificant trek to Crossroads Farm to impart his revelations to her.

"I'll text you, probably tomorrow. Thanks for coming, really."

Abruptly changing the subject, she asks, "Are you disgusted with me?" as she lights an incense candle.

"About what?"

"Acting like a slut."

"Hardly. Just surprised and confused."

"Don't be. It was time. Let's not analyze it."

Glow Bugs

Whoosh.

"Daddy, why are you keeping those lightning bugs inside there?"

"They're not lightning bugs, honey."

"They glow like lightning bugs, Daddy."

"They're painted to light up."

"You paint bugs, Daddy?"

"Sometimes."

Whoosh.

Amanda slowly wakes up in Kent's bedroom. She groggily gets up, drags herself into the bathroom and looks at her sleepy eyes in the mirror. It is then that she remembers a flash from her dream. Or was it the NDE? Something about glow in the dark? She remembers being on the dance floor with Kent at the rave. Yes. She caught a glimpse then. It's the same scene. She struggles to remember. Painting a bug. Lightning bug? Glowing bugs! She walks to the kitchen, grabs a green apple and takes a bite, struggling to reach back into her semi-consciousness.

@Part V

Report to Solarez

Two train crew members, trainmaster Williams, and the two FBI agents sit around a table in the sparse CXT conference room.

After introductions are made, the first field agent begins.

“So there was no damage to your engines or any other railroad property?”

“None that we could find. We found this bag on the walkway by the tracks, but we couldn’t find a person or a body. We’re pretty sure it was a female based on the colors.” The conductor says, pointing to the fabric backpack on the table.

“Did you find anything else besides this backpack?” the lead FBI agent asks.

“I thought I saw a little scratch or two on the lead locomotive, but no real damage.”

“This incident may involve national security, so we’re asking you to keep it confidential. We’ll hold onto the bag as evidence, and we ask that you not report this to the media, or to the Federal Railroad Administration. Everything about this incident stays in this room. Do you understand?”

“But we’re required to file all trespassing accidents with…” the CXT trainmaster begins.

“That could jeopardize our operation. Don’t file anything. Keep my card, and if anyone has questions, call me. There are no reports to be made.”

Looking at the engineer and conductor now, the lead agent adds: “No war stories to any other crew or friends, understood?” The crew members both nod in agreement.

The FBI agent places his card in front of the trainmaster, and then hands one to the crew members also.

“Well, then, uh, are we free to go?” The engineer asks, looking at both agents nervously.

“Absolutely, thank you for your time.”

Once the two agents are back in the unmarked SUV, the lead agent calls Solarez.

"We've taken care of things with CXT. We have the only physical evidence, a backpack presumably left by Amanda Michaels on the trestle with no identification. They assume she drowned after the train sideswiped her."

"Sideswiped?? She was almost killed! Where the hell was the protection I requested? No, I demanded! This operation must be perfect from this point forward. The director will explode when he finds out about this. Yeah, I know she survived, but I still want to know what the hell went wrong!"

"Sir, we've been following her 24/7. We had five agents around her. An agent in a Jon boat, two in the woods nearby, and two in their vehicles. They were in place before she even arrived. We knew she planned to go there because we intercepted her text message to her friend. How were we to guess she'd suddenly walk out on the trestle and dare a train? No way one of our agents could foresee that, or risk running out after her."

"No way to foresee? You knew she was borderline suicidal. So she fell into the river, and then what?"

"We put agents into an ambulance and responded because she needed medical attention. They concluded her injuries were minor enough that she didn't need to go to the ER. Her uncle came and took her away, and we continued our surveillance."

"And?"

"He took her to one of the doctors treating her, Dr. Peter Lucent." In an attempt to point to some better news, the agent adds, "On the plus side, we have a blood sample that our EMT took during her treatment, so we can run a full blood panel."

"Report the results to me ASAP. I also want to fully review all operations immediately—especially those in place to protect Amanda Michaels. I'm setting a meeting for all agents assigned to this project at 8:30 a.m. tomorrow."

"We have a plan in place already, sir. It's not foolproof, but we think it'll work."

"It better work. And, it had better prevent anything like this from happening again. We'll review it in the morning."

"Sir, are you still against sweeping her up and detaining her or any of the others? That would guarantee their safety."

"Absolutely. That would blow the entire op. We're getting closer, I know it. We can and will protect her, and we'll and win this. Over." Solarez abruptly ends the call.

Another Task

The airline has always paid the litigation support vendors that Paul Franklin's law firm has needed to engage in previous cases. This includes Litigation Support Associates, Ryan's innocuous billing entity, which has carried out special projects for Franklin. Franklin decides that if the airline is going to cost his law firm $100,000.00 or more in reduced fees, he's going to use some of their money to find out who will be contributing $100 million to the Hemispheres settlement fund.

Franklin closes his office door before returning to his desk. He taps in Ryan's phone number and reaches him without having to play phone tag.

"I've got a new investigation for you," Franklin tells him. "Find out what airline supplier or vendor is contributing the $100 million. Handle this with complete confidentiality and discretion — no one can know who..."

"Franklin stop. I understand the sensitivity. Give me a week."

Two Judges

The judicial seminar of the D.C. Bar Conference is an annual event held at the Willard, an ornate old-line hotel at 1400 Pennsylvania Avenue, just over a block from the White House.

At the end of each of the two days, many of the judges retire to the reception area on the fourth floor of the hotel. The Peacock Room offers a breathtaking southern-facing veranda. The view in the foreground is the White House. In the distance the jets landing and taking off from Washington National Reagan Airport dot the skyline, and the Washington Monument juts skyward.

"A vodka gimlet, please." Judge Easton requests of the bartender, who's dressed in his white modified tuxedo.

Several other judges stand in the queue for drinks. Turning from the bartender, Judge Easton greets a few of them.

Hovering nearby, Judge Lisa Bondakopf sips her wine. As soon as Judge Easton approaches, she greets her.

"Rhonda, how are you?"

"Lisa, how the hell have you been?" Easton asks her.

The two met more than a decade before at a judicial conference when Judge Bondakopf was still a state court judge and Easton had just been appointed to the D.C. Superior Court Bench. They bonded at "judge school," as they fondly called it

"Talk about high profile. You've got your hands full with the Hemispheres cases don't you? Let's get a better view of the White House. It's so pretty in the evening." Bondakopf leads Easton away from the other judges to the balcony rail affording the best view of the White House. The sun has set behind the buildings of Washington, and in the dusk the White House has been illuminated.

"I never get tired of looking at this view." Bondakopf says.

"It's amazing," Easton agrees.

"How's Andy Michaels doing on the Hemispheres cases?" Bondakopf asks, taking a sip of her wine and glancing over at Easton.

"He's got a tough job on his hands. It's a tightrope walk for him I imagine, given his niece's case. I feel for him every time he's in court."

"We never had this conversation, right? I never should have said anything, but I couldn't help myself..." the federal judge says to Rhonda who quickly turns her head and narrows her eyes toward her friend Lisa. A moment later Lisa leans toward Rhonda's ear and begins to whisper. Rhonda's eyes open wide and she turns toward Lisa. Then Lisa leans in and whispers more. Rhonda now stares out toward the White House again, expressionless.

Both of them stare straight ahead for a few seconds and each take sips of their drinks.

"Be careful, and wait and see how things unfold." Lisa tells her. "I'm going to find my husband. He's on the other side of the veranda. Great seeing you."

Mediating

Angie had been working on contacting each family for information on funeral expenses, lost earnings, and other expenses. Andy set a 3:00 meeting on the third day to review every case and determine a settlement demand figure to give to Franklin. Andy then called each client.

Andy suggested an opening settlement demand between $6 and $10 million dollars for each of the cases in the crash. The one exception was Amanda. He was going to demand $13 million dollars for her because she would have a lifetime of issues to deal with. Angie and Myra prepared a settlement binder on each case, and Andy reviewed them and suggested a few changes. They were hand-delivered to Franklin's office on Thursday, but not a word was heard from Franklin that Friday.

The following Monday, mid-morning, Myra buzzes Andy and says Franklin is on the line.

"Andy, Franklin here. I got all of your demands. We'd like to set up mediation in the next ten days. We're willing to agree to Judge Harris."

Andy has settled cases with Harris in the past, so he agrees, not letting on to Franklin how shocked he is. Franklin suggests that they mediate no less than three cases per day, spread out between 8 a.m. and 6 p.m.

"If you're ready to mediate that quickly, we'll make ourselves ready," Andy tells Franklin. Andy knows these are huge cases and the obstacle to mediating is often the defense attorney, especially since they get paid by the hour. Everything about this situation runs contrary to Franklin's usual operational mode, and Andy ends the call shaking his head in disbelief. The next day, Angie sets up every mediation over the course of five days.

Money Scent

Ryan has studied the information carefully before arranging to meet Franklin at Dumbarton Oaks Café, just north of Georgetown. Ryan knows he has stumbled on tantalizing information and plans to reflect it in a premium on his invoice. As soon as he and Franklin close their menus and the waitress has left the table, Ryan begins.

"Here's what we've got. A $110 million payment received by the airline from 'Embracer-USA, LLC,' which is great information, right?"

"Damn right it is. The airline manufacturer must have some really big problems to pay that kind of money to Hemispheres on a confidential basis. Excellent stuff."

"I'm not done yet. I looked high and low for that entity, and it doesn't exist. Embracer is a manufacturer based in South America that sells jets worldwide, but there is no company named 'Embracer-USA, LLC.' So I did more digging, and I tracked down the bank the electronic transfer came from. According to the bank's ABA code, $110 million traces back to an account connected to the U.S. Treasury, Washington D.C."

Franklin stares back at Ryan, trying to fathom what he has just heard.

"What?" is all he can muster.

"Draw whatever conclusions you want. There is no Embracer-USA and the $110 million was paid from a well-masked account originating from the U.S. Treasury. No question. You may already know what it means, but I don't."

"Totally baffling. But, it may explain how the settlement pot was created."

"Settlement pot?" Ryan asks.

"Oh, yeah, I haven't told you. The airline wants me to try to get every case settled within 30 days. They cobbled together a large settlement fund. It's bizarre."

They switch to small talk and eat their lunch. Franklin asks Ryan to give him a bill for the services rendered to date.

"Given my marching orders, we're going to need to end this operation until further notice. I appreciate you coming through on this last request. I'm sure we'll have some work for you on other cases down the road."

Patent Search

The moment David Owlsley learned that Kent died, his hunch grew into an obsession. He had first believed that Kent secretly recorded Amanda to further his fame or fortune. But the moment Kent died, he had an epiphany. Maybe Kent was on to something. What if there was a connection between Amanda's amazing recovery and her dad's research?

David knew Amanda had told Kent about her dad getting a patent on his cancer tumor invention right out of graduate school, gaining him immediate credibility as a biologist. But he learns some other very interesting things buried in the deleted history on Kent's laptop.

A scan of his recent web activity reveals that Kent had been searching for information about Amanda's dad, cancer tumor research, and especially Biological Blood Services. He had also been searching the United States Patent Office's website, which allows anyone to view the details of U.S. patents.

To determine Kent's acumen in all things relating to surveillance, including bugs, David scours the laptop for any software familiar to even a novice in surveillance. None. Not one program on the laptop associated with the typical off-the-shelf stuff. That seals the deal for David. Kent never bugged Amanda's room. He had been completely wrong.

That being settled, his curiosity turns back to the patent searches. A few words entered in Google, and he locates the U.S. Patent Office search site and Ron Michaels' cancer tumor patent.

Inventor Name: *Michaels, Ron*
United States Patent: *8,164,789*
Title:
Cancer diagnosis and tumor control techniques involving analysis and manipulation of telomerase characteristics
Abstract:
The invention concerns a method for the analysis of cancer cells in a sample of blood, and for attacking the cancer cells through analysis of the RNA components of the telomerase enzyme present in the plasma or

serum of the blood, and by manipulating the telomerase in cancer tumors.
Inventors: *Michaels, Ron (Reston, VA)*
Assigned to*:* *Biological Blood Services LLC (Great Falls, VA)*
Primary U.S Patent Examiner: *Frankel, Arthur*

David then continues reading the claims, which state the specific parts that the U.S. Patent Office agreed was innovative.

"A method of detecting human telomerase reverse transcriptase enzyme (hTERT) RNA extracted from plasma or serum from a human comprising...."

First, David concludes he has no idea what this stuff means, except that it has to do with analyzing blood for cancer cells. RNA is like DNA he assumes. He's never heard of telomerase, so he decides to research it more. David jots down a note:

1. Arthur Frankel, patent examiner?
2. BBS?
3. telomerase enzyme?

Within minutes he determines Frankel is still working as a U.S. patent examiner, that BBS is definitely the company that Amanda's dad worked for, and that a human telomere is a cell enzyme that is a repeating DNA sequence at the end of the body's chromosomes. Biological research on human cancer cells has been focusing on both telomeres and telomerase.

To begin the serious investigative work, he logs into the Wayback Machine website. The Wayback Machine started out as an altruistic non-profit site created to preserve portions of the internet for posterity. The idea was to trawl the internet and randomly save website pages to capture historical snapshots, showing the evolution of individual websites over time. Since web pages are not static and may be constantly updated, the Wayback Machine was used by forensic types and attorneys out to prove what information was on a website at various times over many years. Eventually, its name changed to archive.org – a far more mundane name for the website.

David types in the search box: "Michaels, Ron" and "Inventor Name." This search results in a very interesting two-line reference to a more recent Ron Michaels patent, but despite numerous attempts, David can find no further information about it. The one reference on the page captured by Wayback is:

> *United States Patent Application Serial No. 10/896,321*
> *Michaels, Ron*
> *Suppression & Manipulation of mTOR activity to inhibit or exhibit cell replication*
> *[Application Withdrawn & Sealed]*

Being unfamiliar with patent law, or how a patent application could be "withdrawn," David decides he and Amanda should try to meet this Examiner Frankel, who reviewed the published Ron Michaels patent. Maybe he can explain what the technological innovation means too.

Cut Run

David concocts a tall tale about getting Amanda out of her funk by taking her to visit the Smithsonian Museums. After clearing the day trip with Aunt Barb, he picks her up around noon and they head to the Fairfax-GMU metro station.

"I didn't say much in the farmhouse because I think somebody's bugging it," David says once they are seated on the subway.

"You're kidding. Where do you come up with this stuff?"

"Someone was bugging your hospital room too. I hope you believe me."

"Why should I?" Amanda asks.

David takes some papers out of his backpack.

"I detected the bug at the hospital with computer equipment that's pretty foolproof. But I couldn't tell you about it because right after the accident you were saying anything to anybody. I also thought Kent was doing it, and you'd never believe that. After he died I changed my mind, and now I know for sure it wasn't him cuz I reviewed the search history on his laptop."

"Wait, how did you get the laptop?"

"Don't worry about it. Kent was researching stuff about your dad's job and his cancer patent, stuff like that. I think he stumbled on something, so that's why we're heading to the patent office now."

"So who bugged my room? And what for?"

"I dunno, but I do think it's got something to do with your dad and what he was working on," David whispers as he sizes up the two commuters behind him and those standing in the aisle.

"But what does that have to do with me? I don't know anything about his research, especially now."

"Maybe someone's worried about something you might do, or something you might know. Do you remember anything about your dad's patent, the one he got for the cancer screening stuff?"

"Nope, but I've been having flashbacks about some things."

"Like what?"

"I remember something about my dad's home office and lightning bugs. About four Dorothys like from the Wizard of Oz, except they were all little and one was me. And I remember my little brother Justin. Right, I don't have a brother, I know, I know. But I see myself reading to him. He even played with my car keys. You and everyone else think it's all just a dream, but it's not. It's all vivid, not like a dream at all."

"Played with your car keys? That would mean it was like, in the last year before the crash. I hate to tell you this..."

"David, listen to me. I think NDEs are real. I don't think the flashes are dreams, they're stuff that really happened. Wanna hear something else weird? I remember seeing the doctor drilling into my skull when they were installing my halo."

"What? How can that be?"

"Exactly. I don't think we can explain what happens in NDEs. I know I saw them, like, looking down from above. But how could I know what they were doing or how could I smell them drilling if I was knocked out? I agree with Dr. Lucent. There are just some things we can't explain. Do you think everyone has a soul?"

"I guess I believe in having a soul, but I've never pondered whether it can really leave my body. Or, if it'll exist after I die. Maybe some of that stuff means you're prying memories out of the recesses of your brain or something."

"Do you think I'm crazy? Like about Justin?"

"No. I can't judge anything with what you've been through. Let's switch topics for a second. Here's a copy of the patent your dad got for cancer diagnosis and tumor control techniques. And from what I understand, based on the date and everything, he got that before he even went to work for BBS. Then, I did some research and I found out that he apparently filed for another patent that had to do with something called 'suppression and manipulation of mTOR activity to inhibit or exhibit cell replication.' I have no idea what it means. But when I went to the U.S. patent database, where I found his first patent, there was no reference to this other patent application at all. We need to find out why."

After switching trains at Rosslyn to the blue line, they get off in Alexandria at the King Street stop closest to the patent office, a tall, new, sparkling building of reflective steel and glass. Amanda looks up at the office tower as they approach the entrance, wondering if they're searching for the proverbial needle in a haystack.

Examiner Frankel

After showing their drivers' licenses they get temporary IDs and pass through the metal detector.

"I didn't think about having to show our IDs to get in. Hopefully no one will find us." David says.

"You can't seriously think someone followed us here, do you?"

"Who knows?"

David stops at the first information desk they see inside the cavernous public search room.

"We're looking for a patent examiner."

"Which one?" the information desk assistant asks.

"Arthur Frankel, it says here he's with Art Unit 124."

The assistant looks through a list and says "He's in Building Four, fourth floor, room 433. That's a couple buildings west of here, but you need an appointment."

David looks quizzically at the assistant and over at Amanda.

"Aren't they here every workday? What's it take to get an appointment?"

"Some patent examiners work from their homes part of the week, some don't. I can call and see if he's available." The assistant picks up the phone and dials. After a brief conversation she places the phone back in its cradle.

"You're in luck. He's there and says he can meet you as long as you get over there within the next 15 minutes."

Once they're in the right building and on the appropriate floor, another assistant tells them to head down the hall, make a right and they'll see Room 433. They follow the directions and David taps on the closed door until they hear a voice bark to come in.

Opening the door, they see huge stacks of paper covering a government-issue metal desk and an older fellow with half a head of gray cropped hair and thick reading glasses down at the tip of his nose.

"What can I do for you? You caught me just before my lunch break."

Amanda pipes up. "My dad is Ron Michaels, an inventor. We want to know if he filed any patent applications besides the one we already know about. You were the examiner listed on it."

"Why don't you just ask him if he's your father?" Frankel asks rather brusquely.

"Uh, well, because he died not long ago."

"Well, I see. Sorry about that, I didn't mean to offend you." Frankel offers, softening slightly.

"We wanted to find out what happened to another application that we believe he filed after his first patent was granted. We can't find it listed in the regular patent database," David tells him. He pauses to glance at a piece of paper in his hand, then continues.

"It's titled 'Suppression and Manipulation of mTOR Activity to Inhibit or Exhibit Cell Replication,' and when I did a search I saw it was filed. But it's not in the database. Why is that?" David asks, placing the paper he printed out with the basic application information on Frankel's desk.

Frankel glances at the paper and swivels around in his chair that noticeably squeaks as it turns. He taps several keys on his computer.

"Give me that full inventor name again."

"Ron Michaels, Reston, Virginia."

Frankel scrolls through several screens on his monitor.

"Uh, that application was withdrawn and sealed."

"What does that mean, withdrawn? Does an inventor withdraw it, or who does that?" David asks.

"Uh, it says it was withdrawn under 35 United States Code Section 181."

"I'm sorry, we don't know what or who makes that decision," Amanda says.

"National security. Applications can be sealed for a number of reasons but this was national security. That means even if I could find the application I couldn't give you any information."

"What's that code number again?"

"35 USC 181."

David jots down the numbers on the paper on Frankel's desk.

"Who can have an invention sealed for national security?" David asks.

"I'm not sure," Frankel says. "There's something in the law about which officials can do it, I'm just not familiar with it. But once it's sealed, there's no further public access. That explains why you couldn't find it in the database. Can I do anything else for you?"

"So you still decide if it's a new invention, but the public can't find out?" David asks.

"Well, yeah, it still gets reviewed, but even if it's granted, the public won't know."

Amanda looks at David, crestfallen.

"Wait, but since my dad died, what if the invention gets developed or used?"

"I can't give you any advice on that. You'd have to consult with a patent attorney."

"Wow. Thanks for your, uh, assistance." Amanda says, her voice soaked in sarcasm.

They both walk out of Frankel's office.

Later they are seated on a bench waiting for the subway.

"Now what?" Amanda asks David.

"Well, I think your dad was venturing beyond cancer research. Cell replication also has to do with cell death and cell life. But I don't get how it would affect national security."

Once they grab two seats on the train, David opens his laptop. "Here's the law Frankel was talking about."

> **35 U.S.C. 181--Secrecy of certain inventions, withholding of patent**.
> Whenever publication or disclosure by the publication of an application or by the grant of a patent on an invention in which the Government has a property interest might, in the opinion of the head of the interested Government agency, be detrimental to the national security, the Commissioner of Patents upon being so notified shall order that the invention be kept secret and shall withhold the publication of an application or the grant of a patent therefor under the conditions set forth hereinafter.

David speed-reads through several other provisions that follow.

"It says here that a government official has to renew the request every year."

"Wow, that's pretty spooky. We should talk to my uncle about this, right?"

Foggy Bottom

After they get back on the blue line, Amanda pulls a piece of paper out of her jacket pocket, unfolds it, and looks at the address: *2151 Pennsylvania Avenue, NW, Apartment 3-D, Foggy Bottom stop, blue or orange line*. She folds it back up.

"We're on the blue line, right? I'd like to stop at Foggy Bottom and see a friend of mine. Okay?"

David looks over at her like she is ruining his well-laid plans.

"You know I don't like surprises. Why didn't you mention it before?"

"I wasn't sure I wanted to do it then. It'll only take us 15 minutes."

"What is this sudden mystery stop?"

"She's a potential tutor. I texted her yesterday saying I might stop by sometime in the afternoon once I knew we were going." Amanda leaves a lot out on purpose.

"So, she might not even be there? Is that what you're saying?"

"She said anytime in the afternoon was good."

The escalator carries them to street level, and they head north on 22nd Street, up to Pennsylvania Avenue, then turn right.

They look at the street addresses as they walk. Pennsylvania Avenue is one big study in motion, rushing cars separated by honking yellow taxis, serious-looking people who don't even take time to look to their right or left. Everyone seems to know exactly where they are going, except for the two of them.

"Can it be in that building over there?" David says pointing to the modern office building on the opposite side of the street.

"It's on this side," Amanda says, as they walk past a small Chinese restaurant called Hunan Café. Right next to it is a Thai restaurant called Mehran Restaurant. Amanda sees a partially propped-open door to the left of Mehran Restaurant with "2151" above it.

"This must be it."

They walk in and notice the old-style resident mail slots in the entry with the residents' names organized in rows. Amanda sees "3-D,

Brittney Hayes" and says, "This is her." They look for a button, but there is none.

"I guess we just go up." David says, and they start climbing the dirty stairs, passing a Siamese cat curled up on a ragged welcome mat. "Awww..." Amanda says.

. Once they reach the third floor, they find 3-D and Amanda knocks. No response. After she knocks a second time, the door opens a crack revealing the security chain and a young woman inside. Amanda recognizes her immediately.

"Brittney, hi, it's me, Amanda."

"Okay, hey, come on in." The door closes momentarily as she frees the chain, then the door opens wide, revealing a ramshackle, dirty apartment. As soon as they enter David takes in the clothing, food and other random stuff everywhere. The waif identified as Brittney stands between the door and a stained plaid outdated couch. There's also a guy inside wearing a faded GW hoodie, and he's shaped like a bean pole.

"Oh, this is my friend Jimmy. He was just on his way out."

"Whassup? Just headin' out." Jimmy slowly strides toward the door with a ratty looking backpack slung over one shoulder.

"Catch you later, Britt."

"Have a seat." Brittney says.

Amanda and David both hesitate because the sofa looks so awful.

"You never said goodbye. You left so quickly." Brittney says, sitting in a small chair facing the ratty sofa. David sits on a bar stool by the kitchen counter dividing the small cooking area from the living area.

"I didn't want to stay there any longer than I had to. You did tutor GW students, right?"

"Oh yeah, physics, math, chemistry, and since I double majored at GW, some English too."

"Listen, if you could get to Middleburg, I might want you to tutor me, because I've already missed a lot of school, and I'm not sure I'm going back anytime soon. Could you tutor a high school senior?"

"Sure. I tutored mostly college freshmen, but some high school seniors too," Britt says with a tone that is the opposite of reassuring to David.

"Are you still...uh, using? You look kind of like you haven't slept lately."

Without answering, Brittney ambles over to the messy kitchen. David concludes that Brittney is one of the biggest slobs he has ever encountered. The place looks like it belongs to someone who has decided trashcans are optional.

"That guy Jimmy. Who is he? He isn't a dealer or something is he?" Amanda asks.

"Look, he's a good guy. Occasionally he comes through for me. What about it? It's really not your business."

"Well, it may be if you tutor me. You told me you were over meth. It looks to me like you're not." Brittney looks around, nervously rubbing her left hand across the top of the kitchen counter.

"Look, I can do it. Just tell me when you want me to start. I promise I'll get it together, really." Britt says, tapping her fingers in a pattern on the counter, pinky to index, and then back to pinky again.

"Look, I'll give you a chance, but only if you clean up. I'll call you again in a few days."

"How much would you pay me an hour?"

"I dunno. What do tutors earn?"

"Like $40.00 an hour. How many hours a day would you need help?"

"Well, it depends on if I just need to catch up with what I've missed already, or if I stay out of school awhile longer."

"Look, don't worry. I'll get clean."

David pipes up. "Brittney, why don't you give me Jimmy's phone number. I've got an idea on how to help you. And it'll work."

"What? Who are you exactly?"

"I'm David, I'm one of Amanda's classmates."

Brittney looks down at her cellphone on the counter. She is thinking about it.

"I'll put it this way. If you want to tutor Amanda, give me his number. You won't get the job otherwise." He walks over to her with a pen and piece of paper he's pulled from his backpack.

She recites the phone number for David after scrolling to it on her phone.

"Amanda, we need to get out of here."

"Brittney, I'll get back to you soon. My uncle thinks he may be able to settle my airplane crash case. Get your act together girl, I mean it."

"Wait a second. You're that girl! Hey, you never told me you were her, uh, halo survivor girl..."

"You were high on paxil and who knows what else. And I wasn't looking to make new friends in the psych ward."

"You've really been through some heavy stuff," Britt says, still moving and fidgeting along the kitchen countertop with her fingers.

"I'll get back to you soon, Einstein."

"What?" Britt asks.

"You don't remember telling me you were smarter than Einstein?"

"No, when did I say that? Really? You must be kidding."

"Forget about it. We've gotta go. I'll call you."

They hear the door lock behind them as they walk back into the dingy hall that smells of mildew mixed with musk.

Once they are briskly walking down Pennsylvania Avenue David unloads.

"You've got to be out of your mind! She was in the psych ward with you? You hardly know her. You probably don't even know if she attended GW or was really a tutor."

"Sometimes I just go with my gut. It'll work out, I know it will. What are you going to do with her dealer's phone number?"

The subway doors open at the station and they get in after letting the passengers exit. As soon as they are seated near the doors, David breaks out his laptop, and begins searching. Amanda relaxes, tilting her head back against the vibrating wall of the car, taking in the chatter of several folks talking with each other or on their cell phones. She daydreams about her trip to Paris with Kent. The picture he took of her with the sprinkles from the candied apple.

Just before the metro doors open at the next stop, David snaps the laptop closed and slides it back into his backpack.

"She checks out."

"Who checks out?"

"Brittney, your meth-head tutor. I found a site called tutorme.com and her information is listed there, including her general college education and majors."

"You are one distrustful person, David. Really. A Google search on Brittney?"

"Look, there's a boatload of reasons to be careful when it comes to you. So, yeah, I am careful. Now remember, we visited Air and Space, Natural History, American History Museum and uh, what else?"

Jimmy Bolts

David stops by the farm after school. The smell of fresh pasture grass fills the air, especially since a light rain fell earlier in the morning. David indicates to Amanda that he wants to talk outside the farmhouse, not in it.

"Are you still planning on hiring Brittney?" David asks as they stroll down the pebble driveway.

"Probably. Why?"

"I don't think you have to worry about her getting meth from Jimmy anymore."

"How do you know that?"

"It was pretty simple. He got an anonymous text message."

"David, what did you do?"

David holds up his cell phone and Amanda reads the text message:

Dude, you need to know something. Brittney's a CI for the DEA. You have less than 48 hours to get out of town before the Feds start making arrests.

"You sent that to him? What's a 'CI'?"

"Confidential informant. He's already gone. Told the next-door neighbor he was going to visit a friend on the west coast and he bolted."

There's silence for a little while as they walk. Unseen insects rule the faltering light of day, making incessant sound as dusk falls.

"Are you coming back to M.A? It seems like you've already decided you're not."

"I don't know. You convinced me to begin searching for answers, and that comes first for me. Are you backing out or something?"

"No. I think we're finally making progress. I'll check in with you tomorrow. But how are you going to graduate from M.A. if you just get tutored?"

"Maybe I can take a test on each course if I don't actually go to classes. Uncle Andy'll find out. I don't know why he's still paying for a rent-a-cop to hang out on the porch day and night."

"Because he wants you protected, and I think it's a good idea. Somebody's watching you, it's just a matter of who and why. See ya later," David says as he walks toward his car.

Personal Effects

Before blowing off half a day of work on his portfolio of cases, Andy decided to organize his side mission to pack as much in as possible. Myra arranged an appointment for him to meet with the CEO of Biological Blood Services. He also has an appointment scheduled with Dr. Sid Vance, a respected professor at the Georgetown Cellular Biology and Biotechnology Department – one of his late brother's favorite professors. In the latter meeting he is hoping to pick up some illuminating information; in the former he is hoping to pick up Ron's actual belongings.

Because Andy has never been to BBS, he pulled up an online map to figure out exactly where the place was. Cabin John, Maryland. Hmm. Straight up Canal Road to McArthur Boulevard, bingo.

The security guard at the gate confirms he is an approved visitor and waves him through. Andy navigates the large employee lot, parking close to the modern, three-story building with the small tasteful sign that says "Biological Blood Services." He walks through the automatic double doors and toward the receptionist.

"I have a 2:00 appointment with Mr. Jacoby. My name is Andy Michaels."

"Oh, yes. I have you down here Mr. Michaels. It will just be a minute."

Several magazines are neatly stacked on the modern smoked-glass reception table. There are two low-rise leather couches and several chairs. No one else is in the waiting area.

"I'll buzz you through now and Mr. Jacoby will meet you once you enter."

Andy hears a buzzer as he nears the entry door.

"Andy, it's good to see you again. I met you at Ron's funeral."

"Yes, I remember, and I appreciate you meeting with me today."

"We're in this conference room. I brought Ms. Hendrickson from HR with me to go over Ron's benefits with you." Andy notices that she has an accordion-style file of materials.

"All the materials are in here," she says. "Your late brother did have the right to continue a COBRA health insurance plan, for his daughter I mean. He also had an accidental death benefit that we provide to the employees at no cost. These papers show his beneficiaries."

Then Ms. Hendrickson leans down beside the table and lifts up a large mesh bag. "These are the pictures and other personal belongings from his office. I'm sure you'll want these."

Andy looks at both of them, but doesn't ask any questions. There is an awkward silence.

Then, Jacoby says, "Do you have any other questions for Ms. Hendrickson?"

"No, but I'd like to look at Ron's office if that's okay."

"Ms. Hendrickson, I think that completes the HR side of things. I'm going to speak with Mr. Michaels for a few moments."

"Nice to meet you Mr. Michaels, and my condolences to you," Ms. Hendrickson says as she leaves the room and softly closes the door behind her.

"I know this sounds funny, Andy, but we can't let you look at his workspace. Some of the work we do is classified and requires a security clearance. I'm sure you understand, being an attorney. Andy, your brother was a great guy. I'm so sorry about what happened. But you have to understand my hands are tied here."

"Alright then. Thanks anyway," Andy says cryptically, reaching down for the bag of his brother's belongings. He quickly exits the conference room.

"I'm really sorry I can't do more for you..." Jacoby calls after him, but Andy keeps walking, because sometimes it's just better to say nothing at all.

Telomeres

After stopping to get a latte Andy makes his way to the Cellular Biology and Biotechnology Center at Georgetown University and finds a parking spot. A few minutes later he is knocking on an office door on the third floor of the building. Professor Sid Vance opens the door and greets Andy.

"Thanks so much for meeting with me. Ron talked about you a lot, and I was there when you presented him the Graduate Student Biology Award. I took a picture of you and Ron that day. Coincidentally, just today I picked up that same picture from BBS."

"I'm so sorry about your brother, and your other family members too. I have to say, Ron was one of my all-time favorite students. I'm not exaggerating when I say he was a genius. I've never had a grad student develop a new technique, get a patent, and see it go into use. On a significant cancer detection technique to boot."

Andy looks at the silver-haired man and his tortoise-shell glasses. He figures Vance is probably 65 years old, give or take a few years. Andy takes in some of the office surrounding him. Books of every nature involving cellular biology and biogenetics. Journal articles stacked up all over the desk, some folded open. Typical clutter for a serious scientist.

"I'm really here to find out what Ron's work was most focused on. I take it you're familiar with BBS."

"A number of our grad students are working there," Vance says with a knowing smile.

"Anyway, I met with the CEO, Mike Jacoby. Nice guy, treated me fine. But he refused to show me where Ron worked because some of the research they do is classified."

"Surely you're not surprised by that, are you?"

"Actually I am. He never told me he even got a security clearance, which is weird. I'm his brother and we had no secrets – or so I thought."

"Well Andy, it's no secret that your brother developed biological technology that allowed medical doctors or scientists to analyze cancer cells in a sample of blood. That technology helped predict tumor growth and doubling times."

"Wait. I was hoping you'd explain some of this heavy-duty biology because I don't understand any of it. Would you be willing to take baby steps with me? I'm a lawyer, not a biologist."

"Okay. Let's see. You have to at least understand some basics about DNA, telomeres and telomerase. Each cell has a nucleus with chromosomes that package all the genetic information."

Vance stands up and points to a small color poster on the wall nearby, showing several strands of what looks like a DNA double helix. He is now pointing with his pen at a colorful strand of chromosomes. Hey, Andy thinks, I remember this from high school biology. But Dr. Vance is just getting started.

"Each base has a pair with all the instructions needed to form our entire body structure. But in order to grow and age, our bodies have to duplicate their cells. Is this too heavy for you?" Vance asks.

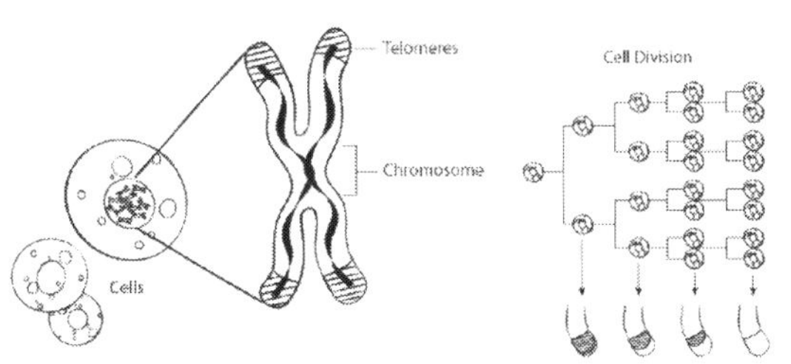

"My brain's turning to jelly, but go ahead."

"So in cell division, every chromosome that is passed along has a special ending or cap which is called a telomere. It's like the plastic tip on the end of a shoelace. But what controls the telomere tips is an enzyme called telomerase. A ton of biological research is being done on the role of telomerase enzymes." Vance again points to the poster on the wall showing cell division.

"Every time a cell divides, some of the telomere is lost. But telomere ends can have loss or addition. The loss during every normal cell division is an erosion, like reducing a wick. But telomerase enzymes can actually add to the telomere tip. It can add more available cell division sequences. We now know that fetal tissue has telomerase. Germ cells have it too. Sounds simple but we don't know how to add telomerase to the telomeres to provide longer cell life." Vance pauses for a second. "Are you still with me?"

"Barely."

"Telomerase is the enzyme that can rewind or speed up a cell's clock. And there's a fine line between uncontrolled abnormal cell replication that happens in cancer cells versus wanting to have cells replicate."

Vance finally sits down, quite satisfied with his lecture.

"Wait a second," Andy says. "Did I hear you say that telomerase can make regular cells last longer? That's where you lost me."

"Look, your brother and hundreds, maybe thousands of researchers worldwide not only want to make telomerase somehow shut down bad cancer cell reproduction, which could potentially cure cancer, but they're also studying how telomerase can replenish DNA sequences in the chromosome end cap – the telomere – so that more cell replications can occur without cell death."

"So, in cancer cells the abnormal cells just go crazy and keep dividing?"

"Well, cancer cells are damaged at the telomere and that damaged pattern divides into tumors. So yes, and telomerase plays an active role in that, but we can't control its impact on telomeres yet, we just know it's there."

"If biologists could control telomeres in healthy cells, what would that do?" Andy asks, still seated in the old wooden chair in front of Vance's desk.

"He who tames the telomere tames cell death. The implications are immense. The cycle of cell aging could be manipulated. It may also help us understand why cancer cells go crazy." Vance then adds matter-of-factly, "But there are big risks once we manipulate the telomeres."

"Why?"

"Telomerase manipulation could inadvertently cause a future cancer in the manipulated cells. We don't know."

"Switch gears a second. Can you tell me what you know about rapamycin and mTOR?"

"Ah...I thought you said you knew nothing about biology? Rapamycin is an interesting macrolide derived from a bacterium."

"I really don't know biology, but it's something Ron talked to me about." Andy is stretching the truth a bit, but figures it may extract more important information from Vance, making his little white lie worthwhile.

"There's lots of cellular biology going on involving rapamycin. It makes a defensive chemical with some interesting properties. The TOR just stands for 'target of rapamycin' and the M stands for 'in mammals.' There were a bunch of recent studies of mice that showed when the mTOR in cells was manipulated, the mice lived 15 percent longer than the non-treated mice. Another study showed that the life cycle of mice was increased by a third with mTOR, when the rapamycin was transfused into the blood plasma."

"How recently has rapamycin been tested on mice, like the last few months, a decade ago, or what?"

"I know it was discovered several decades ago but the studies relating to extension of mice lifespan are fairly recent. It has caused a lot of excitement. Kind of like cord blood. Ron began studying that too when he was still in my classes."

"What's cord blood?"

"Umbilical cord blood. It's full of stem cells. They were simply discarding much of it at the neonatal hospital next door. Your brother arranged to get cord blood they were tossing out."

"I don't get the connection."

"Cord blood is loaded with stem cells. Super cells. The DNA in stem cells can form every part of us," Vance says, pointing first to his chest, his left arm and then his head.

"Dr. Vance, you have really been gracious. Thanks for meeting me. I may come see you again, would that be okay?"

"Sure, no problem."

Andy has a lot to think about.

Self-addressed

Myra drops the overnight box on Andy's desk, just like many other packages they receive several times per week. He checks the return address and finds it's his own. Odd. Opening it, he reaches inside and finds a small knapsack. Inside the bag is an unsealed envelope addressed to no one, and he quickly unfolds the paper inside.

> ***Dear Uncle Andy and Aunt Barbara:***
>
> ***If you're reading this it means I'm gone. I want you to understand that so many things have happened that no matter what I do, I can't understand them. I thought everything would be okay until Kent died. That left me with no more hope. I don't know if this is legal, but I want everything to go to Justin and tell him I love him and I love you guys too.***
>
> ***All my love,***
> ***Amanda***

Tears well up in Andy's eyes. He finds the hand necklace also inside the envelope. Was this left by Amanda at the B&O trestle?

Andy places the note in a small folder and puts it in his one desk drawer that has a lock, where he keeps important personal papers. He puts the necklace in a separate envelope and places it in his pocket. Picking up the overnight pack, he studies the return address again. He never knew Amanda had any personal belongings at the trestle, and he had been wondering if and when any railroad representatives might learn of his niece's identity and come calling. Surveying the backpack from all sides, he locates no identifying label or name anywhere.

How did someone know to send this to me? Andy wonders.

First Mediation

The video interview of the mother describing her daughter Lauren is playing on a large monitor at the end of the conference room. Next to Andy, Mrs. Richmond has her head down and is dabbing her eyes with Kleenex. Beside her sits her husband. Angie sits in a chair behind Andy, providing him support if materials are needed. On the opposite side of the table sits Franklin and two representatives from the airline. And at the head of the table is Mediator Harris, the retired D.C. judge.

At the very end of the emotional presentation is a picture of the Richmond family at Lauren's college graduation, and superimposed along the left side of the screen are the damages they are claiming.

"As you know, we've submitted our settlement demand, and we're here in good faith, ready to resolve this case. Does anyone have any questions?" Andy asks.

Judge Harris looks around with raised eyebrows and repeats, "Any questions?"

Franklin shakes his head.

The judge continues. "I spoke with the airline's representatives before we started, and they are not going to make any opening remarks. We really appreciate your presentation, and Mr. and Mrs. Richmond, I want you to know we're so sorry for your loss. My job today will be to bring the parties together in a settlement. We're going to split up into separate conference rooms, and I'm going to discuss matters with the airline representatives first." The judge stands and motions to the defense side of the table, and they walk out, closing the door behind them.

"Is this how these are always done?" Mrs. Richmond asks Andy.

"Pretty much, yes. After opening statements we both camp out in separate conference rooms and the mediator shuttles back and forth."

After a couple of hours of conveying offers and demands and prodding each side, the mediator returns to Andy's conference room one last time.

"They're saying this is their line in the sand. Why don't you guys talk about it," he says pointing to the number on his notepad, "and I'll be out in the hall. Let me know if we're going to get this settled."

The mediator leaves the room. Andy has written down the number on his notepad and circled it.

"Well, it looks like their top number is $4.3 million."

"I thought you said we wouldn't accept less than $4.5 million," Mr. Richmond replies.

"That's the number I wanted to get for your family. However the question is whether you want the bird in the hand, so to speak, or you want to fight them. Based on my experience this is a significant wrongful death settlement offer. Obviously no amount of money will bring her back or take the pain away."

Mr. Richmond leans over and gently rubs his wife's back in a reassuring way. It's clear that she is going to make the decision. "I don't think I could handle this type of sorrow for weeks and months. Let's take it and move on."

"We'll take it," Mr. Richmond repeats.

Andy privately thinks to himself that he has never had a major case where the settlement came so early and so easily. He quickly realizes the chances are good that every case will indeed settle, then wonders why.

Family Matters

Both Michaels' cases are scheduled for the final day of mediation. Andy visited Amanda at the farm days earlier and explained that she needed to attend. Amanda refused. She told Andy that she would approve the settlement of her own case as long as he and Aunt Barbara approved how she wanted some of the money divided.

"You're also in charge of your parent's case. You need to be there to authorize any settlement." Andy explained.

"Uncle Andy, I trust you. Just get what you think is the best settlement for my parents. The main thing is I want you to get the details worked out with regard to my own case," Amanda told him, and he shuddered to think about working some of those details out.

"Are you going to approve the structured settlement and annuity to cover you for your lifetime, the one I outlined to you?"

"That's fine. Just know that I won't approve anything unless you get the papers for me to sign on my plan. I want all the papers at one time. Can you do that?"

"I don't know yet, but I can try."

Andy and Angie had spent a significant amount of time reviewing the details of Ron and Rochelle's presentation. Andy insisted that he was not going to do a video interview or have any of the family members do one, even though they had done them on every other client. Instead, he and Angie opted for a printed slide show and provided it to Franklin and the insurance representatives of the airline two days before the mediation.

They had decided to seek $7 million each on Ron and Rochelle's death cases and $13 million for Amanda.

When they convene at 2:00 p.m. on Friday afternoon, Franklin immediately asks where Amanda is. Andy replies that she has given him full authority to resolve her and her parents' cases with written powers of attorney. Mediator Harris had been told before the session about the POAs.

"Let's split up and I'll talk with Mr. Franklin's group first," Judge Harris says.

After his usual shuttle diplomacy, Judge Harris returns to the conference room occupied only by Andy and Angie.

"There's no reason for me to hold back anything from you. Their authority doesn't go above $5 million on your brother and sister-in-law's cases. They're offering the entire $5 million on each if you agree to settle below $10 million on Amanda."

"How far below $10 million?" Andy asks.

"I think the highest they'll pay is around $8 million."

Andy turns his chair around and confers with Angie. He then swivels back toward Harris.

"Tell them $8.5 million for Amanda and we're willing to take $5 million each on the other cases."

"Okay let's see if we can get this done."

A few minutes later the judge re-enters the conference room with Franklin.

"Andy, if you accept $8.3 million on your niece's case we'll have a deal." Harris says.

"Alright, we'll make the deal at $8.3 million on Amanda's case and $5 million each on the others."

"Fine. Judge Harris, can you write up summary settlement outlines for us?" Franklin asks.

The judge sits down to complete the settlement forms. Moments later both Franklin and Andy sign and the mediations are over.

As Andy walks to the parking garage with Angie he calls Amanda.

"Just wanted you to know that we settled your case for $8.3 million just now. Also, we settled your parents' cases for $5 million each. I have already talked to a structured settlement broker, and I'll start going through all of the paperwork and getting this done for you. I usually say congratulations, but this time it just seems inappropriate. We still have to have the judge approve your parents' cases because they're wrongful death settlements."

"Does the settlement of my case have to go to court too?" Amanda asks.

"No, you just have to sign the release papers." Andy says as he and Angie approach his Mini Cooper.

"Good. I can't wait to get this over with." Amanda says before they end their call.

Andy and Angie both drop their materials into his backseat.

"Angie, thanks for working your tail off. We still have a fair amount of organizational work to get each case approved, but we've crested the mountaintop."

"I feel like a boulder has been lifted off my shoulders, for sure," she replies.

No Rubberstamps

The first wrongful death settlement hearing before Judge Easton has been set for 10:00 a.m. The court received notice of the hearing about seven days beforehand, and both Andy Michaels and Paul Franklin submitted an agreed recitation of background information in support of a proposed order approving the wrongful death settlement for the Richmond family estate. Judge Easton scans over the proposed order. It's 9:45 a.m.

Just then the judge hears the buzzer at her chambers door. She looks at the monitor that shows a view of the hallway just outside her chambers. It's Tina, Judge Easton realizes, from the clerk's office. Someone on her staff hits the door release and Tina brings in an envelope. Judge Easton pushes the button on her speakerphone for her secretary, Martha.

"Martha, does that pertain to the 10:00 Hemispheres hearing, or is it something else?"

Martha looks down at the sealed business-size envelope. There is no return address. It says "Personal and confidential, to be opened by Judge Easton only."

"It's for you and it says personal and confidential, Judge. I don't know if it's on this case or not, but I'll bring it in." Martha delivers the envelope, and Judge Easton uses her letter opener to slice it open and reads the one-page typed letter inside:

> *Judge Easton:*
> *The settlement being proposed is a complete fraud. Hemispheres is not really paying the money. The U.S. Government is paying and trying to keep it quiet. The government doesn't want anyone to know the truth about the crash. Don't fall for it. Get the truth to the public. They deserve to know.*
> *--Anonymous*

Judge Easton doesn't know what to make of the note. She folds it up and puts it back in the envelope. Right away, she buzzes Tina in the clerk's office.

"Tina, this is Judge Easton. Who delivered this envelope that you just brought up to my chambers? Don't you have a log of some kind?"

"I think it was brought in with a few other letters from Wilkerson Courier Service. But without looking at surveillance video I couldn't be sure. How much homework do you want me to do?"

"Just check with Wilkerson and see if there was anything delivered on the wrongful death settlement on the docket for 10:00 a.m. this morning. Buzz me back as soon as you speak with them. I would like to know before I take the bench."

A few minutes later, Tina buzzes Judge Easton's chambers. Martha patches her through.

"I checked with Wilkerson and they didn't have any delivery for your chambers, so I don't know how it was mixed in with their materials. Sorry I don't know more. Can I do anything else on this?"

"No, thanks," the judge replies.

At 10:00 a.m. sharp Judge Easton takes the bench, and her bailiff handles the usual introductions. Andy Michaels, Angie, and the Richmonds sit on one side of the courtroom. Paul Franklin, one of his paralegals, and a Hemispheres company representative are on the other side.

Franklin approaches the lectern and explains to Judge Easton that Hemispheres has negotiated the settlement through mediation, that Hemispheres believes the settlement is fair and appropriate, and that he has cooperated with Andy Michaels in presenting a wrongful death settlement order by consent of all parties.

Next, Andy requests leave of the bailiff to present Mr. Richmond to explain whether he accepts the settlement on behalf of the estate of his late daughter. On examination from Andy, Mr. Richmond confirms that he is in favor of the settlement, believes that it is in the best interest of the estate, and would like it to be approved. Andy then turns to Judge Easton and asks if she has any questions.

"I do. Mr. Richmond, do you know, under the terms of this settlement, why Hemispheres is paying the sum you have settled for?"

Andy looks over at Franklin quizzically. Then he looks back toward the bench. Certainly a surprising line of questioning to both of them.

"Well, Judge, I guess because they know that their jet crashed and they believe there was some mechanical defect, uh, and therefore they ought to pay. That's what I think." Mr. Richmond responds.

"What I mean is do you know any specific details of why Hemispheres may be liable to your family?" she asks more pointedly.

At this point Andy tries to interject. "Judge Easton, Hemispheres has not even admitted liability in any way in the proposed settlement order so I don't know..."

The judge cuts him off. "Mr. Michaels, let me ask the questions, okay? You're asking me to approve this deal and I want to know. So, neither your lawyer nor the Hemispheres' lawyers have told you why you're being paid the settlement money?"

"Well, our family thinks they're responsible."

The judge then tells the attorneys she has no further questions. "Anything else counsel?" Both Michaels and Franklin shake their heads.

"Counsel, I'm not approving this settlement today. I'm going to take it under advisement."

Franklin finally can't contain himself any longer.

"Your Honor, both of the parties have requested entry of the order, and you just heard Mr. Richmond say that he believes the settlement is reasonable and fair. We don't understand why--..."

"Mr. Franklin, if your side wants to provide more information so the public understands why Hemispheres is so gung-ho on settling all of these cases now, including an admission of liability or explanation of responsibility, I assure you I will sign the order. Until that happens, I'm taking this order under advisement. Is there anything else counsel?"

Franklin, still standing at the attorney lectern turns and looks quizzically at Andy. He then turns back and grudgingly says, "Nothing further, Your Honor."

At least five reporters were in the courtroom and they rush out to file their stories about Judge Easton refusing to enter the first wrongful death settlement order in the Hemispheres crash, despite both parties asking her to approve the deal.

Within an hour CNT is reporting on the hearing.

> "This is Natalee Spalding, reporting for CNT about the resolution of wrongful death settlements in the Hemispheres Airlines crash. Today Judge Easton was scheduled to enter and approve the wrongful death settlement on behalf of victims of the Quarryville Pennsylvania crash, which had only one survivor, Amanda Michaels. However, the judge would

not enter the first settlement order in the case, which would have paid $4.3 million to the Richmond family. The judge simply refused and requested Hemispheres to file additional documents with an admission of liability or some explanation of the cause of the crash. The attorneys have already advised CNT that a number of other cases have been settled but all of the agreements may be stalled. We have our legal analyst Jeff Rossman with us today to help explain this situation. Jeff?"

"Yes, Natalee. It is unusual, but not totally unprecedented. The public might ask if Hemispheres and the victims' families have agreed to settle the cases, why the Judge would refuse. It is rare for a judge to turn down an agreed settlement order where the parties are each in favor. However, in high profile cases involving the public interest or public safety, judges have required some companies to file an admission of liability or to disclose the basis of their responsibility. Is this required in civil wrongful death law? No. The statute involving a wrongful death settlement simply requires that a court review and approve any such agreement. So, it's somewhat of a gray area as to how far a judge can push this."

"Can she force Hemispheres to explain what happened or why?"

"If they want approval, perhaps. To date, Hemispheres has never explained the cause of the crash, and the NTSB has never gone further than the fact that there was an electrical or mechanical malfunction that downed the aircraft. Sometimes judges surprise everyone and this is one of those circumstances."

Outside the courtroom, the Richmond family members are crowded around Andy and Angie. He does his best to explain what he cannot answer. A few minutes later, he and Angie are on the street outside D.C. Superior Court.

"Andy, what's going on? How can she do that?"

"Don't ask me. If I knew, I would have gotten her to enter the order. I don't know who's freaking out worse, us or Franklin and Hemispheres. I certainly want to get the cases closed just like everybody else, but Hemispheres must be having a heart attack. I don't know if she can force them to give an admission of responsibility or tell what they know. I've never had a judge do this."

"I feel so bad for the Richmonds. What happens now?"

"I have no idea. Hemispheres could actually appeal, but I don't think they will. We can do some legal research on it, and I'm sure Hemispheres will be looking into it twice as hard us. Tomorrow's another day — maybe the judge will buckle under the media scrutiny. The families will all start freaking out if she delays the settlements for too long."

Detained

Just before Ryan finishes parallel parking his car in front of his condo, his phone vibrates, indicating a new text message. It's from Franklin: *Job well done. She refused to approve any settlements.*

Ryan stares over his steering wheel with a sick feeling in the pit of his stomach. The same bad feeling he felt during at least two SEAL missions, when unforeseen complications later arose. Why did he go along with Franklin on this? Franklin's motive was strictly money. Ryan rationalizes that he agreed because his own reasons weren't misguided: the public deserved to know the truth.

A car pulls in right behind him on the street. Before he can exit his car a man is standing beside his door, and a woman is standing on the sidewalk. The man motions for him to roll down the window. He retracts it a few inches.

"What can I do for you?" Ryan asks.

The man flips open his badge.

"Josh Miller. FBI."

"What the hell? And she's with you too?"

"Yes. Mr. Ryan we'd like to talk with you at FBI headquarters," the agent says.

"Do I have a choice?" Ryan asks.

"Look, we know who you are, and we know a lot about you. I strongly suggest you come with us so we can do this the easy way. We're going to treat you fairly, we know your background."

Ryan wonders what they know. Hemispheres and the monetary payments? The note? What else?

Ryan gets out of the car and hits the door lock. "Mind telling me what you want to talk about?"

"Let's wait 'til we get to headquarters." Miller says.

Once they are inside a conference room the female agent starts. "You've been eavesdropping on Michaels' law firm and rifling through their trash. Why?"

Ryan isn't sure what else they know. He momentarily pauses, processing information. "I didn't break the law. You know that I do private investigation work. So what?"

"Look, we know Franklin hired you. What does he want to know? All the cases are settling."

Ryan knows she's fishing at this point, and he wants to be very careful.

"I can't tell you what it is he's after because I don't know. I also don't know why you brought me down here."

"Well, it's not legal to bug a law firm or to bug Amanda Michaels, is it, Ryan?"

Ryan looks quizzically at her. "What the hell are you talking about? I haven't bugged them."

"I don't believe you. We think that a professional like yourself planted the listening devices."

"If that's why you brought me down here, you're wasting your time."

The female agent paces back and forth, unsure of her next move.

"Is this about the Hemispheres money?" Ryan teases them.

"What are you talking about?" she asks him, without offering anything.

"Hemispheres is paying a whole lot of money, and it's mighty early in the litigation to cave in."

The female agent becomes agitated. "Look, I have a lot of respect for you. You know who the good guys are and who the bad guys are. And I know what happened to your comrades in Afghanistan."

"Who the hell are you to start some psychological profiling crap to try to influence me? Don't you even dare."

"Don't play with fire Ryan. Some things are best left where they are. You better be telling the truth about the bugs. Because I don't believe you."

"I'm not here to impress or convince you," Ryan says, standing up and taking a step or two toward the conference room door. Both of the agents stare at each other while Ryan nears the door.

"Did you write the note, Ryan?" the female agent shouts.

Ryan wheels around. He thinks she's bluffing. She must not have the goods on him. But Ryan knows it wasn't a crime even if she does know.

"What note?" he asks coyly.

"Don't play with us, Ryan. Keep your nose out of this."

"I take it I'm free to go?"

Hearing no answer, he decides to find his own ride home.

The next morning, Ryan vanishes. His girlfriend reports him missing that evening. She provides the police a key and access to his apartment, where everything seems in order.

@Part VI
Judicial Advice

By midafternoon on the same day of the Hemispheres hearing, Judge Easton has called Judge Bondakopf and invited her to meet for dinner. Bondakopf drops her other plans and agrees to meet her at One Fish, a posh restaurant on Wisconsin Avenue in Georgetown. Because parking will be tough in Georgetown, Bondakopf leaves Alexandria at 5:30, takes the route of least resistance over to the Key Bridge, crosses into Georgetown and finds a private attended parking lot about a block away.

Despite what the public considers a fairly high profile, federal district judges have no regular protection – not even one serving on the secret FISA court. About a block from the parking lot, as she is walking along Wisconsin at M Street, a man walks up beside her. He is in a black full-length trench coat.

"Judge Bondakopf, I'm an FBI agent and I'd like to talk to you a moment." He produces his badge and credentials for her as they continue walking.

"What's this about? How do you know my name or that I would be here at all?"

"I'm not at liberty to answer that, Judge. However, my boss wants to speak with you on a secure cell phone. Agent Solarez, he says you know him?"

The judge stops. Several other pedestrians walking along Wisconsin pass by as she glares at the agent.

"Yes, I know Agent Solarez."

The agent taps in a phone number. "Yes, sir, I'm going to pass the judge the phone now."

"Judge Bondakopf. Agent Solarez here. I'm sorry to have interrupted you this way, but we understand you're going to meet Judge Easton for dinner and..."

"How did you know that?"

"Judge, I don't think that's relevant to what I'm gonna tell you. Judge Easton received a note at her office today before the Hemispheres wrongful death settlement hearing. Someone has suggested to her that the United States paid over $100 million to Hemispheres to help create the settlement fund."

"Is that true?"

"Doesn't matter if it's true or not. But if leaked, this could have devastating consequences on our outstanding operation. You personally know there are national security issues involved with this Hemispheres situation."

"I have no information that the U.S. has paid anything. Are you suggesting that I would give Judge Easton my input involving secret information?"

"No, but she's a friend of yours. She might look to you for guidance. Your recommendation against disclosing such baseless information would be helpful to us."

"I'll tell you what. Let me see what she wants to tell me, and then, well, we know how to find each other, don't we?"

She shoves the phone back to the agent beside her and begins walking again toward the restaurant.

After the judges both receive their drinks, Judge Easton produces an envelope from her purse.

"So, this morning, 15 minutes before the Hemispheres hearing, a courier drops an envelope at my chambers. It's marked personal and confidential, addressed to me. No return address and we can't locate who delivered it. Have a look," Easton says, unfolding the page and placing it in front of Lisa.

Lisa reads the note carefully, folds it back in half and hands it back.

"So that's why you wouldn't approve the deal today."

"Precisely. I've never rejected a death settlement before. But with this bombshell, I refused. That's why I wanted to meet you tonight." Easton says.

"Do you know what kind of monster media storm is going on over your refusal to approve the deal today? It's been on CNT continuously, with various legal analysts all giving their two cents."

"Tell me about it. My law clerks told me it was on Twitter two minutes after I left the bench. Well, do you think I can force Hemispheres to explain a basis for their responsibility? I mean, even if there was no $100 million paid by the government, can I force them to explain to the public why they are settling?"

"Just on the legal issue, I don't know that there's any law that governs whether you can demand an admission of responsibility or not. I mean, making them give a declaration or statement of responsibility seems shaky, but, no, I haven't ever researched it." Bondakopf takes a sip of wine.

"After the hearing, I had my law clerk all over it. There's very little on it. But if it's true that the government paid a huge chunk of the settlement fund without any formal disclosure, that's something the public ought to know. Taxpayer money, right? I don't know what to make of the note or who wanted to blow the whistle." Easton says.

"Hemispheres may refuse. And all those families are probably irate because Michaels made a deal and they want closure. It's certainly a difficult situation."

"If the U.S. paid that money, the public has a right to know. It would mean there's a lot more to this crash than anybody knows. And the tiny bit of information that I had before," Easton says, winking one eye at Bondakopf, "makes me believe what's in the note."

"If you simply back off the demand that Hemispheres give an explanation of their responsibility you will look like you have no backbone," Bondakopf says. "Sometimes just delaying a decision makes you look more brilliant, and maybe just 24 or 48 hours of letting things pan out might be good. I wouldn't disclose any information about what was in the note, though. No reason to. Let them wonder what you're up to."

"I don't want to make those families wait too long. But I don't think a day or two'll hurt." Easton says, taking a long sip of her drink.

Further Reflection

The hallways of the courthouse are typically empty in the afternoons. Martha looks up at the video monitor and notices Judge Bondakopf approaching the door of Judge Easton's chambers. She immediately buzzes her in.

"Good afternoon Martha. Is the judge in?"

"Sure, just one second please." She presses the speaker button. "Judge Bondakopf is here to see you, can she come on back?"

"Sure, send her in," Judge Easton responds through the speakerphone.

"Didn't expect you to come by today. I hope you have some ideas for me." The judge sits down in one of the two client chairs in front of the large desk.

"I've checked on some things, let me put it that way." Bondakopf says. She then lowers her voice into a whisper.

"Here's my idea for you. Reconvene the attorneys and tell them you would like to see both of them in your chambers. Yes, the media will go crazy. So what? Tell counsel you're prepared to approve the deal, but that Hemispheres is going to have to at least reference something in the settlement agreement about the crash being caused by some kind of mechanical or electrical failure. It can be vague. That way, you don't look like you caved. You'll get the admission that you demanded, and Michaels and Franklin and their clients will get what they want."

"But what about the money? What about the hundred million?" Easton asks her.

"It's unsubstantiated. The public doesn't know anything about it and you don't know if there's even a shred of truth to it. You can't go out on a limb on that."

"I think I like it. Thanks."

And that is exactly what Judge Easton did. The next day, the parties reconvened at 3:00 p.m. in her courtroom, and every reporter that had been covering the Hemispheres story was there. Just after court was called to order, Judge Easton asked to see the attorneys in her chambers for some preliminary discussions.

Once in her chambers, Easton scans over the draft settlement agreement—the one previously proposed. There was no admission of liability.

"Gentlemen I've decided that there may be a way we can compromise and move forward here. Mr. Franklin, I want Hemispheres to include a reference in this agreement to an electrical or mechanical cause of the crash. Do you think that's something you can get authority to include?" Franklin looks down at his copy of the settlement agreement, thinking things through.

"What about the explicit admission of liability that you insisted on at the prior hearing?"

"I may be willing to back off from that requirement. Perhaps some language like 'in consideration of the mechanical or electrical blah, blah the parties enter this agreement,' so maybe not the complete admission, but something to serve as the basis of why you entered into the settlement with Mr. Michaels' clients and the other estates. Why don't you go talk with your client?"

With that, Franklin exits her chambers, avoiding eye contact with her or Michaels, his jaw clenched in anger. For a split second he contemplates faking the call to Hemispheres, and advising Easton the offer was rejected. No way, he instantly decides. It will be reported by the media mere seconds after the hearing, his client would go bonkers, his career would be over. Damn, she boxed me in, he concludes. He finds a quiet place down the back hallway and calls Andrews, the CFO.

A few minutes later Franklin returns and asks to speak with Andy Michaels. They discuss the settlement agreement and hammer out the additional section requested by the judge. Once they arrive at a satisfactory version, they present it to Judge Easton.

"This is fine. Why don't you both return to the courtroom. As soon as I have this agreement retyped I will bring it out and have you look it over before I approve it." The attorneys begin to leave her chambers.

"Oh, and counsel, one more thing. When you comment to the media, I expect you to explain that our brief meeting in chambers allowed us to hammer out this agreement, as they will not be happy it occurred in chambers. Do you understand?"

Michaels and Franklin both nod and walk out the door.

Fifteen minutes later, the order is signed and the attorneys – and reporters – empty into the main hall. Several reporters clamber for a copy of the settlement agreement, but are advised the clerk's office will have copies in 30 minutes. Andy tells several reporters only that his clients are "satisfied with the settlement terms."

Newbie

Andy pushes the ignition button, turning off the car. With both his hands still lightly resting on the steering wheel, he turns to Amanda.

"You're 100 percent sure about this?"

"Never been more sure. He doesn't know it was me, right?"

"Correct. An LLC is the buyer and we gave instructions to the realtor to disclose nothing else about the purchaser. You'll be the one telling him."

"Great. Let's go."

They both get out of Andy's car, and he finds the law firm name on the directory once they enter the lobby. They are led into the main conference room of the Reston law firm where several people are sitting.

Amanda presumes a couple of them are real estate agents. One must be the real estate lawyer? Aunt Barbara is there too. After the real estate closing lawyer introduces everybody, Amanda interrupts.

"Where's Kyle Perless?"

The realtor says, "He gave power of attorney to Mr. Regentson, so he won't be attending."

"Really? I thought since he was the seller he had to be here," Amanda says, turning to Andy, bewildered.

"It's the seller's prerogative," Andy confirms.

"Well...okay. I want to go see him right after this."

Andy nods. The real estate attorney hands a stack of papers to Andy and Amanda to start signing.

"You'll see little flags in all the places that Ms. Michaels needs to sign. Feel free to ask me if you have any questions."

Andy starts looking through pages and makes a few comments about them to Amanda.

"See, the purchaser name is Broken Halo, LLC. You need to start signing where indicated."

After signing what seems to be a mountain of paper, Amanda asks Andy, "Where's the papers about Café Loco and his condo?"

Andy locates the papers relating to the payoff and wire transfers.

Once she has finished signing, the others stand, smile and congratulate her. Several shake Amanda's hand before walking from the room.

Andy, Barbara, and Amanda are the only ones left.

"Alright, we've taken care of that. Now I need you to sign the release papers relating to your own settlement," Andy says.

He takes out another folder and shows her the formal release outlining the settlement provisions of her case. Two million dollars will be placed in investment accounts. There will be additional papers relating to the balance of the monies, placed in a structured settlement, which will pay out the millions of dollars in proceeds into timed installment payments in the future.

"This structured settlement approach is a very smart move for your future, given you're only 18." Andy says.

"It'll help assure your college education expenses are covered," Barb says, reaching over and touching Amanda's arm for reassurance. Amanda tries not to cringe, but she hasn't been happy with Barbara since her psych ward stay.

"We hope what you're doing with regard to Mr. Perless is the right thing." Andy says.

"No one can tell me it's not."

Amanda finishes signing all the settlement papers.

"The next important question is, are you coming back to our house?" Barbara asks with a concerned glance toward Andy as they stand in the lobby.

"It's not that I don't appreciate everything, I just want to live on the farm. I hope you understand."

"But you have to finish your senior year at M.A. and then hopefully go to college. You don't have any experience working on or running a horse stable. You can't even drive right now, so how would you shop for your groceries or go to school?"

"There are so many reasons to stay with Barb and Steve and not on the farm," Andy interjects. "You should get back to a routine, and we'll help you with the farm."

"I appreciate everything, really, but I'm staying at Crossroads for now. I know I can hitch a ride with David, or Charlyne or Iris."

"We're not comfortable with you staying there without an adult." Andy says.

"There is an adult there. Mr. Manuel stays in the other house, and Zander lives there."

"They're not family or the kind of adult supervision we're talking about," Barb says. "Don't you think that it would be unsafe for you to stay out there alone?"

"One of us can stay there for the next few nights while we figure things out." Andy says.

"David will stay for the weekend. I already asked him. He just needs to bring his homework." Amanda says.

"What about Kyle Perless, does he stay at the farm sometimes? Oh, but now...hmmm. You should talk with him about all of Kent's belongings at the farmhouse, they're important to him I'm sure." Barbara says.

"I'm going to let Kyle deal with that whenever, or come over whenever he wants, particularly to ride or see the horses. And I don't have any intention of changing the farm help. I want to start some kind of non-profit for people who have brain injuries or paralysis. They could come to the stables, groom the horses and stuff like that."

"That is a nice idea; maybe Andy can help with legalities. But you've never lived on your own before. I just don't see how..." Barbara says before being interrupted by Andy.

"I'm going to hire a security guard again to stay at the farm over the weekend, and then we'll get someone from a professional housesitting service who can stay there and drive Amanda around."

Since Amanda doesn't offer resistance to the suggestion, Andy treats that as a green light to put his plan in place.

"The headmaster at M.A. says you're welcome to return this coming Monday and you can catch up over the next several weeks with a tutor. He offered the name of three tutors who are all M.A. graduates," Barbara says.

"I might have a tutor already. She's a former college tutor at GW." Amanda says.

"How'd you find her?" Andy asks.

"David Owlsley checked her out for me," Amanda says, knowing that she left some details out. But it wasn't a complete lie. "Hey, we've got to get out of here. A bunch of my friends are going to meet us at the farm. We need to pick up some things to celebrate too."

Barbara gives Amanda a big hug in the parking lot, and then explains she needs to return back to work. Amanda asks Andy to take her to Café Loco.

Just after they pull into the parking lot Andy pulls a small clear baggie from his pants pocket and holds it up toward Amanda.

"Where'd you get that?" Amanda asks.

"Someone found it in your backpack, maybe the train crew or someone else there. It got mailed to me with no return address or letter."

Amanda takes the baggie with the hamsa charm necklace from Andy's hand but doesn't take the necklace out of the small plastic baggie.

"Are you going to wear it again?"

"I don't know. I'm not sure if I believe anymore."

"Whether or not you think it offers protection, it's still valuable, so please keep it safe," Andy advises her. "Your note was in the backpack too."

Amanda glances at him, but quickly looks ahead at the dashboard. Andy decides not to dwell on the subject.

Once they walk in the door, Amanda tells Andy she'll be back in a minute. He grabs a seat at an empty table and orders a cup of coffee.

Amanda pushes through the swinging door toward Ramblin' Kyles and hears some guitars playing behind a door. It sounds like Kyle inside, so she taps on the door. The door swings open and Kyle is sitting on a chair holding an acoustic guitar. A kid who looks to be about 13 is facing him.

"Practice that chord pattern, Am-C-G, a few times. I'll be right back," he tells the student, then exits the room, closing the door softly behind him. His shirt looks worn and says "Mott The Hoople" on the front. He has the neck of the guitar in his right hand, just holding it beside him.

"You probably know, right?"

"Know what? About the farm? Why shouldn't I know? I was the one who sold it today."

"I bought it."

"What the...? The realtor just called me to say that the closing was over. They didn't tell me you were the buyer. *You* bought my farm?" he says incredulously.

"Yeah, I really wanted to do it. I wanted you to not have to worry about the money. But that's really not the main thing I came to tell you. I paid off the mortgage on your condo and I paid off your business loan on the café."

"You did what? How can...? I can't accept your money. You can't do that."

"Who says I can't? I did it. I wanted to. And I don't plan to change anything at the farm, but I do have some ideas for the future. I want it to be a place where brain-injury patients can interact with horses."

She suddenly gives him a big unsolicited hug. He reacts awkwardly, still holding the guitar by his side.

"Tell me if you want any of Kent's belongings, clothes, boxes in the closets, anything at all. I mean, I'm not moving anything, but I don't want you to think I...I guess I mean it's yours and I want you to know that."

Kyle has a glazed look in his eyes, and Amanda doesn't know what else to say to him. She notices a couple of tears in his eyes. She can't begin to fathom his grief, her own grief has been overwhelming enough. Amanda feels a twinge of happiness mixed together with tremendous sadness.

"I'm going to have a few friends and my aunt and uncle over tonight at the farmhouse. Would you want to come too?"

"Uh, no, I don't think so. Thanks for asking though."

Amanda walks back to the café and finds her uncle. Kyle follows her.

He ambles over toward Andy. "I don't know what to say. I can't accept this, I'll return the money or pay it back..."

"Kyle, no. It's done, and Amanda has no intention of reversing course. It was her decision, and, that's that. We support her 100%."

They both walk out to Andy's car, leaving Kyle standing in the middle of the café with the acoustic guitar still dangling from his hand.

"You know the deal," Andy says once they are driving through Middleburg. "You're going to go back to Middleburg Academy Monday, right? David says he's going to be your driver. A promise is a promise."

"Yeah, okay." She sighs, and then texts David to confirm when he'll be there to pick her up. Uncle Andy doesn't know that she wants her return to M.A. to be short lived.

"Let's go to the farm. I'm not sure how to do this homeowner stuff." she finally admits.

Housewarming

The night of the closing brought much uncertainty to Andy and Barbara. How would they chaperone their young niece who was living on her own? Since she reached the age of majority they both recognized they had to delicately handle the issue of adult supervision for her at the farmhouse.

Both of them, Barb's husband Steve, Becca, and several of Amanda's friends collected at the farmhouse the evening after the closing. David wanted to bring Jonathan, but Amanda insisted David come alone. David thought that was a bit cold-hearted of her, but couldn't do anything to change her mind.

Amanda was not at all happy about her supposed need for adult supervision. She decided to talk to Brittney about not only tutoring her, but maybe also staying at the farmhouse. After all, Brittney needed help too. And Amanda was now in a position to pay her for tutoring and help her stay out of trouble by keeping her away from her less-than-desirable friends.

Amanda shared her plan with one person: David.

"You're kidding me. Brittney is going to be your tutor and watch over you? Her own life is a wreck. Why don't you find someone else, like one of your relatives?"

They walk from the horse stable back toward the farmhouse along a gravel path. Amanda notices the yellowish sheen of the full moon. She feels remarkably content, more so than ever before that she can recall.

"I don't want one of my relatives staying here. That would be stifling. Can you stay this weekend? Your parents are cool, they'd let you, right?"

"I can ask 'em. I wonder if your aunt and uncle would consider me an adult chaperone."

"It would just be for a couple of days and then I can break the news about Brittney," Amanda says, while sliding her cell phone out of the back pocket of her jeans.

She scrolls through and finds Brittney's phone number.

Can you call me at this number? Want to talk about some stuff. Amanda

A couple minutes later Amanda sees the incoming call from Brittney.

"Tell me again what subjects could you tutor me in if I need help with the end of my senior year." Amanda says.

"Well, any of the sciences or math. What are your classes right now?"

"Chemistry, biology, calculus, English literature, and I think European history."

"How about if I come by tomorrow morning at 10? Gather your course materials together, especially your textbooks if possible, and we'll sit down and figure out a plan."

"Do you have transportation?"

Brittney confirms she has a car.

David stands by listening. He agrees to get all of Amanda's school materials from her aunt's house where it's been collecting dust, and they head back into the farmhouse. They explain to Andy and Barbara about the tutor—but leave out the houseguest part. David motions to Amanda, and they both move into the front foyer. He begins whispering to her.

"I checked her out and she's definitely done a lot of tutoring," David says. "Hey, you didn't forget about getting your medical records, did you? We need to keep searching, keep hunting."

"I'll make an appointment with one of my doctors." Amanda answers.

"Great. It should be your orthopedic doctor since your main problem was your back. I also want to search for info about what your dad was doing in the last few weeks before the Hemispheres jet crash."

"What if we don't get anywhere with this?"

"Nothing ventured, nothing gained." David says.

The small party breaks up by 10:00 p.m. Andy and Barbara know that both Zander and Manuel will be in the guesthouse next to the barn, and that David will be staying for the weekend. Andy lets Amanda know that he plans to hire another security guard by Saturday. Then he and Barbara both leave.

"Well, I guess you get the master bedroom, David, 'cuz I sleep in Kent's room."

"Uh, okay. Being here and knowing that you own this entire farm now, the whole thing is really weird."

"I have a lot of plans, including keeping Manuel and Zander to help with the stable and horses and having people with injuries come to the farm."

"That's a cool idea. It would take some serious organization though."

"Yeah, I couldn't do anything until we settled my case, but now I want to do something with some of the money that makes a difference. I want to make people happy."

"Maybe I'll try to help you out if you really get it going."

"I'll make it happen. G'night."

Amanda walks down the hall toward what is now her room. She reaches for an album, "Dark Side of the Moon" by Pink Floyd, and lays it on the turntable, adjusts the volume to a fairly low level and gets ready for bed. Homeowner. Hmmm, being a homeowner is pretty cool, she concludes.

Tutoring

The next morning is cold but sunny when Amanda and David walk to the horse stable and Amanda introduces him to Voodoo and the other horses. Manuel works diligently grooming one of the horses and stops just briefly to be introduced before getting back to work. Amanda and David then walk along the driveway, their hands shoved inside the pockets of their jackets.

"Looks like somebody's coming. It must be your tutor," David says, looking down the driveway.

A small cloud of dust rises from the car slowly coming toward them.

"What in God's name is she driving? Is that an old Geo Tracker?"

"I don't know much about cars, so I couldn't tell you."

As the car comes to a stop 30 feet away, they see the front passenger door is painted gray, and there is a thick sheet of plastic secured by duct tape over the passenger side window. A few moments later the driver's door opens and Brittney Hayes steps out.

"Good morning. Good to see you guys again." she says. "I'm going to get my books and things out of the back."

She swings a large backpack over one shoulder and walks around the car. David can't help himself.

"That's a pretty, uh, scarred up car you've got there..."

"It gets me where I need to go. And Geos get great gas mileage."

"What's with the plastic over the passenger window? Did you have a wreck?" Amanda asks her.

"No, I bought it that way. It was $500.00 and the engine is still really good. I just have to get some money to get the window fixed."

"Let's go in," Amanda says, starting to walk up the steps to the house. "I really like your purple highlights. When'd you do that?"

"A couple days ago, it's pretty easy. I can show you how if you want."

Once inside, Brittney and Amanda spread everything out on the kitchen table.

"What are your strongest courses?" Brittney asks.

"How would I know?"

"Oh right. Well, you'll need to get your transcript I guess. You're going back to school, what, this coming Monday?"

"Supposedly," Amanda mumbles unenthusiastically.

"I'm coming to pick you up, and, in case you forgot, I will be here at 7:30 a.m." David says from behind the two of them. "Oh, and she was really into English lit and theater. I don't know about her grades in math or science."

They start with chemistry and English literature, and David makes himself scarce by watching ESPN in another room. After a couple of hours Brittney starts collecting her things to leave, stashing books in her big backpack.

"Would you consider staying here at the farm and tutoring me full-time for a while?" Amanda asks.

"Really? Well, I've got my apartment, but I'm month-to-month. And I do have some other students, but I, hmmm, I could consider it."

"Look, I'll pay you enough that you won't have to tutor other people. And you can probably get out of your lease after this month, right?" Amanda counters.

"I don't know if I can do it before the end of the month because of the rent. I don't have enough money," Britt says.

"I can help with that," Amanda says, fingering the shape of the hand charm she put back on for the first time since the trestle incident. She's thinking about how much money she's just put into the settlement accounts she agreed to with her uncle and aunt.

"Let me talk to you tomorrow once I try to figure out what I would do with my other students. I like your hand necklace. Isn't that how they identified you? I think that's what they said in the newspapers."

Amanda doesn't answer her, just stands on the porch watching Brittney get into the ramshackle Geo.

Kyle

Eventually, Kyle calls Amanda and asks if he can come by and they agree on when. For the occasion, she picks up and slides on the peace sign charm bracelet – the one from Paris – from her small jewelry box on the dresser.

She secretly debates keeping Kent's memory book. It was stashed under a bunch of magazines and paperbacks at the bottom of the nightstand drawer. She's feeling guilty, selfish. In her mind, one moment she hands it to Mr. Perless, and in the next she stashes it back in the hiding place. Well, not really a hiding place, but hidden. Sitting on his bed with the book resting on her crossed ankles, she again peruses a number of her favorite pictures ensconced under their clear plastic sheets.

Kent must be around 10 or 12 in a couple of the earliest ones on the very first page. He is dressed in black and appears to be a wizard, surrounded by a bunch of other kids in costumes on Halloween night. He points his wand at one of the other kids, role playing. They are all in someone's den, and bags of candy cover a couch.

But the one that she obsesses over most is Kent with two other boys and a little girl. They're in a semi-circle on the ground in someone's backyard. There's a beach cruiser style bike lying on the ground. The little girl and another boy each proudly hold large turtles with initials painted on the shells. That's what Kent was talking about. His descriptions of the turtle painting are burnished in her brain, but this gives her an actual image.

She flips the page. Kent must be 16 or 17 in this one. He stands beside his surfboard positioned vertically in the sand with two other guys and their boards, the rough surf visible in the background. Their surfboards look wet, and pulling the book closer to her, she can make out the sand on them too. Kent has a good tan; his body looks strong. The handwritten words on the bottom say "VA Beach." She never knew Kent surfed, or hung out at Virginia Beach. He'd never mentioned it.

His mom riding her horse was his selection for the very last picture. Amanda recognizes the background, the open pasture area beside the farmhouse. She wonders why Kent included no pictures of his mom when she was fighting cancer. She figures this was how he remembered her. Riding, happy, enjoying life. She feels like a spy in the House of Kent. Strong emotions cascade over her, but the dominant one is guilt.

Rat-tat-tat. Someone is knocking. Quickly, she lifts the paperbacks and magazines from the bottom of the nightstand drawer and shoves the book back underneath them. Opening the door, she sees Mr. Perless, and behind him his faded green Ford Bronco.

"Hi Mr. Perless, great to see you," she says leaning forward to give him a hug. "Can I help you with anything? I can help carry stuff."

"No, I got it. I'm going to go into the attic first."

"I wasn't sure what you wanted to do with the stuff still in his bedroom. I, um, didn't pack up his clothes, should I?"

"That's fine Amanda. Is it okay if I just leave them?"

"Sure, Mr. Perless. It's fine. I actually wear some of his stuff if you want to know the truth." She confesses. "What about his books and albums, and his stereo? I can pack those up for you too."

"Amanda, just enjoy them. I don't..." He chokes up and can't finish.

"Oh, okay." Amanda can't think of what to say.

Mr. Perless walks down the hallway. She never noticed it before, the pull down cord hanging from the ceiling. He pulls on the cord and the attic stairs appear. He doesn't have his hair in a little pony tail today; it's just a bit long in the back, reaching down over the collar of his long sleeve t-shirt emblazoned on the back with "The Shins, New Slang Tour." She watches him climb the staircase and switch on an unseen light.

"Can I help you with anything?"

"No, I'm fine," he calls down from out of sight.

Unsure what she should do with herself, she wanders around the kitchen for a minute or two. She then heads back to Kent's bedroom, picks up one of his books she's been immersed in, *Fahrenheit 451*, and heads back to the great room. After a while, she hears some rustling and sees Kent's dad navigating down the stairs carrying a box. He goes back up for another and she stands at the bottom peering upwards.

"Mr. Perless, I can help you, hand me the boxes."

"I don't want you lifting any heavy ones," he calls down to her. "That would violate doctor's orders, I'm sure."

Amanda helps carry the lighter boxes to the back of the Bronco. When all the packing is done, Mr. Perless stands on the porch holding his keys, giving the unspoken sign that he's ready to hit the road. There is an awkward silence.

"Are you sure about the stuff in his room?"

"Yes, please. Yes."

Suddenly they burst out of her. Uncontrollable sobs. Mr. Perless slides the keys back in his pants pocket and throws his right arm around her.

"Let's sit down a minute," he says, guiding her back over to the steps leading to the porch. "Sit down and calm yourself."

Her sobs continue, but she musters words through them. "I'm so lost, Mr. Perless. And empty." She wipes the tears from her cheeks with both hands.

"I feel like that too, at some point every day. I find happiness in music, in teaching and sometimes in playing too, but it comes and goes. I knew that getting the settlement finished, and getting the money, wouldn't heal everything for you. I remember my dad used to always say 'money doesn't grow on trees.' But happiness doesn't either. You need to grow happiness from inside yourself, because you can't go on like you are. You're dying inside, and you have to let go. I know, that means in some ways letting go of what you had with Kent."

"Kent told me you could've joined one of the biggest bands in London when you were first writing rock music. He told me you turned down being their guitarist because you preferred to just write music for other bands instead of being tied down to a band with a contract. Is that really true?"

"There was a lot more to it than that. But the truth is I enjoyed hanging out with a lot of different friends in London and just wasn't in to the rock star machine. Some folks say I made a huge mistake. Make sure the fortune you seek is the fortune you need. I chose my path, which is what you need to do now."

"I really want to get my charity going." Amanda says as she wipes off some more tears. "I need to do something that I can feel good about."

"Great. If I can help you with anything let me know. Listen, one time Kent showed me a clip of you playing soccer game in a tournament or state finals, something big. You scored a goal, and the smile you had on your face after that was priceless. You were hugging some of the other players while running back toward midfield. I saw deep happiness in your face, in your teammates' faces. You need things like that. Search and you'll find them again." Kyle says.

"What if we try to teach music to brain injury patients? That might be good therapy. What do you think, Mr. Perless?"

"Just call me Kyle, please. It takes a lot of effort to organize that. And money too."

"My uncle said he'd help. And don't worry about the money; I've got plenty of that now."

"Have you gone back to school yet?"

"No, but I've got a tutor. She's been staying here actually. Don't know where she is right now... Anyway, I might just get tutored through the end of the semester."

"Will you be able to graduate that way?"

"I'm not sure. Probably."

"That would be good. You need to graduate, right? Then what?"

"I'm not sure." Amanda answers, then pauses a second, unsure about telling him. "I've become obsessed with the plane crash, and whether what happened to Kent is connected to it. I don't believe what the cops say about Kent and fentanyl either."

"What do you mean 'connected' to the crash?"

"I'm not sure yet, but I'm going to keep searching 'til I find out."

"Let me know what you find out."

"Where are you going to put all these boxes?"

"In a big walk-in closet I have."

"Are you sure you don't want anything else? Furniture, pictures?"

I don't have a place for it, so no." Kyle pivots back toward the Bronco and gets in. Amanda stands on the front porch and watches the Bronco as it drives down the crushed stone driveway, sending little dust clouds up in the air.

Passed Out

Britt and Amanda had exchanged several text messages. The hourly rate that Amanda offered her was too good to turn down, apparently, along with being able to stay in the master bedroom.

Britt turns up early Sunday afternoon, along with her minimal belongings and explains that she wants to spend several hours getting a feel for how to attack each class. Because there is so much to cover, only a methodical plan will have any chance of working.

Andy has hired the same security outfit that had worked the hospital, even though David is staying at the farmhouse until early Sunday evening. The guard has taken up post on the porch, but once in a while unobtrusively comes inside to use the bathroom.

The tutoring session begins uneventfully. Amanda works through several math problems set out at the end of the chapter. Britt is working forward in the textbook, reviewing things while waiting for Amanda to finish.Suddenly Britt stands up, takes one step, and crumbles to the kitchen floor.

"David! Get in here! Brittney just passed out or something." Amanda kneels down over Britt. Her eyes appear partly opened but roll upwards under her eyelids erratically.

"Hurry!" Amanda again yells. David runs in and crouches beside her.

"Brittney? Can you hear me?" He notices slight twitching movements coming from her arms but no other part of her body. She doesn't respond.

"Call 911. Should we start CPR?" Amanda frantically asks David.

Just then, Brittney's eyes stabilize. She looks up at both of them, glancing back and forth.

"What? Wh-what happened?" Britt finally stammers out.

"Oh God, thank God!" Amanda says.

"You passed out, or had some kind of seizure," David says. "Have you ever had a seizure before?"

"I don't...I don't know. How long was I out?" Britt asks.

"Just a few seconds," David says, "but you should lie down."

Somewhere Amanda finds a washrag, runs freezing cold water over it, and they lay Brittney down on the great room couch. Amanda positions the cold compress on Brittney's forehead.

"Must've been a withdrawal seizure or something," Britt says to her in a near whisper.

"That would make sense," Amanda says, thinking about Brittney and her rehab at the clinic.

"Didn't they wean you off meth at rehab with the drugs they gave you?" David asks.

"I don't know. I'm sorry, I-I don't know what it was." Britt says haltingly.

After another 15 or 20 minutes, Brittney recovers and is again providing Amanda instructions on her math assignments.

"I guess math and meth are a volatile mix," Amanda says looking up from a math problem.

"Not funny." Britt replies.

After David leaves Sunday evening, Amanda and Britt crowd into the bathroom and Britt prepares Amanda's hair for coloring. She segregates the braided areas of hair to be colored, and with artistic precision, brushes in the product.

"We've got to let it set for about 30 minutes. Let's go into the great room and I'll lay a towel behind your head so we don't get the coloring on anything."

Britt gets the remote and turns on a reality show on Bravo about housewives living somewhere.

"Do you like the 'Housewives of Orange County'?" Britt asks Amanda.

"Don't know that I've ever watched it," Amanda answers.

"Oh, yeah, forgot that."

Before they know it, 30 minutes have passed. Brittney shows Amanda how to remove the protective covering from the braids and recommends a certain shampoo and conditioner to maintain the color as long as possible and keep her hair healthy.

A while later, Amanda showers, blow-dries her hair and admires her new look.

"I really like it, we kind of match now." Britt says, when Amanda finally enters the great room.

"Don't think we'd ever be taken for twins, but it definitely makes a statement," Amanda replies.

Pletcher

Closing the bedroom door, Amanda puts on a vinyl record from Kent's collection. She flops down stomach first on the bed. A familiar tone comes from the cell phone on the bed. It's David.

Need to tell you about computer research today. Can I come over?

Y not just call?

In person best.

K, come on over.

In the 30 minutes it takes David to get there, what's left of the daylight fades. Finally she hears a tap on the screen door. As she opens the door, they exchange hellos and he walks into the foyer.

"So, what's up?"

David points with his finger up and around in a circular direction. He is indicating that he doesn't trust that their conversation will be private.

"It's David, he's here to talk to me about some school stuff," Amanda tells Britt. "We're going to see the horses while we talk." They head out the front door.

"When I got your text this morning, I realized you never really planned on coming back to school. You could've told me over the weekend."

Amanda looks down to the ground, refusing eye contact. "I'm sorry. I should've told you, you're right. I just decided I couldn't go back."

"Anyway, you won't believe what I found out. It's about that attorney, Pletcher, who filed your dad's patent applications."

"What? You were investigating that again?"

"A vanishing application? National security? Of course I was."

"So what about him?"

"Brittney gave me a funny look when I got here. Have you told her anything?"

"I don't think so. She knows about my parents and that I'm still looking for answers. But I don't think I've told her anything about you and like, computer hacking or our patent office visit. Why?"

"Okay. Just don't tell her anything else."

"Listen, bad guys could have easily swooped in and killed me already. Don't you think you're being paranoid?"

"Since Kent died, no."

"Let's get back to the patent attorney stuff," she says.

"Okay. I hacked into Pletcher's computer and copied the entire hard drive remotely. He had notes and emails from somebody about organizing a meeting for your dad."

"Are you sure it was for my dad?"

"Well, yeah, it's pretty obvious when it has his last name, and it's about a meeting for licensing his patent."

"Licensing his patent? The one that was withdrawn that we couldn't see?"

"I'm not sure. So, I went through Pletcher's calendar. The day of the crash your dad had an appointment with him and a guy named Mikhail Chapikov."

"What's so earth-shattering about that?"

"Well, Chapikov is Russian or at least it sounds Russian to me. So I searched for Mikhail Chapikov and found one in Moscow who is associated with a company called Russ-med Research.

"Then I looked more into this guy Pletcher," David continues, "and figured out he's a patent attorney in Manhattan. His office is on a floor with an international law firm that he is not actually a member of, but he is listed as 'of counsel.' I called number in his bio and got his voicemail."

"Let's call him again. I can tell him who I am and ask him about all of this." Amanda says while they stand just outside the stables.

"He won't return any phone calls. I've tried three times over the last couple days and he never takes my call or returns it. I told him I was your friend and we just wanted to ask about your dad and if he could help us. We need to go meet this guy face to face."

"I think I need to ask my aunt or uncle. They'll probably freak out and say no, but I have to ask." Amanda says, flipping a gate latch back and forth on the side entrance to the stable. "Do you think this Russian company was involved in my parents' deaths?"

"I don't know. You know how the CSI detectives do it. They look for the last ones to see the victim alive. Pletcher should know exactly what they were trying to license, and that your dad never showed up for the meeting. If you're an attorney with a good client who's a no-show, and you find out his plane crashed that day, wouldn't you call someone?"

"True. But how would we get there?"

"Talk to your uncle. Maybe he'll take us and line up a meeting."

Passenger Seat

"Why do you sit in there?" Britt asks, leaning in through the sport car's front passenger window. Amanda sits statue-like in her pajama bottoms and a t-shirt.

"I don't know. I like the smell. It reminds me of him. Stuff we did together. Do you believe in karma? I mean that everything is already destined to happen whether you know it or not?"

Britt thinks a moment and straightens back up outside the window of the Spider. She has an old faded GW shirt on, shorts, dark-colored socks and a pair of worn slip-on flats.

"I guess I kinda believe in karma, but I also think we can change things. In other words, we have to think positively and seize each day. I don't think it affects everything I do."

"Did I ever tell you about my brother Justin?" Amanda asks, changing subjects suddenly.

"No. Why haven't I heard anything about him or met him?"

"They all think I'm crazy. I mean about him."

"Why's that?"

"Dr. Lucent told me I just made him up or something. I really don't know what to think. When I remember him we're on a bunk bed, he's shaking my car keys and won't give them to me. I have to actually take them back. It's that real. I see flashes of other things too. Some of them I know are real, others I'm not sure."

"That must really bother you, huh?"

"Umm, sometimes, yeah. Did you come out here just to ask me why I'm sitting here?"

"No, I'm going for a run through the woods. Exercise'll be good for me."

Amanda looks Britt up and down. "You're gonna run in those old flats?"

"I don't have anything else, so they'll have to do." Britt takes a few steps away from the car and breaks into a jog. Amanda watches through the windshield as Britt takes off through the open field toward the tree line. She leans back in the passenger seat and closes her eyes, struggling to remember.

Are You My Mother? That's it! That's the book. Justin loved that book. He knew the crane machine wasn't the baby bird's mom!

Unexpected News

Andy texts Amanda and makes arrangements to come over early Tuesday evening. He wants to talk to her about skipping school. Amanda braces herself for a showdown, but something else is keeping her from worrying about it as much as she would have normally.

The Wizard of Oz. Amanda has obsessively watched it since Britt bought it for her after she mentioned the NDE with the four Dorothys. Just maybe there is something in her memory that could be unlocked by watching it.

Britt is on the couch, along with David, who wants to talk with Andy too. Not about school, but about going to New York.

When he first arrived on Tuesday, David had walked through the entire house carrying a small handheld device Amanda thought was a phone. But he wasn't talking on it, he was holding it out in front of him.

Amanda finally asked, "What're you doing?"

He held his index finger up in front of his lips, but never even said "shhh."

"You're so weird," Amanda said, walking back to the great room. She sat next to Britt, who was reading a novel and occasionally looking up at the movie.

David finally sits in a chair beside the couch, and notices that Amanda had lit a scented candle on the coffee table.

"This is one of my favorite parts," Amanda says to anyone listening, as the cowardly lion dashes through the castle hall and leaps, crashing out of the window. They hear a tap on the front door, and then a voice.

"Hello?" It's Andy.

"Come on in, we're watching a movie." Amanda calls out toward the front. Maybe he won't chastise me in front of the others, she thinks.

He sits in the chair opposite David, and notices the movie is *The Wizard of Oz*.

"Can you guys pause the movie so I can talk with Amanda a few minutes?"

David lifts the remote and finds the pause button. "Do you want us to leave you two alone?"

"No, it's okay. Congratulations Amanda. It took a while for us to get it, since it went to your parents' house first."

"Congratulations for what?"

Andy hands her the envelope. "You've been accepted at UVA!"

"What? How?"

"We don't know when you applied, but you've been admitted. Read it."

Amanda's eyes scan over the one-page letter signed by the Dean of Admissions.

Certain that her uncle was going to berate her for failing to return to classes at M.A., she can only muster an uncomfortable grin. She lays the acceptance letter down on the coffee table.

"How'd I get in? I haven't even gone back to school."

"You did really well on your SATs, and you were near the top of your class through your junior year. Apparently you applied to a few others too, including William & Mary, Georgetown, and UNC. Aunt Barbara and I are really proud of you."

"You and your mom went to visit UVA and William & Mary. I do remember that," David says.

"You got accepted to UVA too, right?" Andy asks David.

"Yeah, but I'm pretty sure I'm going to MIT," he answers.

"Well Amanda, maybe you should re-visit UVA. It's a beautiful school, and it's only a two-hour drive down Route 29 to Charlottesville. Either myself or Aunt Barb can take you one weekend if you want to see it, again."

"Maybe..."

"I'm surrounded by serious brains. I had no idea you guys were future scholars," Britt interjects.

"Anyway, the headmaster from M.A. called me today, wondering why you haven't come back." Andy finally gets to the thorny issue Amanda was dreading.

"I'm working with Britt, and she's a great tutor." Amanda says, nodding in Britt's direction. "Also, David and I are working on some things."

"If you don't return now, when will you?" he asks.

"Can't we talk to them? They know about my situation. Maybe if we keep paying tuition, I can study here and just take final exams for each class."

"Mr. Michaels, if they provide the course curriculum I'll do everything possible to have her ready for exams," Britt offers.

"I'll talk to Barb and the headmaster and see what they say." Andy says.

"Britt, we'd like to talk to Amanda's uncle privately for a few minutes," David says, getting up and indicating that he plans to leave the great room for this conversation.

"No problem," Britt says.

"Let's step out onto the porch," David suggests.

Once the three of them are on the porch David says, "I did some digging, and I found the name of the patent attorney in New York who was reviewing the last patent application Amanda's dad filed. There's some strange stuff that we want to tell you about. And, uh, I don't talk about this kind of stuff inside the house because I think it's bugged."

"Really? Why?"

"Well you know the hospital room was bugged. I have every reason to believe this place is too."

"Whoa! Says who?" Andy asks.

"Mr. Michaels, I know what I'm talking about, my dad taught me a lot about security, bugging, how to detect it, all that stuff." David assures Andy, then continues about Ron Michaels. "So, you know about your brother's cancer tumor patent."

"I know about the telomere cancer tumor application. But it was handled by an attorney here in the D.C. area, not New York." Andy responds.

"Well, there was another one. The application was filed but immediately withdrawn under a special federal law that can remove it from public access."

"How'd you find that out?" Andy asks.

"I took Amanda over to the U.S. Patent Office and we met with a patent examiner who reviews those types of patents. I did some digging and found a reference to Ron Michaels' application. It showed the patent attorney's name and a box address. Then I dug some more and found a few pages from the original filing. The attorney's name is Robert Pletcher, and he's in Manhattan. But here's the really interesting part." David stops a moment and looks around the porch for something, but of course no one sees a thing.

He continues, but in a whisper. Andy leans in closer. "I was able to access the calendar on his computer and he was scheduled to meet with your brother on the day of the plane crash. Ron never got to the meeting."

"Have you called him?" Andy inquires.

"Yes, I've left a few messages. But he never called me back, even when I said it was about finding out what happened to Ron Michaels."

"That's why we wanted to talk to you." Amanda says. "We know something's wrong. We want to go to New York with you and meet with him."

"I guess I could call this attorney..." Andy says, thinking it over.

"Why wouldn't he call someone in our family and say something like, 'Hello there, I'm a patent attorney up in New York. I was supposed to meet with your relative and he didn't make it.' We didn't hear a word from him. Isn't that a little strange?" Amanda says.

"Yeah, it is. That's why we should go up there and meet this guy." David says.

"Okay, okay. Let me do some of my own homework on this lawyer. Maybe we can work something out." Andy says. "I looked into some of Ron's research, picked up his personal effects from BBS, and talked to Michael Jacoby, the CEO. He clammed up like an oyster when I asked for details about what Ron did there. Said it was highly classified. Then I also met with one of Ron's former professors from Georgetown, and that really opened my eyes."

"How so?" David asks.

"He gave me a mini-lecture about chromosomes and telomeres. It's all way over my head. Cancer researchers are studying how telomerase enzyme affects cell growth. Ron was exploring the frontiers of cell division. I believe BBS was also studying rapamycin and how it affects cells. BBS sent scientists, including Ron, to Easter Island to get it since that's the only place in the world to find it."

"My dad went to Easter Island?"

"Sure did." Andy says.

"Pletcher has to know why Ron's research was so important. But if he was doing secret research for BBS, why would he be using his own attorney in New York? My findings also make me think Pletcher was meeting with shady Russian contacts too." David offers.

"Would my dad really do that? Try to make some secret deal? I'll never believe it."

"I'm not saying that. All of this is just really weird." David adds. "We need to meet with Pletcher."

@Part VII

Orthopedics

A nurse in a white uniform walks out and calls "Amanda Michaels?" Amanda gets up from the seat beside David, who is surfing on his laptop and listening to music.

"See you after," David says to her, never removing his ear buds.

As Amanda walks down the hall past patient rooms the nurse says, "I've seen you on the news, and it's great to know you're doing so well."

"Thanks."

The nurse removes the chart from the wall holder, waves Amanda inside, and follows her in.

"What's the nature of your visit with Dr. Bodsky today? Are you having orthopedic problems?" she asks.

"No. I just want to talk to him about some of the treatment I had with him before."

The nurse looks up from her pad. "So no new problem?"

"Not really."

"Alright then. Just have a seat."

A minute or two later the door opens.

"How is my famous patient doing? My God you've been through a lot."

Amanda looks up sheepishly, and notices his accent. Maybe British? The problem is that she doesn't remember anything about him or his treatment.

"Actually, I have some questions about what you treated me for. Can you tell me about that?"

"Of course. You were suffering from what is known as a pars defect. Um, let me flip back through your treatment record here, and, yes, you were 12 at the time. It's not unusual for very active young teenagers or preteens to suffer some type of trauma or impact in the very low part of the spine. There's an area called the pars near the top of your buttocks. Problems with the pars interarticularis can also be called spondylolysis. Here's one of your x-rays." He holds the x-ray up toward the light looking at it. "Yeah, you had a noticeable space there.

"Eventually, a vertebra can slip forward because the facets aren't holding it in place. The pars I'm referring to, it's a little gap between the vertebrae on both sides of your spine in your lower back." Bodsky then points to the bony part of the spine near the bottom of a model sitting on a side table. "When this type of injury occurs, these bones become the problem area."

"What causes it?"

"A significant impact, a fall, or just overuse. Gymnasts, weight lifters, and football linemen are especially prone to this kind of problem. Normally we prescribe nine to twelve months of no physical exercise in order to heal the pars-- eliminating all the stress on that area is what works best. But your pain went away much faster, and in three months I cleared you to go back to playing soccer."

"Where are you from?" she asks him.

"South Africa. And, my daughter plays for the M.A. J.V. soccer team."

"Have you ever had anyone get better that quickly?"

"Not that I recall. Like I said, our normal recommendation is almost a year of no physical activity. I'm so sorry about the loss of your parents, but really happy about your recovery, it's amazing."

There is an awkward pause, and Amanda can tell the doctor wants to move on.

"Is there anything I can do for you today?"

"Was there any surgery, any other procedure you did on me before you finished treating me?"

Bodsky looks through her chart again, and then looks on the left side of the page for consultation notes.

"No other procedures, but my notes say you were continuing your regular blood transfusions with home health nursing. Oh, now I remember, you had vWD. That makes sense."

"What's vWD stand for?"

"Von Willebrand Disease. It's a blood disorder that causes excessive bleeding. Yours was fairly minor, but it's something we must watch, especially during a medical procedure or surgery."

"Do you have more details about the transfusions in there?"

"Depends on whether I prescribed it or not," the doctor says while he flips through some other pages. "It appears I didn't, so I guess you or one of your parents mentioned it to me."

"Excessive bleeding, like, if I get cut it never stops? Do you need to be on medication?"

"Oh, it's not total hemophilia. If it was minor, your blood could coagulate, and eventually your body would seal a cut. It just may take considerably longer. There are higher, more serious types of the disease—Types 2 and 3, but you were Type 1."

"Okay."

"Anyway, great to see you. If you need anything else, feel free to call me or come back in. Kathleen out at reception has the copy of your chart you requested."

Amanda stops at reception and Kathleen hands her a folder full of papers. She walks through the double doors of the orthopedic clinic, and she and David get into his car.

"Well, what did you find out?" David asks.

"He says I had something called a pars defect. It's a gap in the bones at the bottom of my spine."

"I told you it was something like that. Any other scoop?"

"He said it usually takes nine months to a year of no physical activity to heal. I recovered in three months and was back to soccer. He said it's the only case he can remember like that. Pretty cool, huh?"

"Pretty cool, but I still have some questions about whether that's a coincidence or whether that means you're special for some reason."

"What're you talking about?"

"I'm wondering whether you are like Wonder Woman, Super Girl, Cat Woman, or maybe all three mixed together," David says with a laugh.

"You found me out. I didn't tell you because I didn't want you to feel inferior. Think you can handle it?"

"Very funny Wonder Woman."

"Did you know I have a blood disease called vWD?" She asks him, becoming serious again.

"No, what's that?"

"The doctor told me I was getting blood transfusions for it through home health nursing. He said it's an excessive bleeding disease, but mine was like a minor case. Here's what's weird. I don't hardly bleed at all. When I get a cut now my blood is like tar. I noticed it awhile ago and even told Dr. Lucent and my uncle about it. If anything, I'm like the opposite of vWD."

"Let's look at the medical records and check online. I'll pull into a café."

After he parks, they order some tea and sit down at a round table.

David turns on his laptop and Amanda opens her medical file on the table and starts to read through it.

"This website says vWD is a form of hemophilia affecting only 1% of the population. It's genetic. 'People with vWD have insufficient or low levels of von Willebrand factor, a blood protein that is necessary for normal blood clotting; thus, they are prone to bleeding...'"

"Dr. Bodsky said he didn't prescribe my blood transfusions, so the reports about them weren't in his file. He just saw the vWD references in his notes," Amanda says skimming through the various pages of the medical records. "Oh, wait, here's a typed part. 'Dad with her today, says Amanda has vWD, Type 1, well controlled.'"

David is still reading the webpage. "It says, 'Almost everybody has vWF, which helps form blood clots to stop bleeding. People with vWD, however, either don't have enough vWF or, if they do, it may not work properly.' Yeah, three types. So you have the mildest, Type 1. That's good."

"But I'm, like, the opposite."

David then begins reading through the medical records himself, and Amanda helps herself to the laptop.

David finally sees for himself that there are no details about the home health nursing service that did the blood transfusions. No company name either.

"We need to find out why you needed blood transfusions. Maybe your uncle knows."

"Uh, obviously for the vWD disease, right?"

"I'm not so sure about that."

Matriculation

"Thanks so much for agreeing to see me," Barbara Simon says to Headmaster Johnson as she takes a seat in his office.

"No need to thank me. It's a pleasure to meet you again. How is Amanda doing?"

"She's coming along well with the help of a full-time tutor, and seems more comfortable with her than coming back to school. We just found out she got accepted to the University of Virginia, which is exciting."

"Fantastic. It's a great college and many of our graduates go there. Does she plan to go?"

"To tell you the truth, we don't know. I'd like to take her to visit. She visited with her mom, but of course has no recollection. And she'd have to graduate from high school for it to even be a consideration."

"Well, yes. And, we're willing to make accommodations. We've had students before who have had a medical crisis or suffered a disability during a school semester. I'm sure all of her teachers will work with her. She can arrange to take a series of exams, and she'll need to continue completing her assignments."

"So she'd be able to graduate, even if she does not physically return to classes?"

"Correct, she just has to keep up through her tutoring and meet each teacher's requirements."

A few minutes later Headmaster Johnson ushers Barbara into the hallway, just as classes are changing. Within 30 minutes, the entire senior class knows Amanda is not returning for her final semester.

Dorothys

Aunt Barbara brought over a shoebox full of old family pictures, banana bread, and a homemade casserole for Amanda. It was nice of her, but Amanda was glad when she left. Back in her bedroom, with the music on, Amanda started randomly pulling out pictures and looking at them, like with the other scrapbooks, hoping for something.

Suddenly she sees the picture. The four Dorothys. It wasn't just a dream or a random NDE after all. Somehow she knew it all along. There she is, sitting on a park bench, smiling broadly, with three other Dorothys. Dressed in blue and white, even with matching baskets for Toto, who appears to be missing.

Wait, where was that park bench? Maybe they were dressed up for Halloween?

Amanda jumps off the bed and trots down the hall where Brittney is reading on the couch. Amanda holds the picture out in front of her, then places it right on top of her open book when she doesn't look at it right away.

"Look. The four Dorothys. I knew it. I just knew it."

"Wow, so it was something from your NDE. Maybe this is a memory breakthrough."

"Could be. I just know I keep remembering it. There were four Dorothys, and when I first came out of my coma I knew what *The Wizard of Oz* was." Amanda lifts the picture back up from Brittney's book.

Brittney places a finger between the pages she was reading and closes up the book, thinking.

"Well, terrible things happened to Dorothy, but she found her way. Bad things happened to you, and you're trying to find your way, kinda like she was. So you have something in common."

"It can't be that simple. There's another reason. I've gotta find the other girls and ask them some questions. Charlyne probably knows who they all are," Amanda says, texting Charlyne and walking back toward the bedroom.

Can u find them? Text them?

They don't go to MA. Gimme an hour.

If u find them, lets meet asap. Cafe Loco.

Why so urgent??

Will xplain later.

Ok, TTYL.

Four Pairs

From inside the bedroom, Amanda hears the front door shut. She walks down the hall to the foyer.

On the floor sit four shoeboxes, each with the top off, revealing new black and yellow running shoes.

"Why'd you get yourself four pairs of the same shoes?"

"I didn't. Two pairs are for you." Britt says, smiling.

"I didn't say I was going to run," Amanda says, walking by the shoes toward the great room. "Plus, you don't know my shoe size."

"Yes I do. I checked your shoes. They should fit, but if not, we can take them back."

A moderate rain falls overnight, seriously dampening the thick pasture grass and, to a lesser degree, the surrounding woods. One thing Amanda has noticed about Brittney: she is steady with her routines. Every morning, like clockwork, she takes off, out of the house, through the pasture, and into the woods, returning maybe a half hour later. She has explained several times how pretty the running path is under the canopy of trees, and how it runs over a small stream, one that Amanda has never seen.

As Britt prepares to leave, she doubles back into the kitchen area. Amanda is reading Shakespeare's *Hamlet* for English Lit, taking notes and highlighting passages.

"Come run with me. It'll be good for you. You can wear the new shoes I got you. From all the rain last night, we may get muddled. Uh, mudded. Oh, you know what I mean." Britt laughs at her own grammar.

"I want to see the stream down there more than I want to run. Gimme a couple minutes."

Amanda gets up and changes into shorts and a comfortable top. A few minutes later she walks out of the bedroom and picks up a pair of shoes in the foyer. As she sits down on the front porch lacing up the shoes, Britt sits down beside her.

"We're going to have to go slow, you know, I'm obviously out of shape." Amanda says.

As they slowly jog beside each other across the pasture Amanda asks Britt something that's been nagging her.

"I haven't heard you talk about your daughter since you started tutoring me. Don't you think about her?"

"I don't like to talk about Sam. It hurts too much. Bobby's got her, and I do check on her." Britt replies. Amanda runs just behind Britt and can't see her facial expression, which is just as well.

"How long has it been since you've seen her?"

"Less than a year. He let me visit her one weekend, and it was amazing. I took her to the zoo."

"Can you ever get partial custody back?"

"Yeah, but I need to be clean for a year, at least." Britt says, a touch out of breath.

"Seems like you've been doing great since you came here. I mean, that's true, right?"

"Yeah. It helps not being around them anymore." Britt says.

They run along a part of the trail with areas of mud from the rainfall the night before. Britt takes a step and mud splatters up and across Amanda's shins and thighs.

"Gee thanks!" Amanda says, between pants.

As they trot through the wooded area Amanda speeds up a little bit when she sees a puddle and purposely smacks her running shoe down, spraying retaliation mud and water all over Brittney, including on her running shirt and her cheek.

"Ha ha! Now you know what it feels like, mud queen." Amanda shouts.

From that point forward, whenever either of them spots a muddy area, they jockey for position to be the first to splatter the other. Eventually their clothes and legs are almost completely covered with mud.

They reach the small wooden platform over the stream. Rivulets of water flow over stones long polished by the stream, which is no wider than 15 feet.

"This is what I've been telling you about," Britt says.

"Let's stop here. I need to rest," Amanda says slowing, then stopping. Britt pulls her cell phone from the elastic sleeve she wears around her upper arm.

"Let's get a couple pictures of us covered in mud." They snap a few, using the timer.

"Didn't you say you did some theater stuff at M.A. before the crash?" Britt asks her.

"I know I did from seeing pictures, but I can't tell you much about it. Did you do theater?"

"Yeah. I did several plays. In *Peter Pan* I was Tinker Bell. Playing a part outside yourself is cool. Kind of lets you branch out into a different personality."

After a short break, they continue their run and return to the house covered with mud.

From that day on, the two regularly jog together through the pasture and the woods. Amanda's endurance and athleticism eclipses Britt's within about 10 days and becomes a running joke between them. After their morning jogs, they spend hours on Amanda's classwork that David brings by each week.

An Extension

Braningham finds Solarez in the hallway after clearing the intensive security screening required to enter the FISA courtroom and judge's chambers.

"I expect some fireworks today about extending and expanding this warrant," Braningham says.

"We have good reasons to want to." Solarez says.

A few minutes later they are inside, addressing Judge Bondakopf.

"All right, we are here on the second requested extension of the warrantless searches on a number of persons under this Affidavit 2165. I'll hear from you, Mr. Braningham," Judge Bondakopf says looking up at him.

"Judge, if we have an ongoing intelligence operation, it's appropriate to ask the court to extend the warrantless search operation because if we notify the targets now, it will jeopardize or compromise this ongoing operation."

"That could be said any time an operation hasn't been completed. If I don't force the disclosures, there are no other checks or balances in this court system."

"Judge, we need more time," Solarez interjects. "One of the targets of the warrantless operations, Kent Perless, died. "

"Wait a second. At the first hearing you told me he was a person of interest. Obviously he was a person of serious interest to somebody."

"Well, it's been listed as an accidental-overdose death. But it's caused problems and we've had to expand the investigation. So that's why we're asking for an additional warrantless search on Robert Pletcher, a New York patent attorney."

"Wait a second. This name wasn't even listed under Affidavit 2165. What does he have to do with anything? And why should I delay the original disclosures?"

"We've learned that Ron Michaels, who died in the crash, was on his way to meet with Pletcher in New York. We've done extensive research on him and his specialty is biological and medical patents. We also learned that he's dealt with a couple of Russian companies and specifically had met with one individual that we are concerned may have been a front for a Russian governmental entity. And Michaels may have met with Pletcher before."

"You assured me at the first hearing that Amanda and Andy Michaels were not targets. But now it sounds like Ron Michaels may have been involved in transferring classified material. Is that what you're saying?"

"We've never completely come to that conclusion Your Honor. Is it possible that he transferred classified biological information to Pletcher at any earlier time? Yes. Until we do further surveillance on Pletcher I can't answer all these questions."

"I'm only going to authorize another 30 days. You'd better have some answers by then, or all of the targets will get the information, including Mr. Pletcher. Do you understand?"

Both Braningham and Solarez nod in agreement. The judge then signs the extension order.

"Have a good day gentlemen," she says.

Inside the secure room in the embassy off Massachusetts Avenue, Jiang takes the headphones off his head and pauses for a second. He then turns to the agent beside him.

"Our worst fears have been confirmed. Michaels had already transferred the biological information to Pletcher, and maybe others. There's no way Pletcher would still be talking with the Russians unless he has the biological formulas. It looks like we underestimated him, he must've been planning this longer than we thought."

"When is Pletcher meeting with the Russians?" Chun asks.

"Soon, but we don't know exactly when. The U.S. agents now have him under surveillance. They know he wants to sell the information." Jiang rubs both of his eyes.

"What about our own source?"

"He promises and promises. Says he has to move ultra-carefully. I'm not convinced he can deliver. It may be he needed Michaels because he was just siphoning information from him," Jiang says.

"Put our people on this in New York," Chun directs. "We can't let the Russians get the technology, especially after what we've invested in this operation. You understand me? We can't let the Americans dominate. Maybe they develop it first, but if we stay with this, we can develop the telomere data independently. Understand?"

"Yes sir, absolutely." Jiang says.

Abbott's Grill

Andy could recall having had drinks with the reclusive senior partner of his own law firm, Hunter Wilson, only once, after a law seminar several years ago. When he called this time Wilson mentioned that one of his former colleagues, Dennis Stratton, who had worked at the U.S. Attorney's office in D.C. with him, had extended the invitation. Andy wondered whether this was some new case opportunity for the firm.

Old Abbott's Grill is purportedly the oldest bar in the capitol city, tracing its existence back to the 1800s when it was a saloon. Situated only a block or two from the White House, all sorts of politicos and big shots frequent its multiple bar areas, including the oyster bar hidden in a back corner.

As he walks in, Andy spots Hunter right inside the large glass and brass double doors, near the maître d' stand.

"Hi Hunter. Is he here yet?"

"No, just walked all the way down the bar and around to the other room and I didn't see them."

"Oh, not just Stratton?" Andy asks.

"He said another attorney might join us too," Wilson says.

"Any idea what he wants?"

"No clue, I'm assuming there's some connection to your Hemispheres settlements."

They snag a small round bar table with four stools that two guys are vacating as they walk by. Once they place their drink order, Andy asks Hunter over the din of the after-work crowd, "How well do you know Stratton?"

"When I was the U.S. Attorney, I helped him get the job over there," Wilson answers.

"Who is he counsel for at the State Department?"

"I don't know really. There are so many lawyers over departments reporting to the Secretary of State. We can ask him when he gets here."

A waitress working the bar area shows up with their drinks.

"How's your niece doing?"

"Thanks for asking. She's being tutored. She could go back to her classes, but she refuses. She is currently living at a farmhouse in Middleburg that she bought. It's a long story, but she insisted on buying it with part of her settlement money, and we couldn't talk her out of it."

"She bought a farm?"

"It was the family farm of this guy she befriended during her hospitalization. He was found dead in his car in one of the pastures. Supposedly an accidental drug overdose."

"You never told me anything about this. You know you can confide in me Andy, really. Is Amanda okay now?"

"Well, thanks. She's been erratic, depressed, and I'm keeping an eye on her as best as I can. But on the bright side, she just got accepted to UVA. We just need to make sure she graduates from high school."

"Hunter, my old friend," Stratton suddenly says from behind Andy. "Great to see you. I'd like to introduce you to Brett Stein, one of my colleagues at the State Department."

Handshakes are exchanged and introductions to Andy are made. Andy eyes Stein, who's in a well-tailored blue suit, white button-down shirt and an understated red tie with an angular striped pattern. He's tall, taller than Andy, with well-groomed short hair, and looks to be no more than 40 years old.

Once they are seated, Stein and Stratton each order a drink, and they order a couple of appetizers too.

Finally, Stratton opens the real conversation. "Andy, congratulations on what appears to be a number of very good settlements you've negotiated for your clients. Obviously a very tough situation for your family though."

"Here, here," Hunter says, raising his glass, and all of them spontaneously raise their glasses. "Is it appropriate to make a toast at all, given Andy's family losses? I say yes, this toast is to Andy's guts and determination, and for bringing all his cases to an early resolution."

They all click their glasses in response.

"I brought Brett along for a specific reason. He's one of the attorneys who works with the CIA." Stratton says.

With this, Andy takes pause.

Stein interjects. "Andy, we understand that you visited Biological Blood Services after you settled the cases. We realize you're curious about your late brother, but some of the things you want to know involve national security."

"Wait. Just going over to talk to Michael Jacoby stepped on the toes of the CIA? Really?" Andy asks.

Stein glares at him for a second, then shoots a quick look at Stratton.

"Look. Sometimes things that seem simple are complicated. We understand you wanted to see the lab where your brother worked. And we understand you have a lot of questions. But some of the research he was involved in is highly classified. What we're trying to gently convey here is, uh, it's deeper than you realize."

"Wait, I'm lost. The CIA doesn't do domestic intelligence. Everybody knows that."

Stratton and Stein glance at each other. Then Stein says, "True. But we can protect U.S. citizens under our counter-intelligence authority."

"Gentlemen, in deference to you both, this is a very vague message. Are you trying to tell my partner specifically not to do something? We're all lawyers and we deal with lines that can or cannot be crossed," Hunter interjects before Andy can respond. "So what line are you talking about, Brett?"

"When the CIA believes we have a national security leak, like with a mole, we'll go to extraordinary lengths to seal the leak."

"Are you accusing my brother Ron of being a mole, a traitor?" Andy asks, his hackles rising with his voice.

"Absolutely not, but what I'm authorized to tell you is that you are innocently putting yourself in the middle of an ongoing, potentially dangerous situation."

"Dangerous in what way?"

"Here's what we're trying to say, Andy. You've done an awesome job on settling the cases. Just let sleeping dogs lie now." Stein says.

Andy feels like he is ready to explode, he has so many questions. But before he can open his mouth, Stein speaks again.

"Andy, let me show you some of the old pictures they have in the basement. Have you seen them before? Several presidents have eaten here."

Stein gets up from the table, and Andy gets the message. He stands and follows Stein past the main dining area and down a stairway to the basement where a private room and the restrooms are situated. And yes, there are a bunch of very old framed pictures there. But they both know that's not why they are down there.

"Did the jet crash because of Ron's work for the government?" Andy first demands of Stein.

Thoughtfully, carefully, Stein measures his words.

"What I can say here is...we've read the NTSB investigation documents. And the FBI has investigated. We believe it was an electrical malfunction, and I can tell you conclusively the CIA and the U.S. Government had nothing to do with the crash."

Andy thinks about that answer. Crafty lawyer lingo, no doubt.

"Obviously, Hemispheres wouldn't have paid my clients unless they knew it was a mechanical or electrical failure." Andy says. "What am I doing that you don't want me to? Amanda and I want to talk to Ron's former patent lawyer in New York, this Pletcher guy."

Stein looks shocked. "How do you know who Pletcher is?"

"My niece did some homework. I'm not sure exactly how she found him. What's the big deal?"

"No, you absolutely need to forget about Pletcher. Do not go to New York, just let it go. Do you understand me?"

Andy stares back at Stein, boiling. But, he still holds his tongue. He knows he is receiving this warning because the CIA has actual concerns for his safety, but there are still way too many unanswered questions.

"Let me just say this," Stein says, "There are times that the agency works for months, even years, to build an operation. They must be built one brick at a time in order to, in this case, expose a mole. The foundation must be rock solid. Just because you believe certain so-called facts doesn't always mean they are real. That's all I can say Michaels."

"You know something you're not telling me. Is it about what my brother did at BBS?"

"Good intelligence work often doesn't involve bullets or bombs. Bullets are overrated. Bullets can shatter the normalcy necessary to lure a mole from their cover."

"Stein, I have no idea what you just said, but you haven't told me a damn thing. What about Kent Perless, Amanda's friend? Was he involved in this somehow? Loudoun detectives say it was an accidental overdose. I don't buy it."

Stein looks pissed off now. "Bush or Obama, Michaels? Where do you fit?" he asks Andy in a mere whisper as a woman walks by toward the ladies room.

"Which Bush?" Andy plays along and whispers back.

"Really?"

"It matters, Stein," Andy says, purposely needling him.

"Okay, the son." Stein grudgingly says, still whispering.

"Lincoln." Andy answers.

"Come on. He wasn't on any of our ballots, Michaels. Where do you fall?"

"Lincoln is on the ballot, Stein. There's a different kind of ballot every day. It's a moral ballot, not a political one." Andy says pointing his index finger close to Stein's chest.

"You think it's about philosophy? What you believe? Ha! I never pictured you as a dreamer, Michaels. Where I live, dreamers get vaporized. There's no nuance, Michaels, it's us against them. There's a line on the pavement."

"Nice, I like the imagery, Stein. Did you take English Literature before Armageddon Studies in grad school? My brother's dead, my sister-in-law's dead and my niece is lucky to have survived. Don't you try to pin philosophy crap on me, and act like you're some amazing patriot and I'm not, because you work for the CIA. Give it a rest."

"You're being the ass, Michaels. I came here for one reason – to help you and your niece, but you won't listen to me. We've been trying to help you both in so many ways you'll never know. Don't go forming a posse now, and definitely don't let your niece either. I'm done for now. I did what I could."

Stein starts down the hall to the foot of the stairway.

"For now? What's that supposed to mean?" Andy asks having cooled down a bit.

"This ain't over, I told you that upstairs. Just listen to me. Please."

Standing on the sidewalk outside, Andy hails a cab. "Things must've got testy between you and Stein. I could tell when you came back." Hunter says, standing next to him.

"It's fine. It was a friendly warning, if such a thing exists. You notice they picked up the tab. They wouldn't have done that unless it was official business." Andy says sarcastically.

"Andy, I really had no idea that this was going to be a meeting about your family, I'm sorry."

"Sure, I understand. Maybe I'll see you at the office tomorrow," Andy says climbing into the taxi.

Ambassador

The world of diplomacy has protocols and formalities. Formalities that stretch back centuries, not merely decades. For this reason, when the U.S. Undersecretary for Public Affairs receives a request from the Chinese ambassador for a formal meeting, accommodations are made. The undersecretary postponed the meeting for a day and a half to be sure he was briefed on all current issues “on the table” between the two nations.

True, some tension between the two powerful nations is to be expected, mainly over trade issues, but the U.S. and China enjoy a symbiotic relationship vital to each nation. Mind boggling billions of dollars flow between the two nations each month. Undersecretary Bauman reviewed the complete dossier his staff prepared, and then covered a number of problem areas with his staff.

The black limousine carries Bauman and his assistant across town to the Chinese Embassy on Wisconsin Avenue in northwest D.C. The Chinese guard waves them past through a wrought-iron gate, and the limo travels down the long road to the unobtrusive building.

"Mr. Undersecretary, it is a pleasure to see you again," says the ambassador, firmly shaking Bauman’s hand. The undersecretary sits in the side seat nearest the ambassador who is at the head of the table, followed by each side’s aides. The undersecretary accepts the hot tea offered to him out of diplomatic protocol, and his counterpart patiently waits to begin until the tea has been poured and the server has left the room. The Chinese ambassador speaks impeccable English, and Bauman speaks passable Chinese himself.

"Mr. Undersecretary, you realize why I have called you here to meet me?"

"I’m assuming to discuss the recent fluctuation of your Yuan in relation to the dollar."

"No. You must know why. Let's be frank and open with each other."

The undersecretary looks back at him, confused. "Mr. Ambassador, you'll have to be more forthright with me. I’m unaware of any situation between our nations."

"Mr. Undersecretary, this comes directly from the premier of the People's Republic of China. The U.S. has something important that we want returned, and we believe we have one of your important assets also."

"Mr. Ambassador, I respectfully request that you provide a clearer explanation so that I can promptly assist with your request."

The ambassador looks flustered. He stares down at the wood conference table, collecting his thoughts.

"Mr. Undersecretary, I am authorized to advise that my government is willing to consider an appropriate trade of assets. We will negotiate in good faith on this matter. I specifically ask you to convey that information back to your government, and we can again meet at the earliest opportunity."

The ambassador pushes back his chair, stands up straight and walks around the table toward the undersecretary with his hand outstretched.

“Thank you for coming, Mr. Undersecretary. I hope we can resolve these issues quickly and satisfactorily for both our nations.”

As the limousine turns onto Wisconsin Avenue Bauman explodes at his aide. "How could you let me be blindsided like that? The ambassador thinks I was hiding the truth about whatever dilemma we are in the midst of. When you briefed me on this meeting, didn’t you check with all our intelligence sources?"

"Yes sir, I assure you we checked with intelligence, counterintelligence, and did our usual due diligence."

"Well, we'll see about that. Somebody held back, probably the CIA. What assets is he referring to? What do we have that they want? Get to the bottom of this as soon as we return, and report to me first thing in the morning."

3/4

Both Stephanie and Rachelle had numerous questions, and Charlyne had few answers for them. She was just the messenger. It's all about that time they dressed up as Dorothys, Charlyne explained, and Amanda's quest for her memory from before the crash. The two girls had agreed to help, but Elizabeth, the fourth Dorothy, had moved to California. The three girls agreed to meet in D.C. since Stephanie lived in D.C., Charlyne in Middleburg and Rachelle now lived in Baltimore. Three out of the four Dorothys would have to suffice.

Stephanie picked Claude's, a restaurant they all knew, under the Whitehurst Freeway at the foot of Georgetown. After warm initial hugs, and placing their orders, Amanda quickly pulls the picture out of her small purse.

"I want to talk about this picture of us dressed up as Dorothys," Amanda says, placing the picture flat on the table for all of them to look at. "Charlyne already told me that it was in sixth grade, at the park bench that used to be on the playground at M.A."

"Yeah, it was Halloween, even though they wouldn't officially call it that because some parents thought we might turn into witches." Charlyne says, laughing.

"That was my last full year at M.A. I remember that day," Stephanie says, smiling and sipping her hot tea. We even walked through the hall together because everyone thought it was so funny. We got the costumes at the same store, and we all slept over at your house for Halloween. Yours was the best neighborhood to trick-or-treat in because there were lots of kids."

"Cool. I actually didn't ask you guys to come here just to find out about why we were all Dorothys. I'm really trying to remember stuff."

David was adamant before they got there that she not disclose any specifics about vWD, or cell biology. David lifts his teacup and sips. Amanda notices he's being invisible, just taking things in.

"I remember how many of the parents talked about us all being Dorothys, and the kids trick-or-treating too." Rachelle says reminiscing.

"What about my house? I've seen pictures, but I don't remember it."

"Your mom was great. She baked cupcakes for us. And she got our beds ready and stuff like that." Stephanie says.

"Did you guys ever see other parts of my house, like my dad's office?"

"I don't remember that," Rachelle replies.

"Me neither," Stephanie adds.

The waitress brings each of their orders, briefly interrupting the conversation.

"I do remember watching a lot of movies at your house." Stephanie says. "And I remember your dad telling us that you needed to stay still for a while because you were getting blood transfusions. That was for your, oh I forgot what it's called."

"I don't remember that. Was there a nurse at my house, or how did I get the transfusions?"

"Your dad did it. I remember him putting some small device on the couch right next to your arm, and you weren't supposed to move for like an hour. If you had to go somewhere, you had to carry the thing with you. I think it was battery-powered or something." Rachelle says.

"Yikes. I hate needles. I know that from my rehab. Where was the needle, in my forearm?"

"Yeah, there was a small thingy with an elastic thing around your arm. We could hear a humming sound. Your dad said it treated your blood and you needed it because of your blood condition." Rachelle adds.

"Did you see the device on my arm more than once?"

"Yeah, not every time, a few times."

"Why're you asking so many questions about it?" Stephanie asks.

"Just hoping something will jog my memory," Amanda lies. David taps her foot under the table and gives her a dagger-like stare meaning shut up, she presumes, so she changes the subject.

Standing outside the restaurant, they all hug each other and agree to keep in touch, shouting over the loud traffic noise from the Whitehurst Freeway above their heads.

"I knew it! Your dad was doing something with your blood." David says excitedly as they walk several blocks to his car.

"Do we really know that? It could've really been for vWD."

"There's no way. Well, I guess there's a way, but he was doing something to your blood. Don't you see? It all makes sense. There was no nurse involved, which is what everyone else would've done. He was doing something. That's why you have these unusual qualities. Who knows what you can survive, maybe anything."

"We still have no idea what my dad was doing—if anything. You're acting like we have proof that he was injecting me with kryptonite or something."

"I'm telling you, we've gotta go meet Pletcher. That's how we'll figure it out, I know it."

"There's one little problem, David. I spoke to my uncle yesterday and he doesn't want us going to New York at all."

"What? Why? We asked him to go along."

"He said we need to leave it to him, it's too dangerous for us to go, so he'll investigate."

"Look, at some point we've got to make our own decisions. Seems like now's the time."

Tour Guide

Finally, after boring introductory remarks, a different speaker takes the microphone at the front of the packed auditorium.

"If your last name begins with A through G, Claire, who's waving her hand over there, will be your tour guide. If your last name begins with H through N, Ashley, on the other side there waving her hand, is your guide."

Amanda and Aunt Barbara immediately stand and start heading toward their guide for the UVA. According to Aunt Barbara, they were lucky to get a slot since it was a Saturday during spring break for many of the nation's high schools.

Amanda has serious misgivings about this whole trip. Especially the part Aunt Barbara and Uncle Andy don't know about. She hopes she doesn't completely freak them out.

Ashley leads the group of perhaps two dozen seniors and parents past a number of colonial buildings designed by Thomas Jefferson and stops in an area with an expansive view across a green open space, where she launches into her first speech.

"Straight ahead of us, across the open lawn is the Rotunda. In 1817 Jefferson laid the Rotunda's cornerstone, along with fellow Virginians James Madison and James Monroe, making it the only U.S. university with three presidents connected to its birth. Jefferson's blueprint called for a central domed Rotunda, modeled after the Roman Pantheon, with 10 pavilions lining the open green space, now called The Lawn. Colonnades connect the pavilions to two rows of student dorm rooms that are highly sought after by fourth year students today. Let's have a look at these coveted dorm rooms along the lawn," she says, guiding the group along the walkway.

Once they near the long row of dorm rooms, Ashley continues, "They're currently all occupied, but let me see if we can get a look at one." A couple of college students sit in rocking chairs in front of one of the doors. "Do you mind if we take a quick look?" she asks one of them.

Aunt Barbara is near the front of the group, keenly interested in the unique Jeffersonian dorm room. This is the moment Amanda has been waiting for, and she quickly dashes around the side of the building, crosses behind it and slips the UVA map David gave her out of her jeans pocket. She quickly studies it, then trots in the direction of their meeting point. After she zigs and zags around two buildings she finds David's Toyota 4-Runner in the parking lot. As soon as she jumps in the passenger seat, David takes off.

"I hope you've got my stuff cuz I don't have any clothes or anything." Amanda says.

"Of course I've got your stuff, including your winter coat. You have your cell phone, right?" he asks.

"Yeah. I can call Uncle Andy or my aunt in what, about an hour?"

David promised that Amanda could make a payphone call within the first hour. There was no reason, Amanda said, to upset them any more than necessary. They'd been through too much already.

"I'm covered till Sunday," David says.

"How?"

"I told my parents your uncle was taking us sightseeing in New York City."

"Nice. Unless they call each other."

"That's highly doubtful. Look, we're going to be followed, not sure how or by who. It'll take 'em a little while to catch up to us. Can you believe a nor'easter is supposed to crush the New York area with up to a foot of snow in the next 24 hours? An April snowstorm, unreal."

"Does that change our plan? I mean the snow?"

"No. I don't think it changes anything, luckily."

"I hope you know what you're doing. We'll probably get caught and never get to New York." Amanda says.

"By who?"

"I don't know, but you say they're always one step away."

"Trust me, we'll get there," he says confidently. Within a few minutes they arrive at the small Charlottesville Airport. David pulls into the short term parking lot, and drives directly toward the second row, looking for a certain parking space.

"I need to get near this particular light pole." David stops the car, looking around cautiously in all directions. As soon as he's got the car parked, he opens his door, stands on the running board, and places something as high as he can on the pole beside the car.

"What're you doing?"

"Nothing." David gets back in the car and closes the door.

"Get in the back seat and change into your disguise." he says. "I won't look."

"Disguise? You never said anything about that."

"You didn't think we could get there without disguising ourselves did you? By the way, you're pregnant, with your second already, we just couldn't wait. There's a strap-on tummy to put under your frumpy looking maternity dress. I get to play the proud papa."

"So we're flying with this disguise stuff?" she asks.

"Nope. We're taking a taxi to the Amtrak station. That's part of the plan to throw them off. We're gonna leave the cell phones here, because I think they're tracking them, and that's how they'll find the car. You can't bring anything."

"What about my wallet, my ID, and some money?" she asks.

"Put it all in this pouch and I'm gonna stash it under the spare tire in the trunk. I've got plenty of cash, and I got you a fake ID. Here, take a look."

"Who's Lori Jane West?"

"You are, duh." David answers, laughing.

"No, I mean is she a real person?"

"No, but that's your name now, so you need to memorize it."

"Lori Jane. Lori Jane. Where are we staying while we're there?"

"A hotel, actually it's more like a bed and breakfast. Can you please change now?"

When she is done, David changes his shirt, dons a curly wig, a Boston Red Sox hat, and a glue-on fake mustache as the crowning touch. He checks himself out in the rearview mirror while Amanda gets back in the front seat and checks her appearance in the vanity mirror.

"I look hilarious with this bulging stomach. And you look like some drunk Red Sox fan that stumbled out of a bar somewhere."

When the cab arrives, David holds the fake baby, who is sleeping, while the driver puts the stroller in the back. David has even outfitted Amanda with a diaper bag, baby formula and all the other accessories necessary for the ruse. At the Amtrak station, David pays the cab driver with cash, they set the stroller up and push their baby into the building. He says the train should be pulling in within 15 minutes.

David finds a pay phone in the small waiting area at the Amtrak station. He puts in the information from the prepaid calling card, gets the phone number for Andy from Amanda, and then hands her the phone.

"You can only talk for a minute."

"Uncle Andy, it's Amanda. I wish I didn't have to leave this message on your voice mail, but I want you to know I'm fine, I'm not hurt. And I haven't been kidnapped either. There's just something I have to take care of, and I'll call you by Sunday. So, don't worry about me and I'll check in with you within two days. Love you."

She hands the phone to David who places it on the cradle. "I hope they don't freak."

Amazingly, the train is actually within three minutes of being on time, and they make their way on board. Amanda holds their baby while David takes care of stowing the lightweight stroller. David locates the conductor, who then guides them to the private sleeper room David reserved. She unlocks the door and explains the various features, including the fold-down bed system.

"We can also serve you food, just buzz us and we'll take your order. If you need anything else let me know."

David rummages through his backpack, breaks out his laptop, flips it open, and waits patiently for it to boot up.

"Well, they already found my car,"

"What? How'd they find it so fast?"

She looks over at his laptop. The video shows two plainclothes men who must be detectives circling the car. One of them checks the door, but it's locked. Then he breaks out a cell phone and can be seen calling someone. A few moments later they disappear off-camera.

"I put a surveillance camera on the lamp pole. They have a surprise in store for them when they come back with a search warrant," he says.

"Oh yeah? What?" she asks.

"The car will be gone. Some guy I found online and paid cash is going to pick it up and drive it back to Reston. He's leaving it in the shopping center parking lot by my house."

Nor'easter

The heavy snow starts falling long before they exit Grand Central station. David especially enjoys the snowy scenery from the train. While he stares out the window, the whole plan clicks through his mind. He relishes the opportunity to answer the burning questions about Amanda and her dad. He also hopes this solidifies his new bond with her. He often feels guilty about Jonathan and Amanda, but it was Amanda's decision.

Later, the massive sized flakes create random patterns visible in the streetlight nearest the window of The Diane, the quaint Manhattan B & B David had booked. He wants to rent a movie on demand, a comedy, something mindless. They settle on *Austin Powers*, the second one. Exhausted from all the logistics, David falls asleep first, still dressed, watching the flick. Amanda realizes she has never been alone with a boy in a hotel room before--at least not that she can remember. She wonders if karma is compelling them together, as she changes into a night shirt. But, since David is out cold, she just points the remote at the TV and turns it off, wondering how David plans to confront Pletcher.

Before first light, David is showered and dressed, and he gently wakes Amanda. He wants to be in position by 7:15 a.m.

Before the appointed time, they encamp themselves in a small breakfast joint diagonally across the street from the brownstone condos where David believes Pletcher lives. The entire sidewalk, street, trees, and bushes are all blanketed in bright white snow. They are both wearing another of the disguises David concocted. Amanda is no longer pregnant, and is now blonde.

An overweight bus-driver type guy sits at the breakfast bar, and beside him another blue collar worker in some unidentifiable uniform carries on a conversation.

"It's almost snowed a foot, I dunno how we're supposed to operate in this." He tells the other uniformed guy.

David walks back to the small table with breakfast for both of them.

"What's the exact plan anyway?" Amanda whispers.

"To wait for him to leave and take pictures of his car and record his license plate. If he drives a car, that is. Or, if he takes off walking toward the subway, we're gonna shadow him."

"How far is the closest subway?"

"Less than two blocks."

They both eat, watching the condo across the street. When they finish, David drops the disposable plates and utensils in a nearby trashcan, then walks back to their table.

At that moment, an incredibly loud boom emanates from the street outside. The windows of the café shake, debris hits the windows. They both instinctively dive to the ground, with David hovering partly over Amanda. A second or two later David crawls a few feet forward and peers through the window of the small restaurant. Pletcher's garage door is completely gone, and fire inside the garage engulfs what is left of a small unidentifiable car. Debris litters the driveway and street.

David ducks his head back down. "A bomb blew up Pletcher's car! I'll bet it activated when he opened the door or started it. The entire garage door is gone."

Amanda raises her head.

"Oh my God! We've got to get out of here! Do you think someone knew we came looking for him?"

"I don't know," he whispers back. "We do need to get out of here, but not suspiciously."

The bus-driver-looking guy and the other café customers have slowly crept back toward the front of the café, but none have the courage to open the front door. They all stare at the fire and destruction across the street. A couple of sirens wail and a police car has just rolled up in the snow-covered street out front. A couple of cops stand beside their patrol car, but aren't moving toward the driveway yet.

"We can't go out the front," David quickly concludes. "Let's walk casually to the back and see if we can get out."

They slowly walk toward the back, past two restroom doors, and see an emergency exit. David pushes the door open and they are in an alleyway. "Don't run," David says. "Act like we're just passing through."

~

The senior agent processes the new information from his field agents about Pletcher's car bombing. The choices become limited.

He responds over the secure wireless communication device, directing his lead field agent.

"Initiate the contingency plan we discussed."

"Yes sir."

"Act immediately."

"Confirmed, sir."

Blasted

Honking taxis crawl through the snow in Manhattan. Combine the closure of one lane of traffic with the usual pushy New York drivers and you end up with snowy gridlock and incessant horn blasts. People who presumably would have normally taken a taxi or bus are now clogging up the slushy sidewalks on foot.

David studies his hand-held GPS as his Red Sox hat slowly turns white with the falling snow. "I changed my mind. We can't take the subway. There are surveillance cameras everywhere. I honestly don't know what to do. Pletcher just got blasted because of us."

"I believe you now." Amanda says.

"We can't go to our hotel room, someone knows we're here."

"So, where are we gonna go?"

"Let's find a busy hotel so I can study the Amtrak schedule and decide if we can get our stuff at the B & B."

His GPS shows a couple of hotels in the area. "Where are we anyway?"

They both look at the street signs on the nearest corner.

"East 78th and 2nd," Amanda says.

They head east down the busy sidewalk after David confirms there is a hotel down 78th Street.

As they walk down the snow-covered street under a partial canopy of trees, Amanda glimpses the unusually serious stare of a guy with a black ski cap maybe 10 feet behind them. As the man walks briskly past her she notices his closed black umbrella. Just then, he lifts the umbrella oddly with his left hand, pointing it forward toward the back of David's left thigh.

Instinctively, she yells, "David! Watch out!"

Just as David wheels to the left and turns back, Amanda hears a sort of whizzing sound. The man suddenly stops, teeters back and forth, and then falls face forward onto the sidewalk with a snow-muffled thud. His umbrella falls ahead of him, forming an elongated depression in the snow.

"David, he was going to jab you!" Amanda screams as she reaches David and they gaze down at the man sprawled face down on the sidewalk. At the same moment, they both notice the blood oozing onto the snow along the edge of his black coat.

"Oh my God!" Amanda blurts out.

David's eyes widen and he turns to his left to study the rows of windows in the building across the street, looking for something, anything. Just as they are contemplating running in any direction, a black SUV slides through the snowy street to a stop at the curb right next to them. A lady jumps out of the front passenger door and flashes her badge.

Amanda recognizes her immediately.

"FBI, get in, fast!"

"Oh my God! Sienna? I thought --"

"No way!" David says in shock.

She throws open the rear door and yells "Now!"

They both leap into the back seat and Sienna jumps in right behind them. The driver steps on the accelerator and fishtails away before Sienna even gets the rear door closed.

"Was someone shooting at us?" David asks incredulously.

"Yes. We had to act immediately." Sienna says.

"That guy was trying to jab David or something. Then we saw blood," Amanda says, still shaken by what has just occurred.

"He must've been an operative for them." Sienna says.

"Them?" David asks, but he gets no response.

The driver begins speeding down the street, power-turns through the snow at the first left, and watches carefully in his rearview mirror. David decides this would be a good time to hunt for his seatbelt.

"Who was firing at us? Why?" David asks.

Sienna cranes her neck around, watching vigilantly and still not answering.

"You disappeared right after Kent died. I thought you were involved. I never imagined you were with the FBI." Amanda says.

"I was there to protect you. We barely managed to extract you just now so we're taking you to a safe house." she advises them.

Amanda catches a flash of her pistol in the holster along her right side under her unzipped coat.

"Charlie, how long will it take us to get there?" she asks the agent driving.

"Under an hour usually, but we've got weather, traffic, and probably a tail this time."

Sienna takes two black scarves out of her coat pocket and explains that she is going to have to blindfold them.

"It's for your protection, so you won't know where the safe house is, and can't be, uh, forced to divulge anything." She then secures the blindfolds.

"How long will we be there? I know it sounds stupid right now, but I have to get back to school Monday. And how will you get us back to Virginia?" David asks Sienna, the analyst in him needing answers.

"We'll get you home safely, but only when we know that hostiles aren't tailing you. You two could have been killed back there. You were in New York to see Pletcher, right?" Sienna asks.

"How'd you know?" David asks.

"It's our business, Mr. Owlsley."

"Yeah, and he got blown up by somebody who didn't want him meeting with us. But he didn't want to meet with us either." David tells her.

"Oh yeah? How do you know that?" Sienna asks him.

"He wouldn't schedule an appointment or return my calls."

"Ahh. I see," she replies, without confirming or denying David's belief.

After a little less than an hour, but what seems much longer, they finally slow to a crawl. Amanda hears the engine sound change.

"I can take these off now," Sienna says, untying the blindfolds.

They are slowly advancing down a long snow-covered rural driveway. In the minimal moonlight, Amanda notices a quaint snowman in the middle of the front yard.

"Nice snowman. Did you help roll it?" Amanda asks her.

"No, Charlie and another agent built it today. There's plenty of down time in this job."

"So, how were you watching us? I had no idea we were being followed." David asks her.

"Don't worry about it."

As they approach the house an overhead garage door goes up and their SUV slowly pulls in.

"It's important you stay here for at least the next 24 hours. We can't let you contact anyone because someone may be listening. We have TVs, a stereo, plenty of food, and some extra clothing," Sienna assures them.

When they enter the safe house, there's one agent downstairs who has what looks to David like a Glock on his holster. Years of warfare video games have made David a virtual weapons expert, despite having almost no experience in firing a real gun. He fired one only once, when his uncle took him to an indoor firing range.

Sienna and the male agent speak momentarily before Sienna asks them to follow her upstairs. She shows them around like a caring relative.

"Don't open the blinds. If you need anything just come downstairs and talk to me or Charlie, the driver. Or ask Jasper who is the other agent downstairs. Do you guys have any questions?"

"Twenty-four hours? And then you'll...what? Take us back to Reston?" David asks.

"I'm going to send one of the agents to get your belongings tomorrow. Do you have the room number and keys?"

David hands over the keys and writes down the room number.

"Do you know why that guy was trying to jab David?" Amanda asks Sienna.

"No, not yet. But we'll definitely find out." Sienna says.

David and Amanda sit together on the bed in Amanda's temporary room. David grabs the remote control and turns on the television. Within seconds they see a report on the car bombing.

"A car bomb exploded today in the garage of Manhattan attorney Robert Pletcher." The video shows the garage door jaggedly blown off and what appears to be the shell of a small car chassis still smoldering.

"New York Police Detective Robert Shiano spoke with Channel 3 News," the anchorman says, as another clip from right in the street near where David and Amanda heard the blast is shown.

"What we can say right now for sure is that there was a bomb that exploded somewhere inside or next to a car owned by Mr. Pletcher. At this time New York Police are not ruling out terrorism, but say that this is definitely an ongoing investigation. They have called on the public to provide information on any unusual activity in or near this residence in the early morning hours before the blast."

A few minutes later Sienna appears with a small briefcase.

"One of our protocols when we have people in protective custody is to take a blood sample. I need to prick your finger. It just takes a second."

David and Amanda look at each other.

"Really? That's weird." David says.

Sienna flips open the case on top of the bed, pulls out a little kit, and says, "Let's go with Amanda first."

Amanda holds out her finger and Sienna pricks it and draws a small amount of blood into a little vial. She then repeats the process with David. She places each of the vials back in the case after marking one for each of them. Below Amanda's name on her vial is the word "Phoenix."

Later, the two of them eat dinner downstairs in the kitchen. Soup and grilled cheese sandwiches. Not gourmet food, but they both are happy to eat.

As they head back upstairs, Sienna calls to them.

"I trust you guys are all set. We'll be down here if you need anything."

"God, I hope I can sleep. This whole thing gives me the creeps." Amanda tells David. "Do you want to watch TV with me?"

"Sure," he says, following her into her room.

They find an old western starring Clint Eastwood. Neither are sure which one it is. Despite Sienna's request, Amanda peeks through the wooden slats of the blinds. The snow still falls, amazingly. She sees another snowman in the backyard too. At least the agents have a playful side.

Urgency

Since Andy had gotten the reassuring voicemail from Amanda, he had become increasingly worried as each hour passed. Nonetheless, he had immediately calmed Barbara down, and persuaded her to leave Charlottesville and come back home. But what if Amanda was really in trouble, and had been *forced* to leave that voicemail?

Early the next morning that Stein calls Andy's cell phone, out of the blue. "Michaels, can we meet? I need to talk to you in person."

"Not today, I'm dealing with an emergency." Andy responds brusquely.

"I know, that's why we need to meet."

"What? How do you know about it?"

"Meet me in 30 minutes at Abbott's Grill. I'll explain."

"Do you know if Amanda is still in Charlottesville? My sister's still there and is freaking out."

"We believe she's in New York City. See you in 30." Stein hangs up.

Andy calls Barb right away and tells her he may have reliable information soon, choosing not to give her any details, and that she should check out and drive back home.

Stein is already at the long bar in Abbott's Grill when Andy arrives. It's late afternoon, but the after-work crowds have not yet gathered. The bartender is right there to wait on them.

"Nothing for me." Andy tells him. He notices Stein has a drink already.

"I'm listening." Andy says.

"Your niece and David Owlsley went to New York to try to meet Pletcher. I told you to warn them."

"I did. They must've gone anyway. Are they safe? How do you know they're in New York?"

"First off, I'm only telling you what you need to know, which is going to be, uh, less than everything. It's simply the way we conduct business, and it's for your own good." He takes a big swig of his drink.

"Are you recording this?" Andy asks him, looking directly at Stein. Stein stares back. "Let me turn that around. Are *you* recording this?"

"Why would I? I don't believe anything that comes out of your mouth."

"Look, we like you and your family. I told you that before, and we hope to have--" Stein says cryptically.

"What the hell? Do you have my niece and David protected or not?"

"Not this second, but I'm confident we will, and when we do, you'll be the first to know. Don't say I didn't warn you."

"My family has been decimated, Stein. Amanda's 18 years old, and guess what? She doesn't do everything she's told. Do you have kids? I don't, but they don't listen sometimes."

"No kids." Stein confirms. "Look, I told you last time we were here, it comes down to us versus them. Us versus the Chinese. Us versus the Russians. Do we make mistakes? Yes, we do, but we didn't cause that crash."

Andy looks over at Stein. "Whoa. I've just represented all of those families on the basis that there was a mechanical failure. Did I just hear what I thought I heard?"

"Yeah, you heard it, but you will never, ever repeat any of this. So what if we funded most of the settlements? Hemispheres knows where that money came from. They didn't need details and you really don't either. Your settlements are solid. Nobody's trying to weasel out of anything, especially not Hemispheres. Your brother was helping us, but he never knew the details--"

"Details? Wait, what was he helping you do?"

"After studying every current BBS research project, we concluded it was his research they were after. We needed to expose their mole, and your brother agreed to help us." Stein takes a sip of his drink, not looking at Andy.

"Finally, a grain of the truth! Who was after Ron's research?"

"At least China. Maybe Russia too, we don't know."

"My brain may blow up. First, how is Pletcher involved? Is he one of their agents or one of ours?"

"You haven't heard the news yet?"

"No, about what?"

"Pletcher was killed by a car bomb today in his garage."

"What the hell? You have to tell me my niece is safe!"

"If I could, I would. As soon as I know we have Amanda and David safe, I'll tell you. And they'll be in protective custody for some time."

"You're a lawyer. Surely you understand the ethical issues you just dumped on me. What about all of my clients?"

"What are you talking about? Have you not heard anything I told you? We're talking about national security, which trumps everything else. I had to tell you about your niece, and that we're all over this. Don't breathe a word of this to a soul – not your family, not your staff, nobody. My contact at the agency told me to meet you and disclose only the absolute minimum. Can we trust you?"

"I don't know how to answer that."

"You better know how. Just in the last 48 hours, we think we isolated the mole. That means that your brother's help mattered, big time. We're grateful as hell too. Oh, the Owlsleys. Would you be willing to talk to the Owlsleys? Not yet, but when we have their son and your niece under our protection?"

"To say what?"

"To give them a plausible explanation."

"You mean make up a cover story for his parents? Now I'm a virtual co-conspirator."

"You make it sound like we're criminals. We have a major op in place right now and we're trying to save them both."

It seems like he should say thanks, but somehow Andy doesn't feel the least bit grateful, so he doesn't speak.

"We can wait on that issue until I have concrete news for you." Stein says. "I'll have more answers in less than 24 hours. Are we good?" He places cash on the bar near the tab the bartender left for him.

Andy looks over at Stein. He is nowhere near "good." His mind whirls. He already feels like some kind of turncoat. The families he represented. His own family. He feels dirty, like someone paid him off or something, even though that wasn't the case.

"What kind of help did you ask Ron for? I don't get it. Was he doing research for you?"

"No, we don't meddle in that. We had a counter-intelligence operation involving leaks at BBS, and we believed secrets about his research on telomeres were being sold to a foreign government. Nothing more. He didn't hesitate to help us. We asked him on very short notice if he would be willing to fly to New York to meet with one of our operatives there. He was part of the bait in our trap."

"That's why he wasn't travelling with Rochelle and Amanda! It was really a complete coincidence they ended up on the same flight. Unbelievable!"

"You've got that right," Stein agrees, "a horrible, tragic coincidence."

"Wait, let me guess. You wanted him to go meet Pletcher. So Pletcher was working for the CIA?"

"Can't answer that with a yes or no. He didn't know why he was going, because we didn't want him to know anything about the scenarios we built to tease out the mole. And then, all hell broke loose. I would tell you more, but the final chapter hasn't been written. Not yet."

Andy lowers his voice to a mere whisper. "The Chinese killed Ron, Rochelle and all those passengers. That's what you're saying. That's the truth isn't it?"

"Don't put words in my mouth, Michaels. I told you before, we didn't cause it. And we didn't do anything wrong either."

Both of them stare down at the copper bar for a few seconds.

"Are we good now?"

"Maybe. It's a lot to digest, and I can't believe how valuable this research must be. As long as you have Amanda safe by tomorrow. We can talk more about legalities then."

Andy gets up and hovers a moment near Stein's bar stool, preparing to leave, but somehow can't bring himself to take the next few steps.

Stein reaches up and places his hand on Andy's upper arm in an unusual gesture.

"Michaels, I'm trusting you here. Not a soul. I promise to explain more when we confirm the mole and have Amanda and David safe."

Amanda lies beside David on the bed, watching Clint Eastwood brood. A nervous tension pervades the room, not because of the storyline of the old western, but from the day's surreal events.

"I guess I should go and try to get some sleep," he says, getting up off the bed.

"Wait. I'm scared."

He stands near the open doorway, while she walks over toward the window.

"We're safer here than we were last night. Here we have the FBI protecting us, last night we could've been killed or--"

Amanda lifts one of the blinds to check on the snowfall. "David! I saw someone, or something."

David quickly walks over and lifts one of the blinds to look.

"What? Where?"

"I saw something. I swear I saw someone running in the snow near those trees."

"I don't see anything. Where?"

"Over by the trees on the right, but—I don't see anything now."

"How sure are you? Should we tell Sienna?"

Looking through the blind again, she seems uncertain. "Can you just stay in here awhile? I noticed there are some playing cards in the night stand." She walks over to it. "Here," she says, sliding it open and pulling out the cards. "Let's play Hearts again. That was fun when we played on the train, before we got into this big mess. Maybe we shouldn't have come, like my Uncle Andy said."

"Easy to say now. Okay, let's play."

Midway through the first game, chaos erupts. Blinding light is followed by a deafening explosion of some type of grenade. Then another, and another. They both instinctively shut their eyes against the painfully bright light.

Suddenly a body launches onto Amanda's, forcing them both off the bed to the floor. Panic stricken, Amanda doesn't struggle. The woman's weight rests directly on top of Amanda, and their heads both face the door below the foot of the bed. Amanda finally cracks open one eye to find near blackness and no electricity. She can just make out the silhouette of her captor's pistol with its long silencer held out in front of them, aimed toward the door. Amanda doesn't dare move, but can't help speaking.

"Sienna? David? Are you mmmfff--" A gloved hand covers her mouth, muffling her words.

"Shhhh!"

A second later, Sienna wheels silently into the bedroom with her pistol drawn ahead of her.

Amanda pulls the gloved hand off her mouth. "Watch--!"

It's too late, her captor fires several rounds upwards at close range and Sienna's body violently shakes and then falls with a terrible thud right into the room near the door.

"Noooo!!" Amanda tries to yell, but she can barely breathe between the shock and the pressure on her back. The gloved hand presses hard against her mouth again. A few seconds pass. Another person slowly climbs the stairs. She can hear the slight creaking sound in the otherwise deafening silence. As she considers breaking free, she hears more whizzing sounds, followed by the unmistakable loud piercing sound of machine gun fire. Finally, the shooting stops and she hears a person tumbling down the long hardwood staircase. She and David may be next, but something tells her probably not. Couldn't they have easily been killed already?

"Three hostiles down," a man suddenly standing inside the doorway says to someone else, himself slightly out of breath. Amanda's eyes focus on him in the darkness, his all black outfit, his night vision goggles, the machine gun in his right hand. He stoops down and checks Sienna for a pulse.

"She's dead," he says with no trace of emotion. Suddenly he hears something from behind the louvered closet doors.

"David. Come out with your hands raised where I can see them," he says loudly with his machine gun trained at the closet. He knows David's name!

"Okay, okay," David says, sliding open both doors and quickly raising his hands.

"They were all MSS agents. Ministry of State Security, China's CIA. We're FBI, and we're extricating you," the guy says.

"What? How can we believe you? They said they were FBI..." David says.

"Not a chance. We have to move, we don't have much time," the woman atop Amanda says, climbing off of her.

"Britt? Britt! What the hell are you..." Amanda haltingly says. She feels dizzy trying to absorb it.

"No way!" David gasps.

"No time to explain now. We've got a plan to get you both out of here alive, but we know this place is wired tight. They didn't kill you; that's a good sign, because they could have. Just follow every direction Jeremy and I give."

"How'd you get in here?" David asks.

"Cut in through the roof, then came down the attic staircase."

"Sienna was their agent? And they killed Pletcher too?" David asks.

"There was no real Pletcher, we created him as bait. Why'd you two have to pull this stunt?" Britt says after a slight delay, then listens to something through her earpiece.

"That makes no sense," David mutters. "We saw that bomb explode and saw the news too."

Britt ignores him, apparently listening to directions.

"Listen up. We're going downstairs, then Jeremy will get to the garage to link up with two other agents. We have 45 seconds to hit the back door, dash to the woods, and take off on the snow scooter. Jeremy and his team will create a diversion."

"Follow right behind me," Britt instructs, and they caravan down the staircase, with Jeremy leading. Both he and Britt have their machine guns drawn. David recognizes the weapon well, down to the silencer and the under-muzzle M-4 grenade launcher. They reach the bottom of the staircase still in darkness, where Jeremy peels off silently toward the front of the house. Britt, followed by the two of them, moves silently in the other direction toward the kitchen area.

To persons unseen, Britt whispers, "15 seconds," and then adds, "Jeremy, at the one count fire your grenade at the snowman in the front yard, I will take out the one in the back."

"3, 2, 1!" Britt crashes out the lower right corner of the kitchen window and fires the M-4's grenade at the snowman in the backyard, reducing it instantly to an uneven clump on the ground. A metal tubular frame, nearly as tall as the snowman was, now stands exposed. Several wires connected to small electronic surveillance devices dangle from the frame.

"I had a feeling about them." Brit says to the network of listening agents.

In the front yard, an explosive device discharges near the highway. Suddenly, the garage door bursts into pieces as a black SUV being driven backwards by Jeremy barrels through it. Gunfire erupts from the woods. The SUV fishtails into a 180-degree turn and continues down the snow covered driveway.

High above the scene, a U.S. controlled drone pinpoints the location of the gunfire from the wooded area adjacent to the driveway. GPS coordinates are conveyed to two agents in sniper positions, who then hone in their gunfire on the hostile agents. A nasty firefight erupts in the woods.

Britt, followed by Amanda and David, burst from the rear door of the home and make a beeline for the thick tree line. Britt has activated a small handheld jamming device in case the MSS has booby-trapped the area with any IEDs. All three jump onto the snow scooter, a snowmobile designed by U.S. intelligence to operate in virtual silence at up to 40 mph. They accelerate through the tree line, guided by Britt, using her night vision goggles. Finally, they break out of the tree line, and Britt steers the scooter onto the snow-covered road. Ahead there is a partially lit panel truck waiting for them with the rear ramp down. Still moving at around 20 miles an hour, Britt runs the scooter right up the ramp and into the rear of the panel truck where she disengages the throttle. A huge airbag deploys in the front of the panel truck and captures them in its midst. A second or two later, the massive airbag retracts, as does the ramp, and the overhead door closes.

A small half-door opens between the truck cab and the trailer. Britt greets the driver and another agent before pulling a fold-down bench seat from the wall of the trailer and securing the snow scooter in place with two large hooks. Then she climbs into the front seat and a different agent climbs into the back, holding a machine gun in his hand and sporting a set of night vision goggles on his forehead.

"Put those shoulder harnesses around yourselves," the agent says. The truck engine starts up moments later and she and David feel the truck pull slowly away.

"Where's Britt?" Amanda asks.

"She's gone. We're responsible for getting you to a real safe house now."

Swimming

The most logical takedown locations had been analyzed over several days before they settled on a choke point one block from the mole's home. The FBI SWAT team, along with several of Solarez' CIA operatives, have taken up positions in the two blocks closest to the mole's home. Unfortunately their careful planning was all for naught: the mole never came home that evening.

A man swims the 1.5K Potomac River course from just south of the Lincoln Memorial to the Arlington Memorial Bridge and back. He has been training for the upcoming triathlon both after work and on weekends. Because the Potomac is notoriously polluted, he wears his full-length wetsuit and black skin-tight swimming cap with a small American flag on the side. As he makes his way to the buoy marking his halfway point under the Arlington Memorial Bridge, he's feeling pretty good.

Even with his swimming goggles on, he never sees the frogman rising slowly behind him. He feels a very slight stinging sensation in the middle of his lower abdomen, from the tiny needle injected there by the specially modified speargun. There is no opportunity for him to feel anything else because he is completely paralyzed.

The frogman then lassoes his leg and tugs him down under the water's surface. River water fills his mouth, his nasal passages, and rushes into his chest.

Nearly motionless, the frogman watches his underwater chronograph and counts down the seconds to ensure the swimmer has drowned. When enough time has elapsed, he releases the lasso from the leg of the swimmer and watches him float back up to the surface. The frogman then proceeds to his launching location at the opposite side of the Potomac about a half-mile away.

Unraveled

At 8:10 a.m. the next morning, Andy's cellphone rings. It's Stein.

"Michaels, I have great news. We have Amanda and David."

"Hallelujah," Andy says with a deep sigh.

"There's a lot more I'd like to go over with you. Can you come to the State Department?"

"Why don't you come over here to my office? I think at this point you owe it to me." Andy says, feeling confident that Stein will do it.

"Okay, I'll grab a taxi. Thirty minutes?"

"Sure. I'll be waiting." Andy looks at his watch and realizes Myra isn't even at the front desk yet. He walks out there and leaves her a note, then walks back to his desk to wait.

About a half an hour later Myra announces that Stein has arrived. Andy greets him in the reception area. Stein leans in slightly and whispers, "We need to take a walk."

Andy raises his eyebrows, but doesn't argue. Stein says nothing until they are on the street. They walk side by side up to M Street and turn eastbound, avoiding the occasional pedestrians passing them.

"We have your niece and David in protective custody, and we are taking them to a safe house. It was pretty dicey from what I've been told. They were kidnapped and we had to put together an armed raid to rescue them."

"You didn't tell me anything about them being held captive."

"I didn't want to freak you out. Lives were lost in the operation. They lost some and we lost one."

Andy looks straight ahead, thinking how much this is outside his realm. They continue their slow walk east, apparently with no destination.

"My niece and David think Ron may have treated her blood with something. What do you know about it?"

"I honestly don't know, but I can tell you this, the Chinese think she was. That's probably why they kidnapped her. They actually drew her blood, most likely under some false pretense. We recovered all of it."

Before Andy can ask another question about Amanda's possible treatments, Stein speaks again.

"The other big news is we exposed the mole. But he was dead before we could arrest him."

"Who killed him?"

"We assume the MSS. They knew that if we arrested him we would surely expose the rest of their U.S. operatives."

"So does that mean you can or can't bring Amanda home?" Andy asks.

"Andy, Alex Erickson drowned last night while swimming in the Potomac."

Andy stops in his tracks as Stein keeps walking. Andy can't move. Stein, realizing he is walking alone, turns and takes a few steps back toward Andy and faces him.

"Stein, that can't be. He wasn't the mole."

Stein simply looks at Andy, says nothing, and then turns, shaking his head. He begins walking again.

"Stein. Talk to me. Tell me it wasn't Alex!"

Stein walks very slowly, refusing to answer. Andy then trots toward him and grabs his left arm.

"How do you know for sure?"

With resignation in his voice, Stein answers. "We know, Michaels. We also know all about how close you and Ron were with him, so I decided to tell you in person, but I...you just have to forget we ever talked about this. No one else will ever know the truth. I'm sure the death certificate will read 'drowning secondary to acute myocardial infarction,' which means 'drowning due to heart attack.'"

Andy feels like a sledgehammer has pummeled his chest. Just breathing seems impossible.

"We're going to develop a cover story about where your niece and David have been. Probably something about Amanda needing emergency medical treatment of some sort and demanding he be with her.

"Last, we're working on a comprehensive deal with the Chinese. If we seal this deal, I believe Amanda and Owlsley will be safe again. We've taken steps already."

"A deal? You're negotiating with the Chinese MSS?" Andy asks him incredulously.

"Oh yeah. We make deals with foreign intelligence agencies on occasion, when it makes sense to both sides. We have some real bargaining chips. Their agents are human beings with families too, and we have some bodies in bags and some live ones too."

Did Andy really hear that? Yes, unfortunately. It seems like just another business deal to Stein. This is not his first rodeo, for sure.

They are near a busy corner, so Stein extends his arm to hail a cab and Andy turns to walk back to his office. He takes a few steps away and stops. Then he pivots back toward Stein.

"What about Amanda's friend, Kent Perless?"

Just then a cab pulls alongside a parked car near the corner, and Stein takes a couple steps toward it.

"The MSS, Michaels. That's one of our major bargaining chips."

"Wait, what's that mean? He was just an innocent victim, right?" Andy asks as Stein reaches for the cab door and opens it.

"We'll talk soon." Stein says and then shuts the door.

Andy steps back up to the sidewalk, unable to focus even on which direction he wants to walk. The pedestrians stream around him. He's thinking about Denise Erickson, their kids. Thinking about all the trips they've been on together. Ron, Alex, and himself, skiing, hanging out, partying in college. Then he rehashes their meeting at the Catacombs too, when he never imagined anything could involve Alex. What made Alex cross that line? Was it jealousy of Ron? Maybe financial stress, with all those kids and private schools and whatever?

He just can't make himself believe Alex sold out. Sold out himself, Ron, hell, his own country. How much did they pay him? Maybe Alex set in motion the crash of the Hemispheres jet. Especially if controlling the BBS research information was what the Chinese were after. Andy finally starts walking back toward his office. Then he thinks of the funeral. Oh God. Not another funeral, this time where he will hide this horrible, twisted secret. Sadness envelopes him, so much so he feels completely exhausted.

He suddenly has the presence of mind to call Barbara and tell her the fantastic news about Amanda being safe and sound. She and Steve are absolutely ecstatic.

After he ends that call and is nearing his law office, Kent Perless, and his dad Kyle slide back into the foreground of his thoughts. It was not an overdose. It was linked to everything else. There's been no closure for Kyle, none whatsoever.

As soon as he gets back to his building, he walks into Angie's office and plops down in a chair.

"Why was that guy here?"

“Amanda and David were actually missing, and that guy was letting me know they’re safe and sound now,” he says, proud that none of it was a lie, just a lot omitted.

“Andy, is everything okay? You look worried.”

“It’s okay. I really think so now.”

“It’s not like you to hold things back from me. Something big is going on, what is it?”

“Things can only get better now. Can I switch the subject back to work?”

“Sure.”

“Can you do some research on the federal whistleblower law, the ‘Qui Tam’ provisions, for those whose efforts are responsible for the government recovering money based on some fraud perpetuated on the government. I’d like it this afternoon if possible.”

“Okay, I guess the discovery answers on the Boyd case can wait. What case is this for?”

“Amanda Michaels.”

"This is certainly not my usual lunch, I mean meeting with an undercover intelligence agent." Judge Bondakopf says with a wry smile. "Obviously you must have something important on your mind. Before you start, I don't need to remind you that I'm not allowed to have ex parte communications on pending cases."

"What’s the exact definition of that anyway?" Steven asks her. "I'm not kidding; I have a reason for asking."

"It's Latin, it means communicating with one party to a lawsuit to the exclusion of the other party.”

"Have you decided on anything yet?" The waitress asks them.

"We're going to need a few more minutes," Judge Bondakopf tells her, as she looks at the menu.

“But in the FISA cases, there is no other party,” Solarez points out.

“I guess you’re right, but I am not authorized to engage in, shall we say, off-the-record communications either.”

They place their order and hand the waitress their menus. A few silent moments pass. Judge Bondakopf doesn’t break the silence, knowing that Solarez is about to impart something weighty.

"Well, I have some major news. We believe we closed down the spying operation at BBS. We were ready to arrest the mole, but that same day he died under mysterious circumstances while swimming in the Potomac River. He was training for a triathlon."

"His name? Not that it will necessarily mean anything to me."

"Alex Erickson. He was actually a close acquaintance of both Ron and Andy Michaels. You may be the first federal judge whose actions proved instrumental in a covert intelligence operation."

"Well that's great, I guess. I probably violated a number of judicial canons barring a judge from showing partiality or bias toward one side in any hearing or trial."

"How could you have not been impartial at a hearing when we never had a real hearing? The entire Pletcher hearing was a ruse."

"Hmmm. It wasn't a real hearing." The judge ponders out loud.

"Nope, it was just supposed to seem like a real hearing so the Chinese..."

"That works for me. How do you know our fake hearing made a difference?"

"There's too much to explain, but it's absolutely clear they believed Pletcher was going to sell the biological research information. When Pletcher died, or I should say when the Pletcher character died, we were able to isolate Erickson."

"Impressive. Now you need to submit the paperwork for my signature notifying those who were under surveillance."

"No problem. They already know anyway."

"They know already? What do you mean? You fought me all the way on notification."

"Well, let's just say that they know, but we'll do the formal part to comply with the law."

The waitress brings their orders so they take a break from the conversation for a few moments.

"So Steven, tell me a little bit about yourself."

Deal Points

Mr. Jang-Chung's black limousine pulls into the gated portion of the White House executive offices in Washington, D.C. for the hastily arranged meeting led by Stein and two other gentlemen from the agency. Stein arranged the secure location to avoid conducting the talks at the Chinese embassy, the FBI headquarters, or at Langley, the CIA headquarters. The six of them sit at the rectangular conference table facing each other. All six speak fluent Chinese and English, except for Stein, who can only muster a few key Chinese phrases. The back channel negotiations had been ongoing for days but got much more serious in the last 24 hours. Stein knew why. The mole had been terminated by his comrades that were now sitting across the table from him. This changed the paradigm. The Chinese realized that their operation was doomed and it was time to move on. That's why they were ready to deal.

"Thank you for coming here today, gentlemen. The first piece of business is the payment of $200 million in reparations for the Hemispheres crash. Then we can discuss the exchanges and any other related terms," Stein advises his peer across the table.

"My country must not pay reparations, Mr. Stein. People's Republic is willing to discuss different methods to accomplish the same thing. We have three offers: The first is that we agree not to dispute the U.S. imposing an anti-dumping tariff on Chinese manufacturers of automotive parts for one calendar year, which will result in hundreds of millions in profits to U.S. company earnings, well in excess of the 200 million dollars you are requesting.

"Second option, PRC reduces, very slightly, the property taxation rate on all U.S. companies with factories in PRC for the next 12 months resulting in more than $200 million in receipts to U.S. companies.

"Or third, the PRC national bank slightly changes the valuation of the Chinese Yuan favorably against U.S. dollar for 12 hours only, and then we re-adjust back, permitting your Federal Reserve to profit on all currency exchanges that occur in the agreed 12 hours, which may result in far greater than $200 million, depending on your transactions. In all scenarios, my nation agrees to no apology, no reparations."

Then, Jang-Chung looks down at the note pad his aide has slid in front of him. He adjusts his reading glasses, and reads the note. "We also would agree to the following exchange - one former special forces soldier from PRC to U.S. for six PRC operatives from U.S., five from New York operation, one from Loudoun operation." His aide then whispers something to him. "You must also confirm whether Loudoun operative is alive."

Stein nods his understanding as his aides on either side of him jot down notes.

"Give us some time to confer."

Stein and his entourage leave the room and step into another nearby conference room.

One detail they had not been sure of was whether the Chinese had swept up Ryan or not, but that mystery was now solved. Clearly the MSS thought Ryan was working for one of the U.S. agencies. They discuss the various offers, and Stein makes a call on a secure line to the director to get his authority to close a deal. The director tells Stein to build in a reverse sweetener in the deal that will return $25 million to the Chinese in one year. It seems counter-intuitive to Stein, but he knows his job is to follow instructions, so he makes notes of the director's instructions. Meanwhile, the Chinese barely say a word to each other, assuming that the room is not secure. After all, it's in the U.S. State Department's control.

Stein and his entourage re-enter the room about 30 minutes later.

"We think that the manipulation of the Yuan during an agreed upon 12-hour period will be satisfactory. However, that is subject to all other terms of the agreement, including a new term that PRC will close down any operation involving Biological Blood Services, and no harm will come to any employee or their families. If PRC honors this agreement for an entire calendar year, the U.S. will return $25 million to PRC. Any violation, and we retain the $25 million."

"You must verify you have the individual who disappeared in Virginia," Jang-Chung refers to their operative who disappeared the night of Kent Perless' death.

"We first need assurance from the PRC that you will return Mr. Ryan alive."

"Yes. You have my assurance, Mr. Stein."

"We have your Loudoun County operative, alive," Stein responds. A look of pleasure comes across Jang-Chung's poker face. It's clear that he was assuming their agent was being returned in a body bag. He turns left and right to his aides who nod to him, obviously happy to receive this unexpected news as well.

Stein gets out a pen and on a yellow pad writes down the deal points:

1. Yuan revaluation – 12 hours;
2. Exchange, as discussed, in U.S., time/place to be determined;
3. Confidential terms;
4. BBS op closed, no further adverse actions by U.S. or PRC;
5. $25 M from U.S. to PRC after one year, if term #4 met.

Stein writes "USA" at the bottom and puts a line under it. He signs it and prints his name and title: "Brett Stein, State Dept. Counsel." Then he passes the yellow pad across the table to Jang-Chung. He and both his aides look down at the notes and briefly confer before he looks across to Stein and nods his head in agreement. He lifts his pen and writes "PRC" beside "USA" and signs his name in Chinese with a flourish.

He respectfully passes it with two hands back to Stein.

"Let's get six copies of the agreement made right away," he directs the aide to his right. "One hour after the 12-hour Yuan revaluation closes, we'll do the exchange at the Roosevelt Bridge. We bring our asset from the Virginia side, you bring your asset from the Washington, D.C. side. We'll deliver the bodies simultaneously to your jet either at Dulles or Washington-National Airport."

"Agreed," Jang-Chung says.

"I'll contact you tomorrow morning to set the valuation timing."

They all rise from the table and walk beside it to shake hands.

"I heard no mention of Mr. Erickson today." Stein whispers to Jang-Chung, wanting to get at least one jab in to his opponent.

Jang-Chung remains expressionless. "I do not know to whom you refer, Mr. Stein. I always appreciate doing business with you."

Whistleblower

Following two separate conversations with Stein, Andy had called Kyle Perless and set up their meeting. Was Kyle one of the most devastated persons in the aftermath of the Hemispheres fiasco? Andy figured that was like asking the Titanic survivors which of them suffered the worst. Kyle was definitely one who was wronged and never compensated. He had been thinking about him ever since Stein all but admitted Kent was murdered at Crossroads Farm. Once Stein conceded the U.S. would recover over $200 million, Andy had pitched his whistleblower deal proposal to Stein and the wheels started turning.

Now he is sitting at the kitchen table in Kyle's small apartment. He notices a rack with multiple guitars and can barely hear some light acoustic music playing through speakers hidden somewhere. Andy has finished going through all of the key terms of the proposal.

"I never even really hired you as my lawyer," Kyle says.

"True, and you absolutely have the right to find someone else to deal with them. You don't have to use me. However, you'll probably have a bigger legal fee and they wouldn't give you the attorney fees back to pay your taxes."

Kyle gets up from the table and paces around the small room, thinking.

"What if I say no? Maybe I'd rather go to the press."

"You have the right to do that, Kyle. But would you really turn down the deal?"

"I don't know. I could go to the press and blow the whole story open. What a story it would be too," Kyle says, but his words lack conviction.

"What good would that do now? The government says they had nothing to do with Kent's death, and I finally believe that. The worst part is your loss. There's nothing...I admit, I can't mitigate that. But they're willing to pay you a lot of money. Why turn it down? To go to the press instead? What do you get by doing that? Will you really learn why some foreign spies killed him? Probably not. And you'll blow the chance of getting this deal."

"Everyone still thinks my son OD'd." Kyle interjects, wanting to protect his son's image. "That's a bald-faced lie."

"We're taking care of that. It'll be part of the deal." Andy says.

Kyle Perless and Andy arrive at the Department of Justice the next day at 10:00 a.m. This time, there is a lawyer Andy has never met before from the Justice Department. The unknown lawyer ends up doing most of the talking while Stein mostly listens with Andy and Kyle.

"Mr. Perless, there's a federal law called the 'Qui Tam' law, which most people call the 'whistleblower law.' We believe that your son's action directly led to the ultimate recovery of $230 million by the United States. Section 7 of the Qui Tam Act is the one that comes into play here because the false act or false claim of a foreign government resulted in an increase of the obligation of the U.S. by that sum of money."

"Let me interrupt you a second," Perless says. "No one told me how the government paid out the $230 million or how they recovered it through Kent's actions. I mean, I'm not questioning it was recovered, but I'd like to know how it happened."

"Mr. Perless, we agree on one essential fact, your son was murdered," interjects Stein. "It wasn't an overdose and it wasn't his fault. We want to see justice done in the best way we can. Exactly what wheels turned, and how it all came about...some of those things cross over into national security. We can't give you all of the details. The deal is the deal."

The DOJ lawyer continues, "Under the whistleblower law, we can compensate the person who brings the losses to our attention. The U.S. can pay the relator, which is your son's estate, anywhere from 15 to 25 percent of the amount recovered plus attorney's fees. We're offering your son's estate $10 million under the Whistleblower Act, out of which you would need to pay your attorney's fees. Under the settlement, all terms will remain confidential indefinitely. Last, we'll need the deal approved by a U.S. District Court judge. Oh, and your portion of the settlement is taxable. Can't do anything about that."

Now it's Andy's turn. "Kyle, you understand that I'm charging you a 25 percent legal fee, but once that fee is paid I am going to use those monies to pay both my firm's taxable consequence and your taxable consequence for getting the settlement money. So you'll essentially be receiving about $7.5 million tax-free."

Kyle Perless flips back and forth through the three-page typed agreement.

"Where does it talk about the death certificate?"

Andy looks through his copy.

"Halfway down on page three. 'The U.S. will assure that the death certificate with regard to Kent Perless will be changed from accidental overdose to homicide – cause unknown.'"

"What if the press finds out about this and wants to ask me questions? What can I tell them?"

"If you look at the next line of the settlement agreement, it says you may simply comment that the medical examiner was asked to conduct a re-examination and determined there were no toxicological results to support any accidental overdose."

"Okay, I'll do it. Where do I sign?"

The DOJ lawyer hands five original copies to Kyle, which he signs one by one. Stein briefly whispers to Andy before shaking his hand leaving the conference room. Andy and Kyle walk through the conference room door and out into the hall of the Justice Department.

"Andy, thanks. I was skeptical at first. I guess I just don't trust the government, but you were right. I had to take the deal. I hate the confidentiality but--"

"I know. I have had numerous major settlements and it truly sucks to be silenced. It's just an evil that no one seems to be able to eliminate."

"How's Amanda doing? I heard she took a trip or something. Is she back yet?"

Andy tries to maintain a calm look. Stein had just advised Andy moments before that Amanda was being dropped off at Crossroads Farm within the next 24 hours. Andy is still concerned about her safety, but Stein said the Chinese assured them that the operation was closed and there were strong anti-retaliation provisions in the deal, whatever that meant.

"Yeah, uh, she went to New York City, but I think she's getting back tonight or tomorrow morning. Anyway, we should have the money to you in less than 10 days, so you need to set up that estate through the circuit court like we talked about. I'll call you in the next few days."

Apologies

Holmes hasn't the foggiest idea why the chief called him in for a meeting at his office on his only day off. He seriously doubts it's for a promotion. When he sees Rogers waiting too, he knows something is messed up. His mind whirls through the possibilities.

After what could hardly be called an explanation, the chief pushes two documents across the desk toward them. On the left is something they have seen many times - a death certificate. Holmes quickly scans it and sees the name "Kent Perless." Scanning down the paper to the cause of death, he sees the words "homicide [amended]." His eyes then move over to the document on the right. It's on Loudon County Police letterhead, addressed to Kyle Perless. It's an apology letter that also explains the death certificate has been changed, and that the police department has reopened their investigation.

"I get the amended death certificate, but why an apology letter? That's not necessary." Holmes says.

"I told you. National security. They can make us do anything. They even drafted that letter, saying it was a 'suggested format.' It's useless arguing with them. So, I'm reopening the investigation."

Rogers can't contain himself. "How're we gonna investigate this? The Feds know what happened. It's a joke."

"Look, I don't want you to do anything. We're opening it, and it will show on the computers as an open, active investigation. But that's it," the chief says with a wry smile. "That'll be all, detectives."

"Unbelievable," Holmes says, as he and Rogers walk down the busy hallway through the middle of the administrative offices, past assistants and other police staff chattering and tapping on their keyboards.

"Days like this make me hate this job," Rogers says.

"Ditto that," Holmes adds.

"Well, I owe you an apology."

"What for?" Holmes asks as they turn down the last hall toward the main entrance.

"For making fun of you the day we were standing out in that pasture beside the car. You told me something was bothering you about the crime scene. I shouldn't have second-guessed you."

"I forgot all about that. Now I've got even more questions. But guess what? We're never going to know. We're just pawns in the Feds' game. And it irritates the hell out of me."

Come Clean

The black town car brought Amanda back to Crossroads Farm early Saturday morning. It turned out the safe house was tucked away in a rural area of Great Falls, Virginia, not terribly far from her farmhouse. Britt was also told to remove her belongings from the farm, including the infamous Geo. She knew that the conversation would be difficult, but that she would have to come clean with Amanda.

Britt finishes loading four boxes of her stuff into the small Geo, along with a duffel bag. She looks up and notices the sun and bright blue sky, only a couple of clouds dotting the horizon. The sweet smell of green pasture grass wafts through the air. As she approaches the porch steps to find Amanda, she turns and sees her on Voodoo, walking slowly near the stable. Manuel watches also, from the far side. Britt walks toward Voodoo and Amanda and meets them halfway between the house and the stable.

"The doctors said riding's out of the question with your condition. You know that though."

"Manuel helped me on. I've just been dying to do it. I'm not going to try to gallop or anything."

"Please let me help you off. I don't want any catastrophes on my watch. We've survived a lot together."

Britt steadies Amanda as she climbs out of the saddle slowly and carefully steps to the ground. Once Amanda is down, she looks directly at Britt, and, oh yeah, if looks could kill, it would have been one hell of a slaughter.

"I don't know if I can ever forgive you. I mean, I thought we were really friends. But everything was fake. Everything you ever said was a lie. How could you?"

They both notice that Manuel has walked toward them. Britt says hello to him, and he takes Voodoo's reins and silently walks him back toward the stable.

"How could I? I saved your life. I saved you from yourself for all those weeks I was here, protecting you, teaching you, tutoring you. You don't even see that. I had a job to do."

"I remember everything you told me. You even said you had done theater. That day we were on the mud run. You asked me if I'd ever 'played a part.' You were just playing me. Why would you do something that dirty? That's like, so vile."

"Maybe I said a few things I shouldn't have. But we do have a bond. I was your friend. Still am, whether you believe me or not."

"My friend? Really? I'm not so sure."

"Listen, you're not going to realize it today. But one day you'll know. Look, I've been re-assigned, outside the U.S. This is...it's my last day with you."

"Wait, do you even have a daughter named Samantha?"

Britt looks at her and then looks down and doesn't say anything.

"I don't believe it. You made that up? That's so cruel, really sick! Were you ever a meth addict? No! You weren't. I get it. You lied about that and you were...you were...planted in my room at the psych ward. How? How could you and the FBI, or the CIA, or whoever, do all that? I bet you made up...wait a second, you even made up the Einstein story about you and your mom and your IQ." Amanda keeps pacing, her face now red with anger. "Who was that drug dealer? He was a plant too. I couldn't believe how gross that apartment was. It was all part of the big scam."

Amanda scowls at Britt, who refuses to deny anything and decides to just let Amanda get it out.

"Then, since you got here, okay, wait, wait. You don't even own that Geo. What is that? CIA property? It was, what, supposed to look pathetic, pitiful, like you couldn't afford a thing! I fell for it so hard, and so did David. Then, oh God, you even faked passing out from withdrawal. What an actor. You were good, so-o-o good. It's like you don't really exist. I bet you're not even Brittney. What's your real name? I HATE YOU! Just leave, leave!" Amanda shouts, then starts sobbing, her head down, chin against her chest.

"Amanda, Amanda," Britt says stepping toward her and momentarily placing both her outstretched hands on Amanda's shoulders.

"No! Don't you dare touch me!" She pushes Britt's hands away, stepping backward.

"You've got to understand something. That was the only way I could protect you. To be with you as close to 24 hours a day as possible. We planned it even before you tried to get killed by the train. Thank God you survived that. We had agents posted here 24/7, we had electronic surveillance, because we thought they might kidnap you. Maybe kill you. We were tasked with saving you and we succeeded, here at the farm, and even in New York, when you and

David pulled your stupid getaway. Their agent was one step away from killing David when our sniper took him out."

"That makes some sense. But why did you have to straight-up lie to us, over and over?"

"Because there was no way to let you in on our ops. Look, my boss told me in our debriefing yesterday that they made a deal that's going to protect you."

"Protect me? I already died! I don't need any of you."

"What's that mean?"

"They don't scare me. I've been close to death too many times. Wait, what about my dad's research? Do I have some kind of super blood now, like David thinks?"

"I really don't know. It's possible you were treated, but nobody knows what your dad actually did."

"Huh, David was right. I can't believe it..."

She turns and walks toward the farmhouse.

"My friend—one of the agents in Westchester, got killed protecting you! We trained together. I know pain too—you're not the only one, Amanda!" Britt shouts at her back.

Amanda stops and turns.

"Jeremy?"

"No, another agent who was outside covering for us. Covering for you."

Amanda stands stone still, looking in Britt's direction.

"I'm sorry," she says, so low Britt can't even hear it. Then, she slowly turns again and walks up the porch steps and into the house.

Britt and the Geo are nowhere to be seen the next time Amanda peers out the window. Amanda decides to take a long, hot shower. But the sadness refuses to wash away, no matter how long the water pulses against her.

Seething

Andy stands inside his small walk-in closet, pushing several suits to the left until he finds the black suit that he only wears to black-tie events or funerals. He realizes he's seething inside, more angry than sad. It's the anger from never getting to confront Alex, being betrayed, wanting to ask how he could have done it. He could've gotten Ron killed. No, he did get Ron killed, whether he intended to or not. He was just as guilty as the lookout or the driver hovering outside a bank robbery who didn't know an accomplice fired a gun inside that killed somebody.

Random thoughts flash through his mind. Ron, Alex, himself, stumbling out of the Catacombs at closing time during college, laughing and joking outside before dividing up and walking home. The time they went helicopter skiing together in the Canadian Rockies, when the guide taught them how to dig each other out in case of a sudden avalanche by finding the homing device each of them had to wear. They actually had to practice digging and finding one of the devices in a big snow-covered field near the helicopter pad. Hell, Alex had been his partner in case of an avi, or if one of them dropped into a snow hole next to a tree and got trapped.

Just as bad was being forced to keep the whole damn thing a secret forever. Not being able to tell a single soul. Torturous.

"What're you doing in here?" Becca asks, startling him as she steps into the open doorway of the closet.

"Nothing, just thinking," he says, lifting the black suit along with its hanger off the closet rod.

"Barb just texted me and wants to know if we want to meet near the church and go together."

"No, I don't want to go with anyone else. We'll just meet them there. Amanda texted me yesterday and said David is giving her a ride."

But what Andy never told Amanda was that her "Uncle" Alex had sold out, and caused untold hardship. She had enjoyed a great relationship with Alex, Denise, and with all his kids too. No, he would never tell her.

Becca is dressed and ready, which is pretty unusual, Andy thinks. She walks away, and he puts on the black pants, white button-down shirt, and looks in the bathroom mirror to tie a conservative, powder-blue tie. On the left side of the sink, he has set the 3 x 5 photo of Ron, himself, and Alex from their ski trip, all three of them standing in front of a helicopter lifting off. He slips it into the outside left pocket of his suit coat, takes his dark sunglasses and slides them in the upper outside breast pocket, checks his look carefully, and walks out of the bathroom. Then, he stops. He wheels around, pulls the photo out of his pocket, balls it up violently in his right hand and tosses it in the bathroom trashcan.

"Okay," he tells Becca as he stalks out of the bathroom, "let's get this day over with."

Graduates

From the lectern in the packed auditorium, Headmaster Johnson, having reached the middle of the alphabet, breaks the fairly routine cadence of calling the graduates' names.

"And, with special pleasure, Amanda Michaels."

As he speaks, the clapping and noise level rises. Amanda climbs the set of stairs at the right of the stage and strides across to shake Headmaster Johnson's hand. He blocks her path partly and then hugs her in a rare show of emotion. After breaking the embrace, Amanda proudly waves the rolled diploma high as she exits the stage, and Johnson calls the next proud graduate.

"Is this the end of us or what? With you going off to MIT and all," Amanda practically yells at David amongst the throngs of graduates celebrating with their families.

"No way. We'll stay in touch, for sure. Let's get a picture." David says.

"Uncle Andy, will you take a picture of David and me please?"

Andy obliges. Then, Amanda gets a bunch of pictures with Andy, the Simons, some adults she doesn't even know, and with Headmaster Johnson and Coach Ricci.

"Hey, Amanda, a bunch of us are doing a group pic," Charlyne says, motioning toward Iris and a bunch of the soccer players who are collecting along a half-wall nearby with the words "Middleburg Academy" visible behind them.

As she walks toward them, Jonathan, her ex-boyfriend, approaches her.

"Good luck at UVA," he says.

"Thanks. What are your plans?"

"Got a scholarship to play lacrosse at Johns Hopkins."

"Great! I wish you the best, really. I do know we had good times together, everyone said so. I just can't remember them. I'll see you again soon, I'm sure."

A smile appears on his face at her recognition of their relationship and vague promise for a future encounter. "Okay, yeah, that'd be great. If not, there's always a reunion."

Several of the soccer players shout at her. “Come on!” Charlyne grabs her hand and pulls her toward the wall.

So she gives Jon a quick grin and turns away with Charlyne, actually feeling bad for the first time about him and their ending. Then she finds herself posing for photos and dealing with a whole different set of emotions.

The Freshman

One Year after the Flight 310 Crash

Angie appears in the doorway to Andy's office. "Natalee Spalding's on line one. I figured you'd want to take it."

"Yeah. Put her through."

"Andy, can we come to your office for a quick interview? We're putting together a special segment for the one year anniversary of the crash tomorrow. We're also interviewing the mayor of Quarryville. We want to cover the progress of the memorial there and the Broken Halo rehab facility in Middleburg."

"Sure, what time?"

They cover some other details, then just before they end the call, Natalee brings up Amanda.

"I wanted to mention that Amanda won't return my calls, so we talked to some of her classmates. Did you know she's dropped some classes? Her friends seem concerned. I thought you'd want to know and wondered if you could convince her to talk to us."

Music blares through unseen speakers to a large area surrounding the frat house just off the UVA grounds in Charlottesville. Students overflow out of the house onto the front porch and lawn, all the way down to the sidewalk. Just outside the front door, Amanda takes another gulp from a large plastic cup filled with vodka and something else unidentified.

A couple of the revelers within earshot of Amanda are talking a bit too loud.

"I saw clips of her on CNT. They're doing a special tomorrow on the crash. I guess this is her twisted celebration," one says to the other.

"She's wasted!" the second guy says as Amanda wobbles a few steps toward them.

"I heard that, screw you, you have no-o-o-o rrright to judge meeee." Amanda slurs at them.

Some guy she just met at the party, but is acting like he owns her, follows right behind her.

"I think I'd...I better...I...I'd better be going hooommme," she garbles at him. Her new escort realizes he's going to need some help.

"Robby, can you find one of the DDs to drive us back to her dorm?"

The frat kid has the decency to escort Amanda into the dorm and to her second floor room. When they reach the door, Amanda turns and sloppily kisses the surprised kid. He leans into her and they engage in a drunken grope. While they are still in their impromptu embrace, Amanda raps hard on the door of her room.

"Who's there?" Margo asks from inside.

"It's me, who'd you think?"

The door opens, and Amanda nearly falls into the room. But she catches herself by wrapping a hand around the doorknob.

"You woke me up." Margo says returning to the mostly dark portion of the room and climbing back into her bed.

"I guess I'll be going now." the frat kid says.

"Thanks – thanks for the ride." Amanda says.

"It's Jerry. My name that is."

"Yeah. Right. Thanks. See ya." The door softly closes. The room is very dark again. Amanda feels around, trying to get her bearings, but falls loudly. The room spins. She crawls over to her bed stand and somehow finds a lamp and turns it on. The lamp illuminates half a dozen empty wine bottles along the ledge above her bed, interspersed with several miscellaneous empty bottles. Margo peeks at the clock: 1:30 a.m.

Too few hours later, Margo awakes for her first class before 8:00 a.m. The room reeks. She sees what appears to be puke all over the side of Amanda's bedspread and the floor next to it. Amanda is sprawled facedown, still under the putrid sheets. Margo finds a can of air freshener and sprays it in a wide swath, and then gets ready for classes in the adjoining bathroom. After showering, she decides to send a text message to Charlyne, who she knows is one of Amanda's high school friends at UVA.

Amanda barfed all over and left it. Not getting up for class. Maybe check on her.

Charlyne receives the text during breakfast at the dining hall. She then texts Amanda herself.

Heard u had a big night. U OK?"

Amanda hears the familiar chime for the second time. This time she decides to look at it even though her head is spinning and throbbing. She sees the text is from Charlyne. She shoves the cell phone back up on the ledge beside her bed without responding.

Sometime later, someone is banging on the door. Amanda refuses to get up at first, but the racket continues.

Finally, she drags herself to the door, opens it, and then without looking, flops back on the bed, barely avoiding the putrid vomit covering the side away from the wall.

The stench nearly overwhelms Charlyne.

"Oh my God! How are you even in this room?" Charlyne asks. Nothing from her friend at all. "You have to get in the shower, you're never going to make your classes."

"Who cares? Leave me alone."

"You need to get cleaned up, eat something."

"I said leave me alone. I'm fine. Go."

"Okay, I'll come back and check on you. You're sure you're okay?"

With no answer, Charlyne finally steps out of the dorm room and closes the door. Within 10 steps she places a phone call to Andy Michaels, whose number she still has programmed into her cell phone.

"Mr. Michaels, there's something wrong with Amanda. Her roommate told me she's been out of it almost every night. I don't know what she did last night, but there's barf all over her bed, her floor, and she won't get up. She's been drinking a lot, I mean a whole lot."

"When did you see her?"

"I just left her dorm room. I don't know what to do. She needs some family here or something. I've gotta get to class. She's in Hancock, it's the McCormick Road area dorms."

Andy looks down at his watch, and looks around his desk. He only has one appointment, and it can be changed.

"I'm leaving now. I should get there in about three hours. If you can just check on her again in the meantime, I'd appreciate it."

"I will. Call me when you get here and I'll come help if I'm not in class."

Andy stops by Angie's office.

"Amanda is spiraling out of control. Charlyne just called. Something about her barfing all over her room, her bed, she won't get up for classes. You need to change my appointment with the Millers at 3:00 p.m."

"You know it's been all over CNT, they're talking about the crash."

"I wonder if that has anything to do with her –" Andy starts, but never finishes. "I'm picking up Becca at the shop, and we're going to drive down. I'm leaving in about 30 minutes, does anything have to go out today?"

"I'll get you anything pressing right away."

When they finally get to the dorm and locate Amanda's room, Charlyne is outside waiting for them in the hall. Another girl is standing there as well. She shakes their hands. Charlyne introduces them to Margo.

"I'm sorry, but I'm not her mother. She hasn't been going to classes. She's been getting drunk, really drunk, for days. You better do something. I can't even go in there it stinks so bad." She walks down the hall to the stairway.

When they enter the room, the smell is overwhelming. Amanda, somehow oblivious to the smell, is sleeping. Andy rousts her. She looks surprised to see him and Becca, but then closes her eyes again.

"We're going to help you clean up." Andy says.

"You didn't need to come here."

"Actually, I think it was a good thing we came," Becca says, placing the new bedspread they had stopped to buy on the desk chair. She also breaks out some spray cleaners to get started on what looks to be a significant cleanup. She surveys the wine and booze bottles lining the window ledge.

Amanda finally crawls out of the bed, still dressed in the jeans and shirt she wore to the party, and unsteadily makes her way to the bathroom.

As soon as she vacates, Becca folds up the vomit-covered bedspread and tosses it out into the hall. Andy collects the empty wine and booze bottles in a trash bag, which Amanda had been displaying like trophies. When the main cleanup is complete, Amanda still hasn't come out. Becca walks over to the bathroom door and lightly taps on it.

"Amanda, can I talk to you?" she asks through the closed door.

"Why? Is this an intervention?" Amanda says from the other side.

"If you're decent just open the door."

The door unlocks. Becca walks in and closes it again. Andy decides to give them some space and carries the bedspread and bottles down to the dumpster beside the dorm.

When he returns to the room, Amanda is dressed and looks halfway presentable. He wonders what Becca could've possibly said to Amanda, but thinks better of asking any questions.

Andy looks her in the eye. "Are you sure you're going to be okay? It's all over the news, reporters will probably keep calling. This isn't going to go away. Are you really okay?"

"Yeah, I keep telling you that."

"If you're so okay, then why are you barfing all over your dorm room?"

"Let's not get into that." Becca interjects. "Let's all go get lunch at Citizen Tavern on the mall, how about that?" Becca waits for a response from Amanda, or even a protest, but hears none.

"That lady, Natalee Spalding, left me a voice message yesterday." Amanda says. "She wanted to interview me today. I didn't call her back. I refuse to relive my pain just so they can share it with the world."

"I can understand that. No one says you need to give an interview. Right, Andy?" Becca asks him.

"Sure, they always push for the emotional story. Don't feel guilty, it's your choice. I'm talking to her to promote Broken Halo, and to help drum up volunteers. Are you ready to go?"

"Yeah, just let me find my phone."

No Closure

Solarez nervously paces back and forth, watching everything on each of the computer monitors in front of the half-dozen analysts, while listening on the active audio feed. Mentally measuring the risks versus the rewards, it comes to him all of a sudden.

"Abort the operation. Now!" he shouts to the analysts in the room, despite the fact he is on the master channel and they all have earpieces. Several turn from their monitors.

"Get him out, however we need to, to a safe house. Abort the remaining operation."

The chief analyst turns back to his monitor, and gives the command to the field operatives.

"Bravo Team. This is Command 5273. Abort operation. Sedate the Phoenix. Confirm."

An immediate whispered confirmation comes back to the analyst. The nondescript man sitting beside Phoenix swiftly plunges a stub hypodermic needle into his thigh as the analysts and Solarez watch on their monitors.

"What? Huh..." Before he can complete a sentence, Phoenix falls slightly forward as the man seated beside him slides the syringe into his trench coat side pocket with one hand and keeps Phoenix from flopping completely forward with the other hand.

"Phoenix neutralized. Confirm extraction coordinates."

"Stand by. Proceed to GPS coordinates in text message. Locate helicopter." Within minutes, a driver and the other operative load the immobile body of the Phoenix onto the helicopter under the wash of the rotor blades.

"Why did you abort?" the chief analyst asks Solarez now that the Phoenix is safely ensconced on the helicopter.

"Don't ask," Solarez says, as he drops his headset on the counter of the ready room and walks down the hall to his office.

Thirty minutes pass.

"Sir, we need you back down here immediately," his chief analyst advises him via phone. Solarez rushes down the hall and back into the room. What could have gone wrong? There should be no risk with the helicopter....

The chief analyst turns to him and Solarez knows something has gone terribly wrong.

"Chief, the jet just crashed somewhere in Pennsylvania. The first report states no survivors. And it gets worse."

"Oh my God, what the hell could be worse?"

"Paul just obtained the final passenger list from Hemispheres. Ron Michaels, Rochelle Michaels and Amanda Michaels were all on the plane."

"How the hell? No! There's no way that can be. No damn way!" Solarez slams his left fist against the wall, something his chief has never seen before. Solarez never, ever loses control. Now he stands with his palms pressed against both sides of his face, eyes closed.

"We have no idea what the entire family was doing – "

"It can't be. Are you sure?" Solarez demands.

"We'll double check. Andy Michaels is the next surviving kin. He's that D.C. lawyer who handled the 9/11 Pentagon cases."

Solarez now drops both arms beside his waist.

"Did you get some other Intel? Is that why you aborted the op?" The chief again asks him.

Solarez never answers.

Just a few hours later, Solarez gazes out one of the two tinted windows, admiring the neatly manicured grounds. This will be my last day, he knows. The thick wooden door opens, and the director of the CIA enters. Everyone in the room gives him their full attention.

The director barely looks at his letter of resignation.

"Not now. However, I'll hold on to it pending what develops in the next several weeks. It is imperative that none of this leaks. Not one word. Do you realize what will occur if any part of this gets out? All the good we've done, all the good we're trying to do, won't matter. It will be irreparable. We will be blamed, bashed, bludgeoned. Won't matter that we aren't responsible. Heads will roll."

Solarez remembers every minute detail of that day. Traumatic events brand themselves on the deep recesses of the brain. Invisible scars that never fade.

He sips his scotch on the rocks and sets it down on the table next to his home office desk. Natalee Spalding discusses the one year anniversary of the Hemispheres crash, the lives lost, during her one-hour special report. She reports on Amanda Michaels, how the sole crash survivor seems to be struggling in her first year at college, withdrawing from one or more college classes at UVA, according to unnamed sources. Solarez downs the scotch, and enjoys the warm burn. He pours another. He passes out face down on top of the bed, never changing out of his work clothes.

Control

"Tell me exactly what happened that day, in the last couple minutes."

"I've told you before." Solarez says with a sigh.

"Only parts. You seem much more troubled now than before. Tell me what you did and how you felt about it."

"We were monitoring everything. I was standing in back of the ready room, near my chief analyst. I just had a feeling. And that's when I aborted the operation."

"A feeling, that's all. Nothing else?"

"Doc, haven't you ever had a hunch? Something just tells you don't. That's all it was. I've gone over it in my mind. Sometimes I can't sleep at night I just keep mulling it over and over. Guilt, blame, shame, every single day. What don't you get about that?" Solarez raises his voice to an angry rasp.

"Calm down please. There have been two separate reviews, and both support your version of events. You've been exonerated, Agent Solarez."

"We had all the exit strategies in place. We got the Phoenix out. I thought everything was okay."

"What's the next thing you remember?"

"Some time passed, 15, maybe 30 minutes. My chief called me back down there and told me the jet went down with no survivors. Of course later we learned there was one."

"Do you feel guilty about the crash, is that what weighs on you?"

"Not at first. We had no intel. But as months passed, I obsessed more and more. We had Amanda Michaels under 24/7 surveillance. I lived her pain through transcripts of her conversations. She'd talk about losing her memory; I knew everything about her, even her whims and wishes. Why didn't I do more? Why didn't I cover all the passenger information in advance with my analysts? I think of new things I could have done all the time. And we still have an ongoing operation..."

"Which is a constant reminder to you?"

"In the worst way."

Solarez throws his head back and stares at the ceiling, trying not to get emotional. He rarely shows any – it's not conducive to his livelihood.

"Haven't you supervised dozens of counter-intelligence operations?"

"About 50."

"There were deaths in some of them, right?"

"Yeah, but we don't usually have a family ripped apart and a teenager we're supposed to protect. She doesn't know the truth, which happens a lot with what I do. So why do I think it's not fair here? She's spiraling down, and I know it's on me."

"You're laying blame on yourself unfairly. Is the guilt getting worse?"

"Yeah. Much worse now. I want to help her, but can't. Protocols, policies prevent me from acting since she's an innocent, we keep them in the dark."

"I've been seeing you every other week since what, about a month after the crash? And not once have I heard anything that indicates you overlooked something. None of the reports pinned any responsibility on you either."

"I know, you keep telling me that. But it was my operation, I conceived it. And when you create a scenario, you have to make sure...you just have to think everything through. And then afterward, I developed a plan to, try to, uh, how do I say this, to help her state of mind."

"Huh? In what way? Does she know you exist?"

"No, of course not, anyway, forget it."

"Perhaps a leave of absence would be the best thing for you now. I can write you up for short term disability."

"Yeah. Lack of control. I need to remain in control. Control..." Solarez mumbles.

"So, yeah, as in you mean you want me to write you up for leave?" The doctor asks Solarez, pulling the scrip pad out of the right desk drawer and placing it on his desktop blotter.

"No, not that. Lack of control, that's what's killing me. Look, there are some things I've solved that I haven't told you about. We, uh, the agency, uncovered the mole, and we believe we've closed down a significant spying operation. We also recovered all the money from the Chinese government."

"Agent Solarez, we went over how my therapy works on day one. You promised me full and complete honesty and disclosure, from the very beginning. I promised you confidentiality. I can't counsel you if we don't have that trust. Yet this is the first time you mention anything about a mole, or recovering money from the Chinese."

"You didn't need to know. It hadn't all happened when I started seeing you either. Anyway, we've been dead in the water on the biological research we've been trying to protect. The whole idea was to maintain our biological supremacy, our exclusivity. It's about cancer research, dying chromosomes. Have you ever heard of telomeres? They control the biological clock on all our cells, and affect aging of the cells. We have promising breakthroughs on this. Anyway, we received intel that proved we had a mole inside a key lab. I devised an elaborate plan to expose the mole, and finally, we got him. Well, actually we had discovered him but they eliminated him before we could."

"What? Slow down. You never told me any of this."

"So, the Phoenix won't work with us. Hell, won't work at all. And he's supposedly on our side. That's a lack of control, you have to agree, right?"

"Well, if this person won't do what you need him to, uh, I would have to say that's a lack of control. What were you expecting him to do?"

Solarez looks past the doctor, staring into nothingness. Yes, Solarez decides. It will involve bucking authority, upending protocols. But maybe, just maybe the director will agree given that the mole was exposed. It's like a eureka moment. Solarez virtually springs up from the patient chaise and walks toward the door. Maybe the director will relent.

"Forget the disability. I'll see you at the next session."

Back at his office, Solarez sketches out some notes and hastily arranges a meeting with the director.

Solarez sits in the large, black leather chair in front of the director, who continues to thumb through the entire dossier just presented to him by Solarez and his team. "Going on a year, and he still won't cooperate? Nothing worked?"

"Psychological or drug techniques weren't an option, we might lose him entirely. So we've tried to reward and induce."

"And that got us?"

"Nothing. That's my point. We need to abandon protocol. Let him win. Agree to his demands. We accomplished the original objective of the operation: to expose the mole."

"And it cost $160 million?"

"We got it back. Besides, the value of Phoenix' research makes that a drop in the bucket."

"But we never put innocents at risk in our covert operations, you know that. They're easy targets. They turn in a heartbeat, and we have history to prove it. Thank God the public never learned about the last two deaths where we strayed. So what's our exit strategy if this plan you've outlined fails to convince him? Or worse, what if he turned on us and we never knew, and that's why he refuses to help?"

"I can't imagine that, but if he refuses us after we cave in, then, uh, enhanced interrogation techniques may be necessary."

"Have you ever made any specific promises to anyone? Protection? New identities? Anything?"

"Nope. Nada. We made a deal with the MSS that included no harm to any person of interest or their family members, and they have a big economic incentive to uphold their end of the deal."

"They could decide the $25 million is not enough, and if they do, the deal means nothing. But, I guess it's a reasonable risk. Look, I'll sign off on it, but nothing is to be disclosed to innocents beyond the minimum necessary to carry out the plan. And we'd better have new research results within 30 days or I'll be accepting your resignation."

"Thank you, you'll have your results."

Healing Heroes

"One of the producers for this year's *Healing Heroes* show called me. They want to do a follow-up feature on us. And they're bringing Dr. Lucent to their studio also. I really want you to be involved, Amanda, it's a great charity." Andy says, having called Amanda at UVA.

"Do I have to? I'm having enough trouble dealing with things already."

"They offered to send a limo to Charlottesville, drive you up this Friday, and drive you back the same evening. They're picking me up too. They were good to you, now you should give back to them."

"Alright, I guess it won't be the worst thing in the world."

"The contact is Tom Peters, so just confirm that before you get in the limo."

Friday arrives. I walk out to the street from my dorm and spot the black SUV limo the producers sent. As I approach the limo, a man stands there beside the stretch SUV.

"I'm Tom Peters, and you must be Amanda Michaels," he says reaching forward to shake my hand.

"Nice to meet you," I say, as he opens the rear door nearest the curb. I slide into one of the smooth leather seats, and Peters climbs in behind me and moves to the opposite side of the spacious limo.

Peters explains where the interview will take place in D.C. and that the limo is equipped with Wi-Fi. After a few more explanations, I slide my laptop out of my backpack and begin some of my homework, figuring I might as well.

The last thing I remember is looking out the tinted window at the Washington cherry blossoms.

My next recollection is a repetitive sound, over and over, just like traveling down railroad tracks. Or is it the vibration of a subway? I just fade in, fade out. It's all fuzzy. Then a man is speaking, but I'm processing the words in slow motion, like some medication or drug I took is still wearing off.

"Amanda? Amanda, do you hear me? Can you hear me?" It's the Healing Heroes guy from the limo. Of course I didn't know it then, but I learned later we were at a farm somewhere in Canada.

"Where am I?" I ask him. I'm in an easy chair of some kind. Tom from the limo is facing me in a chair, and there's a young lady in a white lab coat seated beside him, studying me, which really freaks me out. Then, I notice my feet are hooked together with some sort of plastic restraints.

"Why are my feet hooked together? Who are you? Where are we?" The room looks like a large bedroom in someone's home. "Who's she?" I ask the guy from the limo.

"She's a doctor. Please just calm down," he says in a reassuring voice. "Everything's going to be fine. We have no intention of harming you. We both work for the U.S. government, here's my badge." He flips it open and shows me an FBI badge.

By now I know badges mean nothing. "Look, I know anybody can make a fake badge."

"This lady beside me is a medical doctor. We had to sedate you before we brought you here so you wouldn't be able to divulge this location, voluntarily or otherwise."

"You mean there was never any Healing Heroes interview? So you are... who are you really?"

"I just told you. We work with the FBI."

"You could be anybody. Look, I'm not scared of you, not after everything I've been through. But I don't have any secret information or anything, so you're wasting your time."

Peters glances over at the "doctor" and back at me. "In a moment we're going to give you quite a shock. That's why Dr. Walters is here. I want you to prepare yourself."

"I suppose you're going to make some outrageous demand, for what, money? Or you're going to draw my blood to study and keep me hostage here?"

"If I release you, do you promise that you won't run or anything?"

"Sure, I promise. Just tell me this supposedly shocking news already."

The doctor reaches in a small black medical kit and pulls out a pair of hemostat scissors.

“Please hold your legs still,” she says, and then clips the plastic ankle restraints off my legs.

I stand up and feel light-headed and unsteady. “You drugged me pretty good.”

“You were sedated appropriately, but maybe you should sit back down,” the lady doctor suggests.

I follow her advice and sit back down. "Alright, what is it?"

Peters then reaches into his sport coat, removes a small hand-held walkie-talkie and says, "The finch has been released, you can bring in the Phoenix."

Tom and the doctor stand up like they’re waiting for something, but don’t say anything. They give me a really weird look, and that finally scares me. Then the door opens and Uncle Andy and my dad are walking toward me. *My dad?!*

“Amanda!” The one who I know is my dad shouts as he dashes toward me.

That’s when I faint.

They use some smelling salts on me and eventually I come to.

“She’s back,” the lady doctor says. “Keep her laying down please.”

She moves away and I dreamily see my “twin dads” hovering over top of me. Just like my NDE, I think.

My dad sits down on the bed and starts talking to me. “Amanda, I’ve been waiting for this moment for the last year. They wouldn’t let me contact you at all. I’ve been dying inside.”

Uncle Andy stands at the foot of the bed with a big smile on his face. For a split second, I think about Dorothy waking up back in Kansas after being in Oz.

“So, there wasn’t any crash, right? Mom’s here? And Kent, he’s still alive, and all that stuff was just the worst nightmare, right? Tell me it didn’t happen.”

“I’m not sure she’s totally oriented to her surroundings yet...” the doctor interjects from somewhere, but I just stare into my dad’s eyes, struggling to understand.

"I couldn’t tell you. I’ve been at this safe house since the day of the crash, they had to believe I was dead.”

"What about Mom? Where is Mom?"

My dad doesn't answer me, and he starts to choke up. I know at that moment I wasn't dreaming.

"I'm afraid...she didn't make it. She was on the plane with you." Dad says, standing in front of me now.

"Then how did you survive? You were on the plane too," I say grabbing his forearm, still trying to convince myself he's real.

"She suffered a brain injury, Mr. Michaels," the doctor says, walking over to me. "Her memory from before the crash hasn't come back."

"I was on the last shuttle bus from the gate heading out to the plane, but that's the last thing I recall. They apparently drugged me and diverted the shuttle bus. I want you to know I had no part in any secret plans, and I didn't find out about the jet crash until weeks later when they finally decided to tell me. I knew nothing about Chinese sabotage until today, when the agent told me."

That's when my dad turns and looks toward the open bedroom door, at another guy observing everything, but not saying anything.

"But we buried you. They matched your DNA, and Mom's too."

Uncle Andy finally speaks up. "I'm sure they have easy ways to match it, Amanda, and you know there were only partial remains recovered in that crash."

I notice another woman standing in the doorway next to the other agent. She's fairly young and pretty, in a flowing maternity dress, maybe seven or eight months pregnant.

"Amanda, let me introduce you to Odette," my dad says smiling, as she walks a few more steps into the room.

I snap like a rubber band stretched clear across a room. My fists pummel my dad all over. I'm flailing and punching him, screaming like a wild banshee.

"How could you do this? No, no, you couldn't do this to Mom! You couldn't. No!"

Andy tries to grab my right arm with both his hands, but I swing free. My dad's arms surround his head, he's just defending himself any way he can, while I keep trying to hit, punch, or hurt him. My brain, my heart, everything is going haywire.

"Amanda, stop, stop!"

Peters grabs my left arm, and Uncle Andy finally secures my right arm.

"Doc, give her something!"
And I'm out like a light.

Odie

I just know my brain synapses won't fire right.

Nooo Sir... Sir!...ohhh...Get... jeez..Sir..Get!."
"She's still not here with us..." a voice says.
"Sir...gut...uh...get...uhh...Sir...gut."

When I start to come to I'm restrained to the bed. I try to flail my arms but can't. Dad and Uncle Andy are touching my arms. I can hear them speaking, but my drug-addled mind doesn't understand the words.

"Sir-get it-sir—uhh—get," My dad seems to be saying, which makes no sense.

Uncle Andy tries next: "oh-debt is...oh oh debt..sir, uhhh, get it..."

I try to say "What? Who?" but the words don't come out.

They keep trying to get through to me until they are both almost shouting at me from either side of the bed.

Finally the fog in my brain clears and I can form words again. "What? What are you saying?"

"Sir-uh-get. She's a... *surrogate*." My dad says. "We used my sperm and your mother's egg from the D.C. sperm bank. That agent, Mr. Solarez over there, he worked out everything for me. Odette, or 'Odie' for short, lives nearby. She's carrying the baby and has agreed to nanny for a year. It's going to be a boy! I couldn't contact you to get your opinion, so I had to make the decision on my own. You always wanted a little brother, right?"

I look over at Agent Solarez, who flashes a smile.

"Let's leave them alone now." Andy whispers to Solarez and Odette, and he pulls the door closed behind them.

Andy's not sure, but he thinks he sees a hint of moisture in the corners of Solarez' eyes.

"Is that one of the best things you've ever done in your life?" He asks Solarez.

"Maybe. No, probably. I'll go with probably."

Odette smiles. “That was so special. And meaningful. *Avec plaisir.*” She then takes a seat on the couch, leaving Andy and the agent standing in the hall near the bedroom door.

“Well, what’s the plan now?” Andy asks Solarez.

“Getting you both home safely. Making sure your brother is happy and working on his research. I don’t know if we can bring him back to the U.S. yet.”

“Are you saying you’re not sure he can ever come back?” Andy asks.

“Unfortunately, yes. We’re still not divulging where we are, and it’s critical that you and Amanda not tell anyone that Ron is alive. At least for now. I know that’s going to be hard to do, and we took a huge risk bringing you here. I had to convince the director himself. If we hadn’t found the mole and made the deal he would never have approved this.”

“You’re serious?”

“Of course I’m serious.”

“A couple other questions. Kent Perless. You know the deal we made and how I represented his father?”

“Look, he was just a kid who got caught up in something much more dangerous than he knew.”

“Wasn’t working for anyone?” Andy asks.

“Nope.”

“Stein wouldn’t tell me everything about Pletcher, if he was your agent, or whether the Chinese...”

“There wasn’t ever really a Pletcher. An agent *became* Pletcher, but we essentially created him to help us expose the mole. We created a fictional patent application, and your brother had no idea what he was even meeting Pletcher about. We based his persona on a 30-year-old Brit who died suddenly. We needed them – the mole and whoever he worked for – to believe someone else was going to acquire the technology, and Pletcher was the broker. When your niece and Owlsley went to Manhattan, we had to kill him off, or should I say, kill off his persona. It actually helped us expose their mole, through monitoring their communications, when Pletcher died.”

“Unbelievable. They showed him on TV, a headshot and everything. Wow, that’s crazy.”

“Yeah, building an entire persona takes a lot of effort.” Solarez says.

"What do you remember from the crash?" Dad asks me. He knows nothing except that I survived, they never supplied him any details.

"This rescue guy thought I was dead, but he pulled me out of the broken up fuselage, that's what they tell me. I had a broken neck, so I had to wear this metal halo thing, and I suffered a brain injury that gave me total amnesia about everything before. I still have flashbacks about Mom being with me on the jet, of this guy Kent I met, and about four Dorothys. Do you remember when I dressed up as Dorothy, with three other girls? Like, for Halloween?"

"I'm not sure."

"Okay, doesn't matter. Hey, did you have a home lab with mosquitoes?"

"Yes and no. I had a home office with some lab stuff. I never had mosquitoes, but I did have fruit flies."

"Oh, fruit flies. Did they glow in the dark?"

"I painted some of them, and I looked at them under a black light."

"I knew it! It was in my NDE. Why did you make them glow?"

"I told Steven I wouldn't discuss my research with you," he says lowering his voice to a whisper, "but, I was tracking their lifespans. I would spray different batches of them different colors so I could tell if some were living longer than others. I extended their lifespans by 50%."

"So, making cells last longer and stuff. That's pretty exciting."

"It goes way beyond cancer cells. I figured out how to transfuse stem cell chromosomes, and let's just say there are all kinds of bio-medical applications. We have a lot more to learn, especially about longevity of the human cells that are treated."

My dad then admits he treated me with stem cells and rapamycin in the elixir of blood treatment he concocted.

"You used me as your human guinea pig?"

"No. I transfused myself first for months. Oh, I want you to begin taking enzyme and nutrient pills regularly, Solarez has them."

My dad gives me the longest hug, and tells me he loves me. I then launch into how I met Kent, me buying a horse farm, that I was certifiably crazy for a while, and I just can't stop talking. I cover everything I can think of.

"Dad, how are you going to handle a baby? And when will you come back...?"

"Stop worrying. Leave that to me. Solarez will help me."

Finally, after we talk out everything, we go find Andy and Solarez, and my dad asks me, “Oh, would you like to name the baby? You can start thinking of names.”

“I already have one, Dad.” I say.

“Really?”

Convergence

Everything started getting a lot better after that, even though I didn't know exactly when I'd see my dad again. Solarez promised to keep me posted.

About a month later, I drove up to D.C. from Charlottesville. David took the Amtrak train down from MIT for the big kickoff picnic for the Broken Halo charity. I picked him up at Union Station. I don't know why, but David really loves trains. Everybody else flies. We did have a magical time together on the train going up to New York. I wonder if that's why?

I was sitting in one of the chairs waiting for the train to get in, watching the people all trying to get somewhere. I knew it was going to kill me not to be able to tell David everything I had found out since we were practically soulmates. He actually asked me if we were soulmates in one of our many online chats. I replied that we had a "special connection." I didn't hear from him for almost two days, and I knew I had hurt his feelings. Honestly, I just wasn't sure at first, but the more I thought about it the more I felt bad and I wanted to take it back. I mean, how many soulmates can you have in one life? Isn't there a limit or something? I had already lost one. So, that's what I was stressing about inside.

Even though I couldn't tell him my biggest secrets, we still had a lot of catching up to do on the drive out to Middleburg. Like how Kyle Perless had refused to buy back the farm from me, even though he now had the money to do it. However, he did take me up on the offer to make music part of Broken Halo, and he agreed to run it. So we now had horse therapy and music. Just about anybody who is down and out can qualify – drug addicts in rehab, people with brain injuries. I told him I hate to only come and volunteer every few weekends, but I'll be around a lot more once the summer begins.

Then we got to a touchy subject for me, about Kent. I told him Uncle Andy found out Kent was totally innocent when he negotiated the whistleblower thing. David told me he had known that already, ever since he scoured everything on his laptop.

Jon and his roommate were coming up to visit him at MIT soon, David said, to catch a Red Sox game in Boston. He watched for my reaction, but I just kept looking at the road. I wouldn't take that bait.

He wanted to know who was going to be at Crossroads when we got there, so I told him just about everybody. I explained about the Broken Halo Charity's board that Uncle Andy had put together: himself, Barbara Smithson, from Loudoun Memorial, a rehab doctor, an occupational therapist, and Dr. Lucent. Lucent wouldn't be at the farm for the kickoff though because he was on a signing tour for his new NDE book, the one that included me.

Then David asked if I'd heard from Britt. I turned down the music – I want to say it was the Shins song, "Caring is Creepy" – and I said yeah, she had texted me one time. Some weird five-digit fake number, so I assumed she was overseas. She just said hello, she was thinking about me and would keep in touch. Not sure if I really believed her, I told him. David said she was the best actor ever, she should have been in Hollywood. He asked if I ever did any secret superhero stuff, and we laughed.

We finally got to Crossroads. I drove up the long gravel drive and there were cars parked everywhere, so I just pulled all the way up to the front near the big pasture like, well, like I lived there. I didn't want to get out right away though since we were having such a great conversation. It was so nice, the windows were rolled down, allowing the familiar scent of grilling and pasture grass to come wafting into the car.

David asked me if I knew what I wanted to do yet. He meant like in college, and I told him, no, I had no idea. He said that it's crazy at MIT, they do job fairs even for freshmen. Every big science and technology company shows up. He dug around in his pocket and flipped through some of the cards. He said the most bizarre one was that the FBI was there, and he pulled out a business card and held it between us. He brought it to show to Uncle Andy to ask him if he knew the guy, and what he thought about an internship there.

U.S. DEPARTMENT OF JUSTICE
FEDERAL BUREAU OF INVESTIGATION

Steven Solarez
Special Agent
Washington Division

935 Pennsylvania Ave NW
Washington, DC

Phone: (202) 324-3000
Mobile: (202) 423-3150
E-mail: S.Solarez@dc.fbi.gov

It was Steven Solarez' official FBI business card. I almost lost it, but turned quickly to look at something out my window—there was nothing there of course – and I recovered.

We both notice a large van has pulled up and parked near us. The attendant opens the side door and a built-in ramp lowers an older woman in her wheelchair to the ground. A young girl, maybe 10 or so, hops down from inside the van.

I reach for my door, and so does David.

As soon as we get past the front of my car, I see Uncle Andy walking across the pasture grass and he recognizes the little girl from the van running toward him as fast as she can. She wraps herself around both his legs and Andy beams. We are just within earshot, and I hear her asking Andy to show her the horses.

"Where are the horses, Mister? Did you see Grammy? She's right over there," Gracie says, pointing. "She loves horses too, Mister."

I give my uncle a hug myself and he shakes David's hand and asks how the train trip was. Gracie begins to dart away toward the stables. Suddenly she stops and twirls her small body back to face us.

"Did you save that glow rock I gave you at the park, Mister?"

"Sure did." Uncle Andy says.

"Am I supposed to remember her from before?" I ask, watching her run across the gravel driveway.

"That's a good question," he answers.

Postscript

Thanks very much for reading Taming the Telomeres. If you enjoyed TTT it is appreciated if you can recommend this book to a friend and leave a positive review or comment at your favorite book site. I have written reviews on Amazon over many years, but once I became an author myself I realized how appreciated those positive reviews are, especially to an author. To review Taming the Telomeres on Amazon, please click here.

Comments and emails are also invited at www.RNShapiro.com where my author bio is located, and information behind TTT is posted, including more information about topics like telomere research. Author chapter insights about TTT are also posted on www.Bublish.com.

Will there be another Amanda Michaels telomeres book? Yes, book two of the series is tentatively entitled *Targeting the Telomeres*, and will address a burning question left open in TTT: why Ron Michaels telomere research is so valuable to the major superpowers. Please enjoy the prologue and chapter 1 of *Targeting the Telomeres* on the following pages.

My author website: www.RNShapiro.com
Twitter: @tamingtelomeres
Facebook: taming the telomeres

Pinterest: search: Taming the Telomeres for inspired novel scenes
Check out these playlists on Youtube of Amanda and Andy Michaels:

On Youtube-Taming the Telomeres channel:

Amanda Michaels Playlist 2016

Andy Michaels Playlist 2016

Targeting the Telomeres (Preview)

Sleeper

Prologue

What kind of scum-sucking cockroaches kidnap a defenseless baby, Amanda Michaels thinks while trying to fall asleep. She *will* make them regret that decision.

Lying on the cramped, lower bunk of the sleeper car, she feels with her fingertips along the thin foam-rubber pad masquerading as a mattress. There it is. She tugs on the lower portion of her backpack hiding the loaded pistol with the customized silencer, nestling what constitutes all her belongings in the crook of her right arm. The sheath strapped under the left pant leg of her jeans secures a long KA-Bar serrated edge fixed blade knife. And in the right pocket of her hoodie are two identical burner cell phones. One is her only means of communication with her compatriot, who is also on the train, both of them full-in with their improbable mission. Imagining the linen scent of her favorite candle briefly tricks her olfactory glands into ignoring the foul odors. The elderly Chinese lady on the bunk overhead smells of mildewing clothes. On the lower bunk an arm's length away, a twenty-something Chinese girl sleeps with her jacket over her head. The sleeper car's other occupant, a tiny woman who barely stands five-foot tall and can't weigh 100 pounds, presses her torso against the tiny sink, paper towels surrounding the collar of her shirt, while she works some type of soapy liquid through her dark brown shoulder-length hair. Amanda decides to pass on that shower.

She thinks, all I wanted was to get some of my memory back from before the crash. Not this.

If she's captured, what could Chinese intelligence agents possibly "get" out of her anyhow? Sure, she survived the Hemispheres plane crash, but she doesn't know how or why. Only that it might have had something to do with her dad's research and her being his test subject. To study her telomeres, maybe that's what they would want? Most likely to torture her to learn whatever she knows.

The bullet train hurtling northbound towards Beijing at 180 miles per hour suddenly lurches, causing a metallic screech that soon fades.

Amanda thinks for a moment about a family photo. Of her dad, her, and her mom, sitting on the front porch of the house they lived in before the crash. The one she hopes to recall, that her Uncle Andy showed her. She mentally photoshops her baby brother Justin in too. Nothing can stop fantasies no one else can see.

The sink-showering lady climbs back up to her top bunk, and talks in Chinese with the other older lady.

If my plan fails, I won't have to worry anymore, Amanda decides. Because I'll be dead.

Gag Reflex

Washington, D.C.

The TV in the background startles FBI counter-intelligence Agent Steven Solarez during his early morning ritual of checking the weather on his tablet, sending a swig of burning hot French roast coffee everywhere.

Holy crap, he thinks, listening to the reporter on CNT.

"According to the *Washington Observer*, over 200 million dollars were transferred from the U.S. Government to a Hemispheres Airlines bank account, effectively funding most of the wrongful death claims for the victims of flight 310, which left D.C. for New York City and crashed in Quarryville, Pennsylvania about two years ago. Official sources with the Department of Justice are strenuously denying this claim."

Solarez feels his cell phone vibrating on his waist, slides it off its holster, and reads the incoming text message.

Emergency meeting @ 8:30 AM with Director. Confirm.

His mind whirls. Once the proverbial cat is out of the bag, can you ever shove it back in? This is bad, for sure. But he didn't hear any details of why the money was paid to the airline, so maybe whoever leaked it doesn't have the whole story. Maybe.

He texts his confirmation to his assistant, Dean, then decides to add more.

Find Amanda Michaels now. Tell her not to talk to the reporters. Put two agents on her 24/7.

He smiles knowing she stands far from helpless now. It was a fantastic move on his part to give her training at Quantico once school let out, virtually the same as a field agent undergoes. Weapons, hand-to-hand combat, and avoidance driving techniques. He had to pull a lot of strings for approval, but given the role her father was undertaking, it made sense. Sounds like his idea may prove useful sooner than he thought.

Next, he calls Andy Michaels and braces himself for an onslaught.

"I just heard the report on the radio. Do you know what this'll do to my practice? My reputation? Do you?" Andy barks as soon as he answers, mentally cataloguing every material possession in his

Georgetown home and imagining his lucrative practice going right down the rathole.

"Careful, this isn't a secure line. Yeah, I get how serious this is."

"How about my clients who settled their cases? What if someone decides I knew everything..."

Solarez interrupts him. "Stop! We need to talk in person. You did nothing wrong, so don't start panicking. We're putting protection on Amanda immediately. No one talks to any reporters until we have a solid response plan, hopefully around noon."

"What am I supposed to tell my partners and my staff?"

"Tell them you can't comment now, but you'll issue a statement soon."

"Are you kidding? I can't say that."

"You can't tell them anything until you look into the allegations. Better?"

Andy contemplates this a few seconds. "Completely unconvincing." He tries to come up with a logical explanation, but the more he thinks about it, the more furious and anxious he gets. He was never comfortable with the confidential information the DOJ lawyer had shared with him, that the U.S. did indeed pay the $200 million. His clients trusted him when he recommended they settle their wrongful death claims. Sure, they all were awarded reasonable settlements, but that was before he learned of the secret government payout to the airline. He realized then if anything about sabotage leaked later on, there would be hell to pay.

"What about the press when they start calling?"

"Same thing."

"I want you to call Stein at the Department of Justice to confirm everything is still okay. He assured me all my settlements were legal."

"I'll talk to him."

"My head is ready to explode."

"Tell you what, I have a meeting with the FBI director this morning, but when I'm done I'll call, okay?"

Andy isn't listening. He's still thinking about the news story. Whoever leaked it must have an agenda. Why would the Chinese, who sabotaged the plane, leak it? Makes no sense. Maybe a disgruntled FBI or CIA employee? It's possible, but who, and what was their motive?

"Andy?"

"Of course, yes. Text or call me then."

"We'll work this out," Solarez promises, but Andy has major

doubts. What is it they say about hiding the truth, he thinks? It usually floats back up to the surface no matter how hard you try to weight it down.

To get updates on ***Targeting the Telomeres*** and a release date, please follow the author on his website, www.rnshapiro.com

V5117

Made in the USA
San Bernardino, CA
17 June 2017